Ignis Fatuus

Ignis Fatuus

by

Martin C C Graham

Strategic Book Publishing and Rights Co.

Strategic Book Publishing and Rights Co.
12620 FM 1960, Suite A4-507
Houston TX 77065
www.sbpra.com

ISBN: 978-1-61897-887-5

Dedicated to my wife, family, and friends for their support and patience—especially to my father for teaching me to "get the bull by the horns." Hope this counts, Dad.

My sincerest and humblest apologies to Mr Andrew Ridgely. He won't know or remember what for, but it is a promise I made to myself if the opportunity ever came to do so publicly.

TABLE OF CONTENTS

Chapter 1   Scotland I...1

Chapter 2   The Shire I...3

Chapter 3   Scotland II 11

Chapter 4   The Shire II...17

Chapter 5   Scotland III 33

Chapter 6   The Shire III...36

Chapter 7   The Shire IV 40

Chapter 8   The Shire V...42

Chapter 9   Scotland IV..48

Chapter 10   The Shire VI 51

Chapter 11   The Shire VII..55

Chapter 12   Scotland V 72

Chapter 13   The Shire VIII...76

Chapter 14   The Shire IX 78

Chapter 15   The Shire X 80

Chapter 16   The Shire XI 88

Chapter 17   The Shire XII..92

Chapter 18   The Shire XIII 102

Chapter 19   The Shire XIV 108

Chapter 20   Scotland VI..110

Chapter 21   The Shire XV...114

Chapter 22 The Shire XVI 116

Chapter 23 The Shire XVII...118

Chapter 24 The South Coast I 119

Chapter 25 The Gambia I...127

Chapter 26 Scotland VII 137

Chapter 27 The Shire XVIII..139

Chapter 28 The Gambia II 144

Chapter 29 Scotland VIII 153

Chapter 30 The Gambia III 162

Chapter 31 Scotland IX..164

Chapter 32 The Gambia IV 171

Chapter 33 The Shire XIX 177

Chapter 34 Scotland X...186

Chapter 35 The Shire XX...199

Chapter 36 The South Coast II...202

Chapter 37 The Shire XXI 208

Chapter 38 Scotland XI..215

Chapter 39 The Shire XXII 223

Chapter 40 Northwest France I 230

Chapter 41 The Gambia V 237

Chapter 42 Northwest France II..242

Chapter 43 Morocco 248

Chapter 44 Scotland XII 251

Chapter 45 The Shire XXIII..257

Chapter 46 Gibraltar 262

Chapter 47 Scotland XIII 277

Chapter 48 Northern Spain 289

Chapter 49 Scotland XIV 330

PROLOGUE

The windows of opportunity exist; it's just a matter of recognising them when you see them and having the audacity to slip through before they are slammed shut.

There's no such thing as the perfect crime because, well, what is perfect? The definition of a perfect crime is subjective; my perfect crime will not be the same as yours. That said, allow me to tell you about mine, anyway.

Chapter 1

SCOTLAND I

Calves burning, pumped rigid with blood, complaining with every step up the worn road—if "road" was a fit description for the gravel-strewn scar that switched back and forth across the face of the mountain. Overhead wires hummed as the wind brushed over them and stole the voices of the legs that dangled from the chairlifts on their journey up to the top of the mountain, or at least the end of the lift run. The inappropriately shod feet indicated that the owner was a thrill-seeking tourist clad in denim or, worse, the lurid and bulging bought-for-the-holiday leggings—comfortable, but telling of a less-than-active lifestyle.

A sudden gust of wind caught out what looked like a butterfly. The object, a sweet wrapper, brushed against Connor's chest on its downward spiral to the ground. He looked up at the legs swinging excitedly, hearing wisps of more excited laughter.

Connor stooped carefully to pick up the wrapper. The weight of his backpack shifted, and he leaned hard into his walking pole to maintain his balance. He stood again and pushed the wrapper into his jacket pocket. He untied his neckerchief and wiped his brow. The sweat was drying quickly in the breeze, and he could feel his skin tightening from the salt. Another gust of wind chilled him, the cooling sweat overcoming the complaining muscles as he began to walk.

Walking alone, Connor looked not up, but forward two or three steps, picking out a rock, a ridge or a tussock of grass. As he reached each landmark, he set a new goal, trying not to count the steps, battling against the endless calculations that seeped into the forefront of his mind. Right foot to right foot, one step, seventy steps, one hundred metres, another click on the pace counter. Naismith calculations, Naismith corrections for ascending, temperature difference with altitude, and wind chill.

He stopped and looked up. The Ptarmigan restaurant sat squat and ugly on the shoulders of the abused mountain like a crashed spaceship—both angular and rounded, once a cutting-edge architectural design, purpose-driven with no illusion of aestheticism. Just precast steel, reinforced concrete, and glass, but still a feat of engineering, considering its lofty perch, a welcome harbour on the edge of a stony sea.

Turning, Connor gazed down the side of the mountain, the best part of a climb, looking on the Lilliputian appearance of man behind—matchbox-size buildings, stiff and rectangular. Coloured ants glistened in the watery sunlight and followed each other along the asphalted roads, like cartoons drawn across the panorama. Best of all was the demarcation of the tree line, the frontier above which civilisation hung on, tenuously fighting a continuous battle against the elements. The shackles were falling away; the years of meticulous planning had reached fruition. Ahead lay six months of freedom. It wouldn't be easy, of that he had no doubts, but he hoped that the tree line, as long as he was above it, would keep him safe. He turned again and once more started not counting the steps.

Chapter 2

THE SHIRE I

The fire station stood quiet, the engine in the bay seen through the porthole windows of the red bay doors a caged leviathan. Voices drifted out from the upstairs windows.

The crew sat around the mess deck table. The banter was lighthearted, the conversation surprisingly lofty for periods of time before being dragged down to the gutter humour stereotypically portrayed by the firefighters' counterparts in television documentaries and dramas. Connor sat at what had become the head of the table by nature of the fact that he was sitting there. He pondered the point, actors being firemen, creating the mould for the firemen to grow into. He had joined the fire service twelve years earlier, thus achieving an ambition seeded in his brain the day the brilliant red, bell-ringing fire engine had blazed past an impressionable six-year-old, walking hand-in-hand with his mother along a busy London high street. The realisation of this ambition had followed numerous applications, none of which had borne fruit as they coincided with the endemic unemployment caused by the Thatcher government. Six years in an employment wilderness had seen him hold down two jobs. Luckily, he had survived without having to "sign on," but he had not enjoyed where he was or where he was going.

His last application and a lifeline had been thrown—an acceptance, the recruitment process, and the probation followed by the examinations, promotion, and attendance at the fire service college. His promotion to sub officer had come quickly and had raised expectations, as well as a few eyebrows. Connor enjoyed his work, looking forward each day to the camaraderie among the crew whilst carrying out what he believed to be a worth whilst role in the community. He was proud of his job; he could speak well of it and was often praised for his work, which would bring a blush of embarrassment to his cheeks.

Death and destruction came with the job. He had witnessed both the tears of joy and sadness. He had coped with the peaks and troughs that his experiences showed him, believing that whatever he did could only help a person who was suffering to suffer less, or help the family by acting with the dignity that the dead deserved. That was then. Now, as Connor half listened to the aimless chatter, he realised that the job had changed, the firefighters had changed, the regime had changed, not necessarily for the worse, but beyond what he had joined. He had changed with the job and tried to alter his way of thinking. Health and safety now ruled any actions operationally, whilst political correctness and equality were all that mattered elsewhere. Connor could cope with this, but those around him struggled with the concepts; the inaction at a fire whilst it is "risk assessed" frustrated many firefighters old and young—the seeming inequality of equality, the favouritism bestowed on the previously underrepresented groups (it went beyond parity). It was getting hard to be a working white male nowadays. Connor had nailed his colours to the mast, however; he was committed to his profession. He had reached that stage in his life when a career change was not practical. He had watched as people he knew got big pay rises, company cars, and bonuses. There were no perks in the fire service. Working weekends, bank holidays, nights, and even the millennium night had nearly resulted in a divorce from his wife, Charlotte.

Sure, he got time off. "Four days a week," Charlotte would point out. "How I'd love four days off a week."

Connor had tried to make her understand that having the days off was for working forty-eight hours over four days, more hours than she worked at her five-day-a-week, nine-to-five job. He also pointed out that four days off were not much use if he was on his own at home. He knew lots of firemen who "worked" on their days off. He had done so himself, as they needed the extra money; his take-home pay was quickly absorbed by the mortgage and other bills that seemed to roll in continuously. He often wondered how those around him could afford children. They said things like "you find the money," but children were not on Connor's or Charlotte's event horizon.

Lunch was almost over now, and a heated discussion was taking place over the following question: "If you had the choice, would you rather lose your arms or your legs in an accident?"

Macabre conversations like this were not uncommon, and often sucked in the whole watch's attention. Everyone would chime in with their "logical" choice and then go on to justify their choices with what they believed to be reason. The group would divide and harangue the opposite side until the fence-sitter (there was always one) would try to quantify how much of the arm or leg would be lost or whether a combination was an option. This would broker new ground and take the conversation on a different course until the original question was all but forgotten as more philosophical subjects were tackled. The ultimate goal of such conversations was to snare one of the group, who would take up the baton and reveal some flaw that the rest of the group would seize upon. It was never serious, and in the fullness of time, all the watch members became the butt of the conversational joke. Connor, however, rarely rose to the bait; he'd pitch in, but if he did slip up, he could usually twist enough to muddy the waters and the moment would pass. This was important, as it could get awkward being in charge and ridiculed by the group he was in charge of. His rank was not precious to him, but he wouldn't let it be abused too often. He considered his position in the group a man amongst other men. They would laugh at his jokes, agree with his argument, and listen to his pearls of wisdom, but it was

5

difficult to know whether this was because of his rank or because they genuinely found him funny, fair, and wise. It was hard to be eating, living, laughing, and joking with someone and the next minute be bollocking them—but, he reasoned, that was what he got paid a little bit more than the others to do.

Connor sat at his desk, studying the plans of a building that the crew was going to inspect that afternoon as part of a fire safety visit, when the leading firefighter walked in.

Connor asked, "Everything all right?"

Tony, the leading firefighter who was best described as a gone-to-seed, second-row forward, responded, "Yeah, you?"

"Yeah, what are the boys doing?"

Using the term "boys" caught in Connor's throat a little, although they were all "boys." The political correctness was becoming automatic, but generic terminology would cut no ice with Tony, the leading firefighter. As much as Connor tried to convert him, Tony had always countered, "It's not a fucking inspection hatch. It's a manhole cover. They're not fucking waste operatives, they're dustmen. The day I see a woman come out of the hole in the ground or empty my fucking bins is the day, I might change the way I fucking speak, okay?"

Connor had tried, but there was no arguing with the logic. Tony possessed a sharp tongue and a wit to match, and he had an amazing mind for storing and recalling facts, a walking *Whitaker's Almanack.* Connor liked and respected Tony, a real right-hand man.

Tony continued, "They're servicing the rescue equipment."

Connor refocused on his paperwork. "Oh, right."

Sensing that something was amiss, Tony asked, "Are you all right, Connor? You seem a bit down lately."

Sighing, Connor carried on looking at the paperwork. "Oh, you know. Same old, same old."

"Charlotte giving you grief?"

Connor looked up. "Is it that obvious?"

"Well, you know."

Connor had resigned himself to the fact that there were no secrets in the fire service. Firefighters were in the premier league alongside the fish wives and knitting circle teams when it came to gossiping. He believed that the truth was never as interesting as the speculation that not knowing could generate, so he would attempt to control the rumour mill at its source

"Yeah, she's always banging on, her friends this, her friend's husband that. I can't make her understand. She cannot grasp that if I work my days off, we get more money. But we don't have the time to do anything, and if I don't work extra, we ain't got the money to do it! It's a bloody vicious circle."

Tony's look reflected the understanding of the matter. "Tell me about it."

Connor was now warming to the subject. "The house is a bloody mess, my car's on its last legs, and she's talking about new kitchens or fucking off on holidays. 'Oh, Anne's going to New Zealand for six weeks,' or "Lou and Cilla just got a new car.' Sometimes I could just strangle her and her bloody friends."

Tony, in a placating mood, replied, "Moral high ground, Connor. Just take the moral high ground."

Placation, however, was not what Connor sought. "Moral high ground my arse. Invisible heroes, that's us. Nobody gives a fuck about us until their house goes up or they're mangled up in a car wreck. It's a different story then, all right. They'd give everything and anything then. You put their fire out or cut them out of their car, and you're lucky to get a fucking 'thank you' out of them. There has got to be a better way. Every week I buy my lottery tickets. I'm convinced I'm going to win, and I dream of what I'd do with the money. It wouldn't have to be much, either."

Realising that trying to pour oil on Connor's tempestuousness was not going to work, Tony attempted a diversion: "How much?"

The effect was noticeable in Connor's double take before he replied, "A million would be nice, half a mil' on a big house in

Scotland or Wales or somewhere like that and half a mil' in the bank to live off of. I reckon half or three-quarters of a million would be enough, though. I'm not greedy."

Having side-tracked Connor's rant, Tony saw his opportunity. "Well, one thing's for sure—you're not going to earn it even with all your part-time jobs. You're going to have to win it. The odds are only fourteen million to one!"

Connor smiled. It was just a pipe dream, but he liked to escape to his dream, to walk around in his big house and bigger garden. He had set a personal goal on the size of the property: He should be able to stand in the middle of the garden and throw a half brick as hard as he could in any direction and not annoy his neighbours. That was how big his garden had to be, minimum; anything beyond that would be a bonus. After all, there was no point building a fence around your dreams.

Returning from the tree-filled vista of his dream to the omnipresent, magnolia-daubed reality, Connor returned to work.

"The governor wants us to go to the bank to cash a cheque for the petit cash this afternoon. I was thinking that we'd do the fire safety inspection on Radco's as well. They know we're coming, don't they?"

"Yeah, I phoned them earlier."

"Shouldn't be any problems, should there?"

Connor wasn't keen on the fire safety side of the job, but it was all part of being a firefighter. It wasn't so much the inspections, but the paperwork that each visit would generate and delivering the same old lectures.

"You can't wedge that door open. It's a fire door. Put back that self closer. Service your extinguishers. What do you mean, you don't test your fire alarm?" Connor wouldn't mind, but it was their safety. At the end of the day, he would launch into his closing speech, which pointed out that he would not want to be the person standing in a coroner's court answering questions as to why equipment had been left in such disrepair that someone had lost his life. This usually provoked the right response.

The contravention notice would be served and, after another inspection twenty-eight days later, things were normally put right.

Tony picked up the file and flicked through it to see what he already knew. "No, no problem. I'll do it with one of the lads whilst you go to the bank. I know you don't like them."

Connor smiled. "Cheers, Tone. Did I ever tell you what a wonderful human being you are?"

"Often. I just wish you could convince my wife!"

Connor took a radio, tested it, and crossed the road from the fire engine and headed for the bank. People often stared at his uniform. The reactions amused him. There wasn't much difference between the fire service and police uniforms, and people would often confuse them, which could be embarrassing. That very same mistake was about to occur and start cogs turning in Connor's mind.

Connor hurried across the road and along the pavement towards the bank. Autumn was resisting the onslaught of winter, but a chill northerly wind gusted, a precursor of what the winter would deliver. Connor was glad he had put on his NATO-style pullover. He pushed open the door of the bank as a woman was leaving and held it open for her as she passed through. The woman smiled and thanked him, which Connor acknowledged. As he stepped into the bank, he looked back to catch the woman doing the same. They both smiled knowingly. Connor knew it was the uniform. *Some women,* he thought.

There was a queue in the bank. Connor sighed and joined the back of the line, which had extended beyond the cordon that shaped the customers Indian file, leading to the sign asking the next customer to "wait here." It had stretched back towards the door past the foreign currency till. It was a point of some wonder to Connor that regardless of how busy the rest of the tills were, there was always a teller at the foreign exchange window, pretending to be counting traveller's cheques, but dreaming no doubt of sunnier climes.

Connor's attention was attracted by movement in the corner of his eye. The window alongside the foreign exchange was being unbolted and then folded back, a breach into the inner sanctum. A woman cashier started to load the counter with coloured cloth bags, some containing coins and others containing what Connor assumed was paper currency, judging by the block like shapes showing through the bag material. Five or six bags were stacked on the counter. Connor was standing just a step away. The woman looked at him.

"You're early today."

Connor looked around to see whom the woman was talking to, but there was no one. The woman was talking to him.

"Am I?" Connor replied with a smile. The woman had mistaken him for a bank security collector.

There was a brief pause in which realisation started to dawn on the woman. Then, a look of shock and embarrassment danced across her face. Connor said, "Oops!"

The cashier retrieved the bags and tried to resecure the grill whilst looking around to see if her breach of security had been noticed. She started to mumble, "I thought you were . . ."

The woman's voice trailed off as she hurriedly grabbed back the cash bags and closed the window, trying not to make eye contact with a smiling Connor.

As the line shuffled forward, a seed of an idea formed in his mind.

Chapter 3

SCOTLAND II

As the Ptarmigan restaurant grew closer, a light drizzle pushed around by a strengthening breeze stole the steamy exhalations of Connor's breath and added them to the mist creeping around the mountain. The visibility was worsening—not that this was a problem this side of the peak, but the higher he climbed, the worse it would get. The track on this side of the mountain was well worn, marked with eyesore shacks that housed the snowploughs used during the winter. The continuous whine of the ski lift overhead and the wide path meant Connor could practically walk blindfolded to the restaurant.

Connor reached a concrete footpath. Yards ahead of him stood the restaurant like some World War II gun emplacement. A memory triggered in his mind as he viewed the restaurant again, this time with a touch of scepticism. He had once visited a "secret" nuclear bunker underneath a "farmhouse" built to house the fleeing British government in times of national emergency. He had wondered about the real use of buildings and the power of the government. If they could build bunkers fifteen miles from the centre of London in heavily populated areas without the local community knowing, what could they do in more remote places? Connor shunned the thought and approached a large metal door, well balanced on its hinges that led into a corridor and another set of doors into the restaurant itself. Excellent protection from the weather—or perhaps worse?

Smiling as he loosened the straps on his rucksack and letting it slide to the floor, Connor was so relieved that it felt as if he was floating. He pushed the pack over to the coatrack. He pulled a bicycle padlock from the side pocket and fastened the bag to the racking. He straightened and arched backward, pushing his hips forward with his hands in the small of his back, attempting to counter the miles of stooping forward up the mountain. It felt good. He reached inside his jacket and under his fleece pullover and pulled his tactile vest away from his body. The cold air rushed in and chilled his damp torso. He let the vest go and felt the damp material cling to his skin. Then, he turned and walked to the toilets.

The harsh light against the tile and steel-clad toilet caused Connor to squint until his eyes grew accustomed to the new surroundings. Connor stared into a pitted mirror at his drizzle-dampened face and matted hair, which was reminiscent of a '50s hair cream advertisement. He pushed the button of the hand dryer and directed the nozzle at his face. The warm air felt good as he ruffled his hair, which had been cut respectably short. It wouldn't need cutting for a few months.

The door behind Connor opened. He stopped drying his hair, self-conscious about his preening. An overweight, aged tourist came in. The two men were a step away from each other, yet miles apart in appearance. Connor was broad-shouldered and tight-waisted, whilst the tourist was almost an inverted reflection. Their clothing illustrated their polarity as well. Connor was clad in technically-designed mountain wear, whilst the tourist wore sporting apparel for some sport not at home on a mountainside that had probably cost as much as Connor's.

Connor nodded at the tourist, who grudgingly acknowledged his greeting. Apparently, the courtesy of mountain kinship did not stretch to day-trippers. Connor turned back to the mirror as the hand dryer switched off. Happy with his appearance, he exited the toilets.

Outside in the corridor, a group of people were gathered around Connor's pack. He tensed momentarily until he realised they were just reclaiming their own day packs and jackets. Connor crouched down and pretended to tie his bootlace until the crowd dissipated, allowing a blast of cold air in from the mountain. He crossed to his pack and checked it over before entering the restaurant area.

The restaurant had a lot of windows, with views from three sides, double-glazed with rolled-up steel shutters. Again, the bunker jumped into Connor's mind. Ten to fifteen people had gathered around the tables, sipping hot chocolates and eating sugary pastries. A small group was studying pictures of the snow-clad mountainside from the previous winter. Connor approached the counter, walking past the clear Perspex hatches, displaying gaudy-looking cakes, sweet rewards for suffering a twenty-minute ride in the fresh air. The sugar rush was needed to climb the final 150 metres to the mountaintop.

The checkout was stationed by a forty-something woman, long bored with sitting serving in this airy eyrie.

"Yes, dear?" she asked as Connor approached.

Connor asked for a coffee as he picked up two creamers and a small handful of sugar sachets. The woman jiggled the cup and saucer as she poured the coffee. Connor picked up a chocolate bar as the woman slid his coffee across the counter and asked an exorbitantly inflated price associated with tourist traps the world over, the ultimate market forces economy. Connor dug into his jacket pocket, pulled out a Velcro wallet, and paid with a five-pound note. He received his change (not much) and deposited it in the mountain rescue box. He didn't need the extra weight. The cashier thanked him for his donation. She knew that her job was only safe as long as people kept visiting the mountains. The mountain rescue teams turned potential bad press into heroic news stories—stories that, if left unchecked, would deter all but the most avid adventurers, who were not the type to dally in mountaintop coffee shops. No, the tourist trap needed blue skies, high-calorie snacks, and the frisson of excitement, height, and fresh air as bait.

After reaching the car park at the bottom of the mountain, the only way was up. At this point, the dangers associated with the location were stated when there was little or no choice left, and the party leader, generally the most vocal alpha male tourist, was pressured into making an all too important decision with too little knowledge experience or recourse to suitable other distraction or worse still based on the last time they were here when everything was fine. Not realising that the more times you cross the road, the more chance you have of being run down. A ski lift to the top was all too attractive, and like an ingrained, irrepressible craving, people lined up to play Russian roulette with the elements.

Connor was caught out by the words of gratitude. "Oh, oh that's okay."

The cashier continued, "Are you coming on or off?"

Trying to stay ahead of the conversation and not leave any telltale signs, Connor replied, "Coming off. Just had a couple of days over on Ben Macdui."

"Did you see the "Old Man'?" the woman smirked.

Connor took the reference to the "Old Man," a legendary figure that roamed the mountainside and attracted a mixed press, in his stride. He smiled back. "No, not on this trip."

"You've not had a bad time of the weather. You're lucky. I fear it's going to change for the worse."

"Yeah, I've been lucky."

The contrast of voices was stark: Connor's clipped, dropped-vowel London accent compared with her aggressive, but more rounded Scottish accent. It made Connor believe all the more that the English language was a bad import for Scotland; the bastardised language did not suit the accent. The Gaelic place names on Connor's map, which were almost poetic, were corrupted by an English accent. The Scots, on the other hand, did them the justice they deserved.

The cashier, master of the micro conversation, realised the clock had run out. "Ah well . . ."

Connor picked up his cup and chocolate bar and nodded to the cashier. "Thanks." He moved away to a table across the room, near a window looking down the mountain, but also allowing a line of sight through the vision panel into the foyer and his rucksack. He reached into his pocket and removed a plastic bag. He put the chocolate bar, along with half the sugar sachets, in the bag and returned it to his pocket.

Connor stirred the milk and remaining sugar into his coffee and took his first sip. The hot and sweet beverage had an instant uplifting effect. It had been a long drive up from London, though his beat-up little car had done well. It had taken him hours to reach Glasgow. He'd stayed overnight at a room-only hotel where he didn't look out of place—just a walker or climber getting away from it all.

Connor had parked the car on a back street early that morning. The number plates were false, copied from a car of the same colour and model he had seen an elderly couple driving. He had spent quite some time grinding off the engine block number, as well as the number stamped in the doorframe, and removing the manufacturer's plate. However, this was all overkill, as he had only bought the car a few days earlier and given false details to the car vendor. He knew these details were untraceable.

After parking the car, Connor had reached over and opened the passenger window half an inch, and then lit a nightlight candle and placed it in the footwell. He got out and removed his kit from the boot whilst also taking the cap off a one-gallon petrol container and inserting an eighteen-inch length of mutton cloth to act as a wick into the open spout. He shouldered his pack, closed the boot, and walked away. It was a warm day, half an hour he figured.

He found a sandwich bar down the street, ordered some food, and waited. Halfway through his cup of tea, Connor heard a muffled *crump.* Five minutes later, a fire engine rushed past, followed by a police car. Connor left the sandwich bar and walked back towards the car. "Like a dog to its vomit," he said to himself, but the curiosity of the arsonist was compelling. The car was steaming gently, the rear end burnt back to bare metal. The plastic bumpers and grill had melted off and were a molten plastic mass on the road. The front number plate was only half destroyed, but not enough was left for the police to trace the car. The rear number plate was well on its way to adding to the global warming effect. Connor just walked on past. Halfway down the next street, his keys plonked into an adjacent drain whilst he tied his bootlace.

Chapter 4

THE SHIRE II

Connor climbed back into the fire engine. The driver was just leaning on the wheel, watching the world go by. Easing himself into the lofty perch, Connor said, "That's that done. Heard from Tony?"

The driver shook his head. "No, nothing. There's a job on the radio, though, house fire. Persons reported."

This roused the firefighter's instinctive curiosity. "Where's that?"

The driver relayed the details. "B22. It's gone to four pumps. Station officer Dickens is going on."

Connor nodded and ran through the scenario in his mind. "It would make a change for us to get a job. Perhaps we'll get ordered on."

The driver was more pessimistic. "Knowing our luck, we'll get told to stand by at B22."

Connor's mind ran back to his interview. The physical assessments were over, the hose running had nearly made him sick, the ladders were fine, and the smokehouse was dark and damp—but the competition to get through carrying a five-gallon container of water was enough to displace any fear of claustrophobia. The examiner's preamble that only the first five thought would be accepted had unveiled a survival of the fittest mentality in all the applicants. It was more by luck than judgment that Connor had emerged first.

Connor saw himself sitting in his interview. The normal questions had been asked. Towards the end, the interviewer, an overbearing officer in his full undress uniform, asked Connor, "As a percentage, how often would you expect to be out fire fighting?"

Connor hadn't anticipated this question and answered conservatively, or so he thought. "About fifty percent?"

The interviewer smiled that paternal smile that recognises the hubris of naive youth. "If I said more like three to six percent, would that surprise you?"

Connor was taken aback. The interviewer continued, "Most of your time will be taken up by drills, maintenance, inspections, and studying."

He was right, even though at the time, Connor had believed it was just a test to gauge his reaction. The improvements in fire safety legislation, building control, smoke detectors, and new legislation concerning household furnishings had all diminished the number of fires that occurred. This coupled with the spate of television shows depicting the emergency services and the informational handouts of what to do in the event of a house fire, had reduced the number of so-called "good jobs." In the last six years, they had even changed their name from "fire brigade" to "fire and rescue service," reflecting the number of road accidents they attended.

Connor's mind clicked back as a voice came from the radio. "Bravo 150, Bravo 150 from XI. Over."

Connor picked up the handset. "XI from Bravo 150, go ahead. Over."

The simplex radio system allowed only one person to speak at a time, which took some getting used to. Conversations terminated with the "over" command, indicating that the respondent could carry on.

"Bravo 150, order your appliance to stand by at station Bravo 22. Over."

"XI from Bravo 150, understand. Stand by at Bravo 22? Over."

"Bravo 150, affirmative. Over."

"XI from Bravo 150, all received. Will advise when mobile. Over."

"Bravo 150 all received XI to standby."

With the air of a wise old man and with deadpan delivery, the driver said as he started the vehicle, "Told you, didn't I?"

Connor just shrugged. "Yeah, *c'est la vie*." He picked up a walkie-talkie. "Tony, you receiving? Over."

Tony's voice replied from the speaker, "Go ahead."

"Tone, we've got to go and stand by at Bravo 22. They've got a house fire. Sorry, mate."

Tony replied a little too happily, glad to get out of the inspection, "Okay, be with you in a minute."

Connor put the radio back in its holder. He spoke out to the driver, but not necessarily for him; he realised that the role of the officer in charge was to plan and be prepared to adapt, and it was an option for the firefighters to just move in the direction they were pointed until told to stop.

"It's always the bloody same," Connor said. "You make an appointment, and *bang* in the middle of it you get a bloody shout. It's one of the reasons we shouldn't be doing fire safety. That company doesn't realise how we have to juggle our time. Now we've got a pissed-off manager who has taken time out of his day to show us around, and we're running off halfway through. It would piss me right off if I was that manager, trying to run a business and clowns like us were diving in and out like this." He stopped ranting as Tony and the remainder of the crew returned to the fire engine.

Later that afternoon, Connor and Tony were sitting in the office preparing for the end of the shift and change of watch. Connor was checking the petit cash, and Tony was writing up the fire safety report from the earlier visit. Connor floated a question: "Tone, here's one for you. If you were going to commit a crime, what would you do?"

Tony looked up from his paperwork, wary of committing too early. "Be more specific."

Connor elaborated, "Well, would you hold up a bank or building society, computer fraud, what?"

Tony thought for just a moment before replying, "Well, I can't work our bloody computer, so computer hacking is out. Banks and building societies amount to the same thing—you've got to go in when they're open, so that means guns or violence somewhere along the line, and I haven't got the balls for that. Besides, you need more than yourself. You'd need a gang, and that brings its own problems."

Connor interjected, "What do you mean "its own problems'?"

Tony was warming to the subject. "Well, the more people who are involved, the more people can get caught, fuck up, blab, or spend too quickly. One minute they're in their two-up, two-down house, cheap Ford in the drive—the next, new motor, new house. People ask questions. You'd have to keep it tight . . . two, maybe three people at most. And you'd have to go for cash. Not new money, either—I've heard it's traceable through the serial numbers. Not drugs, gold, or jewellery for the same reasons—plus, you've got to move them through a fence, which means you're going to get ripped off at best or grassed up because you've increased your sphere of liability and control. What you need is information. That's the key to a good crime, good planning, and no surprises. That way it's clean and no one gets hurt. Most of all, though, it has to be worth it."

Connor digested this, and then asked, "And what does 'worth it' mean?"

Tony looked a bit taken aback. "Well, worth it, not a piss-pot amount. Enough that you'd never have to commit a crime again. Most of the crooks in the slammer are recidivists, stupid, or very unlucky. They probably started out small and got braver and braver until they got caught for a piss-ant amount of something that gets them a record. A reputation is formed, and they become one of the usual suspects who get hauled in every time someone sneezes in the wrong place."

Connor pursued the question. "So how much—how much is worth it?"

Tony's hands twisted the pen he was holding as he pondered. "Well, the way I see it is, if I came to work every day for the rest of my working career I'd take at today's pay 25K a year before tax. After the taxman has robbed me, I'm left with, what, 18K? Pay my pension, national insurance that leaves 15K. Multiply that by the number of years in a normal career, thirty? That gives me or someone starting out on their working life an expected earning potential of about 450K. Wow, I hear you say, but say I live in a 100K house. The mortgage will probably cost me about 250 to 300K over twenty-five years, which leaves about 150K to live on, pay the bills, buy new cars, pay for the holidays, that sort of thing. When all's said and done, I'm prepared to work for thirty years to achieve what? A nice semi, a nearly new car, some small amount in savings, and a pension. All that being the case, the crime would have to be worth about 450K. That would allow me to buy the house outright, live the life I'm going to live anyway, but give me back the thirty years I'd have to work in order to be in the same position!"

Now it was Connor's turn to look taken aback. "Fuck me, Tone, you've thought about this before, haven't you?"

Tony smiled devilishly. "It might've crossed my mind before now."

Both Connor and Tony fell into silence. Tony finally broke the pause in the conversation. "What sparked that question, anyway?"

Connor responded, "Oh, you know, I was just thinking that there has to be an easier way. Just look at us. How many A levels have you got?"

Tony, somewhat embarrassed, replied, "Three"

Connor continued with an impressed nod, "You could have gone to Uni', right? All the bloody courses I've been on, I could be accredited with a degree. I look at people who know fuck all about anything pulling down 40K to 50K a year. Then, there are the lucky bastards who get their paths greased for them through their families, friends, and old school ties. You know, that sort of thing."

Tony warmed to the socialist undertones. "The silver spoon gang?"

"Yeah, they're the ones. There's this guy at the rugby club, salt of the earth, streetwise kind of kid, but not the sharpest tool in the shed. You know where I'm coming from?"

"Go on."

"Well, after the game, we're standing in the bar having a beer with some wet-behind-the-ears guy. He'd just left school and was talking about going to college or university, but he was also wondering about work. Trying to live off a government loan and parent handouts wasn't that alluring. Anyway, he's asking me and this other guy what we earn. I'm not that proud—every year our pay rise is printed in the papers, so it's pretty much public knowledge already, but I play him along. Now, he knows what I do, so I ask him how much he thinks I earn. He thinks about it, how it's a tough job—could he do it?—gory sights, that sort of thing. Finally, he says 40K! Well, as you can imagine, I almost choked on my beer. I laughed and said, "In your fucking dreams," so he asks how much and I tell him. Judging by the look on his face, I guess I'd put him off a career in the fire service, especially after I'd told him that was after twelve years of service and two promotions. So then he asks this other guy how much he earns. The guy's had a couple of drinks, but doesn't want to boast, so the kid starts guessing. Now, this guy works in the city—the futures market or something like that.

Tony chided, "What, he sells flowers?"

Connor, a little put out, responded, "Futures, not fuchsias. D'you want to hear this or not?"

Tony could see that he was annoying Connor, but he couldn't let an opportunity like that pass by. Smirking, he apologised, "Yeah, yeah, only joking."

Connor gave Tony a weary glance before continuing. "Well, the kid starts guessing at 50K? No response. 60K? 70K? Still the same, the bloke asks the kid to stop, but he's like a dog with a bone and won't let go. 80K? 90K? The kid keeps pushing, and by now, I'm getting bloody interested. 100K? 110K? The guy finally decides to tell, seeing it as the lesser of two evils. How much do you think he's pulling down a year?

Tony guessed, "150K?"

"Bang on. 150K plus bonuses, and I've just given this bloke a lift to the away game. Six times my annual, and I've been his bloody chauffeur and bought him a beer! He went to a shit school, scraped a couple of O-levels. He's six years younger than me and has never had a blister on his hand, unless he wanks off over his bank balance. Tone, tell me there is something wrong there, or is it just me?"

Tony nodded solemnly. "You're right, it makes you sick."

"Sick? I couldn't taste the beer for bile! So I started thinking, in five years this guy's going to earn what I anticipate will take me thirty years . . ."

"And?"

Connor turned directly to face Tony. "And? And?" He was animated now, to say the least. "I tell you, I could do a holdup for, let's say, 500K. If I stash the cash, even if I got caught and got fifteen years—of which I did, let's say, ten—I'd still be twenty years up on the deal with half a mil' in my pocket."

Tony was rocked a little by Connor's rising passion. "Woe, ten years is serious jail time, and they'd still be all over you when you got out. You wouldn't be able to do anything, not even spend your giro without the Old Bill and the social security checking your receipts.

Connor ceded the point. "Yeah, granted, but this ain't much short of a prison sentence, and I've got nothing to show for it. At least in prison, I could get on a degree course or, even better, come out with a doctorate or something. Look at what's-his-name . . . ? McVicar. Violent crime, long bang-up, and now he's a bloody social anthropologist doing a column for a national newspaper. Do you think that's right?"

Once again, Tony found himself agreeing, but trying to defend the system. "Yeah, I know, but he paid his debt to society."

The fire was rekindled in Connor. "Debt to society? Living in society is just jumping from one debt to another. It's like bailing out your lifeboat, only there is some bastard who keeps stabbing another hole in the bottom, which means you have to bail faster and faster.

Trying to reason, Tony pressed, "But still, ten years—that's a long time away from your family and friends."

Connor nodded, but his eyes were misted as though focused on a distant point. "Well, of course there's a price to pay, but it only has to be paid if you're caught. If there was a way to do a crime that's really perfect, not just—"

There was an explosion of noise, and the gentle half-light was flooded with harsh neon as the station lights came on automatically. Connor looked up at the clock. 5:45. Snapping back to the moment, Connor said, "Fuck it, I wanted to go home on time tonight."

Connor and Tony made the long walk to the pole house, both too long in the tooth to get excited and run. Tony went down the pole first, followed quickly by Connor. They made their way across the appliance bays. The other firefighters were putting on their fire kit, and the bay door was rising automatically. Connor was handed the call out sheet, which he took a moment to study.

The driver climbed up into the cab and asked, "What've we got, Sub?"

Connor focused on the script in his hand. "RTA. Persons trapped. M25 junction 24 to 25."

The driver fired up the appliance. Connor climbed into the cab and slammed the door, looking over his shoulder at the crew squeezed together in the crew cab, struggling into their fire kit. Once he'd counted to make sure all crew members were present, Connor reached for his safety belt and said, "Let's go."

The driver revved the engine, and the appliance rolled forward out of the bays. Connor pressed the foot pedal as the appliance entered the traffic stream and the siren rang out. The siren still stirred something in him; it pulled at the memory string to his childhood. Unfortunately, his reminiscence was broken by the effect the siren had on other drivers, who responded in ways that were beyond belief. Connor listened as the crew shouted at them. He could remember a time when he would have done likewise, but time had mellowed him. Invariably, the driver of the car causing problems to twelve tonnes of fire engine and an irate crew would be a member of the flat cap and driving gloves brigade, a woman who couldn't get any closer to the steering wheel if she tried or some young buck with a stereo output equal to engine output and a parcel shelf so full of speakers that even if he were to use his rear-view mirror, he wouldn't be able to see anything.

The appliance now had a free road and soon joined the slip onto the motorway. The traffic was already backing up in the distance, the tell-tale glare of brake lights and the flashing amber hazard lights revealing that this was a real incident. This fact didn't prevent cars from overtaking the fire engine, a fact that always amazed Connor. They could be rushing headlong into a cloud of poisonous gas or a fuel tanker fire or who knew what, and still some cars would overtake the truck, which was doing eighty miles an hour.

As they drew nearer, the driver steered onto the hard shoulder. This was always a bit hairy; the restricted width and view could easily lend itself to an accident, but this seemed to be tempered by the driver's need to make quick progress. Connor would sit up in his seat, staring ahead and warning the driver who was busy dodging wing mirrors and trying not to slip into the gravel traps. The experienced lorry drivers would get as far over as possible in lane one, but there was always the fear that the siren would startle a driver into jumping into the hard shoulder in front of the appliance. The driver had to expect the unexpected. After all was said and done, it was the driver's licence that would suffer the points of an at-work accident.

The traffic was at a standstill. Farther ahead, Connor could make out the blinking of a blue strobe light. Connor looked back over his shoulder. "Nearly there, fellas," he announced. He picked up the radio handset and called in his attendance. A police officer clad in a luminous motorway jacket was laying out cones to divert the traffic, but he stopped to frantically wave the appliance through. Connor knew that a frantic motorway cop meant that it was serious. The driver knew what to do, but Connor liked to be sure his inner control freak was appeased. Connor's voice was clipped, but calm and authoritative as he directed the driver

"About twenty yards short of the back car. Fend off from here to lane two."

The driver stopped the appliance at an angle pointing towards the central reservation. Connor climbed down from the cab as the rest of the crew dismounted and fell automatically to their individual tasks. Hose reels were run out towards the crash, the pump was engaged, and equipment was unloaded from the rescue locker. Approaching the scene, Connor tried to take it all in: two cars and a lorry nose to tail. One car had run into the back of another, which in turn had run into the back of the lorry, under which it seemed to be wedged. A huddle of people were gathered around the car driver's door, which was still closed. Connor deduced that the driver was still in the vehicle.

A police officer approached Connor. "There's one guy trapped in this car, and the driver of the other car has whiplash, I think."

Connor looked at the officer for a second before surveying the scene. "Just the three vehicles?"

The police officer followed Connor's gaze. "Yeah."

"Ambulance on the way?" Connor asked

"I called them when I called for you," the officer responded whilst gesturing to his colleague to keep the traffic back.

Connor was now next to the car. There was broken glass strewn over the ground from the broken side window. It glinted in and refracted the flashing strobe lights, little spilled diamonds of light that stole Connor's mind for an all-too-brief few seconds—a moment's interlude before he had to refocus on whatever horrific sight might await him in the car. The front end of the car was concertinaed against the underside of the lorry. Connor had an idea from his experience of what kind of injuries to expect.

He eased between the bystanders, who were holding various bits of first aid kit, some with bloodied hands. The driver was conscious, his face covered with cuts from the broken window. His injuries weren't serious. Connor could see that the air bag had deployed and now hung limp from the torn centre of the steering wheel. Looking into the footwell, Connor saw the twisted and mangled wreckage that had trapped the driver's legs. Connor slowly reached into the car through the driver's window, gently took hold of the driver's chin, and cupped the base of his head.

Connor spoke quietly, but assertively. "Do not look at me. Look straight ahead and try not to move your head or neck." Adjusting his tone, he continued, "My name is Connor. I'm from the fire service, and we're going to get you out of here. But first we need to get a neck brace on you, so stay still. Do not try to speak or move, and I'll try not to ask you any questions until the brace is on."

The driver moved his eyes towards Connor. Connor could see that he understood, but he could also see the fear. Still holding the driver's head, Connor looked around to find a member of the crew standing at his elbow.

"See if the back door opens," Connor said, nodding towards the door in question.

The firefighter tried the door. "It's well stuck, Sub."

"Okay. Come and take over from me here."

The firefighter moved around and took over from Connor. The rest of the crew had arrived by then.

Connor called his leading hand to him. "Right, Tony. He's well trapped, so let's get a stiff neck collar on him and some oxygen. Let's get this car chocked and blocked and set up the rescue equipment dump over there." Connor gestured past the throng of firefighters and first aiders. "Make sure someone stays on that hose reel. Let's create some space and keep back those who are doing nothing but gawking and listening in. One air bag has already deployed. We don't know if there are others, so be careful.

The crew fell to their tasks as Connor made his way back to the appliance. The driver was standing alongside the pump bay, getting the final piece of his fire kit on.

Connor had to shout above the noise of the revving engine, which was supplying the hose line. "Radio control, tell them to make pumps two and that the rescue tender is required."

The driver shouted back as he adjusted his tunic and kept an eye on the gauges. "The rescue tender is already on its way. I just heard them book mobile, and I think I saw Bravo 0-nine just go by on the northbound carriageway."

"Okay, good. Just confirm that we need them and get an ETA on the ambulance. This bloke needs help."

Connor pondered the situation. His quandary was that speed is of the essence—the "golden hour" and the "platinum ten minutes" were well-used phrases in rescue work. They were relevant to the survival and long-term recovery chances of the injured person. This was tempered, however, by the need to stabilise the casualty and eliminate as much of the risk as possible. Risk elimination was time-consuming, and time was a commodity that the casualty had short stock of.

Connor had seen many such accidents. He was aware of the risks associated with multiple air bag deployment, glass dust, flesh-dissolving fluroelastomers, explosive charges, and the spilled petrol and oil. A wrong cut could unleash an avalanche of uncontrolled events with who knows what as an outcome, but inaction could be equally disastrous for the casualty.

The air rebounded with the sound of two-tone sirens approaching. Police, ambulances, and more fire crews wove their way through the backed-up traffic, which had already produced a brown haze of smog that hung over the stationary queues.

Connor found an ambulance paramedic, and they spoke briefly about a course of action. The paramedic and her partner got to work on the trapped man. Connor wasn't gung-ho in his approach; he would allow the casualty to be stabilised, while he took the opportunity to organise the crews. He would consult with the ambulance crews and decide on the best means of extrication.

The rescue gear had been set up and laid out, ready for use, including cutters and spreaders that could tear cars open in minutes. The car had been chocked to prevent movement, and the rear door had been removed to allow better access for the paramedics to clamber in and treat the casualty.

The police were hovering around the scene, gathering information and evidence from subjective eyewitnesses and objective sources, such as skid marks on the roadway, which were marked and measured. The police had closed the motorway completely, so the rush hour traffic had come to a standstill. Connor knew that impatient drivers would try to escape the jam and squeeze through lesser roads not designed for the volume of traffic they would be subjected to. Connor could not help but make the comparison to a coronary thrombosis, which would eventually lead to vehicular rigor mortis. *Gonna be late tonight,* Connor thought.

The paramedics were ready. A roof removal and side fold-down would allow maximum access for the driver to be treated and for the crew to get to the footwell area and cut his legs free of the wreckage. Connor briefed the two crews, who in turn took up their position and started the operation. They cut through the window and door pillars, working from front to back. The rear screen popped, and the team lifted the roof away—a two-minute convertible. Tools got to work again, and soon the driver's side was door-less. The footwell exposed a crush of shining metal gripping torn material and bleeding flesh.

Careful incision of the spreaders and cutters inched the metal off and away from the driver's legs. The driver's cries of pains served as cues to stop; the anguished looks of the paramedic crew were the cue to resume.

The rescue was protracted. Lines and bags of fluid were changed, and vital signs were monitored. Various injections were administered, but the painkillers were minimal, as the hospital didn't need a stoned casualty. The fire crews used the driver's pain reaction to tell them when they were cutting too close. The platinum ten minutes was long gone, and the golden hour was all but used up when the driver was finally lifted onto a stretcher and carried to the ambulance parked on the hard shoulder.

Connor was looking amongst the wreckage when Tony said, "All right sub?"

"Yeah, you?"

"Yeah, better than he is, anyway."

"Yeah, gonna be a while before he's up and about," Connor said.

"I suppose he had better cancel his skiing holiday." Tony reached into the car and picked up a skiing brochure.

"I don't know. Have you seen those wheelchair toboggan-type things?"

"Yeah, right. That'll be just what he wants, to swap one pile of fast, out-of-control metal for another. Speaking of fast-moving metal, what the fuck is that?"

Connor looked around to see what Tony was looking at. Another set of flashing blue lights was fast approaching along the hard shoulder, using more than a liberal amount of bullhorn and two- tone wailers. A police car emerged followed by two dark blue lorries, which in turn were followed by another police car. They were brought to a halt by the ambulance parked on the hard shoulder, the array of other emergency vehicles, and the crash itself. There were fifteen seconds of inaction when everyone stared at the little convoy and wondered what was going to happen. Almost simultaneously, the rear doors of both police cars opened, and four flack-jacketed policemen got out. They looked serious, and their semiautomatic rifles underlined their "don't fuck with me" attitude.

A flack-jacketed officer approached one of the motorway police officers, who, after an unsmiling conversation, started shouting at others to clear the hard shoulder. The armed officer returned to his colleagues, who had not moved away from the lorries. A flurry of activity followed, and a great deal of energy was expended in clearing the vehicles from the hard shoulder. As each was moved, the convoy crept forward, lights still flashing. The drivers looked tense, tapping their hands nervously on steering wheels that weren't doing much steering. The armed officers looked agitated as they walked alongside, trying to look in all directions at once.

Only one vehicle barred the convoy's progress, and that was the ambulance with the casualty. At the rear door, a police officer was talking animatedly to the paramedic, pointing to the convoy and then back at the ambulance.

Connor and Tony both looked at the scene along with the rest of the bewildered onlookers. Tony said, "They want to move the ambulance."

Connor nodded as he looked on. "It looks like the paramedics don't want to move just yet."

"They're probably still stabilising the driver." Both Tony and Connor watched the scene from the hard shoulder, having turned their backs to the wreckage that lay behind them. The police officer turned away from the paramedic, who vanished back into the ambulance and approached the convoy, where he spoke to the armed officer. The armed officer then spoke into a headset microphone. A decision must have been reached, as the officers returned to their outrider cars in unison and climbed in. They gunned the throttles and, to Connor's and everyone else's amazement, the front vehicle drove off the hard shoulder and up the embankment.

Connor stared on amazed. "Fucking hell . . ."

"The cars might make it, but surely the lorries will tip. The gradient's too steep," Tony said as the convoy gunned the vehicle engines.

"It looks like they don't agree," Connor said, albeit somewhat redundantly in the face of what they were witnessing. The first police car returned to the hard shoulder on the other side of the ambulance. The first lorry was tilting at a perilous angle, but inched past the ambulance, waved through by a police officer as it descended back to the hard shoulder. The second lorry started to follow. Again, it tilted to a gravity-defying angle as it moved along the embankment. The wheels struggled to maintain traction. The back wheels started to slip and crab towards the ambulance. Losing grip, the driver steered further up the slope and revved the engine, but to no avail. The driver of the following police car saw the problem, drove forward to bring the car's bumper against the rear of the truck, and stopped the lorry from sliding closer to the ambulance. The lorry driver revved the engine again, popping the clutch. He regained traction and sprang the lorry forward and down the slope, past the ambulance and followed by the police car. Having rejoined the carriageway, the convoy regrouped and sped off on the now-empty motorway.

Connor turned to Tony. "What the fuck was all that about?"

"God only knows. That must have been some important cargo."

Another cog started to turn in Connor's mind.

Chapter 5

SCOTLAND III

Connor unlocked his backpack, squatted, and then heaved the pack up and across his back. He adjusted the straps and arranged his clothing until he felt comfortable, and then pulled open the door. A gust of wind reminded him of how cold it was. He watched as the self-closer struggled to close the door against the wind. He adjusted his walking poles and turned up his collar before stepping off the concrete and onto the natural stone stairway leading to the summit. After a couple of steps, his muscles started to complain after their brief respite. Connor smiled. He thought back to the gym and the hours he had put in on the step machine and decided that he needed to shed a few pounds.

It was mid-afternoon, and the sun was veiled in an ominous grey blanket of cloud that constantly threatened rain and made fleeting attempts to deliver. Specks of colour ahead denoted the more adventurous tourist climbing to or scampering down from the summit. Most were ill dressed for the environment and the elements. *No wonder people got caught out,* thought Connor.

Step by step, he climbed the uneven stairway, the walking poles giving extra stability and dispersing the weight off of his knees. The poles were common across Europe and were catching on fast in the UK. Beads of perspiration were starting to trickle down his back, forming a damp stain along the top of his trousers. Connor slowed down and tried to pace himself to allow the cooling wind to evaporate the sweat. Staying dry was important; being wet and cold was not good.

As Connor neared the summit, the rain started—windblown at first, but becoming stronger and harder with every metre he climbed. He pulled up his hood and adjusted the toggles. The rain tapped against the fabric and dripped off of the stiffened rim like a mini waterfall. Tourists scattered down the mountain path towards civilisation, their desire for a brief encounter with the wilderness sated.

He reached the summit and was greeted by a blast of wind strong enough to bring him to a halt. He leaned into the wind, which was driving the rain into his face, and kept going. Squinting ahead, he made out the weather station with the anemometer spinning madly in the gale. He made for the leeward side and stepped into the shelter of the building, which blocked the wind. The sudden loss of resistance caused him to stumble forward.

"Bleak" was the word that came to Connor's mind, and aptly so. The windswept panorama was most definitely bleak, the tussocks of grass bled of colour poking between monolithic boulders strewn over the bedrock of the mountain. The only colour was that of the lichen, which clung to their immovable hosts.

Connor dug into his cargo pocket and pulled out an encapsulated map, which he studied to orientate himself. He took a compass bearing on the Coire Raibert, a mountainside stream that fed into the Loch Avon far below on the south-eastern side of the mountain. He stashed the map and aimed the compass at a conspicuous boulder that was in line with the sight arrow. Connor looked around. Breaks in the clouds caused shafts of light to bounce off Loch Morlich and further still Aviemore. The contrast in weather brought a smile to Connor's hooded face; a sunny day on the summit was the exception, not the norm. Cairn Gorm was not the highest mountain in the world by a long shot, but at 1,245 metres and at such a northerly latitude, it had a climate akin to much higher mountains.

Connor braced himself and stepped from the shelter of the weather station. The wind and the rain met him with renewed vigour, making up for lost time and stealing his hearing. He looked around. The mountaintop was his and his alone. The thrill-seeking tourists were thrilled enough and had headed for the sanctuary below. All alone Connor smiled. Just what he wanted.

Chapter 6

THE SHIRE III

The station was shrouded in an encapsulating dark, which was made all the darker by the oblongs of glazed white that fought off the encroaching night as if it were an invading host. The light poured from the defensive battlements and arrow slits like boiling oil, bright but then cooling and fading away on the tar macadam of the drill yard.

Connor sat at his desk, flipping through some paperwork he was less than interested in. "I hear our man scraped through," he said as he turned another page.

Tony was also reading, but he was simultaneously cross-referencing something and scoring off with a well-chewed biro. "Yeah."

Neither looked up from what he was doing. The conversation did not flow, but came interspersed between bouts of reading or writing

"Went quite well, don't you think?" Connor asked.

Tony replied, "Yeah, but those newer cars still worry me,"

"What, the air bags?"

"Yeah, that and all the other possible blow-your-head-off fucking safety features."

Connor considered the point a moment longer. "Goes with the territory, I suppose."

Tony responded immediately and with sudden passion. "No, it fucking don't. I joined the fire service, not the fucking Russian roulette service. One bad decision and you find yourself with a broken neck or scarred for life."

Connor saw an opportunity to take a shot. "Well, the scarring won't bother you too much, will it?"

With his blood still rising and his pen now discarded, Tony responded, "Granted, I wasn't the best-looking bloke when I joined, but this face is all I've got and I'd like it to stay this way—if that's all right with you?"

Connor suppressed his smile badly, and it stretched his face into too many directions at once. "Okay, okay, calm down."

Tony was obviously upset. "Well."

Connor, having regained his facial control, pursued the monosyllable. "Well?"

The floodgate opened. "It just pisses me off that we pride ourselves on being good at our job. We're underfinanced, but we do a bloody good job with what we've got. But after all's said and done, we're still at best five years behind the car manufacturers and at worst ten. Air bags, carbon fibres, lightweight alloys, dual fuel, and all the time we're practising on fifteen-year-old wreckers. In addition to that, the manufacturers don't give a fuck. Sure, they used to show the safety systems, but now, oh no, people expect them as standard. So you don't get "air bag' stamped on the steering wheel—now you get them exploding out of fucking everywhere. Even the fucking ashtrays have miniature gas struts to open them. Heat them babies up in a fire and, *bang,* automobile acupuncture."

Connor was not expecting such a tirade from his normally staid leading hand, but could not fault what he was saying. "You're not wrong, Tone, you're not wrong."

Tony was still in stride. "I know I'm not, and if that wasn't enough, we try to do our job and we've got a bunch of gung-ho security lorries doing a bit of impromptu off-roading with gun-toting old bill literally riding shotgun. What the fuck was that all about? I just wonder if it's worth the money."

"Yeah, I was thinking about that. Have you ever been to an RTA involving a security van?"

The question distracted Tony. "No, why?"

Connor expanded upon the thought. "Well, suppose one of those lorries had fallen over, or we were called to an RTA with one, say even one that had been ram-raided. How the fuck could we get the driver out, or anyone in the back? Let's face it—they're designed to resist that sort of thing, aren't they?"

Tony considered the point. "Yeah, I suppose so. I've never really given it much thought before."

"I wonder if anybody has. I might ring up HQ and see if they can find out for us."

"How are they going to do that, then?"

Connor responded, "Well, they could talk to other brigades and see if they've had any experience and, if so, how they've dealt with them."

"It's certainly worth a try, but I can't imagine any security firms offering up that kind of info—sort of goes against the grain of what they are trying to do, don't it?

Connor was intrigued by the comment. "How so?"

Tony, taking the role of a parent speaking to a child, replied, "Well, you beef up your lorries or vans to make them all but bombproof, and then tell fifty thousand firefighters that to get in, all they need to do is cut here with this piece of kit. They might as well leave the keys hanging on the wing mirror!"

Connor rose above the admonishing tone and retorted with a health and safety rule. "I see your point, but still they've got a duty of care to their employees, surely?"

"They probably do, but when push comes to shove, they'd probably lose a couple of security guards and pay out the compensation if the crash happened, then have their security vans opened up and robbed by every friend of a friend of a fireman."

"Firefighter."

Tony looked confused. "What?"

Connor returned to his reading. "Firefighter. You said fireman."

Tony, back on the topic of many previous conversations, retorted, "I know what I said and I meant to say it."

Connor smiled at him.

Tony returned to his reading with a suppressed smile and muttered, "Bastard."

Chapter 7

THE SHIRE IV

The night had passed slowly and without event. The morning sun bathed the station building with early warming rays that cast long shadows and left frosted facsimiles cowering within the darkened imprint. Connor hung up the phone just as Tony came back into the office.

"Well, that's that, I suppose," Connor said, as much to the empty office and himself as to Tony as he filled the doorway.

Tony justifiably confused, asked, "What's what?"

Connor replied, "It turns out you were right. All the big security companies keep their cards very close to their chest when it comes to giving info on their vans and lorries. There haven't been that many 'accidents' serious enough that the security guards couldn't get out, although they did have two die in a van after it caught fire—and that was because they were overcome by the smoke before they realised what was going on. Any that are involved in a heist or ram raid are clamped down tighter than a duck's arse by the police. It seems that the employees are expendable in guarding their precious cargoes to the extent that, at the end of the van or lorry's useful life, the security firm doesn't sell them. They have them crushed by a registered contractor!"

Tony nodded sombrely. "Well, that makes sense when you think about it."

"How so?"

Tony was finally coming up to speed. "Use your head. Go out and buy a second-hand van and start posing as a delivery guard, or at least work out the best way to gain access . . ."

Another cog turned in Connor's mind. He took another shot at his long-suffering right-hand man. "Are you sure you're not Mr. Big of the underworld, Tone?"

"What?"

"You seem to have explored a lot of dark avenues. That cherubic face belies the devil behind, I'm sure."

Tony smiled. "Did you know that the devil was a displaced angel?"

"You don't say."

Tony felt he was on a rich vein. "Where angels fear to tread, the devil steps instead."

Connor found himself listening to the rhetoric. "Did you just make that up?"

"Yeah." A smug grin spread across Tony's face.

Connor pretended to look for some lost piece of paper and lifted a seemingly random piece to shield his other hand. "Tony."

Tony stepped closer, thinking that the piece of paper was relevant and being proffered. "Yeah?"

Connor lowered the sheet to expose his hand with an Agincourt salute and said, "Fuck off."

Tony feigned hurt. "Oh, that's right. Very nice. I spout poetry and you spout Anglo-Saxon!"

Chapter 8

THE SHIRE V

The journey home after a night shift was always a pleasure. Midweek was particularly rewarding. The lines of commuter traffic on the opposite carriageway was a small recompense for the long hours and the poor pay, but a payback nonetheless. Ahead of Connor lay four days of rota leave. The crew would leave the station to be replaced by the oncoming crew starting the first of its four shifts. The moods across the parade lines were total opposites for Monday morning oncoming shift, and the Friday evening off going shift was a civvy street comparison.

Connor liked this time of year—winter just moments away, autumn hanging on like the fiery leaves to the host tree or bush, the frost sprinkled round like sugar, the fog-filled hollows and the cold freshness of each lungful of air—even the fug of chimney smoke. Connor could tell what was being burnt: coal, wood, the sickly sweet smell of a garden bonfire, or the acrid smoke as a piece of plastic crept unseen into the blaze.

A good time of year with still better to come, the winter was exciting. There was a selfish pleasure in knowing that he was not missing out by not being out. Nobody else was abroad doing things he knew he should be doing; they were all cosseted away in their cosy homes. If he did venture out, he had the world to himself with so few people braving the weather. No one sauntered around exposing himself. Connor realised it was probably a Freudian flaw in his character, a dislike of dithering, a directness of action that only left him when studying the sea or a patch of pebbles on the beach. Connor could spend hours combing the flotsam and jetsam of the shoreline, an enjoyment only surpassed by settling down with a good book in front of a fire.

The forty-five-minute journey home saw the sun haul its way above the mist, stealing the mysticism from the countryside. Connor arrived home, unloaded his workbag from the car, and opened the side door. (The front door was used by strangers to the house.) The door protested at being opened, yet another job for Connor to address. But not yet—maybe next spring or when Charlotte complained as much as the door did. Every room in the house had its list of jobs to do. Charlotte prioritised the tasks, and Connor attempted to tick them off as time and money allowed. The more difficult jobs had evolved a subset timetable that meshed with other jobs until the domino effect arrived full circle back at the beginning. It was a naturally cold house, north-facing, built around the turn of the twentieth century. It was a farm labourer's house that must have been of average size when it was built, but by modern standards was almost palatial when compared to the timber-framed "prestigious developments" that seemed to spring up at the drop of a hat, shoehorned into any vacant space. The green belt was failing to preserve the sanctuary of the countryside from the suburban sprawl.

The house was empty. Charlotte was at work, so it was just the two cats and a dripping tap for company. The tap was better company than the cats—but, alas, unlike the cats, it was on the list to go. The house had been a good buy; although run-down and unloved, it had transmitted a certain feeling to Connor when he and Charlotte had first viewed it. Three years had passed, and the house had slowly become a home as each room was "temporarily" decorated in anticipation of bigger things in the future. Charlotte was responsible for decorating, while Connor was responsible for the more structural tasks—re-running pipes and wires, ripping out, and re-building. The floorboards and walls had hidden a multitude of DIY sins, which had caused many headaches and more than a few arguments. There was a light at the end of the tunnel, Connor knew, but at this moment he couldn't see it. *Probably a dog leg ahead of me,* Connor thought.

He switched on the kettle, took the broom from the cupboard, and started to sweep the floors. This had become something of a ritual; the amount of dust that accumulated was a perplexing riddle for Connor, and although he couldn't convince Charlotte, the cats were to blame as far as he was concerned.

The kettle clicked off as Connor emptied the dustpan. He poured hot water into a cup and watched the water turn a rusty colour as he steeped the tea holder loaded with a personal blend of loose leaf.

He sat down at the kitchen table with his steaming mug and started to open the mail—credit card bill and bank statement (both in the red), two invoices that were paid by direct debit, and then the usual charity letters asking for donations, and the junk mail. Connor wasn't averse to junk mail, apart from the paper waste it generated. The catalogues of items for sale that promised to "radically improve your life" always amazed him and, on more than one occasion, tempted him, more from curiosity than because of any promised benefits to the purchaser. At the very least, the catalogue would while away a cup of tea and distract him from the depression of his overdrawn bank balance and more pressing bills. He walked to the sink to rinse his now empty cup and looked out of the window. The sun had given up for the day and gone to play behind the clouds. The grass still glistened with dew, and the trees and bushes were in the final throes of shedding their painted autumnal leaves. Connor sighed. It was still a lovely time of the year.

He sat at the dining table, which was strewn with foolscap folders and textbooks. He had paused and was once more staring into the garden through the dining room window, which was a little overdue for a clean, but quite a ways down the list. Four years earlier, Connor had started a degree in environmental studies through the Open University and finals were once again upon him. "Discuss the environmental impact of the third world debt to the African and Asian continents." Half a page of scribbled notes lay in front of him, littered with the names of western multinational companies. He had realised four years earlier that his fire service career would be hampered if he didn't possess a degree of some sort or other. Having studied for all the fire service statutory exams, Connor felt that the usually pursued degrees were not for him and that a degree unrelated fire service would be both refreshing and a fallback position if, as he liked to say, "things went tits up" in his chosen profession. Finding the funding had been difficult. The fire service would sponsor individuals whose degree could be used for the betterment of the organisation; for unrelated subjects, the service would only give time off for course attendance. Part of the course necessitated a year of overseas study or, to accommodate those like Connor who were employed full time, eighteen months of home study. Although the fire service would allow him to take a sabbatical, finances would not. So Connor chose the eighteen-month option to gain the credit he required towards his finals. Finances aside, Charlotte was far from peachy about him traipsing around in foreign country for a year. Third world debts were pretty hard to focus on, especially as a more pressing first world, first-person debt cast a dark shadow over Connor's near future.

Connor's mind flipped to the last few days at work, the talk of money and crime with Tony, and the episodes at the bank and on the motorway. He smiled to himself as he recalled a joke he'd once heard about a God-fearing man who wanted to be rich, but turned down the opportunities that came his way because they were not honest and would capitalise on the labours of others. The man lived his whole life in want, and when he finally ascended to heaven, he decided to take the matter up with God, asking why it was that he had strived to do the right thing and received no earthly reward for the life he led. God's response was that if the man chose not to take advantage of the opportunities that he had arranged for him, that was his fault!

Connor thought about the funny parable and applied it to his life and his recent experiences. It was hard living with a moral code when the immoral dined so well around him.

Connor picked up his pipe and looked at the clock, 12:45. He loaded the bowl with tobacco, lit it, and watched as the tobacco glowed with each pull. The still air of the kitchen became striated with the exhaled smoke. The first pipe of the day was always the best, and putting off that first smoke until after midday heightened the pleasure and satisfied something within him that allowed him to believe that he still had a modicum of self-control, that the drug was not in full control. He smiled as the nicotine kicked in. The slight light-headedness made him recall his school days and his first smoking experiences. The excitement of avoiding capture by the teachers and the camaraderie amongst fellow smokers that bridged the normal divisions created by age all added to the almost sensual experience.

Now, though, there was no excitement—just a need, a craving that must be sated, and the pipe was the latest in a series of evolutionary steps from that first cigarette from someone's offered packet. Connor had experimented with a variety of different smoking mediums in his nicotine pursuits, the only constant being that the nicotine source had become stronger. He'd smoked the usual proprietary brands, dabbled with "roll-ups," and then gone off of the beaten track with less common French cigarettes. This had several advantages, one being that nobody else liked to smoke a full-strength filterless cigarette, the other being the chicness of the brand itself and the continental flair that it lent.

The next step had been cigars. Although Connor enjoyed the smoke, they were never really practical in the workplace because they took too long to smoke; there was no popping out for a quick smoke. In addition to the impracticality, Connor also harboured the private thought that he looked as if he were smoking a dried turd. He moved on to the miniature cigars, or cigarillos, which fitted all of his needs and had been his mainstay for years.

Connor had always secretly hankered for a pipe and had been surprised by Charlotte one Christmas when she gave him one as a present. She believed that it would reduce the amount he smoked, and indeed it had; he was limited as to where and when he could smoke it. Restaurants were out of the question, as were certain pubs in which the clientele would just ridicule the smoker. Connor was old enough, but not old enough not to care just yet. The other limiting factor of smoking a pipe was the amount of time he spent servicing it, and then there was the small matter of keeping it alight. Connor often joked when questioned about the pipe that he had saved himself a fortune in the amount of tobacco he needed, but this had been offset by the number of lighters and amount of lighter fuel he'd had to buy. In fact, he said he always dreaded the budget because he got double-whammied with the pennies spent on tobacco and then the customary increase on fuel. There was, of course, the pleasure that the pipe brought, which outweighed the disadvantages. Connor's local tobacconist was one of the few that still catered to the hardened smoker with a whole wall of tobacco varieties stored in sweet-style jars. The tobacconist weighed the amounts on a pair of polished weighing scales. The whole process took on a reverential feel that filled Connor with a glee shared by the children in the same shop who were literally kids in a sweet shop.

In his stupefied state, Connor picked up his pen and wrote "security van." Next to that, he wrote a list of the various vans he had seen at companies and their individual liveries. Next he wrote the various locations that he'd seen them. The list included banks, building societies, garages, and supermarkets. He wrote a series of questions: "Were they delivering or collecting?", "How much?", and then finally the last question, which he underlined, "How?"

Chapter 9

SCOTLAND IV

The descent down the Lairig Ghru was uneventful. The path was well trodden, but the occasional bit of scrambling was necessary due to the weight of the pack. Alongside the path, the stream was relentlessly noisy and, in combination with the rain that drummed against Connor's hood, rendered him all but deaf to the surrounding world.

Connor kept an eye on the rushing water. He would need to cross at some point and was looking for a good place. He had dismissed several potential sites with the thought that there would be better farther downstream. As yet, they hadn't materialised. The stream fed into Loch Avon, a vast body of water over which towered Cairn Gorm and the mighty Ben Macdui, whose mountainside streams constantly fed it. Connor knew that the use of the word "stream" would cause the natives to roll their eyes, but he wasn't comfortable with the word "burn." It made him feel as if he was trying to ingratiate himself with the locals and, therefore, made him feel more like a foreigner.

The wind had lessened due to the protection that the re-entrant offered, but Connor knew that it would assail him again as soon as he left the mini valley carved by the stream over the millennia. There was a masochistic part of him that was looking forward to feeling the force of the wind once more. The noise of the stream crescendoed as the path dropped down to its level and then faded as the path climbed away. The rain splattering against his hood caused him to hear the occasional shout or peal of laughter, sometimes a distant conversation that caused him to turn around looking for the source of the voices. There was nobody there. It was at times like this, the stories of the "Old Man" of the mountain weren't so hard to believe.

Connor could feel the time creeping by. The sun was invisible behind an opaque shield of cloud. He was climbing down towards the loch, and the shadow of the mountains created its own dusk and night. The stream to his right was widening, and he continued to search for a safe crossing. He scouted the far bank for the start of a path indicated on the map, but the tributaries that added their water to the stream also looked like footpaths. The volume of the stream was continually growing, running deep and fast at the narrower points and slower at the wider points. The water was nearly eighteen inches deep, and Connor's gaiters would not resist the inflow of icy mountain water, which he was keen to avoid.

He looked down to the loch below, a rain-splattered body of water rippled into wavelets by the wind blowing along the glen. It looked grey and unwelcoming. There were still four hundred metres to go. Connor figured that he had missed the path on the other bank, so he decided to try to cross. He lengthened his walking poles. The threaded locking devices were hard to grip with his wet gloves, and the cold had caused the aluminium to contract, reducing the diameter of the poles a little. He eventually had to remove his gloves to get the bezel to twist. After extending the poles to the estimated depth of the water, he retightened them and replaced his gloves. The pause had allowed the cold to creep over his damp body once again.

Connor planted first one pole and then the other into the fast-flowing stream, and then stepped cautiously onto a sticking above the water rock, spreading his weight amongst his three points of contact. He had planned his route all the way across from one rock to another, but the distance between his planned stepping-stones altered along with his perspective from them. Muddy silt stains washed away downstream as he hopped from one rock to another. Five feet from the bank, the stepping-stones ran out, Connor had guessed that the last stone was two or maybe three feet at most—at any rate, a distance easily jumped. Perched as he was on the last stepping-stone, he realised his misjudgment. He looked up and down the stream, but there were no other stepping-stones that would allow him to keep his feet dry. Turning back was not a viable option, either, perched as precariously as he was. The water between him and the bank was flowing more slowly by comparison, an indication of greater depth. The bank had been undercut due to a slight kink as the stream's direction changed. Connor carefully repositioned the walking poles midway into the gap he had to cross. The water came about two feet up the poles. He tensed and kicked hard off of the rock he was standing on and swung his leg through as if on the second stage of the triple jump. The weight came onto his arms and transferred to the poles, which he hoped he had tightened enough. His lead foot made the bank, but he felt his trailing leg kick up the surface of the stream, sinking in until Connor came to a stop halfway onto the bank, his trailing leg submerged to the knee. He threw his arms forward to create enough momentum to roll sideways onto the bank before the weight of his pack pulled him backwards into the stream. He crashed onto his side amongst the rocks and sodden tussocks and heather. He scrambled forward to pull his lower leg from the river and curled up into a foetal position, lying momentarily still to take account of any damage. He could feel the icy water permeating through his sock and into his boots.

"Bollocks," he said aloud to himself and then looked around, a little self-conscious about talking to himself and about the exhibition he had just put on. He conducted a quick self-assessment, in case the adrenalin rush had masked any bodily damage. Thankful to find no apparent injury, he used the walking poles to gingerly raise himself up to the kneeling position. He then struggled to get upright and, in doing so, a wry smile crept across his face.

Hard for me, hard for them, he thought.

Chapter 10

THE SHIRE VI

"Shit," Connor swore aloud at the taps as they grazed his knuckle. "Nothing's ever fucking simple."

He adjusted the wrench and tried again, holding the tap in one hand and the wrench in the other. He applied pressure, and the brass centrepiece grudgingly started to turn. Breathing a sigh of relief, he twisted the last few turns by hand and removed the brass fitting from the tap. He straightened up from being bent over the sink.

Connor's eye caught something moving on the drive. Looking through the window, he saw Charlotte's car backing in. He looked up at the clock. *She's early,* he thought and then returned his attention to the tap. He saw the badly damaged washer, the cause of the drip, and set about prying it off. The side door thumped open to Charlotte's kick.

"Hi," Connor called out, still concentrating on the tap washer. When there was no reply, he looked up. Charlotte was standing at the kitchen entrance, and Connor knew from experience that her expression suggested a problem. He enquired, "You're early. Is there a problem?"

Charlotte's voice was tense, clipped. "We need to talk."

He stopped what he was doing. This was serious. "I'm listening," he replied.

Charlotte was struggling to make eye contact. "This should be hard for me, Connor, but it's not, which convinces me that I'm right. I think we should split up."

Connor felt the words hit him like a punch in the stomach. There was a strange metallic taste in his mouth that had not been there moments earlier. "What?"

Charlotte started to repeat, "I said . . ."

"I heard what you fucking said. Where the fuck did it come from is what I'm asking."

Charlotte started to rebuke Connor, trying to wrest the high ground. "Now, don't start swearing, I've . . ."

"Don't tell me to stop swearing. You walk in here and drop a bombshell like that, and I'm supposed to be cool, calm, and bloody collected? Fuck off, Charlotte. Give me a break."

Connor's retort was just as effective as a retaliatory strike to a preemptive nuclear attack. Charlotte responded with a steady abdicator's speech to the nation, measured and final. "It's something I've been thinking about for the last two or three weeks now. It's not working, Connor. We should never have moved in together. The house is getting me down, you're getting me down, and it's not the same as it was. Everything's changed. *We've* changed, or at least I have, and I'm just not happy anymore. I don't look forward to coming home. I'm still young enough to go out pubbing and clubbing, not stripping walls and sweeping up brick dust every spare hour." Connor was hurt. He knew then that regardless of what he said, the death knell had been struck on the bell of their relationship. There was no recovery from what had been said. It would have been too hard to maintain over the long term, a spectre that would always be willing to step forward from the shadows into the daylight of the moment.

Still, their relationship had been good. There had to be something worth fighting for, surely? Connor tried. "But we knew this when we moved in. We knew there would be sacrifices."

Charlotte was steadfast and adamant in her position. "Sacrifices, sacrifices I've made, but we're no nearer the end. There's no light at the end of the tunnel. Every spare penny is sunk into this money-sucking pit. I haven't bought any new clothes, I can't go out, we haven't had a proper holiday for two years, and when I look around at my friends and what they're doing, I realise that that's what I want to be doing."

Connor reeled from this barrage. He'd watched Charlotte's scornful expression as she talked about her home and the contempt that she felt for it. He knew that Charlotte had been talking to "their" friends and knew that old arguments were about to be resurrected. He also knew that they had gone unresolved last time, so there was little chance they would be resolved now. A sudden wave of apathy swept over him. His self-worth had taken a kicking. He felt alone, very alone.

He looked at his grazed knuckle and then up at Charlotte. There was a mixed bag of emotions pinballing around in his mind and a vacuum in the pit of his stomach. He resigned with a dead and hollow, "Okay"

Caught out by the one word, Charlotte questioned his response. "Okay what?"

"Okay. If that's what you want, okay."

Charlotte was expecting a tirade of abuse and argument and was therefore perplexed all the more by the lack of it and tried to explain. "Connor, can't you see . . ."

The line had been drawn and could not be undrawn, and Connor accepted this. "I've said okay, haven't I? I'm not going to beg. I can see your mind is made up. How are we going to work it?"

Charlotte tried again. "Connor, I don't want to see you hurt, but can't you feel the changes between us?"

Connor felt the anger rising and struggled to keep it in check. "Look, Charlotte, don't ask me to bail you out. I know things haven't been great, but I've mistakenly put it down to work stress and the lack of money, not the house itself. We entered into that with our eyes wide open. You've justified it to yourself, and I'm not going to convince you that you're right. I feel that I've given all I can, but that's obviously not enough. I can't compete with your friends, and I can't supply the lifestyle you want, as you've rightly pointed out. Perhaps I've been too focused on trying to get the house right, perhaps my priorities are different from yours. I thought that was what you wanted. I was wrong, so here we are. What happens now?"

Charlotte had nowhere to go. She was prepared for the fight, not his acquiescence. "Oh, Connor . . ."

Connor cut in with a rising anger tingeing his words. "Look, Charlotte, let's just cut to it, ah?"

Charlotte realised now that the die was cast and she had gotten what she wanted. To try to soften the blow was pointless and too late. "Okay, okay. We'll sell up and split everything. I'll get my stuff together and go back to my parents. You've got nowhere to go, so you can stay here if you want. I'll get in touch with the estate agents and solicitors, unless you want to do something different?"

"Well, give me a nanosecond to think about it."

"I've always hated that sarcasm."

Connor sneered as he laid another trowel full. "Good. I'll keep it in the share-out, then?"

Chapter 11

THE SHIRE VII

The following three months went by in a haze. Connor was operating on autopilot. At work his crew was sympathetic and tried to lift his spirits, which usually involved a dose of double spirits, which in turn led to a downward spiral and rock bottom. The house sold quickly—too quickly for Connor, who had to rush around to find a flat to rent. But the offer on the house was too good to let pass. After everyone had been paid off, Connor was left with £25,000 in the bank, more money than he had ever owned in his life.

He had found a two-bedroom flat close to work, but the rent was nearly £600. On top of this were the bills. Connor quickly realised that he would have to supplement his income, or he would erode his nest egg very quickly. To that end, he started working with a fireman from another watch. They pitched in together to buy a reasonable-looking car and shared it to work for a mini cab firm. Being on opposite shifts allowed them to use the car alternately when the other was on duty, and they exchanged the car when they changed shifts at work. This allowed Connor to have a car and its benefits at only half the expense. The hours were not great, but the job covered his living costs and a bit more, so his savings were growing rather than diminishing.

The second job also had other unplanned perks. Connor had to cut back on his drinking, as he had seen all too often the effects of drunk driving. This allowed him to get his personal life back on track and to focus a little further than the bottom of the glass. He was also meeting people. This was enough of a distraction to keep him from dwelling on the past and had led to two short-term relationships—very short term. He was determined not to be bitten twice.

Nine months on, Connor was back on an even keel. His savings had grown, but so had his familiarity with his situation, and he was not happy. It was as if he had been given a piece of chocolate when hungry instead of a proper meal. He had been putting in the hours, but still felt he was getting too little return for the energy invested.

It was late. Connor was sitting in the cab office, and things were quiet. He dropped the newspaper onto a pile of dog-eared car and soft porn magazines, stood up, and stretched. "I think I'll call it a night," he said to Sandra, the peroxide-blonde fifty something sitting at the controller's desk, the telephone tucked between her chin and shoulder and the ubiquitous cigarette hanging from her pink lips. She gestured for him to wait as she took some final details from the caller.

"There's a job going your way if you're interested?"

Connor approached the desk. Feigning an amorous affection, he said, "Go on then. How could I turn you down?"

She spoke into the phone. "It'll be with you in about five minutes, love, okay?"

She hung up, totally unmoved by Connor's feigned adoration, much too battle-worn from working amongst taxi drivers.

"Pickup at Abbotts Square, the Silmarillion. Woman by the name of Stephanie going to Oakes Cross."

"Cheers, Sandra." Oakes Cross was only a couple of minutes from Connor's flat. "I'll drop off and then I'm going home. I've got a nice bottle of wine waiting for me in the fridge. Interested?" Sandra looked up. "I am, but I don't think my Sam would be too impressed!" she replied with a wry smile.

"Oh well. Some other time, ah?"

"Yeah, and I'll cite you in the divorce case, shall I?"

They both laughed as Connor left the office.

The roads were shining from the light drizzle, and the sheen reflected the distorted images of the brightly-lit pubs and eateries that surrounded Abbotts Square. Connor pulled up outside the Silmarillion, one of the smarter pubs, which had a Tolkien theme that was lost on most of its clientele. Standing in the doorway was a small group of people sheltered under the awning.

Connor rolled down the window and called out, "Cab for Stephanie?"

Three well-dressed women detached from the group. One, a petite brunette said, "That's me."

Stephanie got into the front, and her friends climbed into the back. The car quickly filled with a heady combination of perfumes. Connor liked perfume. For him, it said a lot about a woman—the light, fruity scents of the happy-go-lucky and the heavier, earthy scents of the much more serious, passionate woman. Connor breathed deeply.

"Are you all going to Oakes Cross?"

Stephanie responded, "No, just me. Can you drop these two flirts at Pelham Green? It's *en route*."

"Yeah, no worries," Connor answered with a smile.

Stephanie looked across the street-lit interior of the car. "Nice smile."

Connor, caught off guard, replied, "Sorry?"

Smiling with a flash of teeth, she said, "Don't be, it's nice."

Connor was a bit taken aback. "Is it? I don't get to use it a lot."

A voice from the back chirped, "Ah, poor lamb."

"Bet our Steph could make that smile a permanent fixture," said the other woman in the back as she leaned forward to deliver the line.

Connor, outnumbered and outgunned, shot back, "You reckon?"

The two women in the back tittered like naughty schoolgirls, not drunk, but jolly from the evening's drink and more confident because of it. Stephanie was smiling, but in the darkness, Connor couldn't make out if there was a blush of embarrassment.

Connor was no great wit, and his attempts were, as Charlotte had pointed out often, interpreted as sarcasm. This tended to make Connor seem standoffish, which could be intriguing sometimes, but more often made Connor seem disinterested despite all the other green lights being shown. This was not the usual approach. It could make Connor seem like a bit of an enigma, and it had provoked some women in the past to chat him up. It was something that Connor was aware of, and this "innocence" could be intriguing. Connor was quite relaxed knowing that this was his last job of the night, and a car full of attractive women was a nice job to finish with.

He made small talk, the stock and trade of cab drivers the world over. "You had a nice night, ladies?"

The woman in the back said, "Oh, so-so."

Her backseat colleague supported her. "A free drink on the firm."

Connor nodded approvingly. "That can't be bad. What was it in aid of?"

Stephanie added, "An in-house award. We are top depot in the southeast."

Connor enquired, "Top depot?"

"Yeah, Key Security."

Connor recognised the name. It opened up an avenue of commonality beyond the usual staples of the weather and how long 'til he finished.

"Oh, that's the delivery vans, isn't it?"

"Yeah, that's us. Number one in the southeast," said one of the women in the back

Connor asked as he looked back over his shoulder, "What are you number one for?"

"Ninety-eight percent pickup and delivery rate, all thanks to our Steph, 'The Organiser.'"

Connor feigned admiration. "Well, it sounds like congratulations are in order."

"It's a team thing, hence the night out for everyone." Stephanie stressed the last two words as she twisted to face the two women in the back seat.

"Key Security. That's down on the London Lodge industrial estate by KMC Chemicals?"

"Yeah, that's us." Stephanie sounded intrigued that Connor knew of their whereabouts, and tried to find out how he knew. "I would've thought that it's a bit off your patch. You can't get many jobs down there, can you?"

"The cabbing's only part time."

"Do you work down there, then?"

"Not far. Do you know the fire station?"

"Yeah."

Connor let it hang.

"You're a fireman?" an excited voice from the back asked.

"Only when I'm not cabbing," Connor replied with a hint of resignation.

"Oh wow, do you have a long pole?" The girl fell back into her seat giggling, thinking she'd delivered the most original one-line innuendo ever. Her backseat friend roared in obvious approval, and Stephanie feigned disapproval, but was obviously beaming behind her hands to hide the smile from Connor. Connor smiled, too. It was harmless, and occasionally there was an original line used. There was plenty of material—hoses, axes. Connor had heard many.

The women in the back just carried on baiting him, safe behind the seat barrier. Stephanie tried to be more serious, which was again the usual pattern. She'd say things like, "Isn't it gory?" and "I bet you've seen some sights," and the classic "I couldn't do your job," but was at every opportunity ridiculed by her companions.

Connor just laughed along with them. This was no time for the thoughts that he harboured about who could do the job. Scraping up the victims of fires and accidents wasn't a job for anyone to endure, but given the training and the equipment, it could be done. Connor would say that the real heroes were the people who tried to do something beyond their capacity; after all, he could not do someone else's job unless he was given the training.

Connor started to slow down as he approached the sign indicating Pelham Green. "Whereabouts, ladies?" he asked as he leaned forward and scanned the street.

"Just here on the next corner will be fine," one of the women from the back said.

Connor drove another hundred yards and then steered the car to the kerb. He stopped the car before the two women in the back fumbled with the door handles and climbed, less than gracefully, out of the car into the night. The argument about who was paying ensued good-naturedly. They handed some money to Stephanie through the open window.

"You'll have to let us come and see your pole," one of the women called through the window to Connor. Her friend, no doubt feeling braver now that she was out of the car, added, "Yeah, perhaps we can slide down it?"

The two women laughed and called goodbye as they walked off into the night, leaning against each other for support. Connor dipped the clutch and pulled away from the kerb. "Nice friends."

"Oh, I'm sorry. They're so embarrassing once they've had a drink."

"It's okay. You kind of get used to it. You're right—it is just the drink talking. They'll be as meek as mice back in the office."

Stephanie knew better. "I'd like to think so. Them two have been like that all night, and believe it or not, they're worse at work."

Connor looked across. "Really?"

"Yeah, really. When the drivers and the teams come in, they turn the air blue. I don't know whether it's the uniform or the fact that they know they're safe. I really don't know."

Connor nodded knowingly. "Yeah, the uniform is supposed to be some women's thing, God knows why?"

Stephanie extended the conversation. "There is something, but it depends on what uniform. Police, army, fireman—it has to be one of those. I think subliminally it's a power thing."

Connor laughed.

"What? Was that funny?"

Connor, still chuckling to himself, replied, "Kind of."

"Why?"

He shook his head. "Well, it's just, well . . ."

"Go on."

An intrigued smile crept across Stephanie's lips. Her head tilted slightly, causing her to look up at him. Connor looked briefly away from the road to take in the face of Stephanie, which was smiling demurely at him. Her thinned lips were pumped up with lipstick and liner. She'd dusted her cheeks with blusher, and Connor noticed that the foundation was light and silken and properly applied, not stopping at the chin line, but continuing on and blending down onto her neck and into the hairline. This was something that taxi driving had made Connor aware of; the sideways glance at some of his female customers showed that they applied their makeup looking square at the mirror and paid little or no attention to their profile image or the more shaded neck. Stephanie's whole visage was neatly framed in a bob of dark brown hair.

Connor continued, "I was just thinking how insecure most of us are, big red fire engines, going around in groups, mob-handed. And as for the uniform, it's hardly flattering. I mean wellies, for Christ's sake."

Stephanie pondered the image. "Oh, I don't know."

Shrugging, Connor said, "It must be a woman thing."

The car fell silent for a while. The sodium street lights threw metronomic shadows across the car. Connor reached for the music system and asked, "Do you mind?"

"No, please."

Connor inserted a CD, and a sultry ballad filled the car. Connor started to reach for the "skip track" button.

"No, don't. I like this one, don't you?"

A sad look that told of some distant remembered pain flashed across Connor's face.

"I used to."

Realising she had ventured into an area of personal grief, Stephanie tied to back out. "Oh, I didn't mean to pry. Skip the track if you want."

"No, it's okay. I'll leave it if you like it."

There was a pause as they both listened to the song.

"What's your name, can I ask?" Stephanie blurted out, as if she had been thinking of asking, but was having some sort of internal debate as to whether it would be appropriate and the question just came out. Nonplussed, Connor turned to look at Stephanie. Their eyes met, but any emotion was hidden in the shaded interior.

"Sure, it's Connor."

"I'm Stephanie."

Connor smiled. "I know"

"Oh, of course, stupid of me."

They both smiled at the *faux pas*. Stephanie was glad that the cab was dark enough to hide her blush.

"There's that smile again. It went when you put the CD in, you know."

"Did it?"

"Sad memories?"

Connor looked across again. "Kind of. A long time ago now, though."

"Wife, girlfriend?"

"I thought you weren't going to pry." Connor looked across smiling.

"Oh, don't trust me. I'm way too nosy!"

They both laughed.

"And I thought I could trust you. I hope that doesn't mean you're going to do a runner on me?"

Stephanie pointed down into the dark of the footwell. "What, in these heels?"

Connor looked down but couldn't see in the dark. He did notice the skirt cut above the knee and the slight reflective sheen from the passing street lights.

Stockings or tights? Connor wondered. Then, suddenly conscious that he may have been staring too long, he quickly returned his gaze to the road. Trying to fill the void in the conversation and deflect his pondering stare, he said, "I don't think I'd have the energy to chase you, anyway."

"Shame."

The words hung in the air, Connor blushed both inwardly and outwardly as a flush of heat raced through his body. He wasn't very good at coping with out-and-out come-ons and didn't know what to say. An awkward silence hung between them that not even the sultry, growling tones of Tom Waits could fill.

The track petered out, and a more up-beat number started. "Now this is a bit better." Connor tapped the top of the steering wheel. "This is one of his best hits."

""I prefer "Blue Valentine.""

"You like Tom Waits, then?"

"Yeah, I've got some of his stuff at home. You do, too, it seems?"

"Can't pull the wool over your eyes," he mocked gently.

"Have you got his latest CD?"

"Yeah. I mean, no . . . I mean, I did have."

"What does that mean?" She shot him a quizzical look and furrowed her brow.

Connor explained, "My ex, she took it."

"Ex-wife?"

"There you go again. Yeah, and the thing is she didn't even like him—she just didn't like me, either, so she took it out of spite." Connor pulled the car into the main street of Oakes Cross. "Whereabouts, Stephanie?"

"Second right, Albion Street, number 17."

Connor took the turn and pulled over where Stephanie pointed. "Nice place," he said as he looked at the houses with their postage-stamp gardens decorated with miniature versions of big garden ornaments—aspirational *accoutrements* for a bigger debt to come.

"It's not bad. It keeps the weather out. How much?"

"God knows it's dear around here."

Stephanie started to laugh. "Not the house, the cab fare."

"Nice laugh," he said, and then joined in with her as she searched her bag and removed her purse. "Hey, don't bother about the fare. I was going home and this is on my way. I'm only a way up the road, and it's been nice talking to you."

Slightly taken aback, Stephanie blushed again. "Well, thanks. That's really nice of you. You won't get into trouble with your office, will you?"

"I'll say you did a runner!"

"I'll never be able to book a cab again."

Once more they laughed together. As the laughter petered out and Stephanie reached for the door handle, the interior light flashed on.

"Would you like to come in for a coffee?" It was, again, a blurted-out line that Connor only just heard above the stereo. "Is that a little too forward?" she asked, genuinely embarrassed as she looked towards the floor.

"A little. I was going home to a nice bottle of wine . . ."

He realised that this wasn't the best of replies he could have offered.

Stephanie seemed to have been slipped an honesty pill and said whatever came into her mind. "I've got wine."

"Now *that* is forward."

Stephanie was no longer testing the waters; she had taken the plunge. "Well, you only live once. It's not a dress rehearsal. We could talk some more?"

Connor pondered this, trying not to race ahead of himself. "That will be really nice, thanks."

They smiled at each other and got out of the car. They walked across the pavement to the house.

Looking down at Stephanie's shoes, he commented, "I see what you mean about those heels! Any higher and you'd get a nosebleed."

"They're killing me. I'll be glad to get them off."

They entered the house. Connor stood awkwardly whilst Stephanie undid her shoes in the hall.

"Go through," she told him.

Connor entered the lounge, which let on to an open dining room. He fumbled for the light switch, and Stephanie brushed past and switched the light on for him.

"Sit down. I'll get some wine. Red or white?"

"What's the white?"

"What?"

"What's the white? French, Italian . . . ?"

Stephanie was taken aback by the line of questioning. "Oh, I don't know."

Stephanie went to the small wine rack in the dining room. Connor watched, and before she could even read the label, he had made up his mind. "I'll have red."

"Don't you want to know what the white is now?"

Connor feigning pain in a screwed up face. "Well, it's off the shelf. It will be too warm to drink, whatever it is, so red's fine."

"What, are you some sort of connoisseur?"

"No, no far from it. It's just like being offered a cup of tea or coffee and it's only lukewarm and has too much sugar in it."

"I see. Well, I better make sure the kettle boils properly if I make you a cup, then."

Stephanie laughed and handed Connor a bottle of red. Connor instinctively studied the label.

"Will that be okay for sir?" Stephanie mocked in a wine waiter's plummy voice.

Connor retorted in character, "Thank you, that will be fine."

"I'll just get the corkscrew."

Stephanie vanished into the kitchen. Connor looked around the room, which was comfortably furnished. He was glad to note the not-too-chintzy sofa and armchairs, coffee table strewn with various magazine and an old Sunday newspaper, TV, stereo, and a computer workstation, which looked like it was actually worked at. He furrowed his brow in enquiry.

From the kitchen Stephanie's' voice called out, "Would sir like any particular glass?"

"Are you having a pop at me?"

There was laughter from the kitchen. Stephanie emerged carrying two glasses and a corkscrew; she had removed her jacket to reveal a white cotton blouse undone at the neck. Opaque enough to be decent, transparent enough to intrigue, the blouse was tailored and fitted her well.

Stephanie placed the glasses on the coffee table, exposing the gap between her chest and blouse. Connor diverted his gaze, but not his mind. Stephanie handed Connor the corkscrew, still stooping forward, a stance that Connor thought unnecessary, but not unwelcome. It caused a bundle of synapses to fire off in a variety of directions down innumerable neurological paths to a host of receptors.

"I can't do corkscrews," she said.

Connor took the corkscrew with an adrenalin-fuelled hand and tried to hide the shaking of his hands as he started to open the bottle whilst Stephanie went to the stereo and selected a CD. Tom Waits "entered" the room. Connor poured the wine and handed Stephanie a glass as she sat down beside him.

"Thanks."

"Thank *you.*"

They both took a drink from their glasses.

"I hope you don't take this the wrong way, but you don't make a habit of this, do you? I mean, you know, inviting cab drivers in . . . ." Connor felt himself slipping into hole that he was digging. Starting a sentence that way was always doomed to be negatively received. The more he scrambled to get out, the faster he sank into a pit of verbal quicksand. "Not that it's any of my business. It's just, well, you know . . ."

There was a hiatus. Connor felt he had definitely overstepped the mark and would be seeing the door pretty soon. Stephanie's face looked stern and deadpan, but with exquisite timing, so as to make the moment as uncomfortable as possible without becoming too oppressive for Connor, she cracked into a smile and a mischievous twinkle lit her eyes.

"Haven't you heard about me down at the cab office? I've got three cab drivers locked in my bedroom upstairs." Stephanie paused again, seeing that Connor was struggling to come to terms with Stephanie's sense of what she hoped was humour. "Seriously, you're the first."

"You can't be too careful, you know. There's a lot of fucking weirdoes out there, you know?"

The swear word just came out, which often happened when Connor became passionate or stressed about a subject or situation.

"Sorry," he apologised, looking somewhat embarrassed.

Stephanie smiled. "Don't worry. I swear all the time. You're not a *fucking weirdo,* are you?" She stressed the swear word.

"I don't think so. At least, I haven't been told I am."

"Well, if you can't trust a fireman, who can you trust?"

Connor went serious again, almost edgy. "There are a lot of firemen I wouldn't trust."

"Well, all that aside, you can trust me."

"I thought you said I couldn't earlier?"

"Exactly."

They both laughed again and revisited their glasses, Connor relieved to have survived the dangerous foray into a person's personal life—a person he hardly knew, but badly wanted to know more of. He stepped off onto firmer ground. "What's the computer for?"

"Sometimes I work from home."

"What do you do, exactly?"

"Well, I manage the collection and deliveries. You know, coordinate the pickups and all that."

"Quite important, then?"

Stephanie was matter-of-fact. "I suppose so, but boring, really."

Connor maintained his interest. "A lot of responsibility?"

"Well, the computer does most of the work. The routes vary from time to time, but the distances are known, so we can anticipate arrival times. It only goes square if there's a holdup."

Connor recoiled slightly. "You're very *blasé* about it. I bet the drivers aren't worried about the timetable if they've got a shotgun in their faces!"

"Not that kind of holdup, you arse. I meant a traffic holdup— you know, car accidents or unscheduled roadworks, computer glitches, that kind of thing."

Connor laughed at the over-dramatic image he had conjured up. "Computer glitches?"

"Yeah. The guards carry handhelds, which they use to download details as they do their rounds. These get beamed back to us. What with them and the GPS system, which can blow hot and cold, there is the potential for total confusion. Like the saying goes, 'To err is human, to really foul things up takes a computer.'"

Connor nodded, but he had no real point of reference, as his job was predominantly controlled by pens and paper. The computer had crept into the office, and Connor struggled to remember a time when it hadn't been there; from the evidence that he had witnessed, the "paperless office" was anything but.

Connor was intrigued. "That's a bit dodgy, isn't it?"

"No, not really. Well, not for me, at any rate. I'm here or at the office."

"What about the guards? It must be dodgy for them?"

"They don't give a monkey's. They don't get paid enough to worry. In fact, the company policy is not to put up any resistance if it's a proper holdup. But this is the real world, not Hollywood, and holdups are very rare. The crooks don't know what's in the vans. They could be empty or just moving spent cheques. It's just not worth the risk."

Not content and seeing a flaw in this thinking, he wanted to press the point. "What about if they have inside information."

Stephanie ceded the point. "Yeah, that's about the only time it does happen, but then the ensuing investigation usually ends up pointing the finger at the person or persons responsible for providing the info. They're usually ordinary people who very quickly crack, and then the rest come tumbling down like a house of cards. We may not get the money back, but the gang is usually banged up or put out of commission by their own notoriety."

Connor mused over this last point and returned to his glass. As he swallowed, he said, "That reminds me, we had a job on the M25 once and two lorries had police escorts, guns, the whole lot. They weren't stopping for nobody. I bet they didn't have spent cheques in the back!"

"That was probably a bullion run or cash disposal destined for the Royal Mint. You don't want to mess with them."

"We didn't—they looked far too serious. No sense of humour, some people."

They both drank some more. The wine helped them relax, although they were feeling as if they had known each other for some time. There was no silly small talk, but an ease that allowed serious subjects to be discussed in a lighthearted frame of mind.

Connor broke the silence in the conversation. "I forgot how good this album was."

"I'll burn a copy for you if you want."

"You would? You'd be breaking copyright laws. It would get you into trouble if you were found out."

"And who'd tell?"

Connor teased, "Well, I might, as a fine, upstanding member of society and all."

Stephanie laughed. "I'd take that chance."

There was a certain lilt to Stephanie's voice. Connor felt himself flush and looked at his watch to hide his blushes. "Hey, it's getting late. I'd best be off."

"There's no rush. Have some more wine—there's over half a bottle left."

Connor didn't want to go, but he lacked the confidence to accept what he felt was an invitation without it being spelled out. Assumption was the mother of all fuck ups. This friendship might go somewhere if he was patient and behaved as a gentleman. He did not want to mess things up.

"I'd better not. I've got to drive home. Besides, haven't you got to work tomorrow?

"Yeah, but I'm working from home." Stephanie pointed towards the computer. Connor naturally turned to look where she was pointing. When he turned back, she was inches from his face and staring straight into his eyes. Connor recoiled slightly, and then recovered himself.

"Do you want to be the first taxi driver in my new collection?

She closed the gap and kissed Connor full on the lips, and then pulled back to resume her gaze. Connor tried to speak, but she silenced him with another kiss. Connor tried to place his glass on the floor but, in doing so, dropped and spilled the wine onto the carpet.

"Shit!"

Stephanie looked confused. "It wasn't that bad?"

"No, I mean the wine. I dropped the glass. It will stain the carpet."

Connor and Stephanie looked at the splash of purple soaking into the light-coloured carpet.

"Leave it. Let's hope it becomes a fond memory."

She kissed Connor again pushing him down onto the sofa. Connor didn't resist. He embraced her and breathed deeply. Her perfume was a light citrus with a rich undertone. Connor slid his hands down her back to her tight waist and paused briefly before moving further down. *Stockings,* Connor thought to himself.

Chapter 12

SCOTLAND V

Connor scouted around the southwestern end of Loch Avon. The wind whipped off the water and drove the rain against Connor's left side. The path was running with water, and at times, he felt he was walking along the streambed, except for the occasional muddy indentation of an earlier traveller. The light was trickling away like the water from the west end of the loch, as the sun sank lower behind the imposing bulk of Ben Macdui.

He reached the end of the loch and successfully forded another tributary. He scouted around for a suitable place to camp and considered the small, sandy ledge at the loch's side, but thought better of it; he wasn't sure whether the loch had a "lock" farther down the valley, which might be closed, causing the water to back up and flood the ledge. He didn't want to wake up in a floating world and have to re-camp in the middle of the night. He investigated farther from the loch's edge. The rock sides rose up steeply on three sides. With the loch at his back, he stood on the stage of a natural amphitheatre, an overpowering rock altar, Tolkien's darkest creation made real. The howl of the wind was the screams of dying orcs, slain in battle.

Connor investigated the "Shelter Stone," a natural cave formed by landslide or glacial action. The detritus of previous occupants plus the thoughts of sharing deterred him. The darkness grew, and he moved quickly amongst the boulders. He stopped every now and then to test the ground with a tent peg, prodding the ground to find enough places that would accept the peg and allow him to pitch the tent. Eventually he struck a compromise: a rough piece of tussocky grass high enough to have some natural drainage and not too many subsurface rocks to prevent the guy lines from being run out. Dropping his pack, he felt the relief across his shoulders. He stretched briefly, but the cold wind was quick to remind him of its presence. He unstrapped the buckles on the top of his pack and removed a rolled bundle of nylon. Standing with his back to the wind, he shook out the roll. It unfurled like a sail. Connor pressed his end to the ground and drove two tent pegs with the heel of his boot before moving to the other end to repeat the pegging-down process. Back at the pack, Connor pulled out a two-foot-long bundle, which he emptied next to the tent. He picked up one of the two-foot lengths, and more of the aluminium poles followed, joined as they were by elasticised shock cord. He shook the poles, and they magically grew into a longer pole. He repeated this action twice more until he had three poles, which he proceeded to thread through the webbing seams of the pegged-out tent. With his task complete, Connor tensioned the poles into an arc secured by reinforced loops. A hemispherical dome appeared from the mess of nylon on the ground. He quickly moved around the inner section of the tent, inserting and adjusting the tent pegs to secure the tent from being stolen by the wind.

He stepped back. The inner section of the tent had an almost luminous yellow glow in the fast-fading light and looked as if some alien wood louse had landed, animated by the buffeting of the wind.

Connor returned to his pack and pulled out a second roll of nylon. This green fly sheet was the waterproof membrane that protected the tent's interior from the elements, which at this moment were doing their utmost to soak the yellow dome. Connor cursed under his breath as the wind and the rain seemed to plot against him. The fly sheet billowed high above him into the metal sky like an errant sail cut from its stays. Working from the windward to the leeward side of the tent, he slowly succeeded in securing the fly sheet. With this task complete, he went around fixing the guy lines wherever he could on the rock-strewn ground and then tensioned each line to pull the fly-sheet taut over the framed inner. The rain started to run off. He was content with the pitch; he knew from his research of the sales literature that the tent was ideal for this type of environment, having allegedly been tested in the Himalayas and at both poles.

Connor carefully undid the windward porch and placed the rucksack inside before doing the zip up, then scuttled around to the leeward side again opening the outer porch, he climbed in. He then undid the arched zip of the inner tent, folded down the "door," and spun round so as to be sitting in the inner tent with his feet still in the outer. Connor bent forward, flexing his back hard to do up the outer tent. Instantly, the wind was shut out. He unzipped his jacket and pushed back his hood; he removed his woollen hat and vigorously scratched his head all over to assist the drying and to enliven his scalp. He bent forward again and started to remove his gaiters and unlace his boots. Kicking off the mud-splattered footwear, he cast his mind back to the outdoor shop where he had bought them. £140 of the most technically up-to-date, breathable foot protection money could buy without raising too much suspicion or too many questions. His feet steamed slightly, but they sure felt good out of their confinement.

He removed his jacket and hung it from one of the door toggles. The jacket dripped onto the sodden turf between the inner and the outer. Next came his leggings. Connor tried to not to get the inner tent wet and contorted his body through what felt like advanced yoga positions, reminding him of his days in the front row of his local rugby club. He hung the leggings next to the jacket.

Stripped to his base layers, Connor got fully into the inner tent and closed the door. He lay down on the thick, waterproof base and breathed deeply, systematically stretching his muscles and luxuriating in the feeling of release after tensing. All the while, his body heat generated steam through his sweat-soaked clothing. He stretched again, spread-eagling himself to the four corners of the tent. A feeling of well being came over him, and he laughed out loud before taking another deep breath. He slowly exhaled as he listened to the wind-driven rain blasting and buffeting the tent. Connor rolled over, unzipped the door on the windward side of the tent, and pulled down the rucksack. He dug down the side of the sack and pulled out a rolled-up ground mat. He undid a small plastic knob, and the mat started to expand of its own accord until it was about two inches thick and six feet long. When it was done inflating, he tightened up the screw valve again. He reached into the bag again and pulled out another bundle, this time a sleeping bag—four-season goose down that had cost nearly £200, the value of which could only be realised when someone wanted to pack light and small. He shook it out and laid it on the ground mat. Another bag produced a set of dry clothes. Connor stripped off his leggings, three tops, and socks and placed them in the tent loft, a piece of webbing suspended from the four corners above his head so that they would have the best chance of drying. Connor rubbed himself down with a "pack towel," a super-absorbent sheet of material designed for backpackers. It felt tremendous as he dried away the dampness from the day's exertion. When he was dry again, he started to dress in the clean clothes, his taut body luxuriating in the almost sensuous feel of the fibre. A zip-locked bag produced a fresh pair of socks, which left a small cloud of talcum powder as he pulled them on. The feeling of the talc trickling between his drying toes was pure ecstasy. Sitting up and unzipping the tent door, he reached into his jacket pocket to retrieve the chocolate bar he'd bought from the Ptarmigan restaurant. He did up the door and climbed into his sleeping bag. Once ensconced, he unwrapped the bar. Chilled from the cold, flakes of chocolate splintered into his mouth, which was salivating excessively in anticipation. Connor hadn't realised how hungry he was. The sweetness of the sugar gave him an instant lift; a warm glow of contentment filled his body. It had started.

Chapter 13

THE SHIRE VIII

When Connor awoke, his arm was under his cheek and stretched upwards under the pillow. Opening his eyes, he realised he was lying on the wrong side of the bed. He furrowed his brow as he started to focus on his surroundings, all of which were unfamiliar to him. Slowly, the memories of the previous evening started to permeate his brain. He smiled and rolled onto his back.

"Jesus!"

Standing unbeknownst to him at the side of the bed was Stephanie, dressed in a black silken dressing gown and holding out to Connor a cup of coffee. "Not quite, but definitely heavenly."

Connor was annoyed by his reaction and confused. "You scared the fuck out of me. Sorry, morning."

"Good morning to you, too. Did you know you snore?"

"It's been said, but I've never found it a problem."

"I bet the guys at the station do!"

"They'd have to be pretty light sleepers."

Connor sat up and accepted the proffered cup. He was coming up to speed enough to compete in the verbal dexterity now. "I have my own dormitory. Rank has its privilege and all that."

It was Stephanie who looked confused now. "Rank?"

"Yeah, I'm a sub officer. I'm in charge."

"You didn't say."

"Does it make a difference?"

Stephanie chided, "Well, of course. I would have brought you a biscuit as well."

Connor feigned a cursory search. "You mean you haven't?"

Connor took a sip of coffee and swayed back as Stephanie punched him playfully. "You're up early."

"Not really. It's nine thirty."

"How's the wine stain?

"A happy memory."

Connor smiled a relieved smile. "That's a relief, I was feeling the pressure there for a bit."

"How's the coffee?"

"Tepid."

"Let me warm it up for you."

Stephanie pulled open her dressing gown and straddled Connor roughly.

"Careful, you'll have me spill it. I'll stain the sheets as well."

Connor strained to place the cup on the bedside cabinet. They kissed and rolled so that Connor was on top.

"I guess you'll have something to tell the girls when you get to work?"

"What do you take me for, a kiss and tell? I'm a long way from the playground, you know."

"Oh, I know."

They lay in post-coital embrace, Connor breathing deeply, contentedly.

"You're not going to start snoring, are you?"

"I don't usually snore when I'm awake!" he said lazily.

Chapter 14

THE SHIRE IX

Work for Connor became less attractive over the coming weeks and months; the prospect of at least fifteen more years filled him with dread. Connor contemplated other careers, but wondered how they would stimulate him. Could he break into a career unrelated to his current one? At least where he was, there was the chance that something new and challenging would occur, but there was also the rub. Connor would be once more in a position of danger or responsible for putting others in that same danger, and it was getting harder and harder to justify the risks taken. The public's perception was no longer a valid argument; whatever decision he made in any particular situation would be lambasted—by Health and Safety people for taking unnecessary risks or by the fire crews and press, when they were present, for just standing by. Connor was getting tired of arguing.

On the positive side, Connor's relationship with Stephanie was working out fine. They would meet two or three times a week—no hard-and-fast schedule—and just enjoy their time together. It was not just a casual sex thing, though; they were both past that stage of their lives and found enjoyment together by sharing a meal, a show, or a quiet night in with a bottle of wine and a movie. Sometimes, they just read a passion they were glad to discover was mutual.

This suited Connor, who was still working hard on his Open University coursework and was coming to a particularly difficult section, owing to the fact he had opted not to participate in the six-month self-sponsored field study. This meant that he had to put in extra effort to complete his degree, and a binding relationship was not conducive to that.

Stephanie was equally content. She had worked hard to get where she was within the security industry and indeed was a groundbreaker in a previously male-dominated profession. Unfortunately, this made some life decisions a little more difficult. Not putting herself in a position to have to make those decisions was her way of managing the goldfish-bowl existence she felt she lived in, at least professionally. There might someday be a place in her life for marriage, children, and all the other trimmings, but she was in no driving hurry to get there.

Chapter 15

THE SHIRE X

Connor scoured the local papers. First, he ran his highlighter down the industrial rental property section. He ringed any small industrial lockups that were available on short-term lets. He used his knowledge of the local area to decide whether the address suited his needs. Ideally, he wanted a lockup tucked away at the back of an industrial estate that was busy enough so that his coming and going wouldn't be conspicuous and he wouldn't have to explain what he was doing to anyone. But the sort of place he wanted was in short supply. He had already visited two sites: The first was too small, and the second was located next to a pizza delivery outlet.

Connor's pen stopped at one of the boxes: *Light industrial unit available early next month, terms negotiable. Contact Tel. 1234-5678.*

He tapped the paper. From the area code, he mentally recalled where the site might be. Connor ringed the advert and carried on down the page. There were no other adverts of interest, so he turned to the vehicle section. Once more, he trawled through the small ads, this time on the lookout for vans. The van's age wasn't high on his list of criteria; it was more important for it to be clean and reliable. There were a number of candidates, and one in particular seemed to meet his needs exactly, if the ad could be believed. Connor took out his mobile and started to dial. A voice answered after five rings, "Hello."

Connor spoke in the voice of someone who might be interested, but at the same time was relaxed and casual about the conversation. "Hello, I'm calling about the industrial unit you were advertising in the *Mercury*?"

The voice perked up. "Oh, yes."

"I was wondering where about it was. The ad doesn't say."

"Do you know the area?"

"Yes, a bit."

The man's voice was somewhere between oleaginous and grasping "It's at the rear of the Orchard Farm site, down by Lane Avenue. Do you know it?

Connor paused as he recalled the place described. "Yes, yes, I do. Isn't there a double glazing firm down there?"

"Yeah, that's right."

"Great, it's in the right area. What size is the unit?"

The man was silent, as if awaiting the results of some mental arithmetic. "It's about one hundred and twenty square metres."

Connor tried not to be too keen, wanting to at least have the opportunity to rejecting it. "That sounds about right. Can I come and see it?"

"Course you can. Today?"

Connor thought briefly and, having no reasons not to meet, said, "Okay, what time? About four?"

"That'll be fine. If you go past the double-glazing firm, you'll see a company that sells industrial kitchenware. The unit is next to that, green doors."

"Right, green doors. I'll see you at four. Cheers."

Connor hung up and looked at his watch. 10:30 a.m. He filled the kettle and put it on to boil whilst taking a cup off the draining board, into which he placed the tea strainer. Armed with his cup, he set about phoning the numbers of the van ads. As he expected, the numbers were all mobile phones, and judging by the background noise, the owners were most likely at work. Connor asked them questions and tried to sound as nonchalant as possible; he would be doing the van owners a favour by buying the van off of them, so he had to get a good price. By the end of the last phone call, he had arranged to visit three of the owners later that evening. One of them owned the van that sounded just right, even more so since he'd found out that it was recently taxed and MOTed.

Connor whiled away the day. He met Stephanie for lunch, and she took him on a tour of the work premises. There was a steady flow of vehicles both in and out. The crews moved in and around the vans and the building, quietly loading and unloading their vehicles, all the while being watched by other security guards and remotely operated closed-circuit security cameras.

Stephanie took Connor to the staff restaurant. People they passed smiled and said hello to Stephanie, eyeing warily her friend with the visitor's badge that may have well said "impostor," which was exactly what Connor felt like until they found Stephanie's friend from the taxi ride home. She was less boisterous now, but nonetheless her mischievous sense of humour and ribbing were never too far away. When lunch was over, Stephanie escorted Connor off the site through security. She said goodbye with a peck on the cheek and, with a pickpocket's deftness, removed his visitor's pass

"You won't be needing this."

"I'd forgotten all about it."

"That's what they all say."

"Who's they?"

"All the would-be gangsters." Stephanie was smiling

"It's nice to know that you place me in such esteemed company," he said, feigning both injury and innocence.

"I'll see you tomorrow." It was more a schoolteacher order than a question. Another peck on the cheek and they both went their own way smiling.

Connor drove to the Orchard Farm trading estate, passing the green-doored lockup before turning round and passing it again, parking fifty yards farther up the street. He got out of the car and walked up to a roadside van selling snack food and hot drinks. The vendor seemed almost startled by Connor's sudden appearance, but he managed to compose himself soon enough and wiped the battered mock-wood counter. The epitome of a desperate career move. The burger-van-come-tea-hut had seemed a good investment and the panacea to his recent forced redundancy. Now self-employed with his own patch to ply, he was starting to see the wallpapered-over cracks appear. Blind optimism was becoming a looming reality. His countenance and appearance matched his position and were seemingly linked to the downturn in his trade.

"Yes, mate?"

"A tea, please."

"Sugar?"

"No, thanks."

The vendor, who wore off-white overalls, swung into action, going through a routine he'd carried out thousands of times that culminated in placing the plastic lid on a polystyrene cup and putting the cup onto the counter.

"That'll be fifty pence, please."

Connor handed over the money. He removed the lid and blew on the steaming surface before he asked, "Been busy?"

The man studied Connor for a moment. He spent many long hours interspersed with moments of conversation and activity preparing food and drink, so he recognised the pitch of someone reaching out just to talk and make contact. He had been there. "Well, it's been better. Things have slowed down over the last few months."

"What's the reason for that, then?"

"A few of the units have closed down that were the difference between doing well and, now, just doing."

Connor tried to offer succour. "Still, there's the chance that the units will be filled again soon, I suppose?"

"You'd think, but this is not the des res for new businesses. They're more likely to move to the new site at the north end of the town. Better start-up rates and shorter leases, much more attractive."

The van man leaned forward across the counter, resting on his elbows, adding cold tea stains to his already discoloured sleeves.

"Can't you move up there to where the trade is?" Connor asked.

A resigned look swept over the man's face. "Not that simple. There are already two vans operating up there, so it wouldn't cope with a third van—and I don't want the competition, either."

Connor studied the van man's face. A tiredness that he hadn't seen before had appeared, a weariness born of early mornings and cold breezes stealing into the van. An animal furtiveness due to never quite relaxing, there being only a view in one plain. Customers could steal up on the counter unseen, which meant that the vendor could never study his paper properly or be caught scratching or rooting about in his facial orifices.-

Connor tried his tea, knowing it would be too hot to drink, but he tried out of habit, instantly searing the taste buds on the tip of his tongue—which was just as well, for the tea's sake. The conversation had stopped long enough that to restart it would have meant a new subject, and neither Connor nor the van man looked much in the mood.

"Well, I hope it picks up for you," Connor offered.

"Yeah, cheers. Me, too."

Connor turned and walked back towards his car, holding the lid over his scalding tea and trying not to burn his hand. The van man continued leaning, staring with wind-induced watery eyes, dreaming no doubt of the heady days of queues and sunshine.

Sitting in his car and sipping his super-heated tea, Connor perused his newspaper whilst also watching the comings and goings of the industrial estate. The van man was right; it was quiet. The only people he saw were the nicotine addicts who crept out of the double-glazing company for five minutes of blue-cloud relief. Nobody had passed his car other than when they had driven beyond their drop-off point, and then they had quickly turned their vehicle in the double lay-by, just short of the lockup Connor was interested in.

Connor looked at the clock on his dashboard. The digital light flicked the seconds rhythmically, telling him that the time was 3:40. He heard the van before he saw it, a beat-up white pickup hove into Connor's rear view mirror. It coughed its way down the road 'til it stopped outside the green-doored lockup Connor had come to see. A grey-haired fifty something climbed down from the cab and adjusted his oversized jeans, the waist of which rode high above his belt. The man dug into his pocket and produced a bunch of keys, with which he started to unlock the padlock securing the doors. The padlock removed, the man removed the hasp from the staple and then pushed the door, which folded inwards. The man vanished into the darkness within. A few seconds passed before there was a flicker of light, and then the steady glow of a fluorescent wash lit the inside of the lockup and spilled out into the early evening shade.

Connor climbed out of his car and locked the door before crossing the road towards the lockup. Upon reaching the doors, he looked in. The man was nowhere to be seen. The soft brick walls were white washed with a paint that looked keen to shed itself on anything careless enough to brush against it. The floor, which was strewn with flyers, appeared to have been a stranger to a broom and some housekeeping. At the rear of the lockup was a large whitewashed window built into a breeze-block partition wall, which didn't run the full height to the ceiling but, formed a small office and was apparently hiding the key-holder from Connor's view.

Connor called into the empty void, "Hello?"

A voice responded from the back of the lockup, "Hello there." The man appeared from the office, the dusty white patch on his blue shirt evidence of a wall encounter.

Connor stepped across the threshold. "Hello there. I rang earlier. My name's Alex."

"Hello, mate. You're earlier than I expected—gave me a bit of a fright." The man dusted the arm of his shirt.

"Sorry about that. I got off early and thought I'd come down on the off chance."

"Fair enough. Well, what do you think, then?" He turned with one arm held out, making an arc around the space towards the back.

Connor looked around. "Yeah, not bad, could be what I'm looking for. It's got electric." He pointed to the lights.

"Has it got water?"

"Yeah, of course." The man pointed behind Connor to a Butler sink that Connor hadn't noticed, half hidden behind a pile of cardboard flat packs. He added, "And there's a toilet in here." The man indicated again, this time back through the door from which he'd emerged.

Connor walked farther into the space and turned slowly on the spot, trying to fill the space with the picture in his head. He nodded gently to himself. "Yeah, if we can agree on price, this could do for me."

"Oh right, good. Yeah, price. How long would you want it for?"

"Six, maybe nine months."

"Right, what shall we say?"

The man eyed Connor, trying to gauge his price. "A hundred pounds a week, plus electric?"

It was a question, not a demand, and Connor was not slow to notice. He looked around, his hands stuck rigidly in his trouser pockets. He turned back to the man and shook his head.

"What do you want to use it for?" the man asked.

Connor's face changed slightly—not much, but enough to make the man wish he hadn't asked. The man felt a chill creep down his back.

"Storage, just storage."

The man wanted to ask what kind of storage, but thought better of it. He tried again. "Eighty pounds plus."

Connor considered this latest offer. "Seventy-five all in, cash, two months in advance."

Connor offered his hand. The man reached for it, almost as an automatic reaction, but there was an uncomfortable feeling that the man seemed keen to escape. The two men shook hands. Connor's face cracked into a smile, and instantly the mood lifted and the man relaxed somewhat. Reaching into his jacket pocket and removing his wallet and two prepared folds of money, Connor looked at the man. "That's six hundred, all right?

"Yeah, fine." The man's tongue darted across his dried lips. His face lit up as the inner glow of avarice shone through.

Connor pulled the money away from the man's grasp just as he reached for the bundle of notes. "I can reach you at this afternoon's number?" The man nodded as Connor continued, "I will contact you in two months' time with the next two months' payment. I will be in and out of the country, so I don't have a permanent number you can reach me on. You'll have to trust me."

The statement hung there, waiting to be challenged. The look on Connor's face was less inviting. The man's eyes moved from the money to meet Connor's, and their thoughts crossed. The man felt there was something that was not kosher, but didn't want to push it; he felt there was a profit to be had from it. Connor sensed the man's uncertainty, but at the same time didn't want to expose himself to blackmail, founded or not. A compromise was out there, but could it be found?

Connor pulled another fold of notes from his wallet. "There's another month's rent. If I don't contact you by this time two months from now, you keep it, okay?"

This was most definitely not a question and was not open to negotiation, a take-it-or-leave-it option. The man dipped his eyes and then looked back with a smile across his face. The two men shook hands, and the money exchanged between them. The man worked to separate some keys from the larger bunch he had used to open the doors. Connor pushed the doors closed as the man left and secured them with a drop bar.

Chapter 16

THE SHIRE XI

Connor sat in the staff office at the fire service headquarters. He swapped banter with the officers in the office, picking up pieces of gossip. Each tried to extract more than he revealed. Connor kept an eye on the clock above the door—10:55, five minutes to go. He checked the file on his lap. The next thirty minutes or so could seriously jeopardise his plans for the future. The open-plan office was quietly busy; phones rang and were answered with efficient politeness, but then were often backed, after recognition with a more friendly and jocular greeting. The tapping of keyboards varied from workstation to workstation— the straight-backed, screen-staring secretary's efficiency to the hunchbacked "find the keys" style favoured by the firefighters promoted to office duties. One had suffered from repetitive strain injury, the other from posture-related problems.

A door on the periphery of the office opened and an officer emerged. Connor recognised the officer as divisional officer Clarry, who was responsible for training. He looked around the room 'til he saw Connor.

"Hello, Connor. Come on in."

Connor got up and went to the office door, which Clarry held open. The two shook hands as he entered. Clarry indicated a chair before closing the door behind him. Taking a seat, he arranged another chair so as to sit on Connor's side of the desk— no doubt an interview technique learned at some training course or other. Connor wondered if it was natural or a forced move, and wondered further if it meant anything, bearing in mind that both parties knew the game that was being played.

"So how are things, Connor?"

"Not so bad, thanks, boss."

The officer feigned pain. "Please, Connor. You know me better than that. Joe, please."

"Yeah, sorry, Joe. I guess this just felt more formal and I didn't want to presume, you know?"

"Yes, I understand. So what can I do for you? Bearing in mind that you perceive this to be formal, should I go and sit behind my desk now?"

Both Connor and Joe smiled at this. The mood, although not severe, lightened as both Connor and Joe reflected each other's postures.

"Time off."

The statement was out and hung there whilst Connor studied Joe's reaction. A quizzical look was the only perceivable change. "Time off?"

Connor expanded the statement and explained about his need for a sabbatical.

"I see, and any idea what you want to do?"

"I've been working on a distance learning degree course, and my finals and dissertation involve a field study trip of up to six months."

"Wow, that's quite something. Where's the field study?"

"Africa. The Gambia, to be precise. The degree involves studying the environmental impact of western society on third world countries. You know—mineral extraction, oil, labour, tourism, that sort of thing, the empire-strikes-back, wishy-washy liberal stuff. Bottom line, I need to do the field study, or it means eighteen months of additional course study. I thought that, well, it's been fifteen years and I could do with a change of scenery, maybe recharge my batteries and my enthusiasm!."

Joe considered the information. He had had an inkling the "jungle drums' were never silent, so it came as no real surprise, and he had considered the point in case it was raised beforehand. "I see. Well, first up, I can see no immediate problems. Ordinarily, the person asking for the sabbatical is normally the one who becomes the barrier to taking the break. Have you considered how you are going to live—financially, I mean?"

"Yes, I'm pretty well sorted in that department. Currently, I'm renting, so that can stop when I like. I've been saving hard, and that's in addition to the money I got from the sale of my house. Plus, the cost of living in the Gambia is ridiculously cheap, which is part of the reason I'm going there, I suppose."

Joe nodded as he perused a slim document. "You seem to have it pretty well wrapped up. You do realise that, although we can maintain a place for you in the establishment, we can't guarantee that you'll come back to the place that you left and, in extremis, the rank at which you left. Is that understood? That is quite a sacrifice."

"Yes, I have thought about it, but 'nothing ventured, nothing gained.' And, at the end of the day, I might make my fortune out there and not want to come back."

Both men smiled through the pause that followed. It was difficult for the career man to understand why someone would want to risk his current position for six months in Africa, but he shrugged as if to say "to each his own."

"Okay, Connor. I'll start things going this end. I'll ask you to speak to my secretary and give her the details of your dates, and personnel will no doubt be in touch about your pay details. Is there anything else you need to ask?"

"No thanks, Joe. But thanks for your time and for not trying to talk me out of it. I appreciate your help."

"That's okay, Connor. Could I have talked you out of it?"

"What do you think?"

Again, both men smiled as Connor got up and shook hands with Joe.

"Cheers, Connor. You take care out there."

"I'll try. Thanks again."

Connor left the office. A few heads looked up as he entered the outer office. He waved goodbye to those who were looking his way or tracking him through the office.

Connor exited the building and paused a moment before looking back up at the headquarters that represented both a nemesis and panacea. He took a deep breath before he stepped away, a shadow of a smile creeping across his face.

Chapter 17

THE SHIRE XII

Connor turned to listen as a key entered the lock and the door opened. He returned to preparing the dinner. The small but complete kitchen was strewn with bowls and plates containing vegetables in various stages of preparedness, much like a TV chef would have food ready for use. The draining board contained a selection of washed plates and cutlery. The whole area looked employed, but under control, and Connor moved effortlessly amongst it all.

Stephanie entered the kitchen. "Something smells good." She leaned over Connor's shoulder and planted a kiss on his cheek.

"Well, just you wait 'til I start cooking, then!"

"I meant you."

"Oh, really? Well, wait 'til I have a shower, then!"

"But I like my men dirty."

Connor gave Stephanie a disapproving look, which he couldn't sustain as his face broke into a smile. "How was your day?"

"Busy, yours?"

Trying to keep the mood light, Connor said, "Okay, thanks. I spoke to the OU, and it looks like I could be off in December, if all goes well."

Stephanie pouted and then feigned childlike sadness.

"Ah, Steph. Don't be sad. I won't be gone forever."

He stopped what he was doing, and she stepped into his outstretched arms for a hug. "But six months."

"Six months will fly by. Before you know it, I'll be back and everything will be the same again."

Stephanie didn't respond, but continued to mimic the sad child with pursed lips and looked up at Connor through the top of her eyes. Connor smiled and held her tight as she succumbed to his embrace.

"Besides they say that the sanitation is not that great out there," he said. The statement just hung there, and Connor wondered whether Stephanie would rise to the bait.

She pulled back and looked at him, trying to figure out the relevance of his last comment. "What's that got to do with anything?"

Tongue in cheek, he replied, "Well, you said you like your men dirty. Six months without a proper wash and you won't be able to resist me!" He ducked as she took a swipe at him with the tea towel.

They ate their dinner from their laps in the living room. They both knew it was a bit slummy, but it fitted the mood. A slightly sombre air had descended, and their earlier levity had all but vanished.

Connor shuffled forward on the sofa and stood, balancing the plate and tray in front of him. Once on his feet, he took Stephanie's tray from her and went to the kitchen.

He was leaning over the sink washing the plates when Stephanie reached round and hugged him, resting her face between his shoulder blades. Connor asked, "You all right, hon?"

"I'm sad."

He turned around and embraced her. He looked down into her face and planted a small kiss on the end of her nose. "What are you sad about, honey?" But he well knew.

"You going away and leaving me."

"Hey, come on now. We've talked about this. You know it's something I've got to do. I've put a lot into having this opportunity. Don't make it harder than it is already."

"Oh, I know. It's just, well, you know—six months is a long time, and it's not as if I can even phone. God knows what the phone system's like out there."

Trying to sound upbeat as an antidote to her depressed state, he said, "I know it won't be easy, but I'll phone you whenever I can. We won't be totally incommunicado. There is life outside of Europe!"

Stephanie let go of Connor and returned to the living room. Connor wiped his hands on the tea towel before following. Stephanie was sitting at the computer, going through the start-up procedures.

He perched himself on the arm of the sofa next to her. "What do you want me to do, Stephanie?"

Stephanie paused briefly before continuing to tap at the keyboard. "I know you've got to go, but I can't carry on as though you're not going. I can't hide the fact that I'm not happy."

"You're right. I'm sorry, I'm being selfish. I've worked hard to get to this point, and to be honest, the way things were going, I didn't expect that I'd have to be leaving anyone behind when I went. It's nice to know that you'll miss me, and absence makes the heart grow fonder."

Stephanie countered "Out of sight, out of mind, more like."

"That cuts both ways. I should be more worried, especially with your friends to lead you astray at all those Christmas and New Year's Eve parties."

"Oh, shit. I hadn't thought that you're not going to be here for Christmas!" Stephanie looked even more upset. "You've got one hell of a Christmas present to buy me, do you know that?"

"I'll see what I can do." Connor got up and kissed Stephanie on the neck. "Do you want an early night?" He nuzzled deeper into her neck.

Stephanie pushed him away with her head and said in a business like manner, "Sorry, speaking of Christmas, I've got to make a start on the route pickups for December."

"Do you have to start tonight?"

"Afraid so. This is a critical time for the company. It won't do for the banks and businesses that close over the Christmas period to have bundles of money sitting in their inadequate little safes. They get kind of jumpy about things like that."

"I would have thought people were taking money out of the banks to spend over the Christmas holiday, not putting it in."

"They are, but the places where they spend it will transfer it to a bank or safe holding so as to shift the liability to someone else. Just think about it—how long would you say it takes you to do your average tour around the supermarket for the weekly shop?"

Connor thought about the question before guessing. "I'd say about three quarters of an hour on average."

Stephanie continued the questioning. "Right, and how much do you usually spend?"

Again Connor guessed. "Well, I don't know. It varies—say seventy pounds, something like that."

"No wonder you're slim. Do you buy any food?"

Stephanie was half laughing at Connor's slightly surprised look. Connor retorted with a little sarcasm. "I don't need to buy food. I'm too full of love, and you keep me nourished!"

"Why, thank you, honey. That's so sweet. I didn't realise I kept so much love in the kitchen cupboards!" They laughed together

"Anyway, where is this little quiz going?" Connor enquired

"Well, for the sake of making the maths a bit easier, let's say that on average you take an hour to shop and spend about a hundred pounds each time, right?"

Connor nodded. "Right."

"How many car parking spaces would you say the Oldeston hypermarket has, just roughly?"

Connor tried to visualise the sprawling mass that now stood on what had once been the site of a listed maltings and associated warehousing, which sat alongside the river until, following a failed planning application to convert to character luxury apartments and a shopping complex, a devastating fire had rendered the site derelict and the shopping national took over. This had brought much-needed employment to the area— if minimum-wage shelf stackers, bored checkout staff, and snarled-up roads were what the town needed.

"I would say about a thousand."

"Okay, let's say that during the run-up to Christmas that the store is at optimum capacity in the car park for twelve of the twenty-four hours that it's open. That would mean that there are one thousand people going through the checkouts every hour and, using your miserly budget, spending £100 each, that equals £100,000 per hour. Over a twelve-hour period, that comes to a grand total of £1.2 million a day!."

Connor's face reflected the calculations that were going on behind it. "Jesus, I never thought of it like that. Fuck me, that's a lot of money."

Stephanie was matter-of-fact. "But don't forget that's based on some rough numbers, and it could be less. But at the same time, at Christmas, people tend to spend slightly more than £100 on their shopping, what with presents and all. It could easily be two or three times that amount."

Stephanie had heavily stressed the word "presents" and backed it up with a strong "you know what I'm talking about" look. Connor may have seen it, but it didn't seem to register. He still looked dumbstruck from the mini maths lesson he'd just had.

"Do you know your mouth's open?"

Connor snapped his mouth closed and refocused. "I can't believe that that amount is out there moving around each day. It's almost unbelievable."

"Don't forget, it's not all cash that's being moved. A lot of spending is electronic, and many people still use cheques, but even so, there is still a need to move cheques and counterfoils, as well as the money to the clearing banks. But don't forget, that was based on one store during one twelve-hour period. There are a lot of other businesses out there having similar turnovers—just think about the petrol stations "

"Petrol stations? What do you mean?"

Connor was displaying a very keen interest and a hunger to know more, which Stephanie was happy to feed. Her job was ordinarily quite boring, or if it was interesting, it was usually too sensitive to talk about. This was different: Anyone could make these observations and do the calculations, although the intent might be questionable and might provoke some suspicion from others.

"Well, think about it. How much is a litre of petrol? Multiply that by the average amount a car needs and how long it takes to fill up and pay for your fuel—say five minutes to spend seventy quid. In the run-up to Christmas, there are usually queues to get on a pump that's nearly £840 per hour per pump, so ten pumps over twelve hours is another hundred grand that needs to be moved."

"So you have to plan for the collections to be made. Does that mean that, come the end of the working day, everyone wants their takings collected?"

"That's what they would like, but obviously that's just not practical for all sorts of reasons. Besides, we would need hundreds of vans and crews. No, we have to stagger the collections based on the companies' anticipated takings."

"What does that mean?"

"Well, take our hypermarket. We don't do one collection a day. We could do three or four depending on what they expect to take per hour, but they can also phone in for special request collections if they have had a surge of business through the tills. It's like I said—nobody wants large amounts of cash in their possession for any length of time. There are too many beady-eyed criminals out there."

"I'm almost tempted myself."

"Well, many have been. They're not seeing their loved ones for a lot longer than six months, though. You get longer prison sentences for big-money crimes than you do for murders on a crime-for-crime comparison."

"Would you come and visit me?"

"I don't think it would look too good professionally, do you?"

Connor conceded the point with a shrug of his shoulders and a wry smile. "How long do you think you're going to be?"

"Tonight's just the start. This can take a couple of weeks to do."

Connor was surprised by this statement. "A couple of weeks? Why so long?"

"I have to coordinate the customer requirements along with the routes and the shift patterns, and also build in contingencies for extra collections and drop-offs and no-shows."

"No-shows?"

"Sickness and vehicle breakdowns."

"That happens a lot?"

"Enough to give us serious headaches."

Connor felt his interest rising again. "How do you cope?"

Stephanie sighed. "As best we can. There is an overtime rota, but that struggles to cover the shortfalls, so we have to either get the vans to take on extra deliveries or pickups or we have to put the customer off as best we can. Either way, we end up pissing someone off—either the unions, who argue that we're causing their members extra stress in an already stressful job, or the client, who's getting it in the neck for having more cash on-site than they're insured for. It is a fine line. We can't over-employ, because we would have to let people go when the business drops off. But we have to have enough people to meet the demand and make the outfit look as professional as possible. So that is why tonight I'm working late and will be for the next fortnight or so."

Connor acted suitably rebuked before asking, "What about casual staff?"

"Casual staff? This is a security firm. Who was I talking to when I was talking about transfers of thousands of pounds earlier? 'Wanted part time, short-term-contract delivery teams to collect and drop off large sums of money. Those with aversions to having guns thrust in their faces need not apply.' We'd have every small-time gangster for miles around applying, thinking that Christmas had definitely come early, to say nothing of the exodus of customers."

"I wasn't thinking about that type of casual worker. I was thinking more along the lines of—no, it doesn't matter. I'll say goodnight. You've got enough to do, and I've kept you talking long enough."

Connor leaned forward to kiss Stephanie goodnight. Stephanie leaned away from him. "What type of casual labour were *you* thinking of, then?" Stephanie asked as she climbed up on her high horse.

Connor eyed her warily, as her little outpouring had been acerbic and he didn't want to incur more of the same. "Well, I was thinking, a secure, casual work pool made up of ex-employees, ex–police officers, or police officers who have left the job due to disability—or even people like me!"

"You?" Stephanie started to laugh.

Connor was taken aback to hear her laughing at the thought of him not being trustworthy or able enough to be considered. "Why not? I'm available three or four days a week, and I'm from a trustworthy group of people. And, as it wouldn't be a primary source of employment, I wouldn't be relying on it, but a good rate of pay would make me want to be available for it whenever work was there. I'm pretty sure that I could get a group of interested people who could meet your customers' and your high standards, and in one fell swoop address your staffing problems. It would go some way towards satisfying employees' partners' sexual frustrations."

The last point was lost or just ignored by Stephanie. Her gaze was fixed on the screen of her computer; the flashing cursor pulsed at the point where it was left. But the real computing was going behind her unfocussed gaze. "Do you know, there may be something to what you say? We've advertised before, but we've never actually targeted ex-coppers or professional groups like that. Do you think they might be interested, or are you just winding me up?"

"No, I'm serious. As long as the application process and interview aren't too onerous."

"Oh, God, no. Primarily we are just after a clean bill of health physically and that they have no criminal record. How hard can it be to fill out a few forms and move a few boxes or bags around? I really think you've stumbled onto something here. This might be worth pursuing."

Connor's smile bordered on being smug. "Good. I'm glad. Does that mean we can have an early night after all?"

"Sorry, honey. I don't think your idea, as good as it may be, will be up and running for this year's rounds."

Connor pleaded jocularly, "How about if I make myself available? Could I have an advance on my wages in kind?"

"You wouldn't really want to work on the vans, would you?"

"Well, if the money was right and the bosses were any good, I'd give it some thought, yeah."

"I can't speak for all the bosses, but I know one of them is really good."

"I bet she's one of these career types. You know, always putting her job first at the cost of her home life. I've heard that women like that have minimal sex lives as well."

"Yep, that sounds like the boss I know. Still, a girl's got to do what a girl's got to do." Stephanie returned to her computer. "Night, sweetheart. I'll be up later. Deadlines to meet, numbers to crunch, you know the kind of thing."

Stephanie started typing. Connor shrugged his shoulders, got up, and kissed her on the cheek. "Night, then. Don't work too hard. I wouldn't want you to turn into that boss, you know."

Stephanie smiled. "Why don't you read your book for half an hour, and I'll see if I can get this bit done? Your idea may have got you on the bonus scheme. Did I tell you the firm had a bonus scheme?"

"No, no, you neglected to tell me. Perhaps you can fill me in on the details when you come up?"

"See you in a bit."

Connor went upstairs to the bathroom with a smile on his face.

Chapter 18

THE SHIRE XIII

There was the sound of a van pulling up and the ratchet of a hastily applied hand brake, causing a slight squeal of resistance from the tyres. Connor looked up and stopped sweeping up the pile of litter and dust from the lockup floor. He walked to the wicket door and pulled it open to reveal the side of a white van whose driver was just getting down from the cab. The man looked up to see Connor looking at him.

"Hello, mate. Is this unit 27?"

"Yeah, that's right. Have you got a delivery?"

The driver looked down at his clipboard. "Four boxes. One of them's bloody heavy!"

Connor put down the broom, ducked back into the lockup, and unbolted the three-quarter door. He folded back the larger section, allowing the afternoon sun to light up the inside of the workshop. The driver was folding back the doors of the van and struggling somewhat to clamber up into it, doing a passable impression of a walrus hampered, not only by his bulk (evidence of too many greasy spoon breakfasts and late-night lock-ins), but also the fact that his jeans were on a mission of their own to reveal as much as possible and restrict him at the same time. After he regained his feet, the driver studied the labels of the buff-coloured boxes before pushing them towards Connor like a shepherd separating sheep from the flock. The driver checked his clipboard list against the four packages at his feet.

"That's them, then."

He pushed them towards Connor and then handed Connor the clipboarded paperwork, pointing with the end of a chewed pen. "If you'd sign there—across all four will do."

Connor wrote his signature over the four boxes and handed back the pen and clipboard to the driver before pulling one of the boxes towards him to get a better grip.

"Cheers, mate. Careful, that's the heavy one. I'll give you a hand."

The driver tried to get down, but the boxes had blocked him in, and Connor felt that it would be less aggravation to carry the box himself.

"It's all right, mate. I've got it."

The driver clambered down. This time, gravity worked in his favour; he picked the smallest of the three boxes and followed Connor into the lockup. He stood in the shade of the unopened door, peering around the whitewashed walls. "This is a bit rough, ain't it?"

Connor turned after placing the box on the floor at the rear of the lockup. He looked around as if viewing the workshop for the first time. Even though he'd done a clean-through, it still looked shabby. The plug sockets were dotted around, seemingly random in their placement and connected by a collection of various forms of trunking. He spotted the sites of previous fittings and fixtures, telltale by the outlines showing in the different shades and colours of earlier paintwork. The light fittings were industrial fluorescents that, although turned on, competed with a skin of dust and discolouration as well as the daylight shining through the open door.

"Yeah, it's not too pretty."

"What do you do here?"

"Me? I don't do nothing here. I'm just helping out a mate and waiting for you to turn up with this delivery. There's another two boxes, ain't there?"

Connor had mimicked the driver not sarcastically, but enough for the driver to realise that, when delivering to a bloke in an empty lockup who sounded as wise as the driver was trying to be, it might not be best to ask him what he's up to.

"Oh, right. Hang on." The driver scurried out and was gone a few seconds before returning with the remaining boxes. "There ya go, mate."

Connor had walked to the doors to take the box from him and to block the entrance to discourage any further conversation or impromptu inspection.

"Cheers, you take care now."

"Cheers, mate, and you."

The driver turned and walked out the door as Connor placed the boxes on the ground and then bolted the door shut. Connor turned to the boxes, and one after the other, opened the tops and looked in just to ensure that what he'd expected to arrive actually had. He wouldn't need the equipment for a little while yet.

Over the coming days and weeks, Connor took delivery or went out to purchase a range of items that, if not delivered directly to the lockup, eventually made their way there in the boot of Connor's car. Connor was careful to ensure that the number of direct deliveries was kept to a minimum—not that the products themselves were incriminating, but Connor was keen to avoid face-to-face interaction, which might give someone the ability to associate him with the building or its contents.

Connor's latest acquisition was a digital camera, a middle-of-the-range affair, and he was busy learning its nuances as he sat in his car. The supermarket was busy, and he'd had to wait before securing the parking place that he'd identified as optimum for his purposes. All he had to do now was wait. The magnetic taxi roof light provided a perfect cover for him to wait in his car without arousing too much suspicion.

For Connor, the wait was neither boring nor arduous, as he had developed people watching into something more than a pastime; it was almost a compulsion. Many times, he'd been caught out in pubs or restaurants either watching others or— even better, as far as he was concerned—listening in on their conversations. So he just sat there in the cab and watched. There were no car park security cameras, and even if there had been, he was doing nothing illegal. More importantly, he would not be doing it on a basis regular enough to raise suspicion.

The beauty of using a digital camera was that he didn't have it close to his eye. This meant that no one could creep up on him and catch him out when his attention was focused on what his camera was focused on. Additionally, it would be difficult for anyone to see if he was viewing previous photos or recording new ones. Plus, he could check then and there whether or not he had captured the image he wanted. This was quite invaluable, to say nothing of the fact that a digital camera user could now develop his own pictures without running the risk of exciting some over-inquisitive photo developer at the local chemist. This was all perfect for Connor, who spent an hour and a half busily taking a series of photos of a security delivery van as the driver and his mate went through a well-rehearsed routine of transferring bags and boxes from the van to the building and vice-versa.

It was getting late when Connor collected the van. He had brought cash, hard earned from many a long night and day driving the cab. It was a calculated risk as to whether paying in cash was less memorable to the payee than leaving a direct paper trail in the form of a cheque. The recipient was happy to receive the cash, which Connor knew would be recorded as an amount under the agreed sale price for the purposes of tax returns that, on balance, led Connor to believe that cash had been the best way to pay. The van still had eight months' tax, which had been part of the deal. That meant there was no inconvenience of obtaining insurance or MOT certificates, although Connor would have to register the vehicle's change of ownership, as the seller would probably send off the paperwork to say he was no longer the registered owner. To counter the means of tracing the sale to Connor, he had used a false name and an address of a row of offices that were due to be renovated. He had recently visited them for a fire certificate reinspection. The door had been virtually wedged by the mail, junk and otherwise, behind the door. He figured that a letter from the DVLA would most likely go unnoticed amongst the rest of the mail, and even if it was discovered, the chances of it being sent back by one of the builders was next to zero and a risk he was prepared to take. Even if it were returned, it would be too late and not traceable, anyway.

The shadows were already across the road and creeping well up the walls of the buildings opposite. The air was still warm, but the autumnal chill carried the scent of a bonfire as it crept around the edges, pushing the summer evenings back in the day as the new season stole more of the daylight hours, day by day.

Connor drove the van onto the estate, perhaps a little too cautiously in an attempt not to get involved in an accident— which in turn made him drive in a way that was most likely to cause one, the way one drove when a police car was following him or when his dad was a passenger. Somehow, he arrived at the lockup safely and left the van running as he unlocked the wicket gate and went in to unlock and pull back the main doors, which he secured open with hooks fixed to the brick pillars on either side. He climbed back into the van and reversed it into the lockup. He turned off the engine and closed and secured the gates, taking a final look out of the wicket gate along the deserted service road. He smiled to himself and then closed the door.

Once safely inside, Connor turned on the fluorescent strip lighting, which flickered and buzzed into life, filling the space with pearlescent light. He walked around the van. It ticked as the engine started to cool down, and his hand left a track down the side as he ran it along the dusty bodywork.

Connor felt both the excitement and the foreboding of the situation. They intermingled like first-time sex—the excitement of new experience and thrill tempered by the journey of discovery in territory known only through some very unreliable third- and fourth-hand accounts. He tried to make the view fit the map, the countless crime novels and the newspaper *exposés* and confessionals of "big time" gangsters. He tried to accept that what he was on the verge of doing did not fit the normal bill, if anything ever did. In fact, it was the abnormal nature, the uniqueness, of the situation that provided Connor with his greatest opportunity for success. All that aside, it didn't stop the adrenalin coursing through him. Every action was taking him farther down the road, and soon it would become impossible to turn around. At this point, he had done nothing he couldn't rectify with an apology or a pleading-ignorance shrug of the shoulders. From here on in, though, he would start to create evidence that it would be very difficult to explain away without revealing criminal intent. He started to take his first steps down the road less trod.

Chapter 19

THE SHIRE XIV

Connor, who was getting home from work early, called out to Stephanie, but there was no reply. He dropped his bag in the hall and kicked off his shoes before going to the kitchen to fill the kettle and put it on to boil. He opened various cupboards to collect a cup and a canister of tea. which he used to fill a small stainless steel tea infuser before hanging it from the rim of the cup. He waited for the kettle to boil as he looked out of the window into the garden and noticed that the small patch of grass needed cutting. The wet weather had kept the mower confined in the shed.

Connor picked up the kettle before it had finished boiling and was satisfied to have the switch click to the off position as he poured the boiling liquid into the cup. He replaced the kettle and went into the living room, where he searched for the weekly television guide. He'd nearly reached the point of exasperation when he saw it sticking out from between a pile of papers. Separating the pile, he noticed a file whose title caused him to forget his television guide:

"Collection Schedule: Christmas."

Connor pulled the file out from the pile and opened it. It contained a list of shops, stores, garages, and banks. There were addresses and times, as well as a good number of pencilled notes and crossings-out. His mouth went dry as he wondered how best to use the information. He was just staring at the file in his hands when he heard the front door open.

"Hi, you home?"

Connor quickly shuffled the file amongst the pile whilst pulling out the television guide. "Hi. Yeah, in here."

Stephanie came into the living room, unwinding a scarf from around her neck and then proceeding to shake off her overcoat. He went to meet her, and they kissed hello.

Stephanie was bright and cheery. "How's your day been?"

"Oh, so-so. You know."

"What you doing?"

Connor felt defensive, but didn't show the emotion outwardly. "Well, I am waiting for my tea to draw, and I thought I'd see what delights we had to watch tonight. It's taken me an age to find this." He held up the TV guide whilst indicating the pile of magazines and files he'd had to root amongst.

"Oh, I'm sorry, hon. I should take a lot of that stuff to work."

"No worries. Do you want a cuppa?"

"I could kill for one. I've had a really crap afternoon. We had a couple of drivers book sick, and one of the vans broke down. I've been trying to organise reliefs and cover when I should have been working on the Christmas rotas. At the rate things are going, they won't be done until next Christmas!"

They walked into the living room, and Connor's eyes were automatically drawn to the pile containing the schedule. "Well, you sit down for ten minutes and I'll make you a cup."

Connor went into the kitchen whilst Stephanie plonked herself down into an armchair.

"Teabag or the real stuff?"

"Teabag."

Connor smiled and shook his head as he poured the hot water into the cup again, just as the kettle clicked to off.

Chapter 20

SCOTLAND VI

Connor awoke with a start. A gust of wind had caused the fly sheet to crack like a whip. He lay still to listen carefully and reassure himself that it was just the wind, and also to collect his senses whilst he felt for his head torch. When he located it, he pulled it over his head so that the torch was positioned on his forehead. Content that there were no further noises outside, he switched on the light. The brightness caused him to squint around to find his pullover. His upper torso leaked away the accumulated heat of the sleeping bag. He repositioned the headlamp, having dislodged it whilst pulling on his pullover. His breath steamed in the focused beam. The light flicked around the inside of the tent as he scanned over the contents that he had emptied from his backpack, which now lay somewhat deflated under the foot of his sleeping bag. Against the wall of the tent lay various items of clothing and camping apparel. Incongruous to the jumble were three dark green, plastic-wrapped cuboids. Each measured no more than a couple of medium-size holiday paperbacks. The light of Connor's head torch glinted back off of the transparent sealing tape. A slither of a smile crept over his lips.

He lay back and pondered what more could a man ask for? A roof over his head, all that he needed at his reach, and nobody nearby to worry him or worry about. Or was he being too carefree? He was a hunted man, or was he? He wondered what wake he'd stirred up and who, somewhere, was trying to make sense of the chaos he had created. If things had gone as he'd planned, though, then "chaos" was too strong a word for it. On the journey up to Glasgow, the radio had been woefully short of any national news, as the prime minister was hosting the G8 world leaders. Connor anticipated that this happy coincidence would distract the police forces across the country, as they were pressed to provide officers to police the anticipated protests against world poverty or some other cause that would give them the opportunity to throw bricks and worse at the police and society in general. Connor hadn't taken the opportunity to buy a newspaper lately, but from the leaders he had seen, none concentrated on any robberies. Was the job too small and, therefore, not interesting enough for the nationals? Or was it too embarrassing for the firm? It wouldn't do much for customer confidence to know that somebody had taken them so easily and, as far as he was concerned, vanished so completely.

Connor looked at his watch, and then reached for a bag down by his feet from which he retrieved a tiny personal radio. He unwrapped the wires, inserted the earpiece, and turned on the radio. He scanned through the channels, searching for a news report. He found the BBC news, although the reception was poor, but still there was no mention of a robbery. Even bigger events had overshadowed the G8 visit, and global terrorism had struck another tragic blow. Connor could not help but see the silver lining of this particular cloud, but nonetheless pondered the carnage and suffering his colleagues would have faced on and under the streets of London. He recalled the conversation he'd had about the public not caring about the emergency services until they needed them. He baulked at the rhetoric being spouted by the MPs interviewed for the report, who talked about the professionalism demonstrated by the emergency services, having seemingly forgotten the scathing criticism they doled out when those same professionals had to go cap in hand for their annual pay rise or fight not to have their resources or personnel diminished.

Fuck 'em, Connor thought, removing the earpiece and tucking the radio away. He reached for his water bottle and filled a small kettle, which he placed on a stove in the tent porch, and dug around for his cup and makings for a cup of tea. As strapped as he was for carrying space and weight, he had not compromised on his tea. From a battered plastic lidded box, he took a bag that held the silver tea infuser and started the tea-making ritual. When it was complete, he lay down and turned off the light. The tent was lit by the flame of the stove, which gave a cosy glow that made Connor shiver involuntarily and pull the sleeping bag close around him.

The agitated kettle lid informed him that the water had reached the boil. He allowed it to steam off; sure as he was about the water purity, one could never be too careful. The thought that a diseased, dead sheep lying in the stream around the bend that he had not seen could have serious ramifications for him, travelling alone as he was. He turned on the torch again and searched for a small packet of dried noodles, which he poured into an aluminium dish along with the remaining water from the kettle he had used to make his tea. The inside of the tent was steamed up, and Connor opened the zippered doors a few inches to let the steam out. The tent cooled very quickly, a necessary inconvenience; a steamed-up interior would create condensation, which in turn would impregnate everything and most likely freeze in the nights to come. This would mean some very uncomfortable mornings.

Connor sipped from his mug and gently prodded the biscuit of noodles, which started to separate into individual strands, releasing small pieces of vegetable that bobbed to the top of the decreasing water line. He pondered the events that had brought him to the side of a Scottish mountain and the metaphor of the pea that had just freed itself from the noodle tangle. He thought about how complicated life had become, how everything had become entangled and reliant on everything else. Society needed consumerism as much as consumerism needed society;

it was just a question of where the particular society happened to be. Someone born into a mountain community on the outskirts of the Himalayas might not readily recognize the needs for four-wheel-drive cars or double glazing. That's not to say they wouldn't be useful—more that the peer pressure to own a piece of debt-laden detritus is absent. Sure, the application of market forces—supply and demand or economics in general—could be applied to any form of existence. As such, the strands of the noodles become more entangled. It just took a little hot water to tease the strands apart, and Connor had poured the hot water.

Chapter 21

THE SHIRE XV

There was a mist suspended in the air, but it did not obscure the deep, rich green shine of the drying paint that he had just finished applying to the van. Connor pulled aside the dust mask and lifted the goggles, stepping back to view his work. The fluorescent strip lights reflected in the wet paint. He smiled, pleased with the finish. He disconnected the spray gun from the hose line and switched off the compressor. Then he went to the back room, which he used as a clean work area, unbuttoning his overalls as he went. On the desk was a series of stencilled letters. These he moved aside and uncovered a set of photos, some of which had been enlarged and photocopied. He picked up a ruler and started to take measurements from the photos, which he wrote on a separate sheet of paper under various headings of front, rear, nearside, offside, and roof. Having completed his calculations, he picked up a roll of mirrored paper and some sheets of thin-gauge sheet metal. He began to stick the mirrored paper onto the steel, going to great lengths to avoid any air blisters before attaching thin strips of flexible magnets to the back. When he completed this, he turned the plate over so that the mirror side was uppermost and started to stick on the stencilled letters. After about fifteen minutes, he held up the mirror along the bottom edge. The words read: HATCH HAS TIME DELAY FITTED.

Connor stood up and, carrying the mirror, walked to the rear of the van. He attached the mirror above an aluminium extrusion and stepped back to admire the effect. Connor gave a wry smile.

The effect was simple: He knew that it would not stand up to any form of close scrutiny, but he was confident that it wouldn't have to. For all intents and purposes, it was the rear of a security van. There was a significant enough variety of vehicles for any slight differences to be accepted. Additionally, he thought, *how many people get that close to the vehicle, anyway?* Doing so would surely look suspicious and attract the attention of the guards. Yes, he was content that security vans were only observed in one's peripheral vision, and his van was more than good enough to pass unnoticed. Connor took off the faux-mirrored window as well as the mock aluminium hatch and stored them at the back of the workshop on a bench, which he covered with a dust sheet.

Chapter 22

THE SHIRE XVI

The industrial estate was starting to get busier as the crepuscular light cast by a variety of neons was overcome, only just, by the watery light of the autumnal dawn. The morning was cold. Roof vents and chimneys steamed freely as the heating systems kicked into life. Connor sat waiting. He had just put the blower on to demist the windscreen. The car parks started to fill, and lights flickered on in the buildings as the outside lights turned off. He watched the far end of the main road that serviced the estate. It was from that end that the vans would start to emerge, but it was only five past seven. He didn't expect much activity before 7:30. Reaching into the footwell, Connor picked up a stainless steel flask, from which he poured some hot water into a plastic cup. After securing the lid on the flask, he lowered a tea infuser into the cup. The steam competed with the blower, which fought to keep the windows clear. He bobbed the infuser up and down, watching the liquid grow darker until he was content. Then he removed the silver ball and placed it in a plastic bag. From a small plastic bottle, he added a splash of milk and started to drink his tea, all the while watching the road.

The time passed, and the cup now lay empty on the passenger seat. The glow of headlights indicated that a vehicle was exiting the site. Sure enough, a car passed Connor's. The driver was yawning as he removed his tie—*the night shift*, Connor thought. Four or five more vehicles passed by, the drivers in various states of uniform.

The time had crept on to 7:35. He reached forward and picked up the pen attached to a pad that was stuck to the windscreen. He scribed on the pad to see that the pen was working and wrote down the time. At 7:38, a van appeared, a green livery with gold insignia reminiscent of a high-class delivery van. It passed Connor's car as he feigned reading a piece of paper, but all the while he watched the two-man crew shaking off the early morning start. Slipping the car into gear, he started following the van, an easy task for even an untrained driver. The commuter traffic was starting to build, but the van was prominent enough not to lose. Connor followed for about ten minutes, occasionally noting street names, junctions, or roadside features. Connor completed the roundabout and headed back to the estate, where he parked once more and waited for the next van so that he could repeat the procedure. This he repeated three times that morning, and the whole stakeout four times over the next two weeks. Eventually, Connor had the information he needed.

Back at the workshop, Connor pawed over a large-scale map, onto which he had scribbled a circle in black marker, the centre of which was the industrial estate—the radius of the circle and indicative of ten minutes' travel time. Across the circle, bisecting it at acute angles, were two straight red lines. Where these lines, the main routes from the estate, intersected, he had written down the number of vehicles that had taken that route to complete their rounds against the bisecting lines. He looked at these numbers and the vans' direction of travel, but also at the surrounding roads. One road kept attracting his attention, an "A" road serving a busy town that he knew from experience was prone to the rush-hour holdups at either end of the day. He tapped that part of the map several times before leaving the lockup and setting off in his car to carry out some reconnaissance on the ground.

Chapter 23

THE SHIRE XVII

It was about two o'clock when Connor pulled his car off the main road and into a lay-by just before a five-junction roundabout. He switched off the car and studied the location. It wasn't long before he saw what he was looking for: ten yards beyond the end of the lay-by, an eight-foot white post capped in a once fluorescent orange peaked roof, which had now faded due to the ravages of the weather. It looked as if someone had started to build a bird table and then lost interest. Connor climbed out of the car and shut the door, he reached upwards in the feigned the stretch drivers perform at the end of a long journey. He looked at the marker post and then, nonchalant and without any outward purpose, started to walk towards the post end of the lay-by. At the end of the short length of paved area, Connor stepped onto the grass and walked until he was level with the post. Down at the base of the post, a smaller-cast concrete post stood leaning slightly backward with a white faceplate inscribed with black insignia. Connor studied the information, and a smile crept across his face when he read the word GAS. Looking behind the post, he could see an overgrown ditch in which, approximately a third of the way down, there was a once-white flanged metal pipe almost twelve inches in diameter. Connor shielded his eyes from the sun and scanned the panorama before taking one last look back down at the pipe. Content, he returned to his car and slipped back into the afternoon traffic.

Chapter 24

THE SOUTH COAST I

The wind whipped the wire rigging against the metal masts and flecked the tops of the petrol, green waves with white froth. Boats large and small bobbed gently at their moorings like tethered horses corralled tightly together. They would buck to see out to the wide expanse of the estuary and bigger seas beyond, yearning to stretch their furled and folded sails.

Connor paced along the pontoon walkways, hands pushed deep into the pockets of his canvas jacket, whose collar he had turned up against the wind's icy fingers. The for-sale signs told their own tale. Connor looked only at the more weather-worn. One sign in particular caught his eye, adhered to a motor yacht roughly twenty-five feet in length. *Little Star*'s white hull, trimmed in blue, dipped and bobbed gently against the pontoon walkway, her fenders preventing her hull from being damaged. Connor stood for a while, just studying the little yacht before raising his eye to the horizon, where he saw the white-capped waves breaking on the bow of a working fishing boat. He looked back to the yacht and wondered.

A salesman, clearly uncomfortable away from his heated office, appeared and called out to Connor. "Are you okay there, Sir?"

Connor snapped back to the moment and turned towards the voice. The man had appeared at his side, protected from the weather in a bright yellow jacket with various sailing insignia daubed across it. It had probably been a freebie that he and colleagues used to honey the trap or close the deal.

"I was wondering whether you could tell me a little about her?" Connor indicated the boat tethered at his feet. The wind whipped at the salesman's hair, causing him to finger it back in a well-practised manoeuvre that was as adept as it was futile against the gusting breeze.

"I have the information back in the office. Would you like to . . .?" The salesman pointed along the jetty to a squat office surrounded by various flagpoles, each of which sported flags depicting manufacturer's emblems. Connor gestured to the salesman to lead on and fell into step alongside him. The salesman opened the door for Connor and followed in quickly behind him, helping the self-closer to close against the wind.

A pretty thirty-something blonde looked up from some paperwork and smiled at Connor before looking to the salesman. An unspoken agreement fell into play, and the blonde got up and went to the coffee percolator and started to prepare two cups.

"How do you take your coffee?" the salesman asked as he shed his coat and shook off the cold chill of the wind simultaneously

"Just with a drop of milk, thank you."

The salesman proffered a seat, and Connor removed his jacket before sitting. The salesman was rummaging through a filing cabinet drawer that looked like it needed sorting—probably one of those rainy-day tasks continually put off, even on rainy days.

"Claire, where are the details on *Little Star*?"

Claire looked up from the coffee maker at the salesman. His tone had been somewhat clipped, indicative of his own failing, but attempting to offload the blame. She said, "I thought you moved them to the other drawer."

Connor picked up on the stress placed on *other* and also her slightly retaliatory tone, which he felt reflected more than a professional relationship. The salesman was now rooting through a lower drawer in the cabinet and eventually emerged with a small foolscap folder. Claire delivered the coffee to the table, and Connor thanked her, his eyes catching hers long enough to see her roll her eyes at her boss's behaviour. He smiled. The visual communication was missed by the salesman, who was attempting to brush up on the boat's details. He flicked through the sheets of paper in the open file as he took his seat across from Connor.

He looked up. "I'm Jan by the way . . ." He offered his hand across the desk, and Connor reached out to shake it.

"I'm Connor."

Jan's hand was soft to touch and well manicured, very much a salesman's hands. He started his patter. "Are you local or visiting?"

"I'm just here for a couple of days, visiting, I've always fancied owning a boat, so I thought I'd come down to have a look."

Jan looked at Connor, obviously trying to gauge whether he was serious about a purchase or just trying to pass some time and waste some of his. Still, business was slow and *Little Star* had been on his books longer than he would have liked.

"Well, she's a fine boat to get you started and comes with enough kit to keep you safe. Have you sailed before?"

Connor lied, "Yes, but it was a long time ago."

Jan handed over the file. There were various sheets of paper detailing the specifications, equipment inventory, and inspection and test certificates. But Jan had held back one piece of paper.

Connor looked up. "Well, this all looks okay, but there are no price details."

Jan handed over the piece of paper he had withheld "I think you'll find it's a very reasonable asking price."

Connor took the paper and scanned down to the bottom line, where he saw a price of £8,000. He suppressed a smile and feigned a concerned frown.

"How does that fit your budget?"

Connor knew that, in the boating world, this was very small fish—but, even so, people were hardly breaking down the door.

"It's a bit more than I wanted to pay, what with mooring and maintenance costs year on year."

"Well, if it eases your mind, there are still six months of mooring fees left with this boat, and that also gives you the benefit of extending for another year. This is a very popular harbour, and there is a waiting list to obtain mooring and, between you and me . . ." Jan leaned forward conspiratorially, " . . . a sort-after and saleable asset as long as you pretend that you are passing it on to a relative."

Jan sat back and winked knowingly at Connor. Connor smiled and thought how naive Jan was, considering he had no idea what Connor did for a living. Or was Jan very good at assessing people and their likeliness to be tempted into a deal by a man who was prepared to bend the rules? What did that mean about his honesty when it came to the details and assurances about the boat?

"Well, perhaps we could go and have a closer look and see if it is what I've been looking for?"

Jan smiled and drained his cup, simultaneously trying to put his jacket on—just a little too keenly, thought Connor. Jan went to a large key cabinet and scanned down a list before removing a small set of keys. Connor finished his coffee and stood up, smiling at Claire. "Thanks for the coffee."

Claire smiled back and watched as Connor put on his jacket and was ushered through the door by Jan.

The wind gave the men a welcoming blow, causing both to pull their jackets tight around their necks. The short walk back to the boat was in silence. Connor felt Jan wanted to talk, but the wind meant he would have had to shout, which was not conducive to sales patter. They reached the boat, and Jan stepped from the jetty on board. Connor followed. Jan fiddled with the small bunch of keys and a padlock that secured the hatch, which led below, before finally succeeding with the right key. Jan folded back the hatch and removed a half board, giving access to the dark interior via a steeply pitched ladder too short to descend in the conventional manner, facing the ladder, but too steep to feel particularly comfortable going face out. Only habit would address the awkwardness.

Connor followed Jan's lead and entered the interior. It smelled musty and unused, which was exactly its condition. Jan started to deliver his sales patter, using what he saw as his prompts, rather than referring to the information folder he had brought with him.

"You have two settee berths and a drop-leaf table, and through to the forepeak there are bags of storage, which I think would be better used as two sleeping berths."

Jan stood back to let Connor see past. It was a little too cramped for the men to feel completely comfortable in such close proximity to each other. Connor nodded his agreement, but with a tinge of disinterest that Jan picked up on.

"Are you planning to take others out with you?"

"No, not at first. Perhaps when I've got my sea legs back. It's been a long while, and I'd rather risk my own neck initially before ridiculing myself amongst friends. In time, I'd like to be brave enough to take her out, perhaps even across the channel?"

"Well, that shouldn't be too much of a problem. There is certainly plenty of equipment to get you there and back safely, once you are familiar with it."

There was a slight pause before the end of the sentence that was almost a question about Connor's experience and ability, which Connor responded to with a lie. "I've just enrolled on a day skippers course weekend, which should give me the basics to build on. I've often thought how difficult it must be to learn to play the piano if you don't actually own one. I'm not saying it's impossible, but certainly a lot more difficult."

Connor's response just hung there. Jan was struggling to make the link. He felt there was a thread of logic, but his fear of seeming at a loss to understand ended with him agreeing with a smile and a nod before turning back to safer ground.

"Here there is a gimballed two-burner gas stove next to the sink. Water is foot-pumped from a—" Here was a pause whilst Jan consulted the notes, "—fifty-six-litre freshwater tank, the head is through there." Jan pointed to a small door behind Connor. "Which is a sea toilet. On the port side we have radar, a colour chart plotter, a tiller autopilot, and VHF radio. As you can see, there's plenty of shelf storage."

Connor looked around. He liked the feel of the little boat. She felt sturdy and self-contained, just enough of everything. And there had been some thought into how it all fitted together; space was a premium and used, all the better for being such.

Jan went on reading now, wholly from the notes. "There's a nine-horsepower engine supplied from a twenty-seven-litre tank. The engine was overhauled nine months ago." He was nodding to himself as he read out the details. "Sails, she's cutter-rigged with a storm sail that sets on the inner forestay. The main is slab-reefed with lazy jacks, the furling head sail has a rotostay furler. There's a four-man dinghy with a small outboard, and the batteries are charged via the engine alternator and wind turbine when she's laid up. All in all, that's a lot of boat for not a lot of money." Jan's voice sounded surprised at its own genuineness, and he looked over the boat with renewed interest.

"Well, she's certainly got plenty of everything, but unfortunately that runs to the price as well. Is there any room for manoeuvre there?" At least half of the diatribe had been lost on Connor, a condition he needed to address quickly. Attack was his best form of defence.

"She's very keenly priced. I know for a fact that the owner has dropped the price from £10,500, and he's only selling because of his wife's illness. They are having to move closer to relatives, away from the coast, and the travelling to maintain the boat will be too much for him alone."

Connor appeared unaffected by the sob story and came back with an offer. "I was looking to spend £7,000 tops for a boat to mess about on to get my competence back before moving on to something larger. This is a little beyond what I'd anticipated, so I'm a bit stuck on the finance."

Jan considered these points. He knew the boat had been with him longer than he cared for and was starting to make the stock look a bit stale, but at the same time, he realised now that this was a bargain if the right person came along. Jan had bills to pay like everyone else. "What can you afford to go to?"

The negotiation had now started in earnest. Connor responded, "It's like I said—£7,000 is all I budgeted to buy with. I'll have to pay for a survey and any costs that might come up. How much is a boat survey for something this size? Three, four hundred pound?"

"Connor, I'm confident this boat is in good shape. You can see from this sheaf of maintenance receipts that she's been well looked after, so saying that if you can stretch to £7,700 I'll pick up the survey and any costs it throws up. How's that?"

Connor didn't come straight back. He looked around the small cabin as the boat rocked on the swell. The only noises were the wind whipping the wire cables against the mast and the occasional shriek of the gulls patrolling the marina. This would have been the point in the second-hand car market when, with hands deeply in pockets, the potential buyer would have walked around one last time kicking the tyres. There didn't seem to be a nautical equivalent, unless he retired to the bar for a contemplative gin and tonic.

"£7,300, cash," Connor offered.

This struck a chord with Jan. "£7,500, but I'd need to telephone the owner to agree."

"You'll pay for the survey and anything it throws up?

"Within reason."

Connor smiled. "Okay, you've got a deal."

"Let me just make this phone call. Will that be okay?" Jan pulled his mobile from his pocket, his eyes asking for privacy, which Connor picked up on.

"Sure, no problem. I'll just wait on deck."

"Thanks, it shouldn't take a minute."

Connor climbed out of the cabin and onto the deck as Jan produced another piece of paper from one of the many zipped pockets on his jacket and started to dial the owner's number.

Up above, Connor instinctively placed his hand on the wheel and looked to the head of the mast twenty feet above him, at the spinning battery-charging turbine, before looking out to the horizon. *This is serious,* he thought. He knew next to nothing about sailing and hoped the learning curve would not be too steep.

Jan's voice carried intermittently through the open hatch. "Yes, that's right, Mr. Sally. I have someone who's interested, but can only afford . . ." His voice was momentarily lost to Connor, either through the wind or because he had gone *sotto voce*, conscious that Connor was in close proximity. "Okay, Mr. Sally. I'll do my best, but I can't promise anything."

Connor knew that Jan had squeezed another £500 out of the price from the owner, and although Connor felt a tinge guilty about that fact, it was a dog-eat-dog world. He shrugged it out of his mind as Jan emerged through the hatch and stepped out onto the deck.

"Congratulations, Connor, you are the proud owner of this fine boat."

Connor smiled back at the beaming Jan, and they shook hands.

"If we head back to the office, we can complete some paperwork and finalise the details."

Jan stepped back onto the jetty. Connor followed as they walked back and took one more look over his shoulder to the boat, then a longer look out to the horizon. It did not look inviting.

Chapter 25

THE GAMBIA I

Connor had sold his share in the car back to his colleague, and very quickly the arrangement had been swooped on by one of the other firefighters, who had been circling ever closer, a financially motivated vulture. The mini cab office had seen many coming and goings of drivers working their way through cash-strapped times of their lives. There were only a few hard-core cabbing professionals, and they broke down into two camps: the smart, clean shirt-and-tie brigade who proffered the "sir" and "madam" salutation as they held the door for customers and the nicotine-stained-fingered, shiny-trousers division that beeped their horn outside, rather than knocking at the door to signal their arrival. Both camps had wished Connor well. Neither seemed to understand his motivation for jetting off to Africa, and he had attracted quite a bit of "good-natured" jibing, the kind that would have had serious disciplinary ramifications if it had been made in the fire service.

The day after the leaving do from the fire station, Connor didn't move from the bedroom other than to go to the bathroom. He had pretty much written it off for anything other than making promises never to get in the same state again, promises that were as empty as they were futile in securing relief. God recognised an empty penance. It was the next departure Connor was not looking forward to. The air in the house was particularly sombre, made all the more so through moments of feigned happiness and smiles that cracked too soon when the realisation of the near future returned. Connor had packed and repacked an oversize backpack, which lay on the bed, as well as a carry-on and much smaller pack lying beside it. Tickets, passport, sheets of itinerary, and various amounts of cash in a variety of denominations and currencies protruded from a travel wallet, which Connor placed inside the smaller bag.

He picked up the bags and struggled through the bedroom door and down the stairs. He dropped the bags in the hall and went through to the living room, where Stephanie was sitting, cradling an empty cup in her hands. As Connor entered, she quickly wiped one eye before looking up. Her eyes were a telltale red, and her smile was on the verge of total collapse. They stood together in an embrace. Stephanie buried her face into Connor's shoulder, her body rocking from silent tears. Connor's words of reassurance, at best, fell on deaf ears; at worst, they caused renewed tears. Connor looked at the clock, part of him wishing it on five minutes so he could hear the ring at the door of the mini-cab driver and bring to an end this drawn-out departure. But the minutes ticked by interminably, agonisingly.

As was typical, the cab was late, and Connor had to deliberately slow his departure so as not to appear too hasty. Eventually, the bags were in the car and they shared one more goodbye before he climbed into the car and closed the door. He wound down the window and held out his hand, which Stephanie took hold of.

"I'll ring you as soon as I can, and I'll write. You take care, okay? I'll be back soon—you'll see."

Stephanie nodded and tried once more to smile. She released her grip as the cab revved to pull away and offered a gentle, mournful wave. Connor strained around in his seat to look back for one last glimpse as the cab turned out of the street. He could see that Stephanie was crying again. "I'll be back soon," he said to himself.

The drive to the airport was uneventful. Connor's fears of motorway hold-ups were unfulfilled, but his tenet of "better safe than sorry" was not going to be that easily discarded.

Progress through the airport was the usual organised chaos. People demonstrated the full range of human emotion: the joy and despair of greeting and saying goodbye to loved ones, the anxiety of shepherding family groups past the uniformed officials while displaying the right piece of paper. The worry of luggage being the right weight, the right size, and on the right aeroplane. Queues of people formed snakes across foyers and shuffled forward—or not, depending on queue philosophy. The pointing crowds at the banks of blinking monitors and the omnipresent loudspeaker triggered the *Brave New World* reflex of checking wristwatches.

Connor navigated his way through the *melée* of the check-in, passport, and security before he found himself sitting in the departure lounge at an island coffee bar, sipping an over-frothed, overpriced latte whilst he watched his fellow travellers. Parents chased children to and fro, groups of men and women sat together and apart in the bars, determined to get their holidays off to alcoholic starts. At some point, the holidays would break down over the next fortnight into tears or arguments—and for some cooling off periods in the local gaol or their own personal doghouses. Young couples oblivious to their surrounds snuggled down in each other's company, whilst only yards away examples of their future relationship sat there in silence across the table from each other, or at best tried to distract themselves from their obvious marital problems by buying things they knew they didn't need.

Connor's dissertation had been submitted, and his tutors were more than happy with its content. They were impressed that he had done so well without taking the field trip, as previous students had never scored as well as their counterparts who had committed to the on-the-ground work. This was, of course, indicative of the amount of time Connor had invested in his research and studying; many a long night at the fire station and on the cab rank had been well spent. This meant that this journey was superfluous to his studying, but imperative to his plans.

Connor looked up, somewhat pointlessly, at the loudspeaker when he heard the words "Gambia" and "Brussels" airlines. The message repeated that the flight was about to start boarding. Connor finished his coffee and gathered his holdall, and like some of those around him, started to make his way towards the gate. There was a small queue, which was quickly processed as his co-passengers displayed their boarding cards and passports. Connor noted there were no children and very few older couples. The ingrained prejudices were not easily broken down or forgotten. Still, there were two more stops ahead of him, and he was sure the flight would fill perhaps not so much in Brussels, but in the last hop from Dakar to the Gambian capital, Banjul. At least there was no changeover after Dakar, and the last leg was only forty minutes in duration.

Connor took his seat on the aisle. He had long lost interest in gazing out of the window, especially after visiting BAE Systems as part of his fire service training and seeing the constituent parts of the aircraft being formed and pieced together. In addition, the courses he had taken at the Fire Service College, in which all number of air disasters had been dissected in sometimes graphic detail, to the point where he did not want to watch the wings bounce up and down as the plane accelerated along the runway. If they were going to fall off, he'd rather not watch it happen, and the aisle would allow him to get to the nearest exit quickly. He had seen in video-recorded trials that there would be a fight for survival.

Eleven hours later, Connor emerged from the aircraft, the dry, recycled air replaced by the blanket-like heat of the airport apron. The cement finish reflected the midday sun, causing Connor and his co-passengers to squint and search for their sunglasses whilst they scuttled for the shade of the airport buildings. Immigration and customs lived up to the men in uniform stereotype portrayed by many frustrated didn't-quite-make-it people in uniforms the world over. Connor just bit his lip and resigned himself to accepting this petit level of bureaucracy, knowing that this was just as he had anticipated and, in fact, part of his plan that could prove useful if things were to go wrong.

Connor exited from the terminal building. His backpack had drawn disdainful looks from the plethora of willing hands offering to carry luggage from the perspiring, and often confused, wealthy tourists. He had shown purpose in direction and a don't-fuck-with-me attitude that had kept the run-off-with-your-baggage brigade of "porters" at bay. Connor looked left and right for the taxi rank and saw instead another uniform, this one second-hand-looking, of a smiling, portly man. The original owner of the uniform would have been smaller in stature all around, judging by the let-downs on the trousers and the straining buttons across the stomach.

"Taxi, sir?"

Connor accepted the offer from the attendant. There were some systems he could not buck without getting stitched up more than he would have, anyway, and it might pay to get the scammers on his side.

"Where's a good place to stay that's nearby?" Connor asked.

The attendant looked Connor briefly up and down and then beyond him to see how much time he could invest in this one man. His trade worked out similar to a trawler fisherman: long periods of redundant waiting interspersed with bouts of frantic activity trying to net as many customers as came through the doors. The rush seemed to have ebbed, and there were just the tail-end travellers who, traditionally, were at the wrong end of the tourist "Darwinian evolutionary scale," which meant that they often weren't aware of the appropriate level of recompense for services rendered. This often led to embarrassing silences and bitter disappointment on the porter's behalf. That said, Connor looked friendly when smiling, but edgy when he wasn't, which was intriguing and a little foreboding—something akin to a wet paint sign. There was a personal satisfaction in proving the sign to be wrong, but short of that, one could only lose.

"You want a backpackers' hotel?" the taxi marshal enquired.

"No, something a bit more up-market and air-conditioned."

There was a sheen of perspiration on Connor's forehead and a general layer of grime built up from fifteen hours of travelling that he could almost peel off. It made him itch for a long shower, the temperature of which would not have mattered because he wanted it so badly.

"Well, I would recommend Villa Kato Garden Hotel—enough of everything you want without costing everything you got." The attendant's face broke into a knowing grin that suggested a less than salubrious lone traveller lifestyle.

Connor's smile left his own face quickly enough for the attendant to realise he had misread Connor's needs. He hastily tried to correct his indiscretion. "But on reflection, perhaps you might prefer the Oceana, a bit more expensive, but more refined, more in keeping for you, sir?"

The attendant bowed and looked up at Connor to see whether he had lost his chance of a tip with his little indiscretion. He saw Connor's smile return, which was echoed and amplified in his own face as he turned and waved at some point unseen by Connor and shortly after a small family saloon car over-revved to the kerbside near Connor. The attendant opened the door and leaned in to speak to the driver. The attendant offered to take Connor's backpack as Connor got into the car, but Connor wanted to put the bag into the boot and satisfy himself that it had not been left behind. There was a brief exchange, and a small bundle of *dalasi* passed into the attendant's palm.

"Thank you, sir. You tell the reception that Ali send you, you get extra special service. I promise."

Connor laughed. "Thank you, Ali. I'll try to remember that."

The driver pulled away. The movement pushed Connor back into his seat and kicked up a small cloud of dust, through which Connor could see Ali counting his gains.

The little green taxi sped along one of the few well-kept tarmac roads of the largely unpaved road system. The government recognised the importance of a good first impression for the tourists that used it. It was about twelve miles to the capital, and Connor's driver drove as if practising for an off road rally large amounts of overtaking interspersed with some hair-raising undertaking, accompanied by a comical-sounding horn and wild gesticulation at any vehicle or person that dared to share or compete for his road space. Connor was both alarmed and amused by the experience as he clung to the handles in the back and tried to keep doubts of how roadworthy the vehicle was out of his mind.

The driver was forced to slow as they approached the more built-up area of Banjul, where there was a proliferation of likeminded road users who forced each other into stalemate. This did not stop the cacophony of horn-sounding, arm-waving, and pleas to the gods of the road to take divine retribution on any driver who had committed an infraction of the law they had failed to take advantage of themselves.

The taxi eventually pulled up at the entrance of the Oceana, where there was a polite tug-of-war over Connor's bags between the driver and the doorman. Connor brought this to an end by paying off the taxi driver, who greedily accepted what in reality would represent a couple of days' regular earnings.

Connor followed the doorman, now carrying both bags, to the reception, where they placed the luggage on a gilded trolley that was out of keeping with the surroundings. But on reflection, there was no real theme—more an eclectic mix of the fancy touches from hotels the world over. The foyer seemed to be a test palate for hotel design and contrivance; however, the blend, although somewhat quirky, was also eccentric enough to have been planned that way. Connor couldn't be sure whether the emperor had a fantastic new suit or was parading himself buck-naked down Main Street.

The doorman departed with another of Connor's notes and was replaced by a bellhop, who stood attentively, watching the receptionist gun-dog-like, a heap of energy waiting for the off. The receptionist was smartly attired in a freshly-laundered shirt and well-fitting waistcoat, which signified his position in the hotel hierarchy and the respect he commanded from the underlings who had to bribe their way to the "front of house," where, although they were poorly paid, they could get tip-rich from the fun-seeking tourists. Staffers were safe as long as they did not pursue the guests and remembered regularly, at least once a week, who enabled them to be in their privileged position. A single tip, an almost throwaway amount of money that the average westerner would probably have down the back of their sofa or in an unused ashtray in their car, could well amount to a week's pay here. For this reason, the staff worked hard and maintained "respect" for both the management and the guests to keep a roof over their families' heads and place food on, most probably, a salvaged table. It was a very low point indeed when pride and principles become luxuries.

The smiling receptionist twitched at Connor's attire, but was wily enough to know that millionaires could be hard to spot nowadays. "Can I help you, sir?"

"Yes, I'd like a room, please."

"But of course. How long are you looking to stay, may I ask, sir?" The receptionist was turning the pages of an embossed, but slightly dog-eared register.

"Three days initially. Do you have a room with a view of the ocean?"

"Indeed, sir. Are you staying alone or . . ."

The receptionist looked up from the register as his question trailed off. Connor was aware that travelling alone to this part of the world was not altogether normal and wanted to allay doubts and suspicions whilst not provoking too much interest. He did not want to register on anyone's memory radar.

"Yes, I shall be. I'm going to meet a colleague at Basse Santa Su on the Upper River. I work for a mining company." There was enough credibility, but not enough interesting material for the receptionist to work with, Connor hoped. The receptionist knew enough to know that his country was not rich in mineral or ore deposits, but still the government insisted on employing surveyors on the off chance they might find something.

When the registration was complete and passport details had been recorded, Connor was bid a "good stay" and invited to follow his baggage porter.

The door to the hotel room was quietly closed by the departing porter, and Connor threw himself onto his bed on his back. For two minutes, he just stared at the ceiling and gently rotating fan. He then brought his knees up to his chest and rotated them left and right, hearing a slight click each time from his back, which caused a satisfied smile to appear on his face. He sat up and undid his shirt buttons before getting up to draw back the blinds and pull open the balcony window. There was just enough gentle breeze, which caused Connor to breathe in deeply and again stretch his arms upward to the doorframe whilst taking in the sparkling vista and majesty of the Atlantic Ocean.

Connor turned away from the window and moved back into the room towards the bathroom. As with every hotel bathroom he had seen, there was no window to the real world, so with the pull of a cord, a fluorescent blinked on and an extraction fan screeched to life. Connor banged the fan housing, and the screech settled to a more acceptable volume, which was then in turn drowned out by the drumming of the shower as it beat against the slightly stained enamelled bath.

Connor stripped off, letting his clothes just fall to the floor. He then stepped into the shower. The instant wave of refreshing relief was glorious, as if layers of cling film were being peeled away to allow his skin to luxuriate in the clean, cooling water. Connor looked down, almost expecting to see discoloured water running to the drain plug. He was almost disappointed that there wasn't. He took the soap and lathered himself all over, stripping away the oily residue and replacing it with a lavender perfume from the milky complimentary bar, which rapidly dissolved to un-useable pulp. He became obsessive in his desire to reduce the pulp to a vanishing point somewhere on his body. The shower complete, Connor turned off the taps and stood momentarily, just dripping, before he reached for the towel, which he passed in cursory fashion over his face and torso before wrapping it around his waist. He looked briefly in the mirror and then shut off the light and its noisy accomplice before returning to the balcony.

The gentle flow of air from the open wind was refreshingly cool against his wet skin. His feet left footprints on the tiled balcony. Connor leaned against the cement-rendered wall and enjoyed the uninterrupted view of the ocean and the foreshore, which was dotted with palm leaf–thatched shacks offering a variety of beachside services to those who lounged on the white sand or frolicked in the surf. Immediately below Connor's perch was the hotel swimming pool, for those who preferred more sanitized relaxation and the added benefit of periodic visits from the poolside staff to replenish empty drink vessels. The whole vista sparkled in the mid-afternoon sunshine from the heaving swell of the ocean to the dribbling beads of condensation on the trays of drinks being delivered to the sun loungers' oiled bodies.

He moved back into the shadow of the room and undid various straps on his backpack. He removed rolled-up bundles of clothing, which he shook out and stowed in the wardrobe on coat hangers that had to be teased out of their confused knot.

Having sorted out his wardrobe, he laid a pair of shorts and a cotton shirt over a chair, by which he also dropped his sandals. Connor went back and partially closed the balcony door, then lay back on the bed and fell asleep.

Chapter 26

SCOTLAND VII

The wind was still blowing, and the tent rattled sporadically as rain was forced against it. Connor just lay still, cocooned within the tightly drawn sleeping bag, and took stock of his surroundings. It was early morning. Connor could tell; it was a camping trait to wake early, which was just as well, as getting going was difficult and disproportionately long. Performing each task felt like a yoga exercise. The recently used muscles and unfamiliar sleeping positions meant that calf and hamstring cramps were only a hair trigger away.

Connor wriggled out of the sleeping bag as if in the final stages of moth gestation, so that his upper body was free of the bag's confines. He reached up to check the clothes deposited in the tent "loft" the previous evening. They were cold and slightly damp. He started to make his breakfast, a prepared bag of porridge oats, dried milk, raisins, and sugar. Next, he opened a steel flask and poured the steaming water into the kettle, which he placed on the gently hissing camp stove. The air around his head started to warm, and the condensation vapour from his breath became less obvious.

Connor climbed out of the sleeping bag and folded it open to air for a short while. He searched around for his satellite navigation, which he turned on when he found it so that it could search and fix on the available satellites. He collected other pieces of camping gear, including the plastic-wrapped bundles, and stowed them away in a well-practised and deliberate fashion in the backpack. He rolled up the sleeping bag and wrapped it in a plastic bag before stuffing it into the backpack. The kettle was starting to steam violently, so he switched off the flame and divided the water between the bowl of oats and the mug with the tea infuser hanging from the side. He poured the remainder of the water into the flask. After stirring the oats, he took tentative spoonfuls to the edge of his lip to test the temperature. His eagerness to eat was checked only by his keenness not to scald the inside of his mouth, a very fine equilibrium. Connor took the tea infuser out and sipped the tea without milk. Some tea aficionados thought that milk in tea was a sacrilege. Although Connor wasn't quite that sacrosanct about it, powdered milk was definitely not right.

Chapter 27

THE SHIRE XVIII

It was a cold but dry night. Connor was dressed in a dark pair of denims, a black shirt, and a black army surplus canvas jacket. After parking the car in the lay-by adjacent to the roundabout where he had identified the national gas main, he waited and watched the nighttime traffic pass. He considered the decision to position a lay-by where he was parked. It was close to a town, so not really a stopover for long-distance lorry drivers or for people travelling by car. Connor accepted that there was a need for lay-bys; he just wondered what equation had to be applied to decide where and when, and who created road system maps and actually made the decision.

His thoughts filled a few more minutes as he sat there in his car, the shadows chasing each other around the interior as the headlights of the passing cars shone through the now misting windows. Connor reached down into the passenger footwell and retrieved a small shoulder bag. He rummaged momentarily in the bag and removed a pencil-thin torch, which he clicked on and off to check whether or not it was working. The red filter ensured Connor's night vision wasn't lost. He checked his watch, opened the door of the car, and climbed out. After locking the door, he walked casually along the lay-by. There was nothing to cause him any concern, so he returned to the boot of the car and removed a container of petrol and a handwritten sign with the words GONE FOR PETROL, which he placed on the dashboard in front of the steering wheel.

Once more, Connor walked down the lay-by, this time going beyond the paved section onto the rough grass verge, where he checked the section of road as if waiting to cross. When a gap came that would have allowed someone much slower than Connor to cross, he turned around and quickly scaled the wooden fence. He jumped down into the ditch that accommodated the gas pipe he had reconnoitred earlier. Waiting a few seconds, he allowed his eyes to adjust to the deeper darkness and the now slightly muted sounds of the passing traffic. Once his senses had adjusted, he opened his bag. Using the red-lensed torch, he sought and took out a pistol-shaped battery drill, a bundle of steel wool, and a roll of gaffer tape. From his jacket pocket he took out a small plastic envelope containing a number of fine drill bits, one of which he took out and inserted into the drill. He hand-tightened the chuck. Connor crouched down, positioned the drill against the bottom of the pipe, and started drilling slowly. As the drill steadied, he increased the speed and the pressure. Thirty seconds later, the drill had punctured the steel-walled pipe, and gas was escaping under high pressure. Connor removed the drill and, moving quickly, but not rushing, tore off a piece of tape and stuck it over the hole. The hissing stopped; the tape held. Connor teased out a tuft of the steel wool with another strip of tape stuck over the first so that the wool was exposed on both sides. Slightly above the first hole, he repeated the process each time, releasing a jet of pungent gas; a stenching agent had been added to the normally odourless gas with the intention of indicating to the more aromatically aware that there was a gas leak before levels reached explosive potential. Each time, Connor would wait for the gas to dissipate—not that he was overly concerned about the gas igniting. The only ignition source was the electric spark of the drill, but even if the spark was hot enough, the chances of the stoichiometric mixture being correct were slim indeed, and the fact that the gas was lighter than air left Connor more than sure he was safe.

About thirty minutes passed, and Connor had completed his tenth hole, progressing to the "quarter to" position around the pipe. Connor put the drill back into the bag and teased the remaining wire wool into a two foot long braid, which he laid loosely over the exposed tufts. Gently, he taped each one into place, twisting them together so as to ensure good contact was made. He trailed the remainder to the ground and formed a bird's nest coil directly under the "six o'clock" position of the pipe. From the bag he removed a nine-volt battery, which had been prepared so that a thread of fishing line from a reel had been secured to the base and secured to either side by insulating tape two elastic bands hung limply.

Connor wound the reel of line twice around the pipe so that the battery hung with the terminals facing downward, directly over the nest of wire wool. He produced a metal tent peg from the bag and pushed it firmly through the wire wool nest. Maintaining the tension on the fishing line, he gently stretched the elastic bands downward and slipped them onto the hook of the tent peg. With the fishing line temporarily tied off, he took a roll of food wrap and formed a transparent tent over the pipe, weighted down to offer a modicum of protection from the weather. This task completed, Connor picked up his bag and, keeping the line taut, climbed out of the ditch. He threaded the line through the fence and took a turn around a fencepost, just below the grass line. Back at the edge of the lay-by, Connor took another tent peg and, after securing the line to it, pushed it obliquely into the verge so that the head was away from the ditch, but pointing in the direction of the roundabout. Connor counted the kerbstones back from the end of the lay-by to the tent peg and, though it was a bit of overkill, flattened out a weather-worn drinks tin and placed it over the peg.

Connor had just stepped off the verge back into the lay-by when his car became silhouetted by the headlights of a car pulling up behind. He peered through the screen of his car, trying to make out the car behind and tried to appear as casual as he could. A passing car's lights lit up the new arrival, and the translucent plastic oblong on the roof and fluorescent and reflective signage caused Connor's heart to miss a beat. A shot of adrenaline hit his stomach and almost involuntarily his gait stiffened. Now alongside his car, Connor opened the passenger door and dropped the shoulder bag into the footwell before moving to the back of the car and opening the petrol flap. He removed the cap within, all the time trying to see the activity in the car behind without looking directly at it.

As Connor crouched down to attach the pouring spout to the plastic petrol "can," he noticed that the interior light had come on in the police car when the passenger door opened. He saw the driver in the gentle light. The man looked somewhat bored as he spoke into a handheld microphone, most likely relaying the registration number through the national database. Connor looked up at the driver's colleague as he approached, his features lost totally in the shadow caused by the car headlights. This fact was not lost on the police officer, nor was the stark juxtaposition of Connor's face totally illuminated by the same lights. Connor smiled somewhat lamely and shrugged his shoulders as he stood with the container of petrol. The picture said it all, and no explanation was required or asked for.

"Are you all right there, sir?"

"Yeah, thanks. I could've done without this, but then I guess I've only got myself to blame."

Connor looked at the officer. He, like his partner, looked bored, but had that slight twitch of amusement around his lips, which Connor felt was a suppressed smile caused by his distress. The police officer looked back to his car and Connor followed his eye to see the driver giving the thumbs-up sign, which Connor knew meant that the car had cleared the ownership and tax hurdles in the database.

Connor's heart was still racing. He didn't think he had been seen climbing the fence or stooping at the end of the lay-by, but if he had, his plan was to say he had been caught short after his nocturnal stroll or that he was retying his bootlace— or both, depending on what they had seen and what they asked about. Any investigation at the end of the lay-by or accidental entanglement in the fishing line would force Connor to answer questions not about criminal intent, but terrorism. Both positions would be indefensible and would leave Connor between a rock and a hard place.

The police officer gave Connor a hard stare and said nothing, looking for something suspicious or waiting for an out-of-context remark that might indicate dishonest behaviour. Connor tried to appear slightly embarrassed by the situation and chalk it up to experience as he tipped the dregs of the petrol into the tank and replaced the fuel cap. It was a natural ending. If the officer was going to make a point of the situation, he would. Instead, he just smiled once more.

"Well, as long as you're okay, sir, I'll leave you to it."

"Thanks for stopping to check. I should be okay now."

Connor threw the petrol can into the boot and shut down the lid as the officer retired in silhouette to his warm car. He moved around to the driver's door and climbed in. He held up his hand in a wave as the police car pulled past him and breathed out a controlled sigh of relief, the enormity of the moment washing over him. He sat back and felt the damp patch of sweat on his shirt press against his skin. *That was too close,* he thought— but, then, he had prepared well and the preparation had paid off. Even if there was any connection to his car now that his name was linked to the lay-by, he hoped his planning would cover his tracks.

Chapter 28

THE GAMBIA II

When Connor awoke, he was completely dry and the towel was lying undone about him. The sun was just peeping above the horizon and giving a farewell light show that made him want to take a photo, but if he did, he would never on development recall the actual image with the entire colour and nuance afforded the naked eye. It was still warm, but much more bearable to Connor's English blood. The slight drop in temperature was probably what had woken him up. He struggled to shake off the grip of sleep and lethargy.

He swung his feet off of the bed and reached for the clothes he had laid out earlier. It was an effort both physically and mentally to dress—physically he craved more sleep and, mentally, his brain was telling him that he was too warm to require additional layers. When he finally dressed, he just sat and collected his thoughts before getting up to close the shutters outside the door and shut out the sudden blackness that had chased the sun out of the sky. Connor switched on the bedside lights, and the low-wattage glow formed soft pools of light across the bed and shadows up the walls. He picked up his watch from the bedside table—7:15, he noticed as he slipped the bracelet-style band over his hand and secured the clasp. He turned to the wardrobe and pulled out a soft linen jacket, which even in the short while it had hung free of the backpack's confines had lost most of the severe creases in the high humidity and heat. Putting on the jacket, he looked himself over in the mirror. Satisfied with his not-too-smart but not-too-scruffy appearance, he picked up his wallet and placed it inside his pocket before attaching the dog clip at the end of the retractable fine nylon cord, which was attached to the wallet through the inside pocket buttonhole. He had seen the wallet and securing leash advertised in one of the fall out magazines that came with the weekend newspapers. Whilst he found the magazines annoying for the waste they created, they also held a somewhat have-a-look fascination that he found hard to resist. In Connor's mind, most of the items were a reflection of life itself and almost a pamphlet-size, minimalist study of the social condition of a consumer society. The yin and yang of consumerism—on the one hand were the products that offered to enhance life in some wonderful way, a product that might cure ailments or, at the very least, allow one to cope more ably. Or the product could improve social standing aesthetically or academically. In some instances, a truly wonderful product could achieve all of the above "at an unbelievable, never-to-be-repeated price, offered to specially selected customers who could receive an additional surprise gift if they responded within fourteen days," and all of this printed on recycled paper. Faced with this advertising tsunami and the idea that the panacea for one's woes was within financial grasp, who could resist? However, when the strange package arrived at the door, the eager anticipation very quickly dissipated, all hopes, ambitions, and plans thwarted by the cheap and poorly manufactured piece of brittle plastic or unsuitable tools that were always smaller than envisaged. These items that provided so much hope proved the adage that "you get nothing for nothing." The paradox of the situation was that this life-changing pile of crap now shamed the buyer into stashing it away in some dark corner instead of changing his life. On the one hand, the cheap labour and sweatshop workers that brought the component parts and raw materials together were suffering from the same health problems that the product they made was designed to alleviate due to the lack of control over their working environment and conditions. All this so they could earn enough money to improve their social standing and own some piece of materialistic crap made somewhere further down the consumer food chain. At the same time, the high rollers of the organisation were creaming off the profits regardless of the damaging environmental effects of manufacture and physical human suffering that their "health" products caused, products they most certainly would never contemplate using themselves. This frustrated Connor because, on very rare occasions, he would see a product that he wanted and, against his better judgment, buy it. On more than one occasion, he'd had to chalk a particular purchase up to experience. The wallet-securing leash had been one such product; after much scrutiny, he failed to see how it could fail, and although he felt confident that he could look after himself and his possessions, there was something about this product he had to have. At least it was advertised on recycled paper. It was hard to walk through the Garden of Eden every weekend without sometimes picking the odd apple.

Connor patted himself down and opened the door. Once he had passed through, he secured it with the heavy, well-worn brass key, glad that the key card and flashing red and green lights weren't used in this hotel. It was only a short walk along the corridor and down the stairs to the foyer. Connor could not suppress his thoughts about the lack of fire safety. In particular, the only staircase was, in fire safety parlance, unprotected, a thought that he stowed away. He mentally plotted an escape route—just in case.

The evening foyer was calm and quiet. The receptionist was tidying up the paperwork of the day and looked up briefly as Connor descended the stairs. He smiled and returned to the paperwork. Connor crossed the foyer to the open doors of the restaurant and was greeted by a waistcoated *maître d'*, who welcomed Connor with a beaming smile and slightly subservient demeanour, not the stuffy aloofness that lesser establishments would usually project. Connor thought that the decadence of the wealthier nations filtered to the serving staff of hotels and restaurants to the degree that they themselves had ideas above their station. They, in turn, looked down their nose at those they perceived to be of a lower standing. But they betrayed themselves when they had to deal with real wealth or class, when they transformed their behaviour to an oleaginous, pawing sycophant. This could be dually fascinating and painful to observe. The greeting that Connor received indicated a less-than-full stomach and an opportunity to temporarily address the hunger through either tips or, if need be, table scraps of which the *maître d'* had either a share or first refusal.

Connor was led to a table that was too large for a lone diner, but the serving staff removed the excess flatware to leave it as a one person setting. Connor had chosen the seat for its vantage point of the whole of the restaurant, and also its view through a series of large glass sliding doors across the pool towards the beach. Some of the doors had been left partially open to allow the cooler evening air to steal into the room, and when the noise of the room dipped, he could just make out the rush of the sea as it ran up against the beach.

The restaurant was a little tired-looking, but the bright tablecloths and subtle lighting were enough to distract from the frayed edges, the wear and tear the years had doled out. The other diners filled about a third of the tables. The eclectic mix of tourists indicated that the resort and country had established itself as a popular destination. There was the tail end of the wealthier travelling set, who were reliving the memories of previous visits and finding themselves somewhat disappointed that the expectation failed to meet the reality. There was the middle-age set, who had sent the kids to fend for themselves at university, at work, or at life in general and were either totally thrilled about travelling the less-trod path or struggling with the fact that the facilities and the environment were not facsimiles of their suburban pile transplanted to the beach of another continent. Then there were the rest, the bargain-bucket travellers and tourists with no real expectation other than the experience itself, taking the rough with the smooth and adjusting their tolerance levels to any given situation, not allowing any preconceived ideas to cloud or colour their judgment.

A waiter appeared at Connor's side and proffered a menu followed by a wine list. Connor thanked the waiter, who retired to attend to other business, but he noted that the waiter had tuned in to Connor's presence and moved in a slow orbit around him, waiting to swoop as soon as he was ready to order. The waiter was a lean man in his late twenties or early thirties. Connor had particular difficulty guessing age, and to a degree, this was something he had never felt was an important skill. He could only think it useful in incidents that involved police investigations, something he was keen to avoid in any circumstance, as it only meant pain or suffering for someone somewhere. Connor pondered the waiter and mentally placed him on his possible list. It would be a question of considering how the small pieces of conversational interplay panned out and what vibe he picked up on, if any at all.

Connor perused the selection available and, having decided, put down the menu. Before he could replace it with the wine list, the waiter had returned with his pad and pen at the ready. Connor placed his order whilst scanning the wine list and, like many before him, got lost amongst the myriad of names, none of which struck a chord. He made his final choice based on grape and affordability. The weather was hot, so he chose white—the colder, the better.

The wine was delivered and the ice bucket established; the label was inspected and the cork pulled. The glass was tantalised with a soupçon of the pale amber liquid. Connor raised the glass and breathed deeply the faint aroma of citrus stolen by an over-chilled wine before sipping the liquid, which gave more on the tongue and became butterier as Connor nodded his approval so that the waiter would fill the glass. With the bottle wrapped and submerged in the bucket, the waiter retired to the kitchen through the double swing doors. Connor savoured the wine and thought about the many bottles he'd drunk over the years. The romantic bottles edged with a frisson of excitement, where the conversation came easily and lasted forever. The happy bottles where friends laughed loudly regardless of their surroundings and still smiled through the hangovers that followed as an offering to Bacchus. The melancholic bottles that competed with the tears, and the cups that overflowed with sadness. Then there were just the bottles, the ones drunk the most—the false shoulders of friends that stroked his cheek whilst they wrapped their arms around him and helped him to forget the woes of the day and pushed away the worries of tomorrow. This one, though, was a new bottle, and Connor wondered how it would pan out. Would it be a happy memory like a no-strings one-night stand or a baleful stranger he might expect to steal his wallet or lead him down a dark alley? Connor sipped on, and his thoughts were interrupted by the arrival of his first course, a small plate of couscous pan-fried into two patties, dressed with a hot tomato-based sauce and accompanied by a just-past-its-best garnish of salad leaves and strips of onion. After pushing the salad aside, Connor tucked in. As good as the hotel claimed to be, Connor had witnessed firsthand some of the behind-the-scenes practises in so-called top-class restaurants back in England. A part-time job fitting and maintaining industrial kitchens had opened his eyes to the dark side of the service industry. As he ate, he recollected the nights when he squeezed in the extra work around his duty shifts. Access to the kitchens could only take place after they began to wind down for the evening, which meant starting time was about midnight. The kitchens were always hot and humid, the air spiced with the aromas of the dishes of the day, but there was always that persistent, sickly-sweet smell of rotting vegetable matter and rancid water. Connor could never totally identify the source—perhaps the pools of water, oil, and detritus (as if there had been some sort of food fight) that had accumulated on the floors throughout the evening's hectic service, when time was pressing and tempers were frayed and raw. Or perhaps from the huge pot of stock simmering on a low heat, a gelatinous mass of off cuts and discards with the occasional chicken carcass or defleshed bone.

Spills were common, and wipe-downs of workstations were less than thorough, making way for the next order to be prepared and plated up by the *sous-chef*, who carefully manipulated the food into a semblance of prescribed order as dictated by pictorial references of various dishes hanging above the workstation. Once content with the offering, the *sous-chef* then passed it to the head chef, who, more from habit and enforcement of his or her superior position, would "tut" and have to make some minor adjustment before passing it across the servery to the waiting staff. Here it would be received by the head waiter, who would feel obligated to again meddle with some detail. Prior to clearing the dish for final delivery, the waiters would take the dish and once more adjust the comestible to their own requirement, depending on how much they liked or disliked the final recipient. Four pairs of hands touched the food after it had been cooked. God only knew how many hands had touched it prior to that point—how many hairs, nasal drips, or other bodily fluids, excretions or sloughs of skin had come to rest in the ingredients that had been brought together to make up the overpriced meal that eventually arrived. For these reasons, Connor had promised himself that he would try not to eat out, a point that used to drive Charlotte apoplectic on two fronts: first, trying to get him in the restaurant and, second, trying to get him to choose something from the menu. Still, Connor rarely sent anything back to the kitchen with a complaint or to be adjusted; he just smiled inwardly when he saw someone else commit this *faux pas*. He couldn't say he had ever witnessed it, but he guessed that if someone's food was mauled to pieces *en route* to the table initially, what chance did it have second time around? So when Connor sat with fellow diners determined to put the waiter or chef in his place with a piece of their mind because the soup was too cold or the steak was underdone, Connor imagined retaliatory fingers dipping into and poking the food before nuking it and returning at best with just an apology—at worst, Connor dared not to think. Uncooked food, especially abroad, was something Connor avoided at all costs. He even avoided ice in his drinks. This trip was very important, and Connor could not afford to spend any time laid up with food poisoning, so his meal was far from exciting. Dining for the trip would be a pragmatic exercise in maintaining an operating capacity.

The first course was replaced by the second, and Connor opted for a rather poor brandy instead of a dessert. There had been some small talk between Connor and the waiter. This was necessary on a number of fronts to both parties: It helped the waiter to improve both his English and his chance of a tip, and it allowed Connor to cultivate the relationship and size up the waiter as a potential, but unknowing accomplice in the impending crime. Both parties seemed happy.

Connor was coming to the end of his drink and asked for a refill as well as the bill, which came in the form of a tab. Connor had to sign it and produce his key as proof of hotel residency. During the signing and after confirmation that the meal had been okay, supported by an intentionally boosted tip, Connor made his play.

"Tell me, would you know where I could go to find a guide or someone to show me the sights?"

The question, which was outside the ordinary dinner conversation, caught the waiter off guard. Connor saw the translation difficulties reflected in his face and added, "I have tomorrow free and was hoping to do some sightseeing."

"I see. Yes, I know of someone, yes. It may be a problem, as it is too quick for me to have to talk to him. Maybe ask at reception."

"I understand. It's not a problem. I just thought I'd ask—you know, just on the off chance. But don't worry."

"I would like to help, but it is difficult for me," the waiter said *sotto voce*. His demeanour became furtive and shifty; his eyes flitted around the room and he went through the pretence of sweeping the tablecloth of invisible crumbs.

"I may be able to show you round if you wish. I not starting work until four o'clock tomorrow in the afternoon, but it is not liked that I do this for hotel guests, you understand?"

"Oh, I'm sorry. Of course I understand. I do not want to get you into any trouble. Please forget that I have asked."

The hook was baited; it was just a question as to whether or not the waiter would rise to the bait. The tip had been well received, and separating the tip from a much larger bundle of notes had certainly whetted his appetite for more.

"Perhaps sir could meet me at ten o'clock tomorrow morning by the taxi queue down the street?"

"Why, thank you. That would be fine, as long as you are sure it will be okay. I wouldn't want to get you into any trouble. As I've said, I have a day to kill, and it would be a shame to waste it."

"Tomorrow at ten."

The waiter was definitely uneasy and struggling between more boundaries and protocols than he was comfortable with. He seemed keen to arrange the liaison without losing the deal or jeopardising his job. Connor watched the waiter squirm and was glad to see that he was uncomfortable, as he needed someone who needed his job as much as he needed an opportunity to enhance his income. Connor had hit lucky with this waiter.

"Okay, at ten. What's your name?"

The waiter relaxed a little, and his face once more broke into a smile. "My name is Beril. I will see you tomorrow. Good night, sir."

"Good night, Beril."

Chapter 29

SCOTLAND VIII

The wind had dropped off, but still occasionally sniped amongst the heather and gorse that clad the mountainside in hues of brown and grey. It stole away the corner of the tent as Connor tried to fold it down into his backpack. He bagged the tent poles and strapped them down the side of the bag. He also stowed the cooking stove and saucepans. A flask of hot water lay by the pack, to be put away last for easy access later in the day. Connor unpegged the ground sheet, which protected the bottom of the tent from stones and mud, and sat upon it to complete the packing and take a bearing from his map and compass. Connor looked around, surveying the panorama with his eyes alone. Only wind wraiths kept him company as they brushed against him and whispered in his ear before stealing off to bully the clouds. He felt isolated in his hemispheric prison, both secure in and exposed by his environment. He had slipped a few places on the food chain; in scientific terms, he had now become prey to the authorities. His predatory physiology now exposed inadequacies that his cosseted existence to date had allowed to develop. His senses were starting to heighten with respect to their individual awareness. His eyes picked out the myriad of colours that made up the greys and browns of his surroundings—the subtle flecks of red, purple, silver, green, and deepest blue. The way the watery sun cast a beam against the cold black rock face and transformed it into a nugget of gold, bejewelled with veins of effervescent precious stones caused by the rivulets of water that sought sanctuary in the sea. The almost forgotten muscular reflex that tickled his earlobe in reaction to sounds real or not instinctively caused Connor to turn and face, catlike, the direction of the noise. His olfactory sense sifted parts per million and checked against a catalogue of references to identify any invisible risks, be it the stagnant marsh gas released by a misplaced foot sinking into a guised peat bog or the overpowering stench of a putrefying sheep carcass come to grief from any number of ills and now returning its takings to its lifelong host. Most developed of all was not a sense in the physical, but the metaphysical, the buried deep and neglected receptors of his humanoid past that came bubbling to the fore, now that the distraction of "normal" life had been removed. The blank canvas of his wondering mind could be painted anew—no, better. Like most cash-strapped aspiring artists, his canvas was not blank but over-painted, and from the chaos of the previous amateurish daubs, there came the clarified masterpiece. The renaissance, the realisation, the perspective defined, and the centrepiece just that—centred. Connor could feel himself acclimatising to his environment, and his inner self, his pace, his gait came naturally across all terrain. His body clock dictated his activity and his needs, there being no particular place to go and therefore no particular time to be there. His self-sufficiency gave him the freedom to stay where he was or to move as he chose. It was only the spectres of his mind, the undefined forces that drove him to turn this way or that. Call it fate, luck, or intuition—Connor minded not and cared even less. All that he watched was the weather, the horizons, and his place on the map to stay safe and, where possible, away from pockets of civilisation nestled amongst the glens and confluences of the highlands. That said, interaction was inevitable; the lightening of his backpack meant that his stock of food and fuel was in decline. His gas stove container had finally given out, and he would now have to use his methylated spirit stove until he could find a replacement. This wasn't an immediate concern; even as he stood after a week of self-sufficiency, he was still good.

With a little prudence, he was still at least another week away from needing to replenish. Connor was aware, though, that the weather could close in hard and fast, especially at this time of the year. His map indicated he was about a day and a half, maybe two, from a village big enough to support a selection of stores where he could stock up without arousing too much suspicion.

Connor did up the last remaining clip and hoisted the bag onto his back, and then adjusted it to get the straps into the comfortable zone they had created and to which Connor's shoulders and hips had acclimatised. With one last and a final sweep of the slightly flattened heather, Connor headed off, angling upward to intersect a footpath that cut across the knees of the mountain that had looked down on him during the night. He planned to skirt around the mountain and find a vantage point above the valley, to sit and observe the road and community below for a day or so before slipping down to replenish his stocks and move on. He would take the opportunity to gather any news that might gauge the impact of what he had done.

His aching muscles soon warmed, and he shook off the creakiness of the night's rest. He quickly found his pace and moved steadily across the ground. He had never felt so alive; his body was tight and toned, even more than when he had started thanks to his predominantly dehydrated diet. He mentally registered this fact as potentially significant; the loss of too much body fat would leave him susceptible to the cold and illness, to say nothing of the extra energy he might need if things did go bad. Nonetheless, Connor breathed deeply and smiled as he savoured the clean, crisp air that filtered into his lungs. He was moving with the sun around the mountain. The left hand side of his face was tightening even in the weak winter wash. The sun had soon reached its pinnacle for the day and was already sending out shadows as it flitted amongst the tops of the neighbouring peaks. Connor had not stopped since he had set out in the morning. He knew not why; he would normally take a break every couple of hours and fix himself a brew from the flask of hot water he had prepared before leaving the campsite. Today, though, he had set himself a goal and, as such, some deep-down fear of not achieving it had caused him to plod on. It was unnecessary on a number of fronts, he knew, but still he had pressed on. He had snacked as he went on half a chocolate bar and some raisins, taking drinks from his water bottle. He didn't feel tired so much as sated. He felt he'd achieved both physically and mentally like he used to when coming back from the gym. There was the need to go that little bit farther than last time, that bit quicker to push that extra couple of pounds. It was good to feel the burn sometimes. The fact that Connor had allowed himself to submit to this inner need brought a quizzical frown to his face and, again, a mental note to be mindful of this behaviour. This could be a very unforgiving environment, one that punished severely those who chose to forget that fact.

The shadow was stealing the light from the glen below Connor, herding it up the side of the mountain. Another ten or fifteen minutes would see Connor's spot thrown into shadow. Still, he did not hurry, just sat on his pack absorbing the last of the watery sunshine. Connor looked down and along the glen. A ribbon of tarmac ran through it. The road looked like a discarded bootlace, showing itself where it cut back and forth across the "burn" and then ducking back under cover of the roadside trees and hedges. The traffic was sporadic; there were long periods where nothing moved, and then came chains of three or four vehicles moving nose to tail, the front vehicle dictating the pace while the followers could do little more than grip the steering wheel a bit tighter and curse quietly so that the children didn't hear and they could grass them up to the other parent. There were very few places that would allow overtaking; indeed, even oncoming traffic had to hug the kerb and wince a bit as they passed each other. Connor felt sure that some of the bends would be the final resting place for many a wing mirror.

The village that the road served was a reflection of the road itself: small and quiet, with sufficient facilities to service the local populace—facilities that Connor hoped to take advantage of. Connor could not make out much detail from where he was, but he could see the gentle glow as the lights started to flick on, looking like fireflies captured in glass jars.

Connor shivered involuntarily, which shook him out of what had become almost a trancelike state. He stood and stretched before starting the ritual unpacking and setting up of the tent and campsite. After filling the small kettle from the flask of water he had boiled earlier that day, Connor got the meth's stove going, and very soon the kettle lid was dancing as spouts of steam escaped around it. Connor filled his infuser and set up the insulated cup, into which he poured the water from the kettle before returning the remainder to the flask. This re-boiled water didn't make for great tea, but the plunge into the gloaming and the chill it brought had made Connor realise how cold he was. The tea would keep off the cold whilst he sorted out his requirements before he was confined to his tent. When the tent was up and the ground mat and stuff sack containing his sleeping bag deposited inside, Connor went off to fill his water bottle. He walked back some two hundred metres to where he had crossed a small but bubbling rivulet and, finding a spot amongst the gorse and heather, he filtered the water through a gauze into the bottle. He chose not to use the chemical filter, as he was sure that there was no point upstream where contaminants could enter the watercourse, no habitation or farming to pollute the water with sewage or pesticides. Connor smiled, recalling the many bottles of water he had bought from supermarkets extolling the virtues of sources very similar to the one he was now tapping into. The gauze kept out errant bits of floating leaf and twig, but also the odd grain of sand, as the mountain slowly but surely eroded its potential to a neutral state, which it had done many times before over many millennia. The water was ice-cold, forcing Connor to change hands on the bottle as the cold hand sought the sanctuary of Connor's armpit. Nonetheless, when the bottle was full and he returned to the tent, he started his ablutions. He had spied earlier a likely spot for his latrine and set about preparing the site, excavating as deep a hole as the bedrock would permit. Connor used the squat. As many times as he had used the great outdoors as his latrine, he had not grown accustomed to how exposed he felt. The worry that some other hiker might round the bend was an irrational but constant cause of inner angst. Truth be known, this wasn't confined to the sides of mountains; any toilet other than the one at home made Connor uneasy—the fact that a few layers of laminate and chipboard were all that separated him from the other users of the restroom. But try as he might, he could not source the reason for this unease, which on more than one occasion had seen him aborting the use of the cubicle. He could not recall an event in his childhood, no school bullying or trauma that might have invoked this deep-seated issue, so he was at a loss to address it. As such, being perched as he was, Connor was keen to finish what was necessary. The effects of dehydrated food and hard work took their own effect, but Connor had noticed the regular pattern that had established itself compared to the random and often hurried visits to the toilet he had suffered back in the world of convenience.

When his deed was done, Connor concealed the evidence of his presence as best he could before returning to the stream, where he washed thoroughly and in bodily instalment from head to toe. The icy water caused sharp intakes of breath further chilled by the gentle katabatic sweeping down the mountainside, causing an opaque mist to form and consume the bottom of the glen. The small slice of loofah was abrasive and served to plough the accumulated grime, exposing the dermis to the soap, air, and water. The sanctuary of Connor's waterproof outers seemed disproportionately warm as he recovered his torso, then his lower half, before lathering and massaging his feet and slipping them sockless back into his boots. His ablutions complete, Connor returned to the tent using his head torch to light the way. The sun had gone to be a warm spring morning elsewhere, and the northern hemisphere stars twinkled through the wisps of cloud.

Connor zipped up the outer door of the tent and instantly felt the benefit of being out of the wind. He crouched and undressed again before climbing naked into the inner tent, where he shook out and spread the sleeping bag. He reached back into the porch and pulled out of his backpack the bag containing his nightwear, a set of long john thermal underwear and a separate bag containing the socks, which contained a liberal shake of foot powder. The socks slid on coolly and left a slight perfume in the air. Connor delighted in the feeling of being clean, dry, and relatively hot after the icy bath. His feet tingled as the blood flowed through to the extremities that had borne the brunt of the recent past. He delighted in the unconstrained environment of the woollen socks and the silkiness of the talc within. Connor laid his daywear in the tent loft, the sour smell indicating that it needed washing— an amenity not readily available. He was dubious as to whether the village below him would have a launderette.

The tent grew ever darker, but Connor lay still, comfortable in his cocoon. With one earpiece fitted, he listened to a channel playing classical tunes interspersed with local news items and phases of interference. He felt warm and content and then started to wonder why. After all, he was in a cold and unforgiving climate, a minimalist existence all contained in a backpack that had to be carried. Was it the fact that having so little meant having so little to worry about? Having just the bare essentials, stripped of the baggage and necessities of "normal" life, meant relying on himself and his ability to adapt to the challenges of life and the environment. No long-term goals that could not be achieved until he deemed them convenient, no clock to govern him, no peer group conventions, no cutting the lawn or washing the car, and no Friday evening queues at the local supermarket. This thought shifted Connor's attention to his current stockpile of food, which was low, but still sufficient for two or three days. If weather permitted, he would visit the village in the glen below tomorrow and have his first interaction with someone since the Cairngorms. The thought of food brought a slight hunger pang and reminded him of some menus from his past. Foremost amongst this mental buffet were steaming hot piles of garlic bread. Connor could envisage the golden crust with a slight sprinkling of herbs and could imagine the hot butter dribbling down his fingers. He started to salivate at the thought and turned on his torch to search through his own scant supply of dehydrated food. He was a trifle more than disappointed to see the bland and unappetising selection available. As part of his weight-saving efforts, Connor had re-bagged the various products, thus stripping them of the colourful and enticing, but superfluous packaging. This laid the products bare and made Connor think of the morning after the night before—how the thrill of the evening was tempered by the realm of likely possibility versus necessity, how as the night progressed the packaging became more enticing and exciting. The content might not be particularly healthy, but it was nevertheless an indulgence begging to be sampled. But as always, as with most fast food, the wrapper would fall away to reveal something far from the advertised product, and it then became a pragmatist's meal—"I eat to live, not live to eat." The cold light of day would bring the indulgence into sharper focus when the senses, which had been temporarily muted by the effects of the evening, returned. The down-at-the-heel shoe, the cheap cologne, the bad breath—everything that had gone under the wire was now ringing bells and shouting "look at me," forcing two uncomfortable individuals to disengage from one another as politely as possible considering the intimate knowledge they now shared of each other. They would try not to look at each other's undressed bodies, but at the same time, they wanted to stare unashamedly and remember every last detail as if peeping through the keyhole—only the keyhole did not have a door around it to mask the voyeuristic tendencies.

Connor's thoughts brought him back to the tent, and he removed a smaller clear plastic bag from the food bag. Penned on a panel on the side were the words DUMPLINGS AND GRAVY.

Connor smiled to himself as he said aloud, "Will you still love me in the morning?"

Connor set about making his dinner and resolved that he would buy some fresh bread and perhaps some cheese in the morning.

Chapter 30

THE GAMBIA III

Beril was early. Connor watched from the shadows of a bustling café across the street. With a hot cup of coffee just delivered and a local guidebook for company, he continued to watch the waiter. It was obvious that Beril was still quite nervous. As he stood exposed on the street, the taxi drivers threw quizzical looks at him. He was no threat to their custom, but equally no customer. Beril did not have the solace of a distraction, such as a newspaper to hide behind. Today's news would still be around to affect him tomorrow, and yesterday's newspapers where much cheaper. Once more, Beril looked back towards the hotel in search of Connor.

Connor watched for another five minutes or so before deciding to end Beril's misery. Ten o'clock had passed, and it was approaching quarter past, a sufficient indication, if one were needed, that Beril needed the money. Connor paid the bill and walked out into the street, past Beril's position on the opposite side before crossing and walking back to him. He got within a couple of paces of the skittish would-be guide before he turned around to see his approach.

"Ah, good morning to you, sir. I was getting worried you had forgotten our meeting?"

Connor smiled as he saw the relief replace the anxiety on Beril's face. "Good morning, Beril. I'm sorry. I was early, so I walked on a little and the time slipped past me. Is everything okay?"

"Yes, indeed, but there is much to see. Would you like to take a taxi? I will talk to the drivers for the best price if you wish?"

Connor could see that Beril was keen to arrange this for the novelty of riding in a cab and also to demonstrate to the drivers that had given him the hard stare earlier that he was a man of importance, employed by a wealthy European.

"How long do you think we will need the car for?" Connor enquired.

"To see all the city, I should think it will be the best to offer him twenty dollars. That is more than he would earn on very good day. I have to be at hotel for four o'clock and hopefully by then you will have seen many of the city sights. I arrange?"

Connor agreed with a nod and a smile that was reflected through a toothy grin. Beril approached the drivers, speaking loudly and aggressively demonstrating that Connor was getting a loyal and value-driven guide. That said, there had been no talk of a fee for Beril's services, and Connor felt that the weight of his tip the night before had assured Beril that he would be well remunerated. Connor smiled again, this time to himself at the thought of the effect he and fate were about to have on Beril's life, at least from a financial point of view.

Chapter 31

SCOTLAND IX

Connor woke. Each morning had been similar; the inner glow of the tent had caused that momentary confusion, the disorientation of waking in a strange bed or room following an unplanned stop over at a friend's, when the wine and conversation were flowing. Connor still had to take stock of his surroundings immediate and beyond. It was hard sometimes to judge what exactly had woken him—the rustle of the wind, the constriction of the sleeping bag, the slip of stone caused by sheep, deer, or other. Connor would lie still, ticking off the possibilities until he realised that he probably just woke up due to the pressure on his bladder, which he would try to manage with experimental movements back, front, or foetal—any that would allow blessed relief for a few minutes more. Eventually, Connor would submit to the inevitable and struggle out of his bag and into sufficient clothing to allow him to leave his warm pit and brave the elements.

This morning a silence enveloped the hillside where Connor was pitched—no wind, no bird calls. The glen was cloaked in a mist sufficient to mask the view and, seemingly, the sound of any vehicles scurrying along the low road. Connor looked at his watch; it was only seven o'clock. This was early for Connor to be about, but convenient also. Connor returned to the tent and dressed quickly and minimally. He gathered together his backpack and set off down the hill towards the village, turning frequently to capture a mental image of his tent's position as he drew farther away from it.

An hour later, Connor stepped from the wild, unkempt hillside to the metalled road and immediately felt the benefit of the predictably even roadway. His pace quickened. He walked against the flow of the traffic as much as the bends in the road would allow him, crossing occasionally to avoid the blind side of the bends. That said, Connor received plenty of audible warning to dodge the early morning motorist who would not anticipate someone walking along the verge. The scant police cover would almost definitely be abused by anyone inclined to take another dram "just for the road." The early morning start might not be conducive to the metabolism expelling the last vestiges of alcohol, which might still be affecting judgment if the hangover wasn't having its own effect. The volume of the passing traffic, albeit intermittent, surprised Connor—not that it caused him to recoil, but the coarse assault on the ear was so stark in comparison to the solitude of the glen and mountainside Connor had been roaming for the last two weeks.

The symmetry of civilisation started to surround and converge on Connor. The walls appeared joined by the telegraph poles, which carried their life giving power and communications from far afield. Eventually, the first buildings came into view, and before long the echo of Connor's footfalls rebounded off the lined street into the village. Connor checked his watch. It was now just past eight, and the main street was exhibiting signs of life. Connor mentally ticked off the amenities and shops the village offered. There had been a pub squat with darkened windows; the specials on the board outside had been washed away by the rain. Like many a village pub, it was a local establishment that relied on local customers, not tourists or passing traders. It was a little off the beaten track for that. Likewise, the post office/newsagent/ dry cleaners was more utilitarian than aesthetic, and a light burned behind the windows and through the door, which was heavily adorned with posters of local events and gatherings. A bell tinkled out across the street as a man exited the shop, clasping a paper and calling out some retort to a parting comment with a laugh. The man looked at Connor, a brief quizzical look that turned into a neutral expression—neither a smile nor frown—that preceded an almost imperceptible nod. Connor smiled and nodded back. He continued his tour and came to a grocer's. The proprietor was loading the pavement with a variety of non-perishable's and hanging signs from them that were somewhat dog-eared and showed an earlier price on the reverse side.

Connor kept walking, but the village households were all that remained. Those that fronted onto the road displaying depleted window boxes; those set farther back tried to hide behind the shrubbery of their gardens. There were lights on. Curtains twitched; the occasional door would open and the occupants would exit, casting Connor a suspicious glance or bidding him good morning before setting off to wherever their day was set to take them.

Connor turned on his heel and returned to the post office. He pushed at the door, and the bell told the store of his arrival; the scraping back of a chair informed Connor of the imminent arrival of the storekeeper. Through a vinyl fly-stripped doorway there appeared a lady, as "woman" would have been an inadequate term for someone of her years and station. She was smartly, but comfortably dressed. Although she wore none, half-moon glasses on a neck chain would have looked not out of place on her.

"Good morning. Can I help you? If it's the post office you're wanting, I'm afraid the counter doesn't open for another forty minutes."

She said this whilst looking at a small-faced gold wristwatch instead of the cigarette-advertising clock directly above her head, and then indicated the glass-fronted counter towards the rear of the shop.

"Good morning. Yes, I do need the post office, but I saw your sign for dry cleaning. Not that I have any of that, but I was wondering, do you do ordinary laundering? I've been away in the hills for a few days, and I've still some time to take, but my kit is, well . . ."

Connor tapered off. The lady's expression indicated that she had understood the intent without further detail. She turned and searched through a pile of old blank postcards before turning back to Connor with a look of contentment, the kind of look one displayed after finding something that she remembered having, but whose location she couldn't quite recall.

"There, you could try Mrs Rogers. She takes in washing and ironing mostly through the summer for the holidaymakers, but she may oblige. She's only a wee way down the village. I'd ring first, though."

"Thanks, that's a great help. Is there a phone nearby?"

The lady pointed to the far corner of the shop, well camouflaged by card stands. Connor could just see the yellow-backed telephone symbol.

"You'll want change?" It was more an instruction than a question, but correct nonetheless.

Connor scanned the spread of newspapers and magazines laid on the countertop, looking for a national edition. He selected the only broadsheet on show and asked, "Do you sell cigarette lighters?"

Armed with a handful of coins for the phone and the note, Connor retired to the rear of the store. Someone picked up the phone on the fourth ring, but did not immediately answer. Connor heard the tail end of some shouting and a door slam.

"Hello?" The salutation was as clipped as a one-word greeting could be.

"Good morning, I'm sorry to trouble you. I have just been enquiring in the village and was given your name as someone who might be able to help me out?"

"I'm sorry, who are you?"

The obvious awkwardness existed between two people unknown to one another, trying to communicate for the first time, one of whom had had the privacy of her home interrupted whilst the other tried to conduct the conversation well within earshot of the now very quiet shop.

"I do apologise. This is Mrs. Rogers? Mrs. Jane Rogers?"

"Yes, yes it is?"

"Mrs. Rogers, my name is Connor, and I've just arrived in the village. I was looking for somewhere to get some laundry done, and the lady at the post office suggested I give you a ring. If you can't do it, I understand. It's just that I've been in the hills for a while now, and things are getting . . . well, you know, a bit strong."

Connor felt the mood shift; the tension from when the phone was first answered lifted now that Connor had explained his position, and the echo of the door slamming had faded from the conversation.

"Well, you're in luck, Connor. I was supposed to be away today, but it's been cancelled, so if you pop the stuff around, I'm sure we can sort you out. Did you say you're at the post office?"

"Yes, I am."

"If you ask the lady, Mary, for directions, it will probably be easier than me trying to guide you over the phone. I'll see you soon Connor."

"Yes, great. I'll see you soon."

Connor hung up the phone, gathered up his kit and purchases, and returned to the counter.

"Did you get any luck?" Mary asked.

"Yes, thank you. Mrs Rogers said you would be kind enough to direct me?"

"She did, did she? Well, you go back the way you came this morning," she said, pointing back down the road that had taken Connor into the village, indicating that his arrival had not gone unnoticed. "Just past the pub, you'll notice a track, and when it forks, take the left one. It's the only house there."

"Thanks very much for your help. Just one last thing—I have a package I need to send overseas. What time does the post office counter close today?"

Connor saw that the question had piqued Mary's curiosity, and the implication that he was prepared to return later, rather than upset the post office protocol and opening times, caused her to turn to look at the clock. Although it was still fifteen minutes until opening, she said, "Well, I don't suppose it will get there any later for me opening earlier, but a bird in the hand . . ."

Connor smiled as Mary moved around the counters and through a locked Perspex door, so that she was now in an enclosed workspace within, but separate from the rest of the shop. No doubt there was some requirement dictating this construction, but like most regulation, it looked ridiculous out of context. Once she was safely ensconced, Connor slipped through the serving hatch a small, well-wrapped package about the size of an A5 piece of paper and the thickness of a cigarette packet. The package was already addressed, the destination being the Gambia, West Africa.

Mary read the address and looked up at Connor, who was prepared. "I did some studying out there a while back and have kept in touch ever since with one of the teachers. I'm asked to send bits and pieces for him to use to teach the children. They have very poor teaching facilities."

Mary smiled at the benevolent act. She seemed to like charity—particularly, Connor suspected, when it was demonstrated visibly in others. Connor didn't subscribe to ethnic stereotypes, but there was an air about Mary that made him believe she would be more than willing to put her shoulder to the wheel, but she would be more reluctant to put her hand to her purse so willingly.

Mary placed the package on the scales and read off the prices at varying levels of delivery. Connor opted for the premium and handed over the amount. He saw his package dispatched to an awaiting mailbag.

"Well, thank you very much again for your help. You've been most kind."

"That's quite all right. Enjoy the rest of your day."

Connor felt Mary's eyes follow him all the way out of the shop. He knowing he would be a small piece of gossip for the villagers to kick around for a while, but he had no qualms that they could link him to the activities he wanted to keep secret. In some ways, it was a necessary process; at least now he knew what it was going to cost for each subsequent package, which from now on, he could post anonymously from any post box. *Now,* he thought, *I need to get this kit cleaned.*

Chapter 32

THE GAMBIA IV

The day had been busy, and now Connor felt he needed a shower to wash away the heat and dust of the city. The cab was on the move again, the windows rolled down, but this did little to counteract the oppressive heat; in fact, it intensified the feeling whenever the cab had to slow down or stop. Even Beril was starting to wane. His continuous dialogue had slowed to include only the occasional points of interest that they passed *en route*. All said, though, the day had gone well, and Connor had shot enough film for a two-week holiday and bought a fist-load of postcards and stamps, which he'd affixed already whilst Beril and the driver participated in their afternoon prayers.

Beril spoke to the driver, and the cab slowed to a halt a short walk from the hotel. "I have to walk from here, as I cannot be seen with you. It will cause me too many problems with my job. You have had a good day today?"

Connor focused back on the inside of the car, not having realised how close they were to "home." "Good? Yes, excellent. You are a very good guide, and I hope a good cameraman." Connor was referring to the pictures in which he had posed in front of various landmarks. Beril had taken great delight in directing his model, as well as in keeping at bay the public that seemed to congregate, hands outstretched. Connor reached for his wallet and handed some notes to Beril, indicating they were to pay the driver.

When Beril had paid the driver, and after a series of bobbing-head thank-yous, Connor and Beril exited the cab. Standing in the shadow of a dust-ridden palm tree, Connor held up a clutch of notes and offered them to Beril. The waiter reached out to take them, his eyes wide at the sight of the clutch of money, but Connor didn't relinquish his hold, causing Beril to look inquisitively at him.

"There is a lot of money here, Beril, and you must be very careful with it. Spend it carefully. However, I have some other business you may be able to help me with, which also pays well, but without so much work. Would you be interested?"

Connor let go of the bundle. Beril glanced quickly down at it before stashing the wad into his pocket. "Yes, sir, thank you. I would be most interested, but I am running late for work now. Can we speak later?"

Connor glanced at his watch; it was 3:50.

"Of course. Tomorrow, same time, at the café opposite the taxi rank." Connor pointed back down the street to where he had watched Beril waiting for him this morning.

"Yes, I will see you there. Ten o'clock. Thank you, goodbye."

Connor watched as Beril backed away a sufficient distance before turning and breaking into a trot towards the hotel. Connor smiled. He had just given Beril the best part of three months' salary at the hotel's pay rate, but still he was afraid to arrive late for his shift. This reinforced his belief that he had found the right man for the job. Connor shouldered his bag and walked back to the hotel.

The lobby was dark and blessedly cool as Connor entered, his eyes taking a second to adjust to the darkness from the glare of the sunshine on the street. The lobby was empty, and he had to sound the bell on the reception to rouse a member of the serving staff, who appeared from a door behind the reception, brushing himself down and smiling broadly at Connor.

"Can I help you, sir? Good afternoon."

Connor smiled. The receptionist had obviously been stealing an afternoon nap and was a little flustered by his appearance.

"Good afternoon. I was wondering where or if I could get some camera film developed quickly nearby."

A broad smile broke across the young man's face as he recognised the opportunity to offset the fact that he had been caught sleeping by Connor.

"I can arrange that for you, sir, if you would like. They will be returned for you tomorrow at this time."

Connor was sadly impressed. It was easy to see that the service sector was king and that all must rally to serving, but he knew that schools were struggling to provide pens and paper for lessons. Here his dollars could buy luxury items and services. He felt that he was exploiting and propagating the system that was as oppressive as it was frail. Still, this was part of his struggle to shake off the shackles. He wondered how many would step on him to reach their own goals if the chance presented itself.

Connor handed over four rolls of film, which the receptionist bagged and logged on pre-prepared forms. With that task complete, Connor retrieved his key and made his way to his room to freshen up and rest before dinner.

***

The sun was shining hard through the window; the heat was palpable. Connor felt as though he were wrapped in cling film when, in reality, it was just a cotton sheet. He had to peel it off his body and just lie there trying to cool off as his perspiring body dried, though the humidity in the room just caused him to perspire more. The night had gone well; he'd dined on a passable meal and enjoyed at least two bottles of wine—the thought of which made his head throb and his throat go dry, his tongue suddenly feeling too big for his mouth. Connor looked at his watch—9:15. Beryl would be at the café in forty-five minutes. Connor hauled his body out of bed and took a moment to let the throbbing in his head subside prior to standing.

The water was cool as it washed over his body. To a degree, it lifted some of the hangover, but the vestiges still lurked in the corners and recesses of his head. Any sudden movement would cause some hidden sprite to run amok within his skull with a lump hammer and a metal bin lid. He stepped from the shower, and the relief of the cooling water was negated instantly by the heat that wrapped itself around him. The towel was rough, and Connor brushed himself with it rather than dry himself completely. He poured himself a glass of water and started the process of rehydrating his body. He dressed quickly in a pair of linen trousers and a loose linen shirt to match. He picked up his bum bag and slung it across his shoulder before picking up his key and leaving the room.

Connor bustled down the corridor, passing the room staff as they commenced their daily maintenance routine, sifting through the deeds of the night before and creating small works of art with hand towels and toilet tissue.

Connor breezed through reception, ignoring the offer of breakfast from the waiter standing at the door to the restaurant. It was only when he stepped out into the morning sun that he stopped and realised that his bare head would not withstand the pounding heat. He ducked back under the canopy that led to the hotel reception. His head throbbed as if a pressurised tide was pulling in and out within his skull, crashing against the opposite wall, his pain receptors awash like seaweed thrown against the surf-strewn rocks. Looking at his watch, he realised it would take too long to go back to his room for a hat, and although Beril would probably wait, Connor had invested enough not to want to jeopardise that investment. Out of the corner of his eye, he spied a bucket that held three umbrellas, no doubt for the reception of guests when the rains were on, but by the looks of them, they hadn't been used for some time. Connor took one and, extending it, stepped out into the mid-morning sun and advertised the hotel all the way to the shaded canopy of the coffee bar, where Beril was already waiting.

"Good morning, Beril."

"Good morning, sir. How are you this morning?"

Connor smiled ruefully. His head still throbbed, and even now the heat was uncomfortable, cloying, making Connor yawn for breath. Still, he had to concentrate on the deal he was about to broker with his newfound accomplice. "To be honest, Beril, I have been better. Would you like some coffee?"

"Yes, please, allow me."

Beril called out to the waiter loitering in the darker shade of the shop. The waiter came out, notepad in hand. Beril ordered two coffees, and Connor asked for a bottle of water. The drinks arrived quickly, and Connor drank deeply from the bottle before watering down the Turkish-style coffee in front of him. Still, the caffeine coursed through him, causing him to shudder involuntarily. But the hit was dragging him out of his stupor, the price of which he knew he would pay for later.

"Beril, I have a proposition to make, which I am willing to pay you well for. Would you be interested?" Connor could see that the little man in front of him was interested, but also nervous. Connor went on, "It does not involve anything illegal on your part. I merely need you to forward some mail for me."

Beril looked more relaxed, but still more confused.

"I have the opportunity to fulfil a lifelong ambition back in England, but my family and work believe I am here, something I am keen for them to keep believing. If they find out I have gone off to do this other thing, they will only interfere to the point where I will not be able to do it. So my plan involves the photos that I am having developed from our tour yesterday and the postcards I bought. I will send these to you already stamped and addressed, and you will forward them back to the address in England. For each letter I ask you to send, I will include, let's say, $25 dollars. I think that would be a good price for posting a letter?"

Connor watched Beril, whose face broke into a wide grin. "I, too, think the price is fair. I hope sir will be writing to many of his family!"

Both Connor and Beril laughed, and they finished their drinks before Connor asked for the bill. As Connor was paying, he asked to borrow the waiter's pad so that Beril could write down his address. Beril wrote slowly and deliberately, and then handed over the slip of paper to Connor. Connor studied the address, written in block capitals, but still embellished, denoting a hand and mind trained in the Victorian style. Connor looked up from reading the address, and his smile faded as he looked at the beaming Beril. "I must stress that you must not post the letters from the hotel. You must either take them to the post office or to a reliable posting box. Is that understood, Beril?"

There was a hard edge to what Connor had said, causing Beril to tilt his head slightly in question. "If the hotel itself stamps the envelope, my family may try to contact me through the hotel, who would naturally deny that I am staying there and the game would be up. Is that clear?"

Beril smiled now that he understood the reasoning behind the instruction and nodded at Connor. Connor smiled back and proffered his hand. "It's a deal, then?"

"Yes, it is a deal."

The two men shook hands, a process that left Beril $25 richer.

"A down payment."

"Thank you, sir. Most generous."

"I must get back to the hotel. I shall be leaving tomorrow, but I shall be in touch soon. Good luck, Beril. Goodbye."

"And to you. Goodbye and thank you."

Connor raised the umbrella and stepped back out onto the street—and into the heat radiating up off the pavement. He felt relieved that the business was done and wondered also how often the money behind a crime was used to sponsor third-world families' existence and education, albeit unknowingly. He also wondered how much difference it would make if the source of the money were known.

Chapter 33

THE SHIRE XIX

Connor knew it was risky, very risky, but nevertheless it was a risk he had to take. He looked at his watch to see the slightly luminous hands and dial show 3:15 in the morning. A yawn tried to rise, but Connor stifled it. It was not caused by tiredness, but was most likely due to his hyper-tensive state, anticipation of the day ahead, and the irregular breathing patterns occurring as a result. His body, craving more oxygen thanks to his shallow inhalations, had triggered the yawn reflex. Connor concentrated on his breathing, taking deep breaths and holding them before expelling the depleted lung full.

Connor had parked adjacent to his intended target: a four-foot-wide, green, metal-cased telecom box on the road into the industrial estate. The estate was quiet with very little traffic, but still he waited, watching and listening. The light was crepuscular, the night air still and cool. Connor decided it was time to move. He switched off the courtesy light before opening the driver's door. He climbed out of the car and crossed the pavement to the junction box, where he inserted a T-shaped key into a hole at the top of the door and twisted. He heard the sound of metal sliding over metal until the top of the door sprung slightly, indicating that the catch was open. He checked around before repeating the process for the bottom catch. The door opened a fraction. Connor returned to the car and picked up a canvas satchel bag and returned to the junction box. He reached into the bag and removed a tea-light candle without its foil container, a small can of lighter fluid, and a gas-filled fire lighter. Working quickly, he separated a large bundle of multi-coloured thin wires and nestled the candle amongst them before pouring a small quantity of the lighter fluid along the wire bundle, leaving a respectful gap between the candle and the start of the fuel line. Connor took a last look around. Content that everything was right, he took a deep breath and clicked the fire lighter. A small flame appeared at the end of the nozzle, which he shielded and applied to the candlewick. The candle flame started to grow, and Connor flicked off the fire lighter and watched as the wick darkened to black and a small pool of wax grew around the wick base. He stood, gently pushed the door closed, relocked the bottom catch, and pulled the door slightly open so that he could see the flicker of the candle through the top of the door casement before pushing it tight and locking it.

Connor climbed back into his car, started the engine, and pulled away. He had been lucky; not one vehicle had passed in the time since he had gotten out of the car. He envisaged the candle burning down for the next hour or so before finally igniting the wire insulation. The lighter fuel was a small insurance to help the fire on its way should it need it, but having seen the number of wires crammed into the box, Connor knew it was overkill. Very soon, thick black smoke would start pumping out of the box, the candle would be evaporated by the heat, and the fuel accelerant would never be detected above the hydrocarbon-based insulation. The fire would be put down to overheating caused by localised arcing, the net result being that the telecommunications for the whole estate and some way beyond would be out of service.

Connor woke. The watch he wore showed that a couple of hours had passed. The dark was starting to lift, and the streetlights were winking out. He stretched carefully so as not to touch the inside of the car windows, which were fogged with the moisture of his sleeping breath. He reached forward and started the car, which he let idle for five minutes before switching on the heaters and demisting the windscreen. As the glass cleared, Connor saw the lights come on and people move around through a large, plate-windowed transport café twenty yards or so from where he had parked. The newsagent's adjacent to the café was also lit and a hive of activity; bundles of newspapers were being carried in off the street and sorted onto the shelves and into the paper deliverers' bags. Connor smiled to himself as he remembered the paper round he'd had when he was a young teenager. He shivered involuntarily at the thought of the icy mornings and the dead weight of the bag, which cut into his shoulder as he lugged it around the dark streets. He'd had to come to terms with the peculiarities and idiosyncrasies of gates and letterboxes, not to mention those who lived behind the vast array of doors, porches, and porticos. Connor recoiled inwardly as he remembered the ink-smudged hands and how this would be spread to his face as he tried to wipe away invisible cobwebs strung across the garden paths like gossamer snares. Every day, bar Christmas and Easter, the youth of the day would cripple their young bodies to deliver the news and gossip to the community, but now it seemed that either the youth had woken up to the exploitation or were no longer motivated by the "wage." The rounds were now carried out by the pensioner generation, who strove to increase their miserable state handout and also protect the child deliverers from the twisted machinations of perverted adult minds that lurked in the quiet streets with the well-kept gardens.

Connor was pulled back as the neon OPEN sign flickered to life in the transport café window. He reached for his wallet and climbed out of the car. He locked the door and did up his jacket against the permeating morning cold, his breath steaming and hanging in the still air. He walked to the newsagent and entered the warmth created by the air curtain. He squinted momentarily at the bright light of the shop. The shelves were bedecked with glossy coloured magazines, each trying to shout louder than their neighbour with headlines designed to attract its target audience. Lower down were the fresh printed papers, stacked from right to left—which, whether by design or default, reflected their political leaning. The headlines adorning each front page reflected that leaning with fundamentally the same piece of news being spun each one's ends. Connor picked a paper slightly right of centre and approached the counter. The retailer, who was busy filling in and checking computer-generated forms, stopped and looked up at Connor. "Morning."

"Good morning," Connor replied. He placed the paper on the counter, and the retailer picked it up, searching for the bar code, which he then swiped past the reader. He was looking at the huge display of tobacco products, the neatly arranged packets and boxes that decorated the wall behind the counter. The myriad of colours and designs were, to a large degree, obliterated by the compulsory governmental health warnings—if the prices were not prohibitive enough.

"Ten Marlboro, please."

The retailer barely looked as he reached back to the shelving, removed the packet of cigarettes, and gently threw them onto the paper on the counter. Connor was still looking at the shelf behind the retailer.

"Anything else?" The shopkeeper had things to do. Connor noticed that his tone was somewhat clipped.

"Do you sell book matches?"

The retailer looked this time in order to fulfil this unusual request and located the sleeved booklets of matches. He turned to Connor. "How many?"

"Three."

It was early, Connor realised, but the newsagent's clipped manner was starting to irk him somewhat. It was a growing trend in many of the shops he used. Customers seemed to be an awkward and inconvenient nuisance who interrupted the gossip and cups of coffee being enjoyed by the proprietors or their minions. There were so few outlets that seemed genuinely pleased to hear the telltale tinkle of a bell or its modern-day electronic equivalent. Connor didn't expect to be treated as royalty, just with some common decency and perhaps a meaningless pleasantry about the weather. That was all he asked. Too often, this seemed too much to ask, and the business exchange was a moribund vestige of glory days long past. The impersonality of the computer age manifested itself in many ways.

"Four pound ninety."

"Pardon?"

"Four pound ninety."

"Four pound what?"

"Ninety, please."

Connor felt he shouldn't have to feign deafness to extract a "please," but he was prepared to do it instead of being sarcastic by adding his own please. He handed over a five-pound note and awaited his change, which was dropped into his hand with a small throw. He stared hard at the man, who now looked a little confused and took a half step back from the counter. Connor leaned in. "Thank you!"

It was aggressive and slightly louder than the conversation level in the shop, but then Connor gave an inquiring eyebrow lift and a smile as he looked at the newsagent. Somewhat confused by the display by a person who was clearly "not all there," the retailer automatically responded, "Thank you."

Connor dropped the face, put the ten pence change in the charity box that hung off the till, and left the shop.

The inside of the café was warm and quiet. The radio could be heard through the serving hatch, as could the whistling of the cook, who was bustling away bringing the kitchen up to speed and preparing for the morning onslaught. Connor nursed his tea in both hands, extracting the heat through the marled, off-white china as he looked through the steaming tea at the headlines of his paper. Things were heating up for the impending G8 conference, and various factions were pitching their views both for and against the heads of state summit meeting. Connor couldn't help but smile at the irony of the world's wealthiest nations discussing the plight of the poorest, with full stomachs and in luxurious surroundings. The fact that most of the now debt-ridden countries were at one time or another exploited for their natural wealth and their labour, forced or otherwise, by those who could now offer alms, was a paradox beyond belief. Connor wondered how these heads of state would appreciate having their homes burgled and then being loaned the money to buy back their own property from the burglar at extortionate rates of interest—only then to find that they were being made redundant and forced to live on charity handouts whilst having the loan shark heavies knocking on the door. Still, whilst third world debt was on the agenda, there had to be some hope it could be written off as a bad debt.

Connor's musings were interrupted by the arrival of the waitress with a plate of food. He breathed in deeply and his salivary glands kicked in, anticipating the delight ahead. He had forgotten how hungry he was. The plate in front of him was loaded to overflowing with the "x"-listed products of cholesterol hell. For now, he couldn't have cared less; he knew his future would more than offset this imbalance. The waitress had gone to fetch a knife and fork, and when she returned Connor, asked for a tea refill. He dove into the plate of food with his silverware and, as he progressed, he pepped up the meal with the table condiments in order to keep his palate stimulated, even if his stomach was starting to complain.

Connor mopped the last of the prandial residue from the plate and drained his tea. There was a slight sheen on his forehead that reflected the light from the fluorescent tubes above. He pushed back the chair, got up, and approached the counter to pay. After having done so, he stepped out gratefully into the cold morning air. He inhaled deeply to help ease the congestion he felt in his oesophagus and considered loosening a notch on his belt, but he knew the tightness was temporary and would soon be gone.

The traffic was starting to build, and small queues were forming at the junction with the roundabout. Connor pulled into the lay-by and drove to the far end. He parked the car adjacent to an innocently discarded drinks can. He checked his watch; it was 6:40. He slid across into the passenger seat and opened the door. He swung round so that his feet were on the kerb. Looking down, Connor could see the translucent fishing line running away from the tin towards the ditch. He took out the packet of cigarettes and the book of matches. He removed a cigarette from the pack, placed it between his lips, and lit it. He couldn't resist inhaling the smoke and felt the head rush he'd enjoyed many years earlier and had never forgotten. His experience with nicotine was a happy one, curtailed only by common sense and public scapegoating. Connor leaned forward and wrapped the book of matches around the fishing line, and then placed the lit cigarette so the filter was halfway along the tops of the red match heads and closed the sleeve over the top, holding the cigarette firmly in place. The lit end smoked gently as it burned back towards the book. He laid the book gently on the ground and placed the drinks tin over the top. He smiled when he recalled the film in which he had first seen this impromptu sabotage method employed. Connor twisted back into the car and closed the door, slid back across the front seat to the driver's position, started the car, and eased into the flow of traffic.

He drove quickly through the building morning traffic, back towards the lockup. He parked the car in a car park nearby, which he knew would soon become busy with the site users and would not cause any undue attention. He locked the car and walked the rest of the way back to the lockup, where he slipped quietly and unnoticed inside.

Connor flicked on the lights, which stuttered into life and bathed the van in a white glow. He removed various dustsheets from the van so that the fluorescent tubes' reflection glowed in the fresh, shining paintwork. Moving quickly and purposefully around the lockup, he made a few final touches and adjustments. He placed two boxes in the rear of the van before moving to the back room, where he unzipped a suit bag and removed a navy blue shirt and NATO-style pullover, as well as a pair of black trousers.

Connor undressed and redressed into the uniform colours of the security company, whose insignia he had matched to the van. He looked at himself in a small mirror. Content with what he saw, he bundled his old clothes together and threw them into the back of the van along with the boxes to be disposed of. He climbed into the van and steadied himself, feeling the heat from his hands being cooled on the steering wheel. The cool, quiet interior of the van was comforting, calming. He could hear the voice of reason in his head: *Stay here. No one knows what you've done or are about to do. Just walk away. Go back to your old job. It will be okay.* He shook his head, as if breaking the trance of a hypnotist. It would be okay, he knew, but somehow being "okay" just wasn't enough. This was his moment, the time that many people in life have had to face—the precipice, the crossroads, and the defining point that laid the future path. He hadn't yet decided the destination, nor had he confirmed the itinerary, but Connor had a well-thumbed ticket in his clammy hand, and now more than ever he was determined to use it.

He turned the key, and the engine gunned into life. Connor looked down at the gauges; the fuel tank was full, and the other dials and needles seemed to be operating correctly. He turned on the lights and indicators. He checked that his mirrors and the reflections off the walls all were working properly. Being pulled over by the police for a failed sidelight was not an option on this journey. He killed the lights and climbed out. He took one last walk around the van, inspecting as he went. Content with what he saw, he then turned off the lights to the workshop.

Connor cracked open the wicket gate door and peeped through the gap. All was still and quiet outside; an advantage of being at the end of the estate was the lack of passing traffic. At this time of morning, as he had anticipated, there was none. Connor stepped through the door, fumbled with the padlock, and pulled open the two swing doors. He moved quickly now, as he was most vulnerable. When he returned to the van, he revved the engine and pulled slowly out onto the road, checking that all was still quiet. He drove to the opposite kerb to park. The chill morning air was being fogged by the moisture of the van's exhaust that provided a little unexpected, but welcome, cover he had not anticipated. Once he was out of the van again, he closed the swing doors, which he quickly secured before returning to the van.

Connor felt exposed. His heart raced, and his breathing had shortened not quite to a pant, but not far off. It was like the nightmare of being naked in public, feeling everyone was looking at him, but at the same time taking no notice. It was the rabbit in the field not knowing whether to look to the sky or the hedgerow for approaching predators. He forced himself to breathe deeply and tense all his muscle groups before relaxing and breathing out. He reassured himself that only he knew he was different, and his ability to hide in plain view was key to the whole plan, along with his performance. What *was* a risk was lingering at the arse end of a trading estate in the liveried van of a security firm where, by rights, it had no right to ordinarily be. He slipped the engine into gear and pulled away. Every action now drew him further into the vortex.

Chapter 34

SCOTLAND X

As Connor walked back out of the village, the horizon, rather than growing lighter with the rising sun, produced a slick line of black cloud that more than threatened rain—promised it. Following the directions, Connor climbed the hill and took the left fork. The roadway was unmade, but patched in places where vehicles had scooped out hollows or eroded the edges down the banks. The moss- and lichen-clad trees swayed in the wind, a precursor of the approaching storm front. Connor wondered how he could spend the day whilst his laundry was being done.

He climbed the drive to a solid-looking, whitewashed chalet-style bungalow built into the dark tree-covered hill that towered over the house. The sun had not brought its warming light to bear on the house, which looked colder and sadder for it. The small patch of coarse grass was heavily matted with a velvety, verdant moss. Connor searched the door and frame for a doorbell. There wasn't one, so he was about to reach for the small, but ornate brass knocker when the door started to open. But it came to a halt after opening only two or three inches.

"Would you push?" a voice from the other side of the door called out.

"Pardon?"

"Would you push the door, please? It's stuck."

Connor pushed the door tentatively, scared that it would fly open and hit the person behind, but the shove, which was insufficient, produced a disappointing result—the door seemed less giving than before.

"You'll have to do better than that, or we'll be stuck here all the morning." There was a detectable laugh in the not-very-Scottish voice that came from behind the stuck door.

"Before I possibly break this door, are you Mrs. Rogers?"

"Yes, it is. I trust that you're Connor and that I'm not helping a robber to break into my own house?"

"No, I'm Connor, and I don't believe breaking and entering would, on the back of this performance, be a very profitable line of business, do you?"

"No, maybe not. I'm Jane, by the way."

The glimpse of a face showed through the crack in the door. Connor had taken a grip around the door to pull it back towards the frame before lifting and pushing harder. The door swung freely to reveal a petite, sandy-haired woman dressed casually in jeans and a light fleece shirt that accentuated her curves to their best advantage.

"Hello Jane, nice to see you—at last!"

They both laughed as they took in the person before them.

"Please come in. We rarely use the front door. Getting it fixed has not been one of the priorities, I'm afraid."

Connor stepped across the threshold and bent to undo his boots, which, although not dirty, would not be welcome on the light-coloured carpet that stretched into the house. A brief silence accompanied this moment—should the householder thank the visitor or offer some sort excuse that made it necessary for the boots to be removed? Thankfully, the moment passed. Connor stood, stepped out of the boots, and left them on the mat by the door.

"Would you like some tea?"

Although Jane didn't have a Scottish accent, she employed the same mannerisms and sentence structure, which made for an interesting combination.

"Thank you. If it's not too much trouble, that would be great. I've got quite a thirst now that I've had to break in."

"I'm so sorry about that. My husband keeps promising to fix it, but he's either too busy or too tired. It's not the only thing that needs doing, I can tell you."

The innuendo was delivered deliberately, and Connor had not missed it. For a brief time, their eyes met and the gaze was held. Connor felt his face flush gently. He wasn't sure how to deal with the tension. Almost mercifully, the moment was broken by the phone ringing.

"Excuse me, Connor. Please go through to the kitchen."

Jane pointed towards a door across the hall as she moved towards the ringing phone, and Connor followed her direction. He found himself in a large kitchen, very much in the traditional farmhouse style. A well-built kitchen table doubled as a dining table and stood to one side to make the most of the natural light that seeped through the corner windows, which overlooked the small, but tidy garden. A large and impressive range stood against the far wall and was, in as minimalist a way as possible, heating the kitchen and most probably the rest of the house. It offered little in the way of aesthetics, being as pragmatic as usability allowed, and its presence was testimony to that ethos. It had most likely been installed for the very first occupant of the bungalow. The rest of the kitchen was not the "fitted" variety, but fit it did. Many years of use had forced the nooks and crannies to evolve into integral spaces, and Mrs. Beeton herself would have been pleased to see that everything appeared to have its place and was currently resident.

Connor moved to the window to get away from the door, as he could overhear the conversation and, although Jane spoke in a low voice, it sounded tense.

"No, Steve it's too late now, anyway . . . Mary from the village rang. Someone was enquiring about getting some laundry done . . . Huh, it's okay for you to drop my plans and run as soon as the phone . . . I know . . . Yes . . . I know . . . Well, this will be some extra money, too, won't it? . . . That will be too late, anyway, so you might as well just carry on there . . . Yeah, don't worry about me, as if you ever do . . ."

The silence in the kitchen was deafening; he couldn't help but overhear. Connor scanned the kitchen and spied the kettle on the edge of the range. He filled the kettle from the tap, which had either dechromed from use or had originally been brass, over the deep butler sink. Making more noise than necessary, Connor clattered as he put the lid onto the kettle and the kettle back on the range. He was just about to search for the cups when Jane appeared at the doorway.

"I hope you don't mind. I thought I'd put the kettle on."

"That's okay. Sorry about that. It was my husband," Jane said with a slight flick of her head and an eye roll before moving to the range and removing the kettle. "It's great for heating the house, baking bread, and appearing in *Home and Garden,* but when you just want a cup of tea . . ." She flicked the switch on an electric kettle that Connor had not seen, and it hissed into life. Connor smiled. "Now, the washing?"

Connor picked up the backpack and started to undo the straps. "There's not much, but it does need a bloody good wash. I do rinse it out in the streams where I can, but when I get the chance, I like to get it washed properly."

Jane took the bundle of clothing and involuntarily pulled a face. She recoiled from the stale, almost acrid smell the clothing gave off.

"I'm really sorry about that. I've been wearing it awhile now. Usually, I find a self-serve laundry so as not to inconvenience anyone else . . ." Connor tapered off.

"That certainly is strong." Jane held the load at arm's length and deposited it in the front loader, then poured liquids and powders into the drawer. She paused. "What about the clothes you're wearing? They must need washing, too?"

"Well, they do. They're not as bad, but that would leave me . . ." Connor let the words just hang there. There was no need to complete the sentence; he could see Jane had gotten the point.

"When did you last have a proper shower?" she asked.

Connor tried to recollect the last time. He'd grown accustomed to bathing in the streams and burns he came across at the end of the day. After an arduous day's walk, the desire to wash away the grime of his exertions won out despite the icy chill of the water. Even then, his small bottle of liquid soap was all but empty and, because it was "eco soap," light on perfume and lather.

"I can guess from the pause that it was a while off. Would you care for one? You could borrow a dressing gown, and that would give me a chance to wash those clothes you're in."

It was awkward. Connor was struggling with the conflict of etiquette and social practice. To be all but naked in the house of a woman he had only just met, in the dressing gown of a husband (he assumed) he hadn't met, was not an everyday situation.

"There's no need to worry. My husband's away 'til late tonight, possibly tomorrow, and I won't hold you captive." Jane laughed this sentence out with more than a hint of mischief in her tone. The thought of a hot shower, sweet-smelling soap, and a proper towel swayed Connor into nodding his agreement. Jane led him not to the bathroom as he expected, but a large *en suite* off of the main bedroom.

"Just throw your clothes out and I'll pick them up. I'll sort you out a dressing-gown."

Connor stepped somewhat self-consciously out of his clothing. Everything seemed wrong. He was no prude—far from it. He was rather proud of his body, but not in a show-offish way. His broad shoulders offset any slight flab that had a tendency to accumulate around his waist, but the time spent exerting himself on the mountainside had easily eliminated that, anyway. The fact of the matter was, he was quite surprised—no, *shocked*—at how much weight he had lost. For the first time in many years, Connor could make out the shape of a "six-pack." He smiled to himself as he looked at his figure in the full-length mirror across the room. He had eaten well and constantly since he had reached the mountains and, in anticipation of his exertions, had not caloric counted prior to arriving. That said, the figure reflected back at him was on one hand pleasing, and on the other a little concerning. He was able to survive in the harsh climate through a fine balance of health, strength, and stamina—all of which, to some degree, required him to carry a slight surfeit of body fat. Connor smiled to himself as the idea of a diet fad popped into his head. Take one overweight individual, work out his calorific intake requirements versus metabolic rate, and provide the requisite amount of foodstuffs. Then deposit the person a sufficient distance from a reception point and have him walk back. All the incentives would exist, and the end result would be a slimmer individual. That had to be better than calorie counting and weekly weigh-ins. Absolutely no temptation, maximum motivation, and, depending on the venue, massive calorific intake. Connor recalled reading the diaries of Polar explorers who had walked for many days towards the South Pole, eating chocolate bars and oil-soaked foodstuffs to keep up their work rate, only to find that after their thirty- or forty-day exertions, it worked out that, by normal standards, they had starved themselves for the same period of time.

The thought faded as Connor felt the water and retracted his hand quickly, unused to water temperature above one or two degrees. It felt scalding, and Connor had to condition himself to the luxury of hot running water. The soap cut through the grease that had accumulated on his body, and he was almost embarrassed to see the dirt-stained water running down his legs and off of his body to the drain. Using a long-handled scrubbing brush, he scoured his reddening skin. It brought new meaning to the word "exfoliating." The perfumed soap and hot water were beyond description, and Connor lost himself for a moment. Finally, he wound down the shower valve, and the water reduced to a residual trickle. Connor then searched for a towel and was surprised to see one where he was sure one had not been hanging when he had gotten in the shower. Similarly, he noticed that his discarded clothing had vanished from the floor. Connor smiled wryly to himself as he buffed his skin dry with the towel, revelling in the slightly abrasive texture, glad that the best towels hadn't been laid out. He disliked soft towels; they were far too effete.

Connor padded around the bedroom and spied out through the bedroom window, which looked out onto the garden. It was dull and overcast; consequently, the little lawned area and larger patio looked cold and uninviting. Already, the shadow of the hill behind the house was stealing the little light there was and casting a crepuscular light over the house. Connor shivered involuntarily, but not from the temperature; his was more of an anticipatory shiver at the idea of exposing himself again to the ravages of the oncoming winter. He picked up the dressing gown that had been left on the bed. It was frayed at the cuffs, but it smelled freshly laundered, so he pulled it tightly around him and tied off the belt. He walked barefoot to the kitchen, where Jane was busying herself amongst small piles of clothing, some of which had already been washed, by the looks of things. Jane turned as she became aware of Connor watching her-

"Well, you certainly look better for that, and no doubt probably feel better?"

"Yes, that's a fact. I hadn't realised how bad I'd gotten. My skin actually feels itchy. I must have smelt worse than my clothes?"

The inflexion made a question of the statement, but Jane chose to ignore it, and this left a void in the conversation as they both sought a new line to pick up on. Jane broached a new subject. "How long are you away for?"

"Just a few weeks. I'm sort of doing some research, I suppose."

"Into what, exactly? Man's ability to survive without washing?"

Connor laughed at Jane's comment. "It might look like that, but no. I'm thinking of writing a novel that in part involves survival in the Highlands. It's all very nebulous at the moment, and I'm not sure where it's going, but the last couple of weeks have at least given me some insight and the opportunity to satisfy some wanderlust. Granted, it was a little uncomfortable in parts,"

Connor waffled on. He enjoyed the fact that he was flirting with the truth; it allowed him to come across at least in some part as genuine and also allowed some depth of interrogation. Connor had considered how he would deal with the question if it were raised, and he had practised various scenarios in his head. He was surprised at how easy it came now that he was actually recounting the rouse and that he was almost inviting further questioning. Further questions did not follow, however.

The house now, that Connor considered it, was not that of a bibliophile. Apart from a few magazines, there was scant reading material of any type. This combined with a taciturn attitude that was probably inherent throughout the small communities that dotted the glens. It meant that a man's business was his own, and he should be entitled to keep it that way if he wished. It wouldn't take much to become the village gossip, and it was a fine line that had to be walked so as not to be shackled with that label, especially in such a small village where not much of interest went on, anyway.

Connor stopped talking. The silence was loud; it hung, leaden, amplifying every sound that rippled the air—the gurgle and click of the washing machine, the tick of the clock, the distant hum of a passing car. It got too loud, the pressure palpable. The vacuum of silence sucked out anything that dared to present itself as a thought, any nuance that might flit across the deserted expanse of mind that had gone into temporary shutdown like a deer running through a glade. This was a dangerous time. Connor had had precious little conversation with anyone lately, so there was a longing to talk. This, coupled with the fact that he could so easily bait the hook of inquisitiveness, made Connor feel like a drug or drink addict; he wanted it, and it was there for the taking. Resistance was waning, but he would suffer, so he had to get away from the temptation.

"I've probably taken up too much of your time. You must have things to do apart from my laundry. I'll get out from under your feet if you'd like and come back later when you're done?"

"Well, you can if you like, though I would have thought that a man in your position would want to stay off the streets as much as he can. It may be safe and okay in the hills, but people would talk in the likes of this community, and it wouldn't be long before you're picked up!"

Connor tensed from his head to the very pit of his stomach. A flush ran over his body. His mind raced furiously, recalling the newspapers he'd seen in the village and the reports on his radio. There was no way that Jane could have seen or heard anything. The penny dropped—she wasn't from here. Perhaps she had heard from a friend or relative or worse. Perhaps she had been home and had read or seen a report. No, it was too tenuous a link; the probability of that was way out there. Still, Connor was unsure what she knew. What if she did know? How would he play it? God no, this was descending into a bad plotline from a second-rate movie.

Connor made himself relax. He breathed deeply and forced a smile, trying to look and sound as innocent as possible. "Picked up? Picked up for what?

"For wandering about the street naked but for an old dressing gown. All of your clothes are in the wash!"

Connor almost slumped in relief. He'd totally forgotten his current state and now felt foolish as he sat there. There was nothing he could do but laugh. "So you think I run around naked in the mountains, do you?"

"Well, whatever does it for you."

The playfulness was there on both sides of the conversation. They were each in their own way lonely—Connor through isolation and Jane through neglect. Connor grew more relaxed in Jane's company

"You think that's what does it for me, do you?"

"What you do in the privacy of your own mountainside is up to you."

Connor laughed out loud.

"What are you laughing at?"

Jane was smiling at Connor, an inquisitive smile, as though the sound of laughter in response to her conversation was an alien experience

"I was just thinking, if I were to indulge in a bit of naturism and someone were to walk around the hill and see me, could you imagine? It's awfully cold up there. There's snow on the ground in some parts."

"I should think you have nothing to worry about in *that* department." Jane delivered the line and instantly realised she had crossed another. Another silence was born, and there it hung. This time, it was Jane who struggled with the wordless pause. The awkwardness prevailed. Connor realised that Jane had taken more than his dirty clothes whilst he was in the shower.

"Are you hungry at all? Maybe I could fix you something to eat? Another cup of tea as well?"

She had identified the way out of the moment, and Connor was happy to follow.

"Yes, that would be nice. If you really don't mind, I was going to go to the pub I'd seen on the way up here. But, as you so rightly point out, perhaps the folk would not take too kindly to me wandering around dressed as I am."

"It's not that we're old fashioned, but a line has to be drawn somewhere, and at this time of the year, you'd be lucky to get anything hot to eat in the pub. The tourist trade is a little slow and the locals . . . well, pubs are pubs as far as they're concerned, and they're unwilling to pay the tourist rates for food they can easily get at home."

"I can appreciate that, but, to be honest, any food that hasn't been dehydrated would be good. I'd be more than prepared to pay over the odds for a fresh sandwich. I've got a real craving for bread at the moment."

"Well, I made a loaf only yesterday that shouldn't be too bad, and I could top up the stock in the pot and heat you up some soup if you fancy that?"

There was a comfortable air between the two of them, Connor mused. It was a rare association that sometimes occurred between two people previously unknown to each other, thrown together for whatever reason. They just clicked. This was one of those occasions. Both Connor and Jane were relaxed and content in each other's company and now, in a semi-dressed state, he was going to break bread with Jane. Eating with or in front of strangers usually made him uncomfortable. It was one of his unexplained traits, probably rooted somewhere in his "caveman" subconscious. Today, that feeling was missing. The pair sat opposite one another and ate the hot soup. The washing machine gently hummed in the background as it went through the cycles, building to the climatic spin and shudder as it slowed. The range ticked as the temperature increased. The arrow on the gauge nudged higher towards the edge of the red crescent at the far end of the scale, and the room started to grow warmer.

Connor pushed his empty bowl away, a sheen of perspiration on his brow from eating and from wearing a dressing gown designed for cold mornings. His appetite was sated. He picked up the bowl and plate and carried them to the sink.

He turned to find Jane standing right behind him. She reached up and pulled him towards her, and they embraced in a kiss—awkward at first, laced with tension, but then the tension eased and the lips softened, the embrace tightened, and their two bodies melded together. It was a pent-up passion, a suppressed emotion allowed to demonstrate itself unbridled. Their hands ran over each other's bodies. Connor's dressing gown parted; his arousal was obvious, and Jane raised herself onto him and squeezed gently with her cotton-clad thighs. The kissing was hard and penetrating. Jane threw back her head. Her neck cried out to be kissed, and Connor obliged, nipping her scented skin gently from shoulder to ear.

Connor felt Jane's body tense. He pulled away to find Jane's eyes glazed with tears. "What is it? What's the matter?"

"I'm sorry, this is wrong. I can't do this. I'm sorry."

Connor released his hold and they separated. The moment had gone, and the room felt a little cooler and a lot quieter. He re-tied his dressing gown. "Are you okay, Jane?"

Jane had her back to him and was looking out the window into the darkening garden. She turned. "Yes, I'm fine. I'm sorry, Connor, I don't know what . . ."

Jane didn't finish the sentence; it just faded. She didn't need to finish; both knew what was being said without needing to say it aloud.

"I understand. You're right. Please, let's forget it happened. We're both in a place at the moment where it might feel right, but we'd only regret it later."

The words were right, but the feelings both harboured were not reflected in them. The temptation to be locked together in embrace, skin to skin, consuming each other, was towering. Only a tissue of moral fibre prevented the glowing embers between them from blowing into an all-consuming fire.

The washing machine door lock clicked. Both Connor and Jane looked towards it and then at each other. Smiles crept across their faces, quickly followed by silent laughs. It was enough; the moment was broken and the opportunity gone, but not spurned, their short relationship shorter than the lifespan of a mayfly's. It was to each their own regarding what they took from their moment together, and the line had not been crossed. Had it been, then they would have trodden a different path, the journey back from which would have been much more difficult.

The sun had been long hidden by the time Connor left. The warmth and comforting glow of the bungalow were hard to leave behind, especially knowing that a cold tent on the side of a mountain was all that waited for him. It had been a little awkward to say goodbye, as their emotions had been a roller coaster in the short time they had spent together. The business like formality of paying for the washing service was embarrassingly difficult.

Connor trudged down the drive, his breath sending out clouds of vapour before him. He reached the road. Instead of turning right back towards the hill, he headed back towards the town. Connor stopped at the phone box and called the number on the card. The connection rang four times before being answered.

"Hello, Jane?"

"Connor."

"Hi. Look, about today—I know it didn't start too well with your husband. I mean . . . and . . . well, perhaps that made you a little vulnerable and, well, what happened. The reason I'm ringing is because this would have been too awkward face to face, and you'd never have accepted, so before you wash or hang up the dressing gown, check the pockets. I'd like you to treat yourself to something nice when you go on your shopping trip, I'm sorry I eavesdropped. I hope today was a nice day for you. It was for me, so I hope you buy something that will remind you of today and put a smile on that beautiful face. You take care, Jane, and thanks again."

Connor didn't wait for a response. He didn't want an argument; polite or otherwise, he knew he'd taken a huge chance getting anywhere near involved. His gift had been given wholeheartedly, but it also bound Jane over to silence. There was only so much she could earn taking in washing.

Connor hung the phone in its cradle, shouldered his pack, and set off back the way he'd come to his cold home on the hill as the last vestige of sunlight climbed up and off of the peak.

Chapter 35

THE SHIRE XX

Connor merged the van into the traffic flow. He felt as if there was a huge arrow affixed to the roof saying, "look at me," and Connor had to contain this thought, as preposterous as it was. He was conscious that the "arrow" was symbolic of some other oversight that might be giving him away. This was the first time the van had actually been out in the natural light of the street, and Connor had to shake off the nagging doubts and paranoia that something was amiss. It was too late now, anyway.

On the dashboard in front of him, secured by a bulldog clip, was a list of addresses and times. The first time on the list was 8:45. He checked his watch; it showed 8:15. Connor switched on the radio and tuned into a local station. The tail end of a song faded out and gave way to an overzealous, too loud, too early in the morning breakfast show host trying hard to upstage his part by mimicking the hosts of national radio shows. His attempts to shoehorn happiness into every listener's life were abrasive to say the least. Even bad news was met with a "shit happens, isn't it a pity" approach that might be okay as long as the listener wasn't the recipient. At that moment, a large percentage of work-bound commuters were probably cursing the presenter's jolly way of delivering news about a serious accident that was snarling up large parts of the area and inanely adding in what he believed to be a helpful piece of advice, to "avoid the area if at all possible."

Connor knew that his fuse had ignited, and he could imagine the scene of ignited gas escaping, burning as a huge roadside flame similar to those seen off oilrigs. The road would have been closed as emergency workers converged to play their respective parts. Fire crews would be standing by with their covering hose lines, police officers working frantically to control and divert traffic, which at that time of day and at that particular junction would create havoc. Avoiding the area would be sound advice, but if someone did have to go anywhere, the intersection would invariably form part of the journey.

Connor smiled to himself briefly; he was in the lighter-than-usual traffic on the town side of the incident he had fashioned. The smile faded as he thought about the enormity of the task ahead. He checked his watch as he drew up to a set of traffic lights. It was approaching 8:30, and he estimated he was about five minutes from his first point of call. It would be okay to be early, but more plausible to be late. Connor decided to drive past the garage forecourt of the national supermarket on the outskirts of the town, his intended stop, and continue into the town itself. He decided to carry out some last-minute reconnaissance of the next three sites on his list. He was familiar with each of the venues, having watched them from afar over the last few months. From various locations he had watched the activity in and around his intended "targets." He had spent many hours at cafes, bus stops, and shops, even in drive-bys. He had sighted all the closed-circuit cameras and, most importantly, the timings and positionings of the security collections. Stephanie's list had given him the starting points, and whenever they were available, Connor would note the timings for specific locations. Of course, there was no defined pattern—or at least that was what he initially thought, but he reasoned that human nature being what it is would eventually create an inadvertent pattern. Not a conscious process, but one that fitted a natural flow, be it a likely circuit, an accommodation of some external factor, complacency, or plain laziness. Connor knew there were no guarantees, and the teams were unsure of their routes until they were issued at the start of each shift. This, and the fact that teams were forbidden to carry mobile phones, would ensure that no inside planning could assist a potential heist. Even so, Connor gleaned information from his observations and was in a position to make an informed guess that, coupled with the chaos of traffic and communication breakdown, should be sufficient to muddy the water if doubt was cast. Or at least he hoped so.

Chapter 36

THE SOUTH COAST III

The waves lapped against the hull as Connor's boat lay tethered alongside the pontoon. He pulled himself up off the boardwalk by the thin, stainless steel wire rope that ran around the circumference of the fibreglass hull and deck. The rope cut into his hand, shiny white and cold as it was. The boat dipped gently as it absorbed his weight, and then it came to, level again. He stepped into the cockpit and set about unlocking the hatch and extracting the sliding board that let onto the small set of steps down into the cabin below. He descended into the dank and musty air of the cabin. He popped the hatch in the middle of the cabin roof, or the deck head. He smiled to himself at the terminology of the sea, the transition of language steeped in the history of a very brave body of souls who had risked all in appalling conditions. In some cases, they gained riches beyond compare, but mostly the beneficiaries were those who took risk only with their wallets and reaped their reward off the backs and ultimate sacrifice of less fortunate individuals.

The air started to flow through the stuffy interior as Connor sought to connect the battery, hidden behind a removable panel underneath the steps he had just descended. Once he had made the connection, he pushed the priming lever, feeling the resistance of fluid under pressure through the lever. He flicked a series of switches and then turned a key. The engine coughed and eventually spluttered into life, expelling a dense cloud of black diesel smoke before settling into a rhythmic cycle. Connor moved about the boat, checking levels and flicking switches until he was content that all was well and as he wanted it. He went aloft, gauged the wind, and let slip the stern rope before loosing the bowline. The prow of the boat turned out into the open water as he revved the engine, and the little boat chugged towards the sea lock that guarded the marina from the estuary's tidal flow.

With a cheery wave, Connor exited the sea lock. The lock keeper reciprocated from his lofty perch. Connor hauled in the fenders and dropped them down into the cabin to be properly stowed later. The estuary wound its way out to sea, and as Connor followed the green marker buoys, the vista changed accordingly, cutting from east to west, showing the promontories and the grandiose homes that clung to them. The small boat motored under a sweeping bridge that caused Connor to admire the ability of man and then to ponder the significance of the same structure in any war-torn state. As the boat passed under, he spied the spindle-like arrow that pointed back from the top of the masthead over his right shoulder. A following wind off the starboard quarter would allow him to come to terms with the boat. Many hours reading and playing simulation games could come close to, but never replace the real thing. There was no start again or reset button.

Connor prepared to raise his mainsail. He threw a hitch on the wheel and, cutting the engine speed, slipped off the protective shroud that was wrapped around the boom. The nylon sheet lay folded over the boom. He wound the extending line around a winch and then wound the winch handle so that the sail, reluctantly at first, crept up the mast. The effort of winding soon had Connor breathing hard, but eventually the sail was fully extended and taut at the mast. The wind kept pushing the sail, lifting the boom against the kicker. Connor locked off the line before letting go of the boom stay and controlled the line so that the boom pushed towards the port beam. The sail filled and bellied out in the wind. Connor looked at the wind speed gauge and saw that the wind was blowing between nine and twelve knots. He cut the engine. As the puttering ceased and the taint of diesel exhaust left the boat, an air of serenity descended. The only sounds were the thrum of the wind on the lines and the gentle slap of the rippled sea striking the prow.

Connor released the hitch and took control of the wheel, steering the boat harder into the wind. He watched forward across the bows of the boat to the sea ahead. He looked at the compass built into the wheel housing and also at the windex on the masthead, and steered the boat to accommodate all three points of reference.

Connor sheeted in the mainsail and felt the boat pick up half a knot or so. *Little Star* heeled to the starboard, and he shifted to the upside of the cockpit, locking his foot against the wheel housing. *Little Star* shot out of the estuary and hit the sea proper. The wind shifted slightly to come fully across the port side of the boat. Connor responded by steering off a little, but the speed didn't seem to drop any. Connor studied the windex, which stayed steady, and the boat's wash, which he was pleased to see was pretty straight, streaming out from the stern. The view ahead was clear, and only the distant horizon showed any activity with the steel monoliths ploughing the waves, hauling their containerised loads. The rust-stained hulls of the virtually crewless vessel displayed a heartless character, the stains akin to the tear-streaked elephants of some backwater circus. Pure functionality, pride long gone, just the drudgery of the day, the convenient flag beating the taxman. The purged bilges ejected crude sludge to contaminate all unfortunate enough to come across it. The make-do-and-mend mentality merely tipped its hat to the regulations, preferring to run the gauntlet with the local port and harbour authorities. Time was money—luxury cars or cheap plastic ducks for the bath, novelty surprises for Christmas crackers, or illegal drugs. They all sat alongside one another in their temporary metal box homes.

Content that all was well, Connor set the auto tiller and as the light turned green, he let go of the wheel. Connor waited a moment. He knew that all should be well. He understood the concept; it was just felt unnatural for him to let go and invest his trust in electronics. However, he knew he would have to sooner or later, so he surrendered and ducked down into the cabin.

The relatively dark and windless conditions caught Connor somewhat by surprise. He kicked a fender as his eyes adjusted to the gloom, and he could feel his face taut from the breeze and the sun that had been glinting off of the water. He picked up the fenders and wrestled them into a locker below the main seating. Then, he took a seat and reached for the radio handset. Taking a breath, he pushed the transmit button.

"Portsmouth Coastguard, Portsmouth Coastguard, this is *Little Star*. Do you receive? Over."

Connor waited. There was just silence, apart from the lapping of the waves against the prow of the boat.

"Portsmouth Coastguard, Portsmouth Coastguard, this is *Little Star*. Do you receive? Over."

The small, ear-level speaker gave a tinny response. "*Little Star, Little Star,* this is Portsmouth Coastguard. Go ahead. Over."

"Portsmouth Coastguard, good afternoon. For your information, I will be leaving port authority waters on a southerly course, intentions of reaching Saint-Malo. Over."

"Good afternoon, *Little Star*. Your message all received. Headed south for Saint-Malo. There are no issues for you to be concerned about, and we wish you a safe trip. Over, out."

Connor hung up the microphone in the cradle and turned up the volume for the cockpit speaker. He scanned the laminated chart that showed the channel crossing in black chinagraph pencil and the compass bearing scrawled alongside. It was ten past twelve. With the speed as it was, he predicted fourteen hours of sailing. He crossed to the stove and played with the gas cylinder and the dials trying to light the hob under the kettle, which sat in a restraining frame over the gently swaying gimballed stove. Collecting together the makings for a cup of tea, he peered at the small and restrictive view offered by the porthole windows studded about the cabin. It was a mind jam to be below as the boat ploughed on, powered only by the wind and the wizardry of electronics. This was not something that someone with such a controlling nature could be content with. All said and done though, it was necessary if *Little Star* was going to make decent progress and would mean that Connor would not have to keep hauling to every time he wanted to go below.

When his tea was finally made, Connor resumed his position in the cockpit and took control of the helm. The sky was still strewn with a thin cloud covering. Occasional shafts of golden sunlight broke through and struck the furrowed sea like some huge golden girder being consumed by a furnace.

The radio chirped with the interplay between the various vessels as they boxed the compass across the busiest sea channel in the world. This fact was staggering, given the number of seagoing vessels and available routes. Why would so many traverse this small, almost eye-of-a-needle, route? It was just one of those facts that people accepted, all the more for the seeming importance of it being called the English Channel, a patriotic throwback to the days when England, Britain, really did rule the waves. At the start of a fourteen-hour crossing, the grey-green open sewer of a body of water was not so nostalgically inspiring. Connor would not, he decided, be imposing his historical birthright connections with Britannia on any fellow seafarers he came across.

Connor's confidence in the handling of the boat grew and became less by the book. He experimented with the ability of the boat to cope with his toying at the controls, sometimes to excess, and the boat would come up to stall in the wind. Connor would wrestle it back onto course, deciding that just getting there was the aim, but, like a scab that could not be left alone, he would start playing with it again and pushing the boat harder to the wind. Content that he had reached a zenith of ability, he set about unfurling the headsail and sheeting it in on the starboard winch. The sail went taut and then bellied ever so slightly.

Connor felt the little boat surge forward. The bow of the boat lifted a little and stole a few more degrees to the starboard side. Looking down at the gauges, Connor was pleased to note that *Little Star* had increased her speed to nine knots and had trimmed, by his rough reckoning, three quarters of an hour off of his journey. Time, though wasn't an essential element, but old habits die hard. *How many times*, he wondered, had he stressed about getting out on time, arriving early, and inevitably shouting at Charlotte, demonstrating bouts of road rage by cursing the driving public who dared to be using the highway at the same time as he? It was this thought that allowed Connor to sit back and let out a long, slow breath, absorbing the tranquillity of his world, his clock, and his destiny. The knot of tension that had crept into the nape of his neck unwound as Connor rolled his shoulders. As if on cue, an arrow of light illuminated the boat and warmed his face as he squinted up at the masthead, at the tear in the sheet of clouds and the blue sky beyond.

Chapter 37

THE SHIRE XXI

Connor's heart was bursting through his chest—at least it felt that way. He was sure that, were he to look down, he would see the pumping organ stretching his pullover. He took a deep breath as he pulled onto the forecourt and circled to the rear of the kiosk shop. Out of sight of the busy forecourt, Connor collected his thoughts and pulled on the crash hat, obscuring his face with the semi-opaque reinforced visor. He picked up a pad and, from a batch of headed paper, took an official-looking A4 sheet, which he clipped to a battered-looking clipboard. With one last deep breath, he exited the van.

The morning air was still fresh, and the car exhausts produced steam as they sped away from the garage. Connor's exhalations added to the steam. He walked the few steps to a matt-painted, metal-sheeted door and knocked with the ball of his hand. While he waited, he feigned the actions of a cold man stamping his feet and fidgeting. Although he should have been feeling the chilled air, the adrenaline coursing through his body was sufficient to numb the needles being stuck in him. The door swung open, and a harassed-looking woman looked out at Connor.

"Morning," Connor offered.

"Morning. We're a bit behind cashing up. Could you give us a minute?"

"Well, before you rush about, you need to read this." Connor proffered the sheet of A4, which the woman took whilst looking at Connor for the first time proper.

"Are you new?"

"No, not really. I normally work out of a different depot, but due to what's going on . . ." Connor indicated the letter the woman was now holding, "I've been sent over to help cover the rounds."

Connor watched the woman read the letter.

Dear Customer,

Following a fire in a telecommunications cabinet that services our building, our delivery and collection services have been severely disrupted.

Consequently, the electronic data docking system cannot be employed, which means our delivery teams will revert to the traditional receipt docket that will be annotated and signed at point of contact.

Due to the communication breakdown, links to our central server have been similarly disrupted. This means that you will receive two visits today; one will collect only and the other will deliver.

We of course realise that these arrangements are unprecedented, but wish to assure you that our normal high levels of security are in force. If you are in any way concerned or unhappy with these arrangements, we will understand completely. Should you choose not to deposit with the delivery team, you will not be charged. We felt that we should attempt to provide a level of service in order to alleviate any of your security concerns you may have with keeping monies on your site.

Please feel free to use the emergency contact number, 1234 1234 56, for additional details and for information about when we anticipate resuming our normal service.

Once again, we apologise for the current circumstances and wish to ensure you that we are doing all we can to address them.

Signed,

A. Lesley

"It seems like everything's gone crazy this morning. The traffic jam into town has stopped my relief from getting here. She's over an hour late already. Now this!"

The woman looked Connor up and down before looking over his shoulder to the van parked behind him. She clearly had doubts; this was outside her realm of decision making. Connor stood calmly, or as calmly as he could, feigning a nonchalant disregard for the woman and her predicament. He looked at his watch so that the woman noticed, an attempt to turn up the pressure on her to make a decision.

"I've got to make a phone call. I'm not quite sure what to do about this."

"No, that's okay really. You take your time. We were anticipating people being unsure about what to do."

The woman retired to the rear of the service area and indicated for Connor to follow. She held the door until he was in the building. Connor found himself in a long, narrow room almost the width of the building. There were no windows and only one other door, which Connor knew would lead to the store. The lights buzzed gently overhead and shone down onto the chaos strewn below. Piles of product in various stages of unwrap covered the work surfaces and floor space. Paperwork was dotted about; lists were stuck to available wall space. A computer screen glowed above a keyboard, bedecked with the omnipresent sticky notes, little yellow memory-joggers that framed the glass screen like paper shingles. Connor's heart jumped as he saw a grey plastic box lying open at the far end of the room beneath a wall mounted safe with its door ajar.

The woman was dialling a number on a wall phone, holding the phone in the crook of her neck as she finger-followed a telephone number on a list beside the handset.

"Hello, Jenny? It's Kate. Are you all right?"

"What, still? Whatever is it?"

"A gas main? God."

"No, don't worry about that. But, well, the security collection is here. I haven't finished the cashing up yet . . ."

"No, it was a busy night, and this morning—well, you know how this morning's been going. Anyway, the guard has handed me a letter. Can I read it to you?"

The woman read the letter, somewhat embarrassed that Connor was standing well within earshot.

"Yeah, that's all. Oh, no, it all looks okay. Yeah, yeah."

Connor guessed that he was the subject of the one-sided conversation, especially given that the woman had subconsciously looked him up and down before the last response.

"Okay, I just wanted to check. You know, just to be on the safe side."

Connor sensed the woman relax as she bid her goodbyes. She turned back to Connor after replacing the receiver. "I'm going to be about ten minutes. Do you want a cup of tea?" She indicated towards a hot drinks dispenser

"Thanks. Yes, I will."

"You can relax a bit if you want." The woman indicated Connor's helmet by looking at it and pointing to her own head.

"If you don't mind, I'll take the tea and go back to the van whilst you finish up here. You give me a shout when you're done. I don't know the area very well, and I need to check the route."

"Okay, that'll be fine."

Connor pushed the button marked TEA – WHITE. A paper cup dropped into sight and was instantly filled with water. He took the cup carefully, the paper wall already hot, and placed the cup on the clipboard whilst negotiating the door. He cast a short glance up at the security camera, blinking silently from the far corner of the ceiling and wall.

Connor sat back in the driver's seat and breathed a sigh of relief. He absentmindedly sipped at the tea and scalded the inside of his mouth. He swore to himself and almost upset the contents of the cup into his lap. He swore again and put the cup down on the floor. He checked his watch and pretended to study the map propped upon the steering wheel.

The minutes crept by. Connor saw the flicker of movement out of the corner of his eye and looked up to see the woman waving to him from the doorway. He picked up the clipboard and climbed down from the van. Back inside the building, the grey box was now closed, as was the safe. Connor placed his clipboard on the pile of canned drinks atop the table and shuffled together three pieces of headed paper, between which was a leaf of carbonised paper.

Tutting and with some disdain, Connor said, "I thought these days were long gone." He started to fill in the various boxes with sufficient complacency, but due regard also, up until the point where he held the board for the woman to sign. Once she had done so, Connor countersigned, timed, and dated the top copy before detaching it and handing it over. Connor's hands were hot and clammy, and the handle of the box was cold by comparison.

"Right, that's all then. I might be back later if you are expecting any deliveries today, so see you then."

"Well, I hope not. I was supposed to finish an hour ago now, but if the traffic is as bad as they say, I could be here all day!"

"Anyway, all the best."

"Yes, goodbye."

Connor felt as though he was rushing, but was equally conscious to make inappropriate small talk. He wanted to be bland, nondescript, a beige emulsion of a man who, if linked to any security camera footage, would be next to indistinguishable from a million other "average Joes" who served a world of people who thought themselves better than the small cogs of the machine. Connor was happy to be a small cog. He knew the importance of small cogs—easily overlooked, a complacency that corporations and individuals failed to realise. No cog was put in without good reason, and through careful design, they served well. But the moment something overstressed that cog, it spun too fast or stopped working altogether. How often it turned out that the system would come crashing down, the reliance on the small cog realised too late.

To enhance his false persona, Connor had added a waistline at least four inches thicker than his own and a seen-better-days pair of trousers with a sheen on the seat and small collection of stains. A small piece of onion in his pocket was sufficient to give a slight body odour smell, not overpowering, but enough to distance others and keep them away. Connor walked towards the van, aware that he was being watched. He walked to the rear and, once slightly out of sight, banged on the rear door, which responded by opening as if from within. Truth be known, it was just a simple matter of timing, opening the door simultaneously with the corresponding knock. Connor placed the box inside the van, closed the door, and went round to the driver's door, waving to the woman as he went. Once back in the cab, he started the engine, all the time watching the woman through the opaque glass. Finally, she went in and closed the door.

Connor breathed a huge sigh of relief. His whole body felt clammy; rivulets of sweat trickled down to the small of his back. He could feel a damp band growing around the waist strap of the theatrical "belly" he wore. He started the engine and pulled the van away from the forecourt. The radio DJ was still pushing out the traffic message, and although the rush hour should have been easing up, the congestion had caused chaos that was being overstated in terms of gridlock. Connor knew the brief; the burning gas in itself would not be a problem. Sure, it would look spectacular, and the police would have cordoned off the road approaches, hence the traffic chaos. It would be a watching brief for the fire service, though, until the main could be "valved down" by the national grid gas operators. Until then, the fire crews would just stand by ensuring that any surrounding risks were safe. Putting out the fire would only result in a bigger problem: leaking gas at high pressure. Connor looked at his watch. It was 9:20. *At least the fire crews will be earning overtime out of it.* He smiled to himself.

Chapter 38

SCOTLAND XI

Connor awoke. He was cold—not in a chilly way, although frost was visible on the inside of the tent's fly sheet, but cold in a fundamental body core way. He took stock of his body: He felt clammy, and there was an itch in both his throat and his eyes that neither swallowing nor rubbing alleviated. He swore to himself. At best, he thought, he'd caught a cold; at worst, this was the onset of a bout of flu. Whatever the outcome, it meant he had to move, and move quickly, to a better location. Because he was perched on the side of the mountain and close to the village, he was more exposed than he would have liked. If it was flu and he was laid up for a few days or even a week, the locals might notice and get inquisitive.

Sitting up, he tried to keep in the heat of the sleeping bag by pulling it up over his shoulders and fumbling with the lighter and the gas control on the stove. It lit on the second flick of the lighter, and an indigo flame ignited. The heat rose almost instantly. He felt the small hairs on his face moving in reaction. The remnants of the evening meal were still present; the crumbs of bread and the hunk of cheese were drying out and sweating, respectively. For a moment, he considered that he might be having a reaction to the cheese—food poisoning, perhaps. It mattered not; the prognosis was the same. Connor filled the small kettle from the remains of the flask and added cold water from his bottle. He set this on the stove to boil and gathered together his walking garb. He dressed and undressed as much as he could whilst still inside the sleeping bag, to the point where he only needed to wear his trousers after leaving the silky cocoon. He stashed the nightclothes into their own separate plastic bag and pushed them into the backpack, followed by his sleeping bag. The regime of packing and unpacking the tent and his kit was well oiled; everything went in a set order, in a designated place. The previous day's purchases had added bulk and he had to push a little harder, but in it went until all that remained was the cooking set and the tent to go.

The kettle was steaming, and the lid was being lifted by the expanding liquid and jets of steam. Connor poured some of the water into the flask and closed the lid before shaking it to warm the flask walls. He then poured this water into the dinner-stained bowl he had retrieved from outside the tent and quickly swished it round to remove as much of the residue as possible. He set it aside to soak whilst he filled the flask completely and also filled his lidded cup, to which he added his tea diffuser. He swished the bowl one last time before emptying the water and poured the remainder of the kettle's contents onto the oats and milk powder mix he had placed in the bowl. He stirred a good dose of sugar into the steaming white mush. It was too hot to eat initially, but it would cool rapidly; the last spoonful was always cold. Connor held his spoon, waiting for the porridge to cool sufficiently or his patience to run out before he speed fed himself. There was no time to go strolling in the woods whilst it cooled.

When the porridge was gone, he made up the stove set and stowed it away. He took his tea and, whilst drinking, he studied the map he had unfolded. He felt tired and unmotivated to move; he was definitely coming down with something. Connor saw what he hoped he would find on the map, a small oblong with an arrow pointing at it saying "Mountain Rescue Hut." The "bothy," as they were known locally, were charity-maintained shelters that had been a blessing and life-saving sanctuary to many who had crossed the mountain wilderness of Scotland. They varied in nature from simple, stone-floored huts with tin roofs to more grandiose ex–hunting lodges willed to the Bothy Association. Due to their location, their upkeep was at best pragmatic; the charity funds could not run to, carting excesses of building materials across inhospitable terrain. So repairs were not always in keeping with the original design or structure. Aesthetics gave way to durability.

His mind made up, Connor wrestled the tent and the last of his kit into his backpack. This slight effort had raised his body temperature; a sheen of sweat had crept across his forehead, and any extra effort caused a throb of pressure about his head. Connor checked his bearing and picked out a rocky escarpment on the flank of a hill a mile or so away. The sky was leaden and threatened rain. The wind, which was of many minds as to what it wanted to do, buffeted all and sundry. Connor took an already weary step on the first of the five miles towards his intended shelter. He strived for his walking pattern, but was frustrated by the tussocked grass and water-saturated low areas that forced extra yards on his journey or forced him to speed up when he found his feet sinking into the mire. His anger started to rise, and he berated the scenery with an Anglo-Saxon turn of phrase that a Roman wall had been successful in keeping in abeyance for many years.

The weather finally broke. The first spits of rain were fat and hit with a density that promised more. Connor looked to the sky and cursed again. His pack felt leaden and more burdensome than usual. His legs ached from the effort as he moved across the moor at a slow and torturous pace that seemed negligible on the folded map. But slowly, too slowly, he approached his goal.

The wind was growing in strength and blew into his face. *Typical,* Connor thought. The wind-borne rain caused him to squint ahead and further reduced the distance he could see, the greyed out vista obscured to within a couple of hundred metres. Connor was becoming frustrated by the need to continually keep checking compass and map to stay *en route*. The wind kept trying to steal the map from his hand as he tried to set his bearing on the compass and find a suitable destination point. His head was throbbing. Had the weather been slightly better, he would have succumbed to the temptation to pitch his tent and ride out the hostile conditions. But he also knew that, as bad as the bothy shelters could be, it would be better to be within a sturdy, four-walled shelter than his tent if his health deteriorated.

Connor eventually came to a track he had been aiming for. Admittedly, he had begun to doubt its existence—or thought that perhaps he had missed it. Another trick of weather and the feverish state of his mind. He had deliberately aimed for a part of the track where, once he turned onto it, he would soon pass a hanging loch that indicated he was headed to the bothy and not away from it. Many times, he had read about lost souls who had found the path they needed only to wander off in the wrong direction, and impending disasters convinced them that they were going the right way. It was the ability to make right decisions by way of second nature that often meant the difference between success and failure, a skill heavily drilled in many a basic training course. Connor allowed himself a weak smile for having made this automatic decision and once more concentrated on the task at hand to reach the sanctuary that his map promised him. After turning onto the path, he was just short of ninety degrees to the wind. The side of his hood was being pressed to his face, and the rain was amplified by the stretched nylon over his ear. Connor unrolled his fleece hat to lift the hood from his ear.

Twenty-five minutes later, the bothy revealed itself fleetingly as Connor crowned a slight rise that allowed him to peek down the glen. Snuggled amongst the folds and re-entries of the hill, the angular slope of a roof shone a sleek black. He relaxed a little; at least the bothy existed and he would soon be out of the weather. He could get on with getting ill or better in as comfortable a shelter as a bleak Scottish mountain could offer. A small stream had formed in the deteriorating weather and bubbled across his path. Connor stopped and reached around for his water bottle, which he released from its pocket. He took a few steps up the hill from the path until he reached the small pool that the stream was filling and flowing through. He took a small cone of pliable plastic and folded it into a half-funnel shape, which he then inserted into the neck of the bottle to fill it. The plastic funnel sped up the process and kept out the water-borne grit, flotsam, and jetsam being washed down the watercourse. When the bottle was full, he cupped his hands and threw some of the icy water onto his face. It was refreshing and washed away the sweat-strewn salt that streaked his face. It also served to remind Connor of how hot his skin had become. Wiping his face, he stood up and cleared his nose to the ground. These efforts caused his head to throb more, as if a tsunami of molasses were flowing through his skull. Once he was back on the path again, he turned a bend to see the bothy standing unimpeded in his view. He had hit lucky. This must have been the four-star end of the bothy market. Obviously an ex–hunting lodge, this chalet-style wooden building stood incongruously on the hill side, the faded cedar shingles glowing in hues of red or white, showing the movement of the bleaching sun and washing rain.

Connor stepped onto the porch covered deck area at the door and let his pack slip from his back. The shadow of the building was a welcome relief after the hours of battling the elements. He fumbled in the side pocket of the pack to remove a knife too large to be deemed a pocketknife, but large enough to be bordering illegal. It was the size that would make you consider the value of your body parts and whether you would be willing to sacrifice any in order to take anything from the knife wielder.

Connor pushed back his hood and then unfolded the rather ugly-looking saw-edged blade of the knife before reaching for the latch and opening the door. The door swung back on hinges that were somewhat reluctant to carry out their designed function, complaining like a union official at an imposed shift change. Connor was pleased to some extent at the noise generated by the door, as it announced his arrival to anyone who might be present.

He stepped over the threshold and listened. It was the silence of an empty building; only the buffeting of the wind and rain could be heard. Connor called out to the empty rooms he could see and was pleased not to receive any reply. He grew slightly more confident as he moved through the building, cautious at first, but with growing assurance as he realised he was alone. A steep-pitched ladder-come-stair at the end of the building gave access to an open-plan roof space illuminated by a plastic glazed roof-light. Having scanned the upper floor from the top of the ladder, he descended. Once back on the ground, he folded away his knife. The adrenalin generated from the search started to subside, and the malaise crept back, serving as a reminder of how ill he had become. He rested with his head against the ladder whilst he waited for the throbbing to relent. The pine interior of the shelter creaked to the machinations of the wind, but it felt safe within the confines of the bothy and reminiscent of an unused sauna. Connor closed his eyes and drifted into the relaxing calm of the darkness. Although he was still standing, it was preferable to the effort of having to move and set up his bedding.

A while passed—it could have been a minute or tens of minutes. Connor couldn't tell, much less care. Something caused him to come to the task at hand; the effort of inertia was overcome by the power of the mind just as his body seemed ready to relinquish the fight.

Connor struggled back to the door and dragged his backpack in before exiting the bothy once more. Leaning against a post that supported the weather porch roof, he fumbled with his fly and relieved himself onto the scrubby piece of coarse grass that abutted the deck on which he stood. His urine was dark and smelled acrid. He watched it splash onto the ground and soak away to leave an off-white froth, which was whipped by the wind. Connor redressed himself and returned to the bothy, closing the braced door and securing the simple, but heavy latch. The sudden lack of wind caused his face to glow, as the radiated heat was no longer stolen by the wind chill. He pulled his water bottle from the backpack and took a long drink. The water tasted earthy with a metallic tang that he attributed to whatever illness he was suffering.

Although out of the wind and rain, Connor felt a chill run through his body that juxtaposed the glowing heat from his forehead. The cold water hit his stomach, and he felt his bowels react to the chilled liquid. An overwhelming urge to defecate pushed through him. He tensed and clenched his buttocks, but it felt hot and loose.

"Not now," Connor said out loud to himself, but knew he that no mind-over-matter was going to stop the inevitable evacuation. He made for the door, but *en route*, spied a metal wastepaper bin used for emptying embers from the fireplace. He placed it in the corner of the room, unfastened his trousers, and squatted awkwardly against the junction of the two walls, over the bin, and expelled the hot liquid that burnt within. Connor was conscious of his predicament and prayed that nobody else would choose the moment to arrive. With tissues from his jacket pocket, he set about cleaning himself, although his stomach and lower bowel continued to complain audibly. Using a rusted shovel next to the fireplace, Connor scooped up some of the ashes and tipped them into the bucket before placing it outside, having neither the strength nor inclination to bury the contents as he was supposed to.

Connor dragged his backpack to the far end of the bothy to a through-room aligned roughly east to west, with a window at both ends to let in a reasonable amount of light even on this dark-skied day. He unstrapped the bag and dropped the tent to one side, then spread out his camp mat and sleeping bag along with his sleeping clothes. After finding his towel, he stripped away his layers and then patted his sweat-dampened body dry before donning the fresh clothes he had prepared. He climbed into the sleeping bag and rested briefly, semi-recumbent against the wall, which was washed in the watery light shining through the western window. He reached into the backpack and pulled out his flask, as well as a small plastic box from which he took a blown plastic sheet of pills and a sachet. He popped out two pills and struggled to swallow them without liquid before emptying the sachet into the thermos cup and pouring on some of the flask's contents. Connor breathed in the lemon-scented liquid before sipping the contents, benefiting from the warmth as the liquid ran down his throat. He drained the last of the cup and wriggled down into the bag, positioning the water bottle on the floor next to his shoulder. He withdrew his hand into the bag and pulled up the zip.

The wind and rain continued to lash at the windows. Connor watched the rivulets run down the window until his eyelids grew too heavy and he lapsed into sleep.

Chapter 39

THE SHIRE XXII

The weight of the last two boxes was significant—not in a weighty, coin-heavy way, but paper-heavy in a dense, packed lump. However, earning these two boxes had been the most fraught of the three visits he had made. As such, Connor had decided not to push his luck. He stashed six boxes in the rear of the van—two from the petrol station, two from a small post office community store, and the last two from the town bank. Connor's nerve endings were frayed almost to the point of numbness. Luck had played more than a fair share in the outcome of the morning. The senior bank clerk had made two phone calls before offering over the boxes. The pressure of other people trying to do their own jobs and poor communications, predominantly people's inability to communicate clearly, had created an environment for a little manufactured disruption to allow Connor's plan to work. Enough was enough, though.

A series of predetermined parking locations, which provided cover to one side of the vehicle—then the other, as well as the rear—allowed Connor to remove the security company identification logos and signage without raising the suspicion of a vehicle driving off the road a security collection vehicle only to reappear as otherwise moments later. Still, hiding in plain view was a working strategy, and he had selected the locations to avoid the "nosy-do-gooder" as much as possible. Back behind the wheel, Connor drove for some miles as he sequentially stripped off his security guard uniform. Within two hours of leaving the bank, he was just another van driver of just another van. He drove into an off-road lay-by, busy with other trucks, vans, and sleeping sales reps. A bright yellow flag flapped from a precarious pole strapped to a seedy-looking mobile home, which had been converted to "Sam's Caff." Connor got out of the van and walked over to the café.

The cigarette smoke–smelling interior fought with the pervasive bacon frying and the stale cooking fat, which seemed to positively ooze from the thin walls. The seating area was littered with an array of individuals being just that—individual, sitting alone together. There wasn't sufficient space to sit alone, and, therefore, total strangers were forced to sit together at the worn tables. They tried to stay as far apart as was possible. The choice was simple: Take the food and drink back to the car or sit with a stranger. For many, after hours behind the wheel, the change of view and the chance for some external stimulation was more than welcome, especially for the regulars who knew "Sam"—if Sam was the person eponymous on the flag and personified behind the counter serving.

Connor wound a circuit through the plastic-backed chairs occupied by NHS resuscitation candidates of the future to gain access the hole-in-the-wall counter and serving hatch. A middle-aged, sour-faced man stood almost scowling at Connor. By way of greeting, he wiped the countertop aimlessly, asking for Connor's order. Connor ordered a tea, and the man went through the ritual of reviving the depleted teapot with hot water and gouts of steam pressure before transferring the liquid to an oversize mug. He proffered the milk jug at the cup, instead of asking and looked enquiringly at Connor, who played along and just nodded. The man ploughed the cup across the countertop, through the morning's residue, and held out an open hand. Fascinated by this non-communication, Connor deposited a one-pound coin into the man's palm. The man turned and made change, which he handed back to the waiting Connor.

After retreating to the back of the cabin to find a seat and picking up a discarded newspaper *en route*, Connor sat across from man in a checked shirt who was doing his utmost to ignore his screaming arteries, as he went with some gusto at the plate of fried everything set before him. Looking at it around the edge of his newspaper made Connor regret somewhat his own cholesterol indulgencies earlier, but he reasoned that he would soon be eating in the land of Sparta if the day panned out as expected, and pure lard on a plate would not be enough for him to gain weight.

"Sam" seemed to have relaxed a bit and was enjoying a bit of over-the-counter banter with a couple of his regulars, perhaps now believing that anyone who came into his establishment without a waistbelt overhang or a cigarette might not necessarily be from the Environmental Health Department. Connor relaxed also. He could feel the tension seeping slowly away from between his shoulder blades and the base of his neck, which many of his co-diners interpreted with knowing looks and small nods of understanding as the product of a hard stint at the wheel. Many of those present had probably been affected by Connor's act of commuter terrorism that morning, and the paradox of the event was that it had probably cost more in lost productivity than the unknown sum of money now languishing in the back of his van. Still, he could justify his motives to himself. Not that they would stand up as any form of mitigation—and he wasn't anticipating any plaudits, either—but he wondered how things would be managed publicly. He looked at the red-topped newspaper before him. The front-page stories were far from front-page stories, and he could imagine the angle the editors would take on his own mini crime wave. Of course, the sum of money involved would have a large bearing on the amount of media interest generated, and, paradoxically, the greater the sum, the less publicity the heist would get. It wouldn't do either the banks or the establishments concerned many favours for their public and shareholders to know that their money was "given" away without so much as a threat. The security firms would not like the fallibility of their systems to be highlighted, either. The police would also be in a difficult position. Of course, they wouldn't suppress the information, but they couldn't shout it from the rooftops if they very soon realised they had few or less leads to work on. The question of economics would again come into play regarding the amount invested in detection versus the likelihood of recovery and prosecution. Connor pondered these points and again looked at the front page. It was all sex and sleaze; his story would most likely register as a points drift in the shares section against the banks and insurance sector. Connor smiled to himself. He fell between stalls—not a Ronnie Biggs, a Leeson, or a Robin Hood, more a daring opportunist? No, it was more than that—a criminal mastermind? Much less than that. All in all, the press would only focus on the chagrined victims if they caught hold of the story; public sympathy for the "establishment"' was never great. Not smug, but generally more content with his justification for his actions, Connor braved the stony silence of the counter for a second cup of tea. The change in "Sam" was dramatic—the surly man who had served earlier had morphed into a happy, chatty butterfly. He gave out pleases and thank-yous on a buy-one-get-one offer, and Connor found this mood swing worrying. He wondered whether or not he preferred the "grumpier" version from earlier.

Connor retook his seat and checked his watch. It was coming up to three o'clock—another couple of hours to kill before the activity around the lockup would start to slow and dusk would be coming on, allowing Connor to get back to the sanctuary of the lockup, behind closed doors. The windows around the Cabin had been covered in some form of opaque vinyl—whether to stop people seeing out or in, Connor hadn't decided. Previously, someone had attempted to scratch away some of the covering, which Connor looked through now with the newspaper discarded only to see six motorcycle police officers pull up. Connor's inner calm bolted, and he nearly choked into his tea, to the point where the two men he was currently sharing the table with looked up from their food.

"Wrong hole," Connor spluttered and took a breath. The two men returned to their meals and, Connor surreptitiously spied through the scratched vinyl. The leather-clad officers were clustered together, receiving a briefing from a central officer who was standing with his back to the cabin, but whether he was pointing at it or past it towards the van, Connor wasn't quite sure. Two of the officers broke away from the group and approached the cabin. Connor hunkered down in his seat. The two officers entered the cabin and surveyed all within, and there was a lull in the café conversation in response.

"Yes, gents, what's it to be?" Sam's voice rung out loud and clear by way of welcome to the officers—and as a warning to all patrons who might need to know that the police were in attendance. The officers approached the counter and ordered six teas. Connor went into a free fall of relief. Driver training, he realised. His relief must have been palpable, as the man across the table once more gave Connor a skewed look. Connor took the hint, finished his tea, and made his way out of the cabin. He walked up the lay-by and passed the array of parked vehicles before he reached his van and, after a quick circuit, got in and gunned the engine. The number plates were a concern. He had been as meticulous as possible with his targets so as to park and avoid surveillance cameras, but they were everywhere nowadays. He had calculated the risk and had figured security cameras would not be in the equation too much on the actual day. After he got back to the lockup, the van would probably never see the light of day again—at least not with Connor behind the wheel.

Connor pulled away, checking his mirrors to make sure that the motorcycle officers weren't discarding their teas and hurriedly starting their bikes for pursuit. Connor realised this was retribution for his earlier smugness and vowed he would not fall into the same relaxed frame of mind again. The job was far from over. There was a long way to go—a whole lifetime, in fact, and although he had invested much time to this point, it had only been a few hours since the real clock had started ticking. Up until this moment, no real crime had been committed, at least as far as anyone was aware. It would only be an unfolding of circumstances that would reveal what had occurred. From now on, though, the machine would be asking questions, prying and probing, trying to make sense of reports that would be filed by confused security guards returning empty-handed from their proposed collection points. The microscopic investigation of any scrap of information would be catalogued and placed on a table like the pieces of jigsaw, which some champion puzzler would have to put together. It had been Connor who had made the puzzle; he was the only one who had the full picture, and he had gone as far as he could to make damn sure that there were as many parts of the puzzle missing as possible. It had been chaos that had allowed his plan to come off. Connor had gleaned this outcome from participation in and observation of incidents and exercises over his years in the service. Case studies and debriefings time and time again had thrown up the same old lesson: "poor communications." Of course, in the context of an emergency, everyone adapts and gets by; it's only after that people realise it could have been better. The lack of communication leaves people isolated against a wall of mounting pressure to do something. Strangely, it is braver to do nothing in these circumstances, but try getting that to sit when a potential "heroic" action, which these circumstances sometimes throw up. The glowing adoration that can be reaped is a difficult motivator to harness and takes a strong manager. The damnation that would befall that individual if, due to inaction, the situation got worse would be tremendous—so you're damned if you do and damned if you don't. Most people do and try to justify their thought process. Give this option to the unschooled or inexperienced, and they will make bad decisions. This circumstance was the crux of Connor's plan—investing in the responsible person to make the call and, given the uniqueness of the circumstances, letting that person make a decision without sufficient guidance due to little or no communicative support, all the while trying to feel pressurised to make a decision that, if not made, they would be questioned over for placing the organisation at risk. It would be some time before Connor would find out how successful he had or had not been.

Chapter 40

NORTHWEST FRANCE I

The twinkling of the harbour lights was a welcome sight. The crossing had been reasonably uneventful, although the onset of night and the crossing of the ferry lanes into Saint-Malo had brought a frisson of excitement. Connor had resorted once more to the engine to power the boat into the port some two miles up the estuary, and the sail lay roughly folded and secured to the boom.

Connor had been fortunate with the tide, which was flowing in his favour and still had an hour or so to run before reaching the high mark. *Little Star* followed the marker buoys into the small-walled Port-en-Bessin, and Connor gently eased the boat against the floating jetty. Connor slipped the engine into neutral and moved quickly fore and aft to secure the mooring lines and adjust the hanging height of the fenders. With the boat secure, he set about making up the sails, ensuring that they were well stowed against the weather in his absence. Once all was as Connor wanted, he cut the engine. He stood on the rail and scanned the harbour, which had wound down for the day. Retiring below the silence was welcome; the glow of the lights created a cosy atmosphere of an old-world snug bar, to which Connor soon added the glow and hiss from a boiling kettle. Whilst the water came to a boil, Connor set about making his bed, unballing a sleeping bag and digging out a pillow from behind cupboard doors set into the various bulkheads that made up the main cabin space. Everything was slightly musty, but

Connor was not overly concerned; he felt that if he didn't get to bed soon, he would fall asleep standing.

A ping from the kettle's metal body and an attempt at a whistle indicated that the kettle was reaching a boil, so Connor prepared the tea and pot. He warmed the pot first before going into his ritual, pouring the hot water from the teapot into the mug so as to warm that, too. The leaves let out a sweet, earthy aroma as the hot water was added. He breathed this in before fixing the lid and a battered tea cosy to the pot. Tipping the remainder of the hot water into a bowl, Connor took a flannel bath. The soap and water freshened his tired eyes and slaked away the airborne salt from the crossing. Once he had dried off and changed into some light cotton shorts and a T-shirt, he went back on deck. The sky was dark, though no starlight could be seen. The water of the small harbour was still and reflecting the scattered marker lights, which hung randomly around the perimeter of the harbour. There was no movement and nobody about, and Connor felt self-conscious as he relieved himself over the side of the boat. The sound of his urine hitting the water seemed to echo around, and he hurried to finish the job. His ablutions now complete, he returned below, put in place the weatherboard, and drew the hatch to, leaving a small gap for ventilation.

Connor poured out a cup of tea, climbed onto the bed, and wrapped the sleeping bag around his legs. The tea was hot and lifted the spirits. He hugged the mug and looked around. Everything was going according to plan and as it should be; slowly, the various phases were linking up, and soon all the preparatory work would come into play to form a whole picture. Of course, his plan was somewhat over-detailed, but the potential for failure always existed. Connor was keen to exert maximal control. There would be no consolation of saying "If only I'd . . ."; there would be no second chance to get it right. This was an all-or-nothing attempt to take the chance. The only gamble was whether or not it would all be worth it, the only variable being the undetermined sum that could be reaped from the whole activity. Applying a business mindset, it was akin to starting a new business: the identification and research into the market followed by the initial investment for start-up costs, and then the wait to see if it all came together with a healthy turnover and positive profit margin. You didn't know 'til you knew. At least Connor didn't have to carry the burden of other people's expectations; he wasn't answerable to partners, shareholders, or banks, although, were it to go wrong, he would be out of pocket and answerable to some much more powerful individuals. This was why he had covered the planning stage from a multitude of angles and applied a variety of scenarios to test the resilience of the component parts. Of course, there was doubt. Was he too close? Did he want it to work so much that the trees and the woods were indistinguishable from each other? Connor hoped not; he really hoped not.

Connor awoke. For a brief few moments, he luxuriated in the bliss of perfection. He was comfortable, neither too hot nor cold. He focused on the small clock across the cabin and saw that it was still early, though he felt rested. The light, crepuscular and timid, filtered through the small porthole windows and opaque, tinted deck hatches. The shadowy interior and gentle rocking made Connor want to snuggle down and enjoy the moment longer, especially when he heard the first few drops of rain strike the deck above.

The boat bobbed gently against the jetty, and the wire rigging became agitated enough by the rising wind to ping against the masts around the harbour. Connor thought about the day ahead and how another series of pieces would be fitted into the puzzle. The sleeping bag started to grow warm and constricting, to the point where he sat up to be half in, half out. After some small stretches, he shook the bag off, dressed, and stowed away the bedding. He set about converting the cabin back into a seating-come-dining area whilst waiting for the kettle to boil and the grill to reach operating temperature for toast.

Ten minutes later, he sat down to a steaming cup of tea and a few rounds of toast. The butter melted gently into the crisped browned bread. Connor studied the few pamphlets he had on various timetables for ferries, trains, and buses. When he had finished his breakfast, he cleared away the cup and plate quickly and refreshed himself with a wash and brush-up.

Connor jumped down onto the jetty and checked the mooring lines before walking back towards the collection of squat buildings. He figured that amongst them would be the harbourmaster's office. Sure enough, a battered door led into a countered office area with an array of nautical paraphernalia to suggest that whoever worked here was responsible for the control and movements of the vessels in and out. A noise came from behind an ajar door that led off of the office towards the back of the building. It sounded like someone struggling to move a heavy and reluctant piece of furniture. Connor waited patiently. The exertions from the back were interspersed with some rather guttural language beyond Connor's capacity to interpret, but truth be known, he understood fully the intent and meaning, frustration being a universal language.

"*Merde!*"

The door at the back of the office slammed shut. Two seconds later, it opened again to allow the entrance of the harbourmaster into the office.

"*Ah, bonjour, monsieur,*" Connor offered "*Ça va?*"

The harbourmaster looked up, surprised to see Connor standing there, and examined him keenly. "*S'il vous plaît, monsieur, s'il vous plaît.*"

The small but broad-chested man waved Connor to follow him back the way he had just come, and Connor was obliged to follow. The master launched into a tirade of language whose meaning Connor could only guess at 'til he felt he had to interject. "*Pardonnez-moi, monsieur, je ne comprends pas. Je suis anglais, et mon français est très petit. C'est possible pour vous parler retard, s'il vous plaît?*"

The harbourmaster stopped and turned quickly. "*Pardonnez-moi monsieur,* I am sorry, *très stupide. S'il vous plaît, aidez-moi?* You help me please?"

A smile grew across the salt-and-pepper beard that grew up into a thick, white shock of hair. It was a disarmingly friendly face when it was smiling, but there was also a more sinister one lurking not too far underneath. Connor could tell that the owner was no fool when it came to employing the right face for the right moment.

Behind the door was a collection of nautical equipment reminiscent of a boat jumble, amongst which were filing cabinets, cupboards, and shelving, all overflowing with bits of paper files, the importance of which Connor could not ascertain. Connor had to squeeze around the half-open door before the harbourmaster could shut it to allow access to the indicated corner.

"Please, *je m'appelle Jean.*"

"*Je m'appelle Connor.*"

The two men shook hands. It was an awkward introduction, but Connor felt it addressed some sort of Gallic necessity, especially because there was so little personal space between them. Jean beckoned Connor to follow between some racking to the nub of the problem. Jean had been trying to retrieve some item or gain some access when a small series of events had led a number of items, including a filing cabinet and two outboard motors, to become locked together. Jean's previous labours, which Connor had been privy to, had resulted in further dislocation of the room, to such a point that it was now almost unnavigable without climbing over or through the stored items. It was just a question of enough hands, enough to hold one thing out of the way long enough to move something else. Ten minutes later, having followed one another's direction and suggestion, the room was sufficiently clear for them to stand at a respectful distance from each other and survey their collective labours.

"*Bien, très bien. Merci, mon ami.* Thank you, Connor."

"*Mon* pleasure, *monsieur.*"

Jean held the door for Connor, and Connor passed through back into the office. Jean followed, sucking on a small cut on the back of his hand.

"Now, Connor, how may I help you?"

"I arrived last night from England. I am on my vacation and looking to leave my boat here for maybe two weeks. Is that possible?"

"But, of course, *mon ami,* of course. Yours is the vessel at the end of the jetty, *non?*" Jean pointed out towards the harbour over Connor's' shoulder.

"Yes, that is mine, *Little Star.*" Connor mimicked Jean

"She is a pretty little thing. I was going to come to visit you later after I had finished my . . . filing, and the rain had stopped." Jean indicated with his thumb over his shoulder to the store behind with a dismissive little shrug. Reaching into a drawer, Jean removed a pad and searched for a working pen. Eventually, armed with one, he set about filling out the paperwork.

Five minutes later, the paperwork was complete, and Connor held a receipt for the two-week mooring fee. Jean led Connor to the door and out onto the quayside.

"Move your boat to the far side. It should be sheltered there. You can take up any berth you wish. I only have one or two reservations, and with the English weather you have brought for your vacation, I do not think I will have many visitors!" Jean laughed out loud at his joke at Connor's' expense. The twinkle in his eye showed he meant no harm.

Connor retorted, "My friend, in England this *is* good weather! At least you will be able to get your filing done?"

"*Touché, mon ami, touché.* Have a happy vacation."

"*Merci, monsieur, au revoir.*"

"*A bientôt.*"

Connor returned to his boat and fired up the engine before letting loose the mooring lines. At the wheel, he revved the engine gently and steered away from the floating jetty. He navigated the boat across the harbour to the berths that Jean had pointed out. Having secured the boat, he went below to finish his preparations.

As the kettle approached a boil, Connor moved around the interior, stowing things away and packing the bits and pieces he would need to take with him into a small backpack. He kept his money and passport separate inside a zipped traveller's wallet, which he would carry in a zipped cargo pocket of his jacket. The kettle called to Connor that it was boiling, and Connor set about making his tea. Whilst it was drawing, he disconnected the gas supply, emptied the small fridge of its contents, and left the door ajar. The tea steamed gently in the cup, and Connor took a cautious sip whilst once more studying the set of timetables in front of him. They were more indicative of how much time his journey could take. There was no pressure to be anywhere at any particular time, and the variety of transport he intended to take would depend on where and when he got to any given location. In fact, the more random his journey seemed, the less association there would be between the boat, where he came from, and where he was eventually heading.

After finishing his tea, Connor washed the cup and stowed it away. He checked that the fuel to the engine was switched off and flicked the isolator for the electric circuits. The hum of the fridge stopped. He took one last look around before ascending to the deck. Once he had put down his pack, he fitted the weatherboard and drew the hatch closed, securing both together with a combination padlock. He patted his jacket pocket to ensure that his wallet was there, then shouldered his pack and climbed down off of the boat. He looked along the boat once more before turning his back on *Little Star* and setting off down the jetty, to the bus stop in the town beyond the harbour.

Chapter 41

THE GAMBIA V

Connor had lain awake for some time, looking periodically at his watch and ticking away the minutes and hours. The darkness of the room was fading as shades of grey, and colour started to bleed into the furnishings that made up the decor. The sound of the ocean was rhythmic and predictable, although it created its own hiatus as Connor waited for the next wave to wash over the beach, delivering or stealing the millions of imperceptible grains of sand that, many millennia ago, had created or dissolved the continent and shoreline.

A sharp, metallic dragging sound interrupted the tranquillity, causing Connor to get out of bed and go to the window. Pulling open the shutters, he looked out onto the poolside to see the sun loungers being reorganised. The early-rising employee was rearranging the chairs like some sun-worshipping druid. He realigned them with the onset of the sun's first warming rays back through the 180 degrees from where they had been vacated the day before.

Connor picked up a bottle of water from his bedside cabinet and went to sit on the small veranda. The backpack was propped against the bottom of the bed and waiting for the wash bag and shorts that Connor had slept in. Alongside were the clothes Connor had laid out for the day ahead. It was still far too early, and Connor didn't mind just sitting in the early morning shade, collecting his thoughts for the day ahead.

A gentle breeze moving along the coast flicked the parasol umbrellas that stood sentinel round the pool like spindly mushrooms. Connor wondered whether there were mushrooms in this part of Africa and, if there weren't, what the indigenous population would think of them as a foodstuff. They were a strange foodstuff, he mused, the food of the dead. As much as he loved them, he understood the revulsion that some people had for them. He smiled at the recollection of his first station officer at his first fire station. As the "new boy" and the lowest of the low, certain duties befell him, and being the mess manager was one. Collecting the mess fees from the watch members and doing the "messing"—or shopping, in normal parlance—was all part of the responsibilities. But these duties had to be carried out with due deference to the individuals' rank and time in service and their own particular likes and dislikes. Full-fat milk or skimmed, margarine or butter, and streaky or rinded bacon. But the one that always made Connor smile was the fact that the station officer liked his mushrooms peeled. Seeing grown men, he amongst them, trying to remove the paper-thin covering of the fungi and cursing all the way was comical, almost surreal compared to the blood-and-guts environment in which they worked. The top of their promotional tree had an aversion to unpeeled mushrooms.

The hour hand moved on. The pool attendant had swept the poolside and was now doing imperceptible things to the pool itself with some Heath Robinson suction device. *Time to go,* thought Connor. He went back into the shade and coolness of the room. He showered and dressed, collected his bag, and checked his appearance in the mirror before exiting the room with one last scan around to ensure that he had left nothing behind. The corridor was deserted, as was the reception into which Connor descended. The breakfast room was closed and the waiter absent, though the tables were ready for the onslaught of those who, in this environment, least needed it.

Connor stood at the reception and broke the silence by sounding the chromed bell on the counter. A minute or so passed with no development, prompting Connor to sound the bell with a little less guilt. At the far side of the lobby, a door opened and a man appeared with a confused look on his face. The look was of a man checking to see whether or not he was hearing things against his better judgment and now, having been proved aurally right, was questioning the visual evidence that now presented itself. Somewhat bemusedly, the man crossed the open space, bidding Connor good morning as he did. A customer up at this hour of the morning was unusual to the say the least, unless there were flights to catch, in which case he had normally been forewarned.

"I am sorry to have kept you, sir. How may I help you."

"I'd like to settle my bill, please," Connor replied.

"I am sorry. I was not told you would be leaving early. I have nothing prepared." The night porter looked a little perturbed by the request.

"I have to meet a friend today and wanted to get away before it got too hot." Connor handed over his room key, and the man checked the number.

"One moment, please."

The man turned and hung up the key, checking the small cubbyhole beside the hook. He vanished momentarily to locate the required paperwork, which he returned with and presented to Connor to check.

"Is this okay, sir?"

Connor scanned through the handwritten lines, next to which were numerical amounts that seemed ballpark. Truth be known, he would pay even if overcharged; his need to get away with the least amount of fuss or show was worth much more than a few pounds here or there.

"That looks fine," Connor said as he returned the bill.

The porter smiled and started to add the various figures together. Two or three minutes passed before the final figure was presented to Connor, who had removed his wallet in preparation to pay. Connor counted off a number of notes and handed them over to the porter, who looked pleased to receive currency instead of a credit card, which would have meant wrestling with the electronic world. He made change, which Connor declined, taking just the receipt instead.

"Thank you. Goodbye," Connor said, as he shouldered his bag and folded the receipt roughly into his pocket.

"Thank you, sir. Goodbye to you." The porter watched Connor cross the reception and step out into the brightening light of the day.

Once outside, Connor stood briefly to watch the activities of the early morning risers. The sun was already starting to take hold. The first shimmers were radiating from the distant road, through which lorries were emerging, they also trying to take advantage of the early morning cool. Connor turned down the street and made his way to the small café he had used to meet Beril. The proprietor swiftly supplied a pot of hot, sweet coffee as well as a dry, but sweet bread and a small bowl of viscous honey. The taxi rank Connor watched was empty. The people who were out at this time of the morning could not afford the drivers' fares even allowing for the deduction of the tourist rate. Connor alternatively sipped his coffee and the bottled water he had brought from the hotel. The coffee was strong and coursed through him, purging the last vestiges of sleep from his body. He had eaten some of the cake, but the effort of keeping the flies at bay was too much and too off putting, so he had moved the plate away to another table.

Halfway through his second cup of coffee, Connor saw a taxi pull up to the front of the rank. He pulled a note from his wallet and tucked it under the cup and saucer, knowing well that the proprietor had seen this from the shadows in the back of the shop. Connor got up and left.

The early bird caught the worm as far as the taxi driver was concerned. His small car barrelled along the highroad towards the airport, and he wore a smile as wide as his windscreen. Connor sat in the back, watching the world come to life whilst enjoying the cooling breeze through the window. The taxi soon reached the airport, and Connor paid the driver before entering the terminal building. Like airports the world over, they rarely conformed to local time. Their agenda was much bigger than the needs of the service industries that kept the airport working. Tired-looking employees were carrying out their respective roles, maintaining the flow of customers through the airport. The customers were doing their thing, trying to make themselves as comfortable as possible on chairs and in spaces patently not designed for long waits—or trying to cut into queues just so they could be first in the next queue.

Connor got his bearings and then made for the ticket bureau. To his relief, the small queue in front of him diminished quickly. He was greeted with the beaming smile of a youthful man, who was to all the world exquisitely happy in his job. He smiled back at the man.

"Good morning. I would like a flight to Morocco please," Connor said.

The attendant's faced faltered for a second. "Certainly, sir, let me check for you."

The man tapped away at a keyboard and studied the monitor. He seemed to dismiss one without consultation, or maybe he had made some data entry error. "Which airport were you hoping to fly to, sir?"

"To Casablanca-Anfa airport."

"Well, I have two options. There is a direct flight to Casablanca-Anfa airport that does not leave for two days' time, or at four o'clock this afternoon there is a flight to Cairo and a link from there to Tangier Ibn Battouta. It arrives at three tomorrow afternoon. Would that be convenient, sir?"

Connor hadn't expected to be as lucky as he had, so he was glad to accept the second choice. At least he would be moving rather than stuck in the already overcrowded airport and closer to his final destination than he had hoped. He bought his ticket and was soon part of the waiting masses on the uncomfortable chairs of departure.

Chapter 42

NORTHWEST FRANCE II

Connor had walked about half a mile up from the little harbour, towards the town centre. Morning commuters passed by in their Peugeots, Citroëns, and Renaults ranging from shiny new to advanced decay. The occupants reflected, in their attire, the condition of their respective vehicles—from city slick to country artisan.

The village was quietly going about its business; people stopped and greeted each other cheek to cheek, which was both intimate and insincere at the same time. The *boulangerie* looked too small for the volume of customers it was trying to serve. The shutters of the other stores were being rolled up and the awnings being stretched complainingly from their overnight casements in anticipation of the noon sun, which at this point did not look like it was going to make an appearance.

The shabby and the chic were starting their rounds, either toting shopping bags and pushing prams or sporting designer bags and toy dogs on a diamante leash. A shopkeeper looked on at his customers—those that spent a little and searched for every bargain, those that spent a lot and allowed their dogs to foul the pavement outside his shop front—with disdain.

Connor checked his watch as he leaned against the one of the supports of the bus shelter. The bus routes of the buses were shown on the rear wall amidst the graffiti of some disaffected youth who had used a confused Anglo-French turn of phrase to register his or her angst with the world. Connor had chosen a bigger town, some fifteen kilometres on, to ride the bus to, and someone had chosen to burn the town, most likely with a cigarette end, through the protective Perspex. Just before the bus arrived, Connor was joined by two women in their mid-fifties armed with their shopping bags. They greeted Connor, who responded in kind and then feigned a search of his backpack to prevent further exchange.

The bus arrived, and Connor ceded his place in the queue to the women, who thanked him, and followed them onto the bus. Having bought his ticket, he took a seat midway along and sat against the window. The bus pulled away and trundled through the village. It eventually broke free of the buildings and pushed inland along tree-lined roads that cut straight across the countryside, where French farmers plied their trade and earned their subsidies. The road ran through a host of villages, all with the same combination of pretty and utilitarian buildings. There seemed to be no thought to the aesthetics and no consideration of the venerability of some of the edifices, which had to suffer the indignity of a concrete- and asbestos-clad barn, cheek by jowl with its own ornate iron-worked railings and crafted stone masonry. It was as if a child had been allowed to submit a school project of house styles through the ages and used it as a town plan—a block of flats next to a thatched cottage, a hobnailed boot next to an expensive trainer.

Eventually, the bus broached the outskirts of Bayeux, and Connor was amongst the large percentage of occupants preparing to disembark. The bus driver negotiated the narrow roads and turns with a professional flair that bordered on arrogance, arriving at a square at the centre of the town. A bright and bustling market was in full swing, and the stalls and canopies were a riot of colour even though the skies were overcast and grey. Connor waited for everyone to pass before following behind. He stepped down off the bus and into the throng of the market crowd.

The market bustled with the activity of the shoppers. This was clearly a market of some renown, and the patrons moved with efficiency amongst the stalls, chatting amiably, but with a gimlet eye to the price, freshness and gram on the scale of value. Already, shopping bags and baskets were burgeoning with the viands, comestibles, and the ubiquitous, aerial-like batons of bread.

Connor breathed deep the heady aromas that swam amongst the crowd, stirred and eddied by the bodies' turbulence—the acrid scent of roasting coffee and scorched beans, the pungent onions and garlic counterpoint to the hot and yeasty baked bread. A passing smoker pulling hard on his cigarette, the contrail blue-hazed and heady. There was the salty tang of the fish stall, which glistened and sparkled from water and ice, then the rattling as the mussels were stirred so the monger could shave their beards. One could see the destiny of these blue-black nuggets in the rising clouds of steam from the corner stall, where bowls of *moules marinières* were being consumed by the traders, whose stalls were set and being looked after whilst they stole away for an early lunch. Connor smiled when he thought of the British alternative—the hot dogs, burgers, and chips. He was brought back to the present by a change of wind direction, which carried with it the unmistakeable stink of a French sewer, the rancid and sickly-sweet stench of rotting effluent that painted the inside of a person's nasal cavities and lived there long after he or she moved on, so Connor did.

Nearly completing a circuit of the market, Connor came across the taxi rank he was seeking. A small group of men stood at the side of the front cab, smoking and gesticulating at some object that commanded their attention, which at the moment seemed to be the back page of a newspaper being passed amongst them. Connor approached the group who, sensing his presence, moved from the front cab, allowing Connor to speak to the driver. The rest of the group waited at the edge of earshot to see what fare was picked up so they could no doubt debate animatedly the best route.

"*Cherbourg, s'il vous plaît, monsieur. Combien?*"

Connor's French was not great, but he purposely feigned it to be worse. If the driver took the fare, Connor did not want to have to engage in a "franglais" conversation for the next thirty or forty miles.

The driver was in his early forties and, from what Connor could deduce, a full-time taxi driver. He had a road-weary face and a nothing-will-surprise-me demeanour. The human interface had, over the years, eroded the emotion of shock from him. The automaton role and mundane conversation had taken its toll. Still, this fare would at least mean an early day.

"*Quatre-vingt euros*—about eighty euros." (Connor's puzzled look had prompted the English translation.)

"*C'est bon,*" Connor replied and climbed into the back of the large Renault as the driver started his engine and flicked away the remnants of cigarette through the window.

The Renault barrelled along the national route in seemingly arrow-straight sections, and the driver seemed to respond to Connor's desire for silence. After Connor's broken French-English explanation that he was touring the war beaches and landing grounds, a comfortable silence ensued. Connor just watched the countryside tumble by 'til it gave way to the built-up grey tumble of Cherbourg's industrial suburbs.

The taxi driver enquired, "*Ou est* . . . whereabouts?"

It was a timely request as Connor pointed at a roadside sign depicting the ferry terminal. "*Le bateau pour la Manche, s'il vous plaît*." The taxi driver smiled, and Connor guessed that his French, although descriptive, was not as it should be.

The road signs began offering directions in English as well as in French, and Connor watched the driver follow the constructed route into the ferry port designed to manage the flow of vehicular traffic. The taxi passed holding areas for lorries sectioned off from the tourist traffic and offering better facilities, no doubt the product of the French drivers' demands and probably the sacrificial burning of a vehicle or two. The taxi pulled into the front of a large square building, which once would have looked fresh and stark rising from the reclaimed flats of the harbour, but time had passed since it had been the "new kid on the block." The ravages of the costal climate were biting deep into the facade of the building. The corrugated plastic coating was starting to fail and peel away, and the rust staining that showed against the once-white fascia signified the decay that was taking place, a cancer the rust would spread and contaminate all around it. It was a throwaway building, though, and as long as the decay was such that it corresponded with the expected lifespan and usability, nobody cared. It would be bulldozed away and replaced with another "new kid." The accountants had infiltrated the world of architecture and trimmed aesthetics to the bone, balancing corporate image against cost-effectiveness, repair versus replacement. They left their mark on the balance sheet, and their physical presence was minimally pragmatic.

Connor climbed out of the taxi and handed the driver ninety euros before retrieving his backpack. The driver bid Connor *bon voyage* and drove off across the large open expanse beyond the ticket office. Seagulls soared and dived in the on shore breeze, which carried either specks of rain or flecks of spray off the waves as they eroded the harbour walls. The birds were stark white against the leaden sky and landed; their beaks and feet glowed luminous. They cried mournfully to each other, only to intersperse their dirge with alarming shrieks as they scavenged the shoreline for food scraps, which they clamoured for.

A slap of breeze blew against Connor and pushed him through the entrance of the ticketing office. The air curtain washed him with warm, recycled air. The company liveries hung above the desks and portals of the ticket booths and extolled the virtues of their competitiveness against their neighbours in the small space available to them. There were no queues. It was approaching lunchtime, and the French still observed the sanctity of the lunch "hour," a concept that was lost in time to the colder climate of their British cousins. Still, commercial competition was eroding away values and traditions. The lure of lucre created greater pangs than hunger, but it was a moveable feast, and the sullen expression of the woman at the desk showed more the want of a decent lunch than an hour's overtime.

A brief exchange saw Connor leave the desk with a ticket for the afternoon, sailing to Portsmouth. He had two hours to kill before boarding, so he toured the limited facilities before settling down with a large coffee and a discarded newspaper at a fixed-down table by a salt-stained window. The semi-opaque view let on to the empty key and the port entrance beyond. The view inside the room was tired and no more exciting—not even when orange laminate had been fashionable. Connor tried not to watch the clock.

Chapter 43

MOROCCO

Connor had been lucky, although he felt far from it. He was travel-weary, and the accumulated grime of airport departure lounges and the subsequent flights had left a tangible residue that demanded a hot shower and a bar of soap. No, Connor had been lucky that his flights had connected and that he had the luxury of a spare seat next to him on this leg to Tangier. This allowed him to flip up the dividing arm and spread out to a semi-recumbent position.

The airplane had skirted the northern expanses of the Sahara Desert and was now crossing the Atlas mountain range on its descent to Tangiers Ibn Battouta airport. Wisps of candy-floss cloud streaked past the porthole-style window that Connor squinted through. The pitch and whine of the engine changed as the airplane continued its descent, and Connor swallowed again to unblock his ears. The plane hit the runway hard, and the engines screamed in their reverse thrust efforts to bring the shuddering hulk of a vehicle to a taxiing pace. Once it had slowed down, the plane lumbered across the runways, following an indecipherable set of runway markings and arrows. The plane drew to a halt outside a low-slung arm of a building, which crept out from a hub. The cabin crew set about opening the compartment doors, allowing the tube of passengers and their motley collection of hand luggage to disembark. Connor could not shake the anticipation of cool, fresh air as the cabin doors were opened, but instead there was just a pause as nature decided which of the two climates needed to be balanced and, as often as not, the status quo prevailed. Connor climbed down to the runway and squinted from the glare off the cement, even though the sun was a few hours past its zenith. Connor followed Indian-file the people ahead of him and made the shade of the terminal building, which offered no more comfort. Whether the air-conditioning was inadequate or absent entirely was anyone's guess. The added cacophony of the waiting travellers and overpowering speaker system built a bazaar-like atmosphere that made Connor draw a breath before entering into the maddening crowd.

Connor had felt his patience being peeled away, strip by strip. The collectively unruly and self-righteous behaviour of his fellow passengers had taken its toll, and now Connor had become as bullish and uncaring as the next man, literally. Due to his size and being a product of first-world culture, Connor commanded his own little pocket of space. The fear of being pickpocketed had caused Connor to react, *over*react, to being touched or bumped into—something that was inevitable at a baggage reclaim conveyor belt, but had surprised a particularly persistent and pushy young man, who had found himself propelled backward against his will and intended direction. Tired and travel sore as he was, Connor had puffed out and used his physique aggressively and without reserve to control the space around him. The luggage drifted by, and the collection of baggage melded into an Eton mess of belongings. Suddenly, people could not recognise bags that they had lived with and toted around as their own. They would paw and remove items that others had identified from afar as being theirs, but were also not a hundred percent sure, either—the result being that the person having removed an item would, on realisation, be quite *blasé* about putting it back onto the carousel and careless about how they did it, if indeed they did. Eventually Connor's backpack emerged from the depths of the airport carousel and rolled around to him. He had considered just leaving it and walking away—such was the anxiety he found himself suffering—but the loss of his wallet and travel documents was something he could not allow to happen. Having to show up at the local embassy or consulate would scupper entirely the convoluted travel itinerary he had set for himself. By comparison, a bag full of mostly dirty clothing and a wash kit and shaving tackle would be a negligible loss. However, they might try to track the owner against the flight manifest, especially with the threat of aircraft-delivered terrorism, so he had to wait and claim his bag. Additionally, going through border control without baggage would attract unwanted attention.

Thirty minutes later, Connor exited the building into the full glare of the late afternoon sun. The front of the building was as chaotic as the inside, only here the chaos was caused by the multitude of vehicles battling to achieve the best position at the terminal exit. Connor drifted down past the building confines, glad to be free of the madness behind him. He actually considered just walking into town, as he had no written agenda to follow, but good sense took over. He could easily wander into a no-go area and bring on a world of pain he could easily avoid.

At the tail end of the traffic scrum, Connor spied a lone taxi driver who seemed to be enjoying a *siesta* and was unconcerned with the melee for clients going on behind him. Connor rapped on the roof and disturbed the would-be driver from his slumber. A pained look replaced the blissfully neutral sleeping posed and then a more aggressive "who the fuck are you" look stole across the driver's face. Connor brandished a fistful of dirham, which caught the driver's attention.

"How much to the harbour for the ferry? *Le port, le bateau pour Espagne?*"

The barrage of questions and the juxtaposition of tranquillity and aggressive interrogation, and the sight of so much money, had created the desired confusion. Connor was soon travelling through the late afternoon towards the port of Tangiers, the wind blowing through the window, offering blessed relief from the arid heat.

Chapter 44

SCOTLAND XII

Connor awoke. Unsure of what had woken him, he lay still and just listened. There was no noise beyond the wind as it sought the nooks and crannies of the bothy. The sleeping bag was sodden and cold. Whenever Connor moved, the ache was total, across his whole body. His eyes felt pressurised from behind, and his throat burned with an insistent itch that no amount of his depleting water supply could suppress. The sleeping bag was uncomfortable due to the sweat-induced dampness; any movement caused the bag to suck the heat from his body. Connor just lay still, curled up in the foetal position he stared at the floor and wall joint and just studied what he saw in minute detail. His field of vision was monopolised. His reluctance to move and the nausea that movement caused meant that Connor just stared on, so his eyes sought distraction and started to create patterns in the discoloured wood. A dog and an elf hid along with a crocodile and floating iron, which would slide out of focus with each prolonged blink. The boredom and pain fought with each other for dominance. The static position would, over time, create pressure points that grew in intensity until Connor ceded to their insistence and moved the offending arm or leg, which in turn reset the clock for another part of his body to start complaining.

Connor listened to the wind as it played around the building. His water bottle was at his side, and he struggled to bring his arms out of their cocoon. He picked up the bottle and drank the remainder of the chilled liquid. His throat cooled and his thirst momentarily abated. He just dropped the bottle as the cold water hit his stomach. The chilled water sucked the heat from his body, and the blood at his periphery rushed to his core to deal with the hostile invasion. He realised the error of his ways too late. He felt the onset of excessive salivation and the cramping deep in his bowel. He knew what was coming and struggled to release himself from the python-like grip of the clinging, damp sleeping bag. His whole body complained against the forced moves, and his head throbbed from the tide that seemed to be crashing against the pain sensors, which had been ripped raw by a cat o' nine and lay exposed. Connor fell through the rooms to the door of the bothy, using the walls and doorframes as both support and guides, his legs and eyes failing to fulfil their usual roles. Assisted by the wind, he clicked the latch the door, which flew open. Stumbling out onto a brightly lit weather porch, he promptly ejected the cold water from his stomach. With every retch, his head throbbed all the more, causing a vicious cycle. The convulsions brought up less and less, until Connor was just dry. Lights danced in his eyes, and the flush of perspiration across his face chilled with a blast of wind. He stumbled back into the bothy and leaned against the inside of the closed door. He shook involuntarily, crossed to the stair-come-ladder, and rested against it, trying to take stock of his condition and his position. The temptation to just collapse back into the sleeping bag was huge, just to stop the dizzying surges of painful pressure that were sloshing through his head like an overrun storm drain.

Forcing himself to concentrate, he returned to his sleeping bag and unzipped it fully to allow it to air before picking up his water bottle and filtering kit. He sank his feet into his cold boots, but could not face the trauma of tying the laces; he tucked them loosely inside the boot cuff. Steadying himself after being bent over, Connor returned to the door. He was buffeted again by the wind when he opened it. He picked up the shovel with the broken handle that stood propped against the wall and the metal bin he'd left on the porch step. The physical and mental efforts were huge and not helped by the distasteful task of burying his own turd.

Connor saw a small mound of pine needles in the lee of a tree trunk and scooped a shovelful into the bucket in an attempt to disguise the contents. Walking back towards the stream he had used the day earlier, he scanned left and right for a suitable place to empty his bucket. Having decided that no place was perfect, he chose a spot a few metres off the path and set about scraping a deep enough hole. It took an inordinate amount of time to produce a hole, which he felt should have been at least twice as deep, but the strata of rock he had struck had set the depth. Connor emptied the bucket and inadvertently produced a nest effect in the scrape hole. Keen to be away, he back-filled the hole and, getting up from his labours, felt the ill effects of his exertions. On his face was a sheen of perspiration, and his torso, damp with sweat, was hypersensitive to any pressure, even the weight of his jacket. A hundred metres or so farther on, Connor reached the small stream that cut across the path. From the downhill side, he shovelled a bladeful of stones into the bucket and quarter-filled it with water, which he then swirled around, the scouring effect cleaning out the bucket. He carried it back down the path and emptied. Returning to the stream, he sat on the upturned bucket, using his jacket as a cushion. With a small bar of soap, he set about washing himself—head, face, and hands first which he quickly dried with a small flannel travel towel before moving on to his torso. He cleaned himself as best as he could in sections—chest and shoulders, abdomen and back. He dried off as quickly as he could. The wind bit deep the exposed wet flesh. The effort was tremendous, but at least the cold and freshness were exhilaratingly distracting. Connor left his T-shirt to soak under a rock in the stream down from where he sat and wrapped himself in the jacket before repeating the washing operation for his lower half. But for his boots, he sat naked from the waist down as he went about the rest of his ablutions. Even though he was nauseated and in pain, he could not help but picture himself like some leprechaun with his pot of gold hiding in the mountains. He wondered what any wandering souls would think if they walked around the bend in the path only to be confronted by a half-naked man sitting on a wastepaper bin with half a broken shovel and a pile of wet clothes.

Connor washed his hands once more. The soap lathered excessively, even though it was an environmentally safe brand and not known for its lathering quality. The soft water of the burn helped his little bar to outdo itself. The slight perfume was organic and buttery, which was as welcome as it was repugnant to Connor. Reminiscent of lilies on the turn, the heady perfume clashed with the tinge of decay. To him, the scent played havoc with his senses; the buttery scent threw memories of food into his mind, and this visualisation made his stomach lurch in anticipation of another imminent expulsion. At least his stale, malodorous sweat had been washed away.

Connor took a moment just to sit and concentrate on his breathing, and to bring himself into balance before struggling with the exertions of completing his redressing. Coming to a stand, he removed the water bottle from his pocket and faced upstream. Pushing off of his own thigh, he propelled himself over the initial steep incline to a small plateau. He climbed on for a few more metres before going through the bottle-filling procedure. Connor took a cautious sip and rinsed his mouth of the acidic residue of his earlier expulsion. He took another mouthful and held it momentarily, allowing it to warm before swallowing. He waited, half expecting a recurrence of his earlier episode, but the moment passed without event. He took some more water to quench his thirst before filling the bottle once more. Connor slipped back down the stream to his temporary bathroom, where he collected his clothes, shovel, and bin before returning to the bothy.

The wind had eased and the cloud cover was breaking, allowing laser shafts of sunlight to pierce the mountainside. The solar searchlights scanned the surrounding countryside, picking out the relief-coloured palette; the hues that made up the predominant colour were given their few minutes of fame as they shone lost into space. The bright light bleached out the bothy's golden browns into a yellowed white, and the heat of the rays warmed Connor's shoulders as he reached the porch. He put down the bin and propped the broken shovel against the wall before opening the door and entering the bothy. The scent of the resinous wood assailed his senses; the aromatic wood had maintained its powerful aroma after many years and seasons. Connor set about hanging his damp clothing up around the room using whatever hook he could find. The various clothing items bedecking the walls and ledges created something of a festive air, not that Connor was of a mind to appreciate it.

Connor looked to his sleeping bag and yearned just to lie down and curl into a sleeping ball, but he knew also that he had to eat something to give himself the energy to fight this infection. He set about finding his stove and starting his kettle to boil. Then he rooted amongst the various plastic bags that held a variety of foodstuffs. As he read and considered the contents of the bags, he couldn't help but visualise the cooked product and felt the bilious juices rising in his throat, causing him to stop and look away until he had cleared his mind and could continue. There were beads of sweat once again on his brow when finally Connor found his two packets of paracetamol-laced flu remedy. The directions were written alongside the written promise that the restorative was a panacea. Keen as he was to accept the snake oil–salesman charm, he knew that liquids and rest were the best course of medicine, and he had to resign himself to them.

The small aluminium kettle was coming to a boil. He emptied the sachets of powder into the insulated cup along with three sachets of the cafeteria sugar. The steam curled up from the cup and filled the room with a sweet, lemony fragrance. He turned out the flame on the stove and arranged the bottle of water and blister pack of pain-relief drugs to be close at hand. He got back into the sleeping back and sat with his back against the wall, cradling the drink, from which he took tentative sips. Each small mouthful caused a salivation frenzy that Connor felt was the precursor to another episode of vomiting. The effort of getting up again would be huge, so he sought an alternative and hurriedly emptied a plastic bag of its contents in case he could not control the muscular contractions. As the contractions subsided and his head grew clearer of the pulsating pain that each bout caused, he would force himself to drink some more—once again starting the cycle. As uncomfortable as the process was, Connor felt that soon the painkiller would kick in, speeded up by the hot liquid and sugar. The deep-set cold ache would start to subside and allow him to rest easily—in a peaceful sleep, he hoped.

Time lapsed, measured only by the cooling of the drink in the insulated mug. The sun crept further around the room, and the rays stole over the lower part of Connor's sleeping bag, heating his legs. He stared at the residue in the cup and took one last sip, recoiling at the violent sweetness. He threw the cup as his head throbbed massively from the sugar rush. A contraction spread from his stomach through his oesophagus to his throat. Connor sank down into his bag and instinctively adopted the foetal position. The pain started to ebb over time, and he dragged up the fold of the sleeping bag over his shoulders, but gave up on the zip as it refused to rise to the top. Though fuelled with the hot, sugared liquid, Connor's body still shivered in muscular spasms. The tension at the base of his neck caused his head to spin so that he closed his eyes, hoping to reach the sanctuary of sleep and escape from the vice he felt his head was in.

Chapter 45

THE SHIRE XXIII

Connor pulled hard to overcome the resistance of the lockup doors and then assisted them with their own weighted momentum to close against each other. Outside, the site was quiet and the neon lights were on again, sending out their orange halos. The engine ticked in the quiet. The floor was wet from the drips that rolled down the vehicle side and fell from the sills. Connor turned and rested with his back against the doors. He closed his eyes and just waited in the sanctuary of darkness. Slowly, his breathing came back to normal. He pushed himself up away from the doors and fumbled for the light switch, which flooded the confines with a brightness all the brighter because of the darkness that preceded it.

Connor opened the back of the van, the doors now wide open. The six boxes sat there, nonchalant, uncaring, and disinterested. The pain that these boxes had caused already to those who had given them up was unrecorded and immeasurable compared to the pain they could cause Connor. A wash of fear flushed through his mind at the implications of being discovered and caught, almost to the point that he expected to hear the squeal of brakes and a megaphonic voice telling him that the building was surrounded. Once more he closed his eyes and regained his breathing and composure. Back in self-control, Connor focused on the task at hand. The boxes still sat there, displaying his guilt like Jacob Marley's chains. He brushed past his own growing melancholia and took up two of the boxes. At the back of the lockup, he placed each box on a set of scales and, as he weighed each box, he arranged them so they ran left to right, lightest to heaviest. With the order arranged, he took the lightest of the boxes and placed it on the workbench. He focused the beam of light to illuminate his subject matter fully. Connor carried out a thorough examination of the box, tapping and feeling his way around, scrutinising every indent hole and casting. His inspection complete and four areas marked with an indelible marker, he took up a battery-powered drill and, slowly and gently, started to drill through the plastic casing at one of the marked spots. Strings of plastic and shards of metal spun from the drill bit and deposited in a small heap at the drill end. Thirty seconds saw the bit penetrate the case. Connor stopped and removed the bit and swept away the deposits. He fed the end of a fibre optic camera into the hole. The device had been an expensive acquisition, but it was about to prove its worth. The view as it was tantalising— coloured bundles of plastic-wrapped paper brought a smile to Connor's face. He removed the camera and picked up a can with a small plastic hose attached. He started to shake it vigorously. After inserting the hose into the hole, he sprayed the contents into the case. A rush of off-white, aerated liquid rushed down the hose and vanished into the case. Connor sprayed for some ten seconds before the liquid started to emerge from the hole. He stopped and removed the hose; the liquid continued to expand out of the hole, a honeycombed mass of insect-like product that slowly settled and set. Connor waited a couple of minutes before repeating the procedure at the second, third, and finally the fourth marked spot on the case.

An hour later, Connor sat back and surveyed his work: All six boxes stood on the work bench, distended and swollen from the internal pressure of the expanding foam. The air was heavy with the petroleum-based plastic chemicals that now oozed from the cases in some form of grotesque sci-fi creation. Connor turned away from the bench and unwrapped some disposable overalls, which he put on along with latex gloves, a facemask, and goggles. Content that he was well protected, he took up a small hand grinder and switched it on. He fought against the gyrating effect of the spinning disc as he placed it against the security latches. The process gave off an acrid smoke, followed by a spray of bright sparks. Midway through, there was a small thud, and luminescent yellow liquid sprayed through the joint.

Another hour passed, and the end result was a smoke-laden atmosphere and Pollock-esque worktop sprayed with explosions of paint and shards of plastic and expanded foam. Connor took a small jemmy bar and worked at the latches to open and separate the two halves of the cases. The foam had formed to the shape of the insides, but slips of coloured paper showed through the castings. The foam had prevented the protective paint from polluting the contents, and Connor cut away the outer layers of foam with a sharpened knife. He hunched over his work like a knife-wielding amateur surgeon of the early nineteenth century with a freshly delivered corpse on the slab.

As Connor cut away a piece of foam to reveal the contents inside, his excitement grew against his better judgment. He tried to keep in check the mounting anticipation and deliberately slow down his pace to an archaeological speed of excavation. He extracted plastic- and paper-wrapped packages from the foam cases, and he could see past the crusting foam covering that, amongst receipts and counterfoils, there was the object of his long labour. Bundles of notes, sorted into their various denominations, formed a pile amongst the detritus of the exposing operation.

The clock spun on 'til all six of the cases had been dissected and their various treasures set free to leave a block of cash beyond Connor's expectation. His excitement over the size of his haul was tinged with what he knew would be a proportionate effort to repatriate the monies to its rightful owners. But he couldn't help but keep glancing at the pile as he sifted through the rubbish and off-cuts of foam, which he divided into paper or plastic bags as according to the makeup of the rubbish he was disposing of. Four large sacks saw the job done, and with the last of the paper sacks open beside him, Connor picked up the first of the bundles and examined the package carefully, dusting away any of the dried foam residue. He placed any with the protective paint on in the cross shredder and smiled as he thought of the cost of his particular brand of confetti. At the end of the exercise, he stripped out of the protective overalls and added them to the sacks, which he in turn rebagged into bright yellow plastic bags prominently marked BIOHAZARD. As he taped the bags shut, he looked at the fruits of his labour: a cube of money that, without counting, appeared to be at least twice what he had expected, perhaps even more. He broke the cube into smaller, book-size piles, which he wrapped heavily in plastic kitchen wrap before covering with the outer cover of a hardback book from which the pages had been removed, and then in a layer of gift wrapping before stowing them into a waiting rucksack. To the casual observer, the four blocks looked as Connor wanted: like gift-wrapped books ready to be delivered to their waiting bibliophile. He attached labels without adding any details as to the recipient—at least, no details that required explanation.

Having slept in the back of the van, Connor awoke the following day and set about the final stages of evidence removal. He connected the jet wash up, plugged it in, and started jetting off the water-based emulsion paint. Great swathes of the deep green gave way to the original base paint beneath. Soon, the van had been restored to its former state and well beyond recognition in connection to its most recent employ.

Having retrieved his car, Connor visited a local shopping mall and stocked up on a number of products, which he ticked off a list as he purchased them. Content with his purchases, he made his way back to the lockup. Approaching the lockup always caused a feeling of trepidation, a fear (be it rational or not) that the peace and quiet was about to erupt into the chaos of two-tones and blue flashing lights. This fear caused Connor to be somewhat skittish in his approach. He entered the wicket gate and, content that there had been no external interference, set about clearing out any reference to his criminal activities and inhabitancy. He spent a couple of hours working around the car, eradicating any identification he could find. He stowed the yellow biological waste bags, which he had lifted from the fire station over some months, in the boot of the car. He scrawled a brief and unsigned note to the lockup owner with some half-baked excuse, apologising for the inconvenience of leaving the van and equipment and offering him the opportunity to benefit however he may from their disposal. Sure, that money-grabbing mind-set would see to it that any residual evidence would soon disappear, and any contact to Connor would be impossible.

Connor pulled away from the lockup for the last time with little residual sentiment. The lockup had always represented a substantial risk, the one weak link in the chain. He was not saddened to see it diminish in his rear view mirror.

Before starting his journey north, he made a detour to the general hospital. He skirted around the perimeter road with one eye on the tall, silver-coloured chimney, taking any service road that seemed to head towards it. Connor eventually pulled up alongside a row of lidded wheelie bins. When he was sure that no one was about, he took the yellow bags from his boot and placed them amongst the many other biological waste bags that filled the bins. Even the most suspicious of minds would have to contemplate whether their curiosity was worth running the gauntlet that the apocryphal cat had, in case the outcomes were literally tied. The residual remnants now disposed of, Connor got into his car and started driving north.

Chapter 46

GIBRALTAR

Connor could feel the heat of the metal deck through the soles of his shoes. It was late in the day, and the transition through the port had been painless—other than the bone-crunching heat that bled him dry.

Connor had bought a ticket for the forty-minute crossing by rather rudely interjecting himself into a small party of German travellers, who had decided to cross at the same time of day. The ferry would be soon under way. The ferryman, seemed to disregard the timetable and had an eye to the tides, the horizon, and the promise of an evening of alcohol and associated pleasures on the non-Muslim side of the straits.

The crossing went smoothly. Connor leaned against the stern rail and watched the wake of the boat being stolen by the tidal flow through the bottlenecked strait separating the Mediterranean from the Atlantic. Soon, the ferry was slowing on its approach to the Gibraltar harbour, and the exhaust from the engine was being buffeted down onto the stern platform, causing Connor to move along the rail of the starboard side of the boat. It was still light, easily enough light to read by, but the port was already lit with pole-mounted floodlights. In typical British fashion, the reception was ordered and uniformed, and this little piece of Britain, as in all ex-pat communities, waved the flag high and proud

Connor filed through the passport control with slightly less scrutiny than those presenting passports from outside the UK.

Connor had no prepared excuse for travel from Morocco, so he tried to look as natural as possible. He was travelling and studying. He knew he could bore the official that showed any interest in him with a brief synopsis of his thesis. The fact that he was taking advantage of a window in his studying and the chance to experience a little bit of "Blighty" would be sufficient to appease the inquisitive nature of an ex-pat with a hankering for the shores of home. The weather of the Mediterranean was becoming less predictable, but it would be many a long day before the continental mainland inhabitant of Europe found the weather diverse enough to be an interesting topic of conversation. So grey skies and cups of tea were evocative and would always strike a resonant chord, even though the skies above were clear and cobalt blue, the air was laced with citrus and strong coffee and the surrounding conversations, which sounded both exotic and angry.

Connor slipped his passport back into his pocket and took in his surroundings. He had a long haul ahead of him; the route over the Pyrenées was his eventual goal. The day had been long, and the cooling air of the mountain passes was a blessed relief from the constant and penetrating heat of the past few weeks. To breathe the crisp, cool air scented with the verdant trees and snow-capped peaks would be bliss itself, compared to the canned heat and synthetic coolness of the omnipresent air-conditioning systems that hung like carbuncles from the sides of buildings. The units thrummed away in a physical depiction of being, in the scheme of global warming, a contributor greater than the sum of its parts. The rich grew cooler from its input while the poor suffered from its output, a true demarcation between the haves and the have-nots. The high tide mark stopped at some point before the air-conditioning units started. The risk to those without the luxury of cold air was quite real, and erosion of their living space was an ever present and growing threat as the tides and the rivers edged closer to their domains and life support systems, be they their crop fields or city support infrastructures. Long before the silken, fancy footwear of the rich were soiled by the effluent of the masses, they would have abandoned their abodes for the high grounds the second homes, the boltholes in the country, whilst the general population suffered the consequences of the consumer age. *Noah, where art thou? Would your dove return or find itself the amusing soupçon on the table of the rich and famous?*

The streets were starting to cool as Connor sought out a place for the night. His Spanish was poor, but fortunately the signs were multilingual in recognition of the diversity of travellers in this cosmopolitan gateway to Europe. He avoided the mainstream hotels and looked for the sort of accommodation that was not going to require him to surrender his passport or credit card. His approach had been to say that he had lost his wallet to thieving Moroccan pickpockets and that he had been forwarded cash by the British embassy in anticipation of a wired transfer, and that he would be able to collect emergency documentation replacement tomorrow. Connor had recognised those hoteliers who looked suspicious or circumspect early on and made his apologies and excuses so as not to burden them with his problem, for which they seemed grateful. He sought a cross between the grasping and the benevolent, someone who was willing to profit from his misfortune, but could also be the charitable Samaritan by offering him shelter and succour for the night. Connor cared not which he came upon first; both had their pluses and minuses. The grasper would overcharge, but not ask questions or want to know what happened; the Samaritan would be fair, but would want to pour over the details of how he managed to find himself in such a state. On reflection, the grasper sounded a more desirable host, so Connor searched on.

It was approaching nine o'clock when Connor found himself dumping his bag on the bed of a small back bedroom in a frayed-at-the-edges bed-and-breakfast that asked for cash in advance of accommodation. It was only a couple of degrees removed from being called seedy and didn't seem to care either way.

He turned on the bedside light and checked his watch. It was getting late, and he hadn't eaten. He had spied two or three likely restaurants close by, and as his grumbling stomach reminded him to take advantage of their proximity.

After a quick freshening up in the small en suite, Connor was once more out on the street and walking towards the glow of the veranda's restaurants that shone brightly in the dark streets and beneath the black night sky. Connor studied the menu posted on a stand outside the restaurant, which was sparsely populated, to be generous. Conscious that he was being eyed by the waiters within, whose attention was torn between the potential customer and the much more interesting football match on the television perched high above the bar at the back of the seating area. He decided that the football would be a welcome distraction that would allow him to dine quietly and, he hoped, pass through without being a more pressing memory than the success or failure of their chosen football team. Connor took a seat just off of the street.

The meal was basic. The service was just service, and Connor's tip was reasonable—not over-generous or miserly, so that the waiter would not remember him for either good or bad reasons. With some solid sustenance and a bottle of wine inside him, Connor was sated and roamed a little before turning for "home." He had taken account of the car hire outlet a few streets from where he was staying, and it was large enough to cope with one-way hire deals. Connor would be back in the morning.

The sun stole gently through the shutters and light curtains despite their combined efforts. Connor rolled over in his bed and felt the pressure shift across his shoulders to his back, and the coolness of the sheets was a welcome relief. He started to think about the day ahead. He figured he had two days of hard driving ahead of him and smiled to himself about the mini adventure that would end—or, indeed, start—on the edge of the English Channel.

Breakfast was on offer in the small room at the front of the house, through which Connor had to cross to exit onto the street. Showered and as together as he could be, he cast a glance at the table offering: a variety of uninspiring breakfast cereals and dried rolls and a small selection of sliced meats that looked positively dangerous as well as uninviting.

Connor took his leave and emerged onto the street with his backpack slung over one shoulder. The sun was crawling up into the sky and casting sundial shadows across the whitewashed streets. He walked down the street past the restaurant from the night before, which was all locked up and dark, marginally less inviting than it had been the night before.

The car hire shop was closed. Connor dropped his backpack against the shop window and sat on the low wall that ran opposite the darkened shop. The sign indicated that the shop should be open, but the door was definitely locked shut, and the interior was desolate as a car hire shop could be. A few sad and dog-eared posters showed blissfully happy families enjoying the thrill of convertible cars and open roads. There was a small table with a pile of insurance pitch pamphlets hemmed in by four sun-faded chairs. Checking his watch, Connor saw that it was twenty-five minutes past the opening time. A few people strode up the street and raised Connor's hope, only to dash that hope as they walked on by, watching Connor out of the corners of their eyes. Twenty minutes later, he spied a hopeful who turned out to be the key-holder. The man stopped at the door and opened up. He flicked away a cigarette as he opened the door and entered the office. Connor picked up his backpack and followed the man into the shadowed interior, much to the key-holder's surprise.

A flurry of paperwork and scribbled pen saw Connor emerge with the keys of an overpowered mid-range BMW. He went on a short walk with the car hire representative to a backstreet car park and, following a cursory talk, Connor signed the acceptance paperwork and dropped his backpack into the boot of the car.

With a curt wave, he pulled out of the car park and back onto the streets of the town.

Connor stopped at a small store selling a variety of products and, in true European fashion, an open-style fridge hummed and rattled outside. The cool insides contained a myriad of luridly coloured drinks. Entering the store, he breathed the mixed air of plastic wrapping and peppered, spiced meats that hung in the window, chilled by an over-loud air-conditioning system that, at this time of day, blew around unwelcome, chilled air. Connor picked up two plastic-wrapped six-packs of water. The weight of the large bottles tested the tensile strength of the binding wrapping. After picking up a few bananas, some oranges, cheese, bread rolls, a large bag of what Connor hoped was crisps, and a variety of chocolate bars, Connor paid the matriarch of the family business. He took two trips to carry his purchases to his car. Once the purchases were sitting in the footwell, he gunned the engine and set out on his journey north.

The sun was still low in the sky, and as Connor drove through the maze of streets to the start of the autopista, his car dipped through the shadows cast by the roadside buildings like a dolphin dipping through the bow wave of a fast moving boat. Connor put on his sunglasses, but quickly removed them, as they made the strobing effect worse; the rapid pupil dilation was causing Connor to slow down more than he cared to, especially given the long journey that lay ahead. Once he had left British-controlled Gibraltar, the road opened a little, and he pushed the accelerator a little harder. The car responded with ease. Soon Connor was barrelling along the A376 "Autovía del Mediterráneo," spurning the A377 for the prettier coastal road. Sure, time was important, but as the hackneyed phrase went, it was not the destination, but the journey that was important. There was enough aesthetic appreciation in Connor to warrant the extra time it would take.

The road rose and dipped to and from the coastline, hairpin bends interspersed with sweeping straight sections of road that ran protected from the azure sea, sometimes only just by the mass of mountain that supported it. Poseidon received his occasional offering, and another roadside shrine was erected in memory of the reckless, the barrier repaired and the skid marks erased. The views were beguiling and probably complicit in the tragedies the road experienced—perhaps a silent siren, enticing the hapless traveller to pull off the road permanently. Multi-coloured swathes of blue, turquoise, and indigo mixed and danced along the coast, occasionally exploding into the white froth of fresh foam sought by advertising agencies the world over to demonstrate the cleaning brilliance of their respective products. The sun cut the airborne spray and refracted its invisible beam into its constituent parts whilst shovelling heaps of splintered diamonds across the rippling, seething mass of sea that bleached out towards the horizon.

It was a beautiful route, and Connor sped along in search of more, a panoramic junkie chasing his next hit. Every now and then the hit would come interspersed with the withdrawal symptom, the mundane, the banal vistas that the authorities had allowed to grow in between the visual highs. Run-down conurbations linked by pragmatically designed industrial processing plants, all chimneys and silos. But as the authorities wrested back the control, recognising the value of the coastline, they sold out to the developers, who in turn produced the white, windowed boxes described as stunning, luxurious, and prestigious so that sun-seeking tourists could hang their towels over the balcony for a couple of weeks.

The Costa del Sol was synonymous with crime culture, or it had been. Recent extraditions had put paid to the absconding criminal, large or small, and probably accounted for some of the more flamboyant properties that were on the real estate agents' books. But there was still more than enough money in the area for it to maintain its attraction to the *nouveau riche*, who dripped jewellery and for all their wealth lived a lifestyle that would rely on medical intervention, private of course, to keep them on the mortal coil. They fell broadly into two sets: the careless, who indulged in all the vices that money could throw at them, and the vain, who pursued every avenue to "enhance" their public Dorian Gray, as long as it didn't involve perspiration and would be in vogue only long enough not to get bored by the regime. The super set with their dedication to Helios, Sola, Ra, the wheeled chariot they worshipped as it crossed the sky and daubed the brethren's skin a hue they wore as a show of wealth.

Fuengirola, Puerto Banus, passed by as Malaga drew ever closer, and the views over the harbours and ports ceded their moorings of the salt-encrusted bleached paint fishing boats to the super-sleek chromed and leather opulence of the multi-engine-powered boats. All the optional extras, mini floating palaces, the jetsam from burgeoning bank accounts and tax write-offs, crewed by the prettiest people money could, and definitely did, buy. Cut free of the showy streets of the Malaganese town where the roads were choked with the improbably rich driving the impractically cumbersome, in which driving mirrors were rarely used for that purpose, Connor eventually reached the A45 national route and pushed the accelerator hard. He had over a thousand kilometres ahead of him.

The kilometres tripped over on the speedometer. For Connor, used to the Imperial mile, the numbers seemed unusually large, but for balance they reduced rapidly and time was the only constant across the two systems. The sun crawled towards, through, and past its zenith. Connor shifted the sun visor around to the side window. His arm rested on the edge of the wound-down window and was in its own neutral temperature zone created by the warming sun and cooling breeze. The passenger footwell and seat were littered with on-the-move snacking, discarded wrappers, browning apple cores, and banana skins—consumption to satisfy boredom more than hunger. He was a one-man epitome of society, a waste-producing, fossil fuel–using, self-serving consumer, moving from A to B in order to deprive others and benefit himself. *Fuck it,* Connor thought. He had tried to inform those around him about the catastrophic effects their actions were having on the environment and how this would lead to the breakdown of society and the degradation of humanity. He had suffered the jibes and the taunts, knowing that people couldn't make the link of turning off "this one light" or "that tap" and the demise of the world's land masses and the migration of the environmental immigrant. He knew that, when push came to shove, it would be every man for himself. Connor felt that today's society was not as noble to acknowledge the women and children protocols of a bygone age. So, yes, he was being selfish. He had given, he'd donated financially and physically to many causes, he'd done his bit and paid his dues. Most of all, he'd done more than most. He had saved lives— not many, but when people had gotten themselves into the predicaments that life sometimes threw up, Connor had been there, in the heat and smoke, on the dark, rain-swept roadside, and most of all in their lost and confused state when he held out the hand that could guide them back to safety. Now, though, he felt things had moved on. He had become convinced that Darwin was right, that the species would continue through the fittest, but that fitness should be interpreted much more holistically than just mind and body, but in perception as well. The ability to know that changes were coming and to be best prepared to meet them, what the government of the day called contingency planning. History showed that this foresight was often mocked and, at worst, ridiculed as excessive or scaremongering. The reflective would say that apathy was an easy path to one's already known end. Noah built his ark and the Pharaoh took guidance from the brightly adorned Joseph. The Thames barrier and flood defences, the stock piling of EEC foodstuffs, the mountains of grain and lakes of wine were the biblical parables in modernity.

Connor shrugged off his guilt. He knew he was on no invite list for when the balloon went up; he knew he would be among the masses time shot back into the dark ages of existence. He realised that on his treadmill, life would never allow him to shake off the shackles that tied him down. He was prepared to swim, but not wearing the irons cast by others. So like many before   and he was sure many of the present would follow— he would create his fortune, initially through crime. Not the crime of tyranny, oppression, and exploitation. Not the crime of personal deprivation, but the crime that society exposed itself to and thrives on every day: pressure. The need to move something from one place to another without having sufficient means or resources. It manifested itself through time, ability, competence (and not necessarily the lack of), as those with ample amounts of these attributes relied on others to implement them. The smaller the cog, the faster it spun. So in pursuit of squeezing out the last possible bit of productivity, the system forgot that the process was worked somewhere by someone under pressure. All Connor had to do was exploit that pinch point, make these "small cogs" choose the option they believed was the best for the corporate good. Of course, it would be argued that they most probably operated outside of the protocols and that page 79 of the standard practises (volume one) clearly stated . . . . But that would just exemplify the point. The processes were fine if learned and followed, but the one vital point so often overlooked was the human element. The work-a-day employee was not an automaton who followed religiously the script to the letter. Everybody liked to freewheel a little and take control of their own destiny; the individual's capacity to do this allowed organisations to flow more easily and work around the little glitches that existed in every system. Indeed, this type of practice was encouraged in the design stage to highlight these areas and address them accordingly. Over time, however, the little "efficiency changes" that crept in were not holistic, and although they flattened one wrinkle they often rucked up the carpet of process elsewhere. Add to this a management mentality that just wanted results, where output and productivity were king, and the hierarchy from that point down would deliver in the most pragmatic way possible. All would be fine and dandy until something went wrong. Then, the finger of blame would be pointed and the scapegoat sought, saddled, and sent into the desert of the unemployed. Of course, there would be an internal review and recommendations made and, in part, adopted. But organisations were fluid and had scant time to ensure that all the holes were adequately stoppered. So, once again, the employees—whether happy with their lot and conscientious in their approach or malevolent and miserable, resenting the organisation profiting from the sweat of their brow—would be responsible for making it happen. Connor recognised that this was the way in, the chain with the built-in weak links. All he had to do was stress that link sufficiently. Every day, industry and business witnessed the links breaking; whether it came to public notice was a matter of scale and importance or the efforts of undercover reporters. There were a myriad of health and safety failures filed each day, and newspapers claxoned the ineptitude of those who should know better, demonstrating their ability to have done. The queen suffering night time visits to her very bed chamber other than by those she would expect, governments losing data and suffering security breaches of the highest order, nuclear power station failures, bow doors not being shut, aircraft flying too close to each other, space vehicles being programmed with differing SI units—the list goes on, but as sure as eggs the common denominator would be an employee somewhere making a decision that as either time-pressured or an inherited practice that didn't account for the confluence of unusual factors. All Connor had to do was create those conditions and apply a little pressure. He would, of course, play the role of subordinate and give due deference to the person on the spot, pander to his ego—letting him make the decision, letting him stay in control and weigh up the options, letting his vainglory drive him into showing this pissant deliveryman that he was important enough to make the call. In doing so accept the forced card, pride riding the horse as it hurtled towards the mother of all fences.

But for the moment, at least the enormity of the fence looked sufficiently diminished by distance.

The motorways had blurred into a mass of letters and numbers: A92, E902, A1, E5. Madrid was a distant feature that he had skirted round and was now approaching. Yet another toll road control with Bilbao being the next major city to be ticked off before the French border. The temperature had dropped, most likely due to the time of the day, but Connor couldn't help but think it was due to the northerly latitude. Connor had rolled the window up and felt his face tingle as it warmed now, draft-free. Cars passing on the southbound carriageway had their lights on and a sheen of rain around their windscreens. The temperature gauge showed a drop in the outside temperature, and before long the first raindrops started to fall. Connor smiled and tried to recall the last time he had seen rain. It had been back in England and seemed a whole lifetime ago.

Beyond the tollbooth, Connor pulled onto a garage forecourt and refuelled he car. He used the toilets and, on his way back to the car, stopped to let the rain fall gently on him. It wasn't cold; there was a breeze that earlier would have been laden with the dry dust of the parched land, but now it was heady with the scent of fresh rain, an organic aroma, a wholesome petrichor. People passed Connor and eyed him suspiciously, wondering why this man was just standing with his hands on his hips and his face to the sky, but the world was full of craziness and nobody had the time or inclination to stare too long, much less enquire. Connor returned to his car and opened the boot. He pulled out a pack towel from amongst his stuff and dried his face and arms before getting back in the car and returning to the flow of the red tailed traffic.

The road rose to meet the ever darkening night, the coloured stripe of indigo that washed out as it seeped down the paper sky until it met the blanched rock of the Pyrenées, which stood like a hammered mouth of busted teeth. A bar code of shadows cast by the setting sun sucked the bloody red out of the low-slung light. Connor's car powered along the metalled ribbon, which wound its way amongst the rocky outcrops like discarded silken finery on an unmade bed.

Each mile brought him closer to his crime; every minute ticked, every turn of the rubber-shod wheel propelled him to his carefully laid plan and, he hoped, the freedom beyond. Connor wondered where he was as a person, analysing the path and predicament that had led him to this juncture in his life. He was on the cusp of a commitment that would simultaneously shake him free from the burden of debt and work whilst pitching headlong beyond the pale, thrown by his own moral guardians from the sanctuary of safety into the badlands. The torment of his upbringing wrestled with his conscience. "Thou shalt not steal." The Catholic guilt streak was ploughed deep and indelible to the justifications brought to test the biblical standpoint. Everybody knew that behind every great fortune was a great crime, and it was the fading memory of time that made cutthroat murderers of the past the eccentric nobility of today. Every acre of prime real estate had a tale to tell—how it was grabbed from some subsistence farmer by a bullish, sword-wielding knight of yore, pitching the unfortunate family onto the common land, where their pleas went unheard by the local magistrate—especially when the local magistrate also wielded a sword of his own, to his own end. It's a rare fortune that has been made through sheer endeavour, hard work, and good fortune. Even now, lands were grabbed and assets lost, if not to the gun-toting militia, then to the pen pushers and bean counters. Connor smiled at the thought of similarities between the then and now and how civilisation now was not far removed. It invariably ended with the heavies banging at the door and leaving the helpless owners either watching as their goods and chattels were carted off or being chaperoned to the local police station to face charges, bailed to return and face the ignominy of being listed un-creditworthy. The creditors had most likely had their pound of flesh, surgically cut indeed, avoiding any trace of fat having employed the very best of surgeons. Once sated, they had decided to return the remainder of the meal unfit to eat and ask compensation for it. It was a poor justification, Connor knew, but he would take solace wherever he could find it or invent it. He had worked hard to create the opening he was about to exploit, having identified the situation and studied the potential of success—and, most importantly, given life a fair crack of the whip to reward him for his labours. He knew he could bow to the societal norm, keep his head down, and shuffle along to the inevitable end, but something in him burned, burned hot. He could not identify what it was, but he could feel its heat. Connor felt he would be famous. Something deep down waited to come to the fore and shine bright. He had flirted with the limelight of the public glare, having been interviewed on national television for his role in a public interest story, but that was not how it was going to be. Not for him, the tail-end Charlie slot on the ten o'clock news. No, he would be further up the schedule than that.

The heat in the car, the lateness of the hour, and the time behind the wheel were all taking their toll, and Connor was looking for a place to pull over.

The engine pinked as it cooled, and the night darkened around Connor's car. The boot light shone bright on the virtually empty space, from which he removed two microfibre fleece blankets. Gone were the days of tartan and tassels. Looking up into the night sky, already strewn with pinpricks of light like sackcloth dusted with icing sugar, he urinated into the roadside vegetation. The drips from the evening rain dropped randomly onto him from the overhanging branches, which framed his view of the heavens. Connor washed his hands using the bottled water and a small bottle of liquid soap lifted from his hotel. After shaking his hands dry, he climbed into the passenger side of the car and adjusted the seat to the horizontal before arranging the blankets to cover himself as best as possible. The inside of the car was still warm from the exertions and heat of the day, but the skies were clearing and Connor had no doubt the night temperature would soon drop. He hoped he would be beyond its discomforting chill. A few twists and turns saw him as comfortable as his surroundings would allow. He relaxed, letting the lazy waves of sleep ebb and flow through him, the gentle pull lowering his weighted eyelids to a twitching close. He took in a deep and contented breath, and his last memory was of the lavender perfume from his hands, which clutched the blanket under his chin.

Chapter 47

SCOTLAND XIII

Connor awoke suddenly. The room was in darkness, and he struggled for his bearings and release from the twisted sleeping bag. A noise. The last residue of sleep scuttled away like cockroaches from the disturbing light. A flush of adrenalin was countered by the leaden-limbed, head-spinning effects of his illness. Connor fumbled for his torch as the sound of stomping feet on the porch reverberated through the building and the enclosing night, amplifying the sound beyond the numbers making them. He twisted the ferrule, and the light shone out and lit the room, causing the stomping to stop and an uneasy quiet to follow. Connor scouted around the room 'til his eye rested on the rucksack propped against the far wall. He cursed himself under his breath.

Connor heard the latch on the door to the bothy click, and shod feet entered along with what sounded like a suppressed giggle—along with a similarly suppressed rebuke aimed at the giggler. Connor stared at the door, the ever-decreasing circles of light centred brightly on the cold japanned black latch. An avalanche of thoughts and fears crashed through his mind. Who was on the other side of the door? He was exposed, vulnerable, and weak from whatever illness was coursing through his body, let alone the threat that came from outside. He had seen the evidence in previous bothies of drug usage, various cooking-up and delivery paraphernalia he had swept into the fireplaces before laying out his kit. The ubiquitous half-pint vodka bottles were carelessly discarded in and around these mountainside havens. The thought of some drug- or alcohol-fuelled yob starting trouble was, in his present condition, the very last thing he needed. The tension mounted the longer the silence continued. Connor strained to hear, his ears almost moving at the slightest creak or shuffle. His mind raced at the thought of a group of drug users skulking over the countryside to the sanctuary, out of the reach of the police and the prying public, their appetite increasing the closer they got to their eventual drug Shangri-La—only now to be frustrated by an interloper, their hit being taken from them.

"Hello there?" called a voice from beyond the closed dark door, a male voice.

"Hello," Connor replied, his voice cracking from prolonged disuse.

"We're sorry to waken you. We got caught out by the weather. We'll be away upstairs. Is there anyone else here?"

Connor cleared his throat and thought rapidly. The voice sounded friendly, polite, and educated.

"No. It's only us." He emphasised the "us." The door to his room was still shut, so there was no way his visitors could tell how many were bunking down in the room. Likewise, Connor could only guess at the number who had just arrived.

"Right, sorry again. Good night."

"Good night."

Connor flopped back into the sleeping bag and listened. He could hear more whispered conversation, then the sound of footsteps ascending the stairs. The timber floor squeaked under the visitors' footfall, and from what Connor could deduce, there were two people. He listened as they dropped bags and shuffled around, the metallic ring of cooking equipment being set up and the nylon *swish* of sleeping bags being pulled from compression stuff sacks and jackets being taken off and shaken. All the time the visitors chatted, sotto voce. Connor listened intently, having turned off his light to concentrate his hearing and his mind. There were definitely two voices, judging from the flow of the conversation. The voice of the man he had spoken to and of the other person a woman, he guessed from the pitch and softer tones—sounded Scottish. Connor relaxed a little more and lay still, just thinking and listening as the pair moved around above. He turned on his light once more and struggled to sit up in his sleeping bag. He shone the torch around the room, the beam illuminating the various bits of kit garish and discarded like underwear on a first date. He crawled out of the bag; the chilled air rushed in to fill the compressed body shape Connor had left behind.

Connor reached into his rucksack and felt through the pockets until his hand felt the spare pack of laces he had stowed out of habit, ever since he'd had a pair that kept snapping on a walk many years ago. Now, though, he just carried the spare laces, the paradox being that he had kept his in good order, so the chances of needing the spares was minimal—but once bitten . . . . He flicked one of the laces from its paper sheaf and stretched it out before tying a slipknot over the latch on the door. Content that it was secure, he sought the security mesh from a side pocket, wrapped it around the rucksack, and secured it with the padlock.

The cold air carried the vapour trail from Connor's breath, and the light from his torch cast shadows and flashed the light awkwardly around the room. He picked up his coat, wrapped it around his shoulders, and proceeded to set up the stove. The smell of gas, eggy and pungent, reached his nose briefly before he struck a flame on the lighter, and the hiss of the gas changed to a puttering purr and an indigo flame danced around the gas ring. The light from the flame threw larger-than-life shadows around the room, up the walls, and across the ceiling. The heat was welcome and eased some of the tension that had stolen into his neck and shoulders. The kettle squashed the flame so that just the tips of yellow stole round the base and smutted the sides of the aluminium pot. Soon, little gusts of steam rattled the lid of the kettle and added to the vapour-laden air. All the time, Connor was preparing his mug for the hot water, the silver diffuser loaded and waiting suspended from the side of the cup. The words of the recently arrived were playing on his mind. "Caught out by the weather." Connor walked over to the opaque window out of habit more than expectation; the night was pushed up hard against the outside. Connor placed the torch against the sheet plastic, and the light refracted through the dirty sheet. A small amount stole out into the night and, through the weak glow, a shadow fell and then vanished, then another followed suit until it was a continuous pattern. Connor stared hard at the shadow show until the realisation of what he was watching dawned on him. *How long has it been snowing,* he wondered? He looked instinctively to his watch, but it offered no point of reference. He returned to his sleeping bag and the kettle. Once he had poured the boiling water into the cup, he sat down with his back against the wall and threw the opened bag over his legs.

The tea was hot and aromatic; the heat from the liquid warmed his face as he sipped from the cup. The stove gave a gentle glow as Connor had adjusted the flame to its lowest setting. The first pang of hunger stirred, and he contemplated the last time he had eaten. The thought of eating and the return of an appetite could only be a good thing, demonstrating in some way the start of the recovery phase. Connor's mind turned to what food he had available. He still felt weak, and the thought of cooking anything proper was as appealing as it was not. The soiled pots and pans, as well as the drain on his water supply, were not an attractive proposition. He searched through his pockets of his jacket until his hands patted a dense lump, which turned out to be a plastic bag containing into a half-eaten chocolate bar. He peeled away some of the wrapper and took a small bite. Connor's mouth flooded with saliva and ached as he chewed the sugary morsel that melted around his teeth and tongue. After swallowing, he washed away the residue with the hot tea, feeling the chocolaty liquid descend through his oesophagus. He waited to see if there was any reaction. The chocolate and hot tea were an aggressive assault on a system that had been purged and had lain empty for as long as Connor's had, and they would not have been the recommended first convalescent meal. As such, the slight nausea was not unexpected, and his body reacted to the sugar rush with a flush of heat that brought a glow to his skin. As the feeling subsided, he took another bite from the bar, followed by a mouthful of tea from the cup, and continued in this fashion until the bar was gone and the cup drained. He turned off the stove and the room was once more enveloped in darkness. Connor wormed down into his sleeping bag, listening again to the shuffling and voices coming from beyond the ceiling. Connor fought the lethargy that was creeping over him until he was content that the pair above was also surrendering to the exertions of their day. Then he let go to enter into a blacker black.

The banging of a door and voices. Confusion tumbled around Connor's head as his eyes struggled to adjust to the brightness of the new morning light. Looking at his watch, he was surprised to see that the hour hand had crept on to ten o'clock. He lay still, listening. The couple with whom he had shared the bothy were now outside and setting themselves to leave, making the final adjustments to their clothing and their backpacks. They were talking to each other, but Connor could make no sense of the words. As he listened, they must have set off, as their voices grew fainter and then dropped off the edge of hearing. He lay there listening; the creak of the building's timbers was the only sound. The wind had dropped away during the night, and the fall of snow had deadened and insulated any noise to silence. As he lay still, he started to take stock of his physical condition. Gone were the dull ache and tension across his shoulders and neck, likewise the sensitivity of his skin—but mostly the nausea and swirling headache. He had slept well, obviously, not having woken as his "guests" had prepared to leave. He had a flash of guilt. Had the door slamming been a reaction to him not responding to their goodbyes? He wondered whether this was the case before casting aside the thought, taking solace from the fact that he had not engaged with the pair any more than he had. Rolling over, Connor felt a dull ache in his lower back and recognised simultaneously the need to relieve himself. Slowly, he set about preparing himself to venture outside, slipping on his coat, leggings, and now dry boots before retrieving his nearly empty water bottle, which he drained before untying the lace from the latch. It felt good to stand straight without feeling dizzy or requiring the support of the wall, and he breathed in deep the pine-scented, cool air. He noticed as his chest expanded how much his waist had shrunk. He had to adjust the leggings belt tighter to keep them from slipping down.

Connor opened the door to the bothy and squinted out into the glittering whiteness. The sun had breached the tops of the pines, which were laden heavy with snow. The rays of light bounced off of the surface and ricocheted, casting light on areas normally deep in shadow. Only under, where the boughs of the trees and bushes were thickest, had the snow not penetrated, but as compensation had drifted up against the trunks and rocks to greater depths. As Connor's eyes adjusted to the monochrome vista, he started to make out the footprints left by the couple and followed them away with his eyes, around the bend where he too would soon tread. There was no sign of their corresponding approaching footprints, but they could easily have been covered by the snow that fell following their arrival.

Connor stepped off the veranda. The snow came above the top of his boot, so he calculated that at least six or seven inches had fallen. Adjusting his stride, he stepped in the couple's snow prints and set off down the path.

He had always loved the snow—the innocence of its loveliness, the way in which, left to its own devices, it covered the ugly and enhanced the beautiful, turning a pig's ear into a silken purse. In a strange way, he loved the destruction and disruption it brought, how it converted the ordinary to the extraordinary. It was, after all, those who were unprepared that suffered most when science, the gods, or fate—depending whether a person trusted in Darwin, religion or not—had it in for them, so it was important for Connor to have his wits about him. It never failed to amaze him, the unpreparedness of people and how quick they were to try to offset their own stupidity. More often than not, they brought predicament onto others. Buying homes on flood plains might be financially unavoidable, but being surprised by the floods when they happened—why? It was like having a great view from a seaside chalk cliff, then being upset that the council was doing little to preserve the rapidly depreciating house value and shrinking lawn. Climbing into cars on January mornings and wondering why they found themselves later contemplating the effects of hypothermia, dressed in clothes suitable for the office and not a howling, snow-ripped gale. It was nevertheless a trait of the human condition, and Connor jokingly considered it the "suicide gene." It was, he believed, present in all. It was the compulsion to touch wet paint, to pour the water from the unblocked sink trap back into the sink before replacing the trap. It was that moment which, post-event, one can recall thinking about, but failed to act on in time to prevent calamity. It was akin to being advised or directed by someone not qualified or competent, but who can see the impending danger through unbiased and neutral eyes—and who thinks, justifiably, that you must know best. The tilting scaffold board across the roof joists, the bare foot and the upturned plug, which only come together after stubbing toes on door edges or bed legs—of course, you should have been wearing slippers. Life was dangerous enough without playing dare with the Grim Reaper's scythe. Connor's mind raced on before his thoughts were broken by the softest of sounds, running water. He dug down through the snow to reveal the running stream and, once he had done so, left his water bottle pushed into the snowbank before going off to relieve the cold-induced ache in his bladder. He resisted the almost primal urge not to piss straight and stared at the almost dark orange stain his urine left in the snow, feeling the pain in his lower back ebb with the emptying of his bladder. He resolved that he needed to take on more water. With this in mind, he filled his water bottle halfway and sipped the icy liquid as he surveyed the scene around him. The beauty was absolute. The whiteness was startlingly bright and caused him to squint involuntary when looking towards the sun. Each tiny, hexagonal crystallised snowflake burst with sunlight, a prism of colour that leaned towards the ultraviolet end of the spectrum and gave a sheen impossible to paint or capture. The deformation of shape, the blurring of edges, the creation of delicate statuary the night had brought in its black sack and spilled over the countryside before him. How the snow had built on the windward side of obstacles and grown back into the snow-laden wind, leaving a shadow on the leeward that would offer respite to the foraging animals that wandered amongst the new fall. All the time Connor was snatched back from just sitting and gazing as, from the corner of his eye, he would see movement, and his natural reaction was to turn and track the cascade of snow that tipped from its branch or ledge and vanished into the white carpet below.

Connor felt the chill of the water spreading through his stomach and decided to stop drinking for fear of inducing cramps, especially in his frail state. After filling his bottle to the brim, he walked back to the bothy, stepping again in the path of prints as he went. Back on the veranda, he kicked the snow out of the welts of his boots before crossing the threshold. Once inside and before he shut the door, he noticed two brown ovals on the small table on which the bothy book stood, which was now bathed in the light reflected from the snow. He approached the table and smiled at the present that had been left: two eggs, with the date of their delivery (today's date, Connor confirmed by checking his watch) written on the shell in pencil. It was a small thing but not uncommon; visitors to the huts would often leave surplus items in the hope that followers would find a use for them, and this was a find that Connor particularly welcomed. His appetite was returning, and he salivated at the thought of how to serve the eggs. He smiled also at the thought of the deliverers of this treat and the care they must have gone to in order to transport the delicate cargo across such a wild terrain. Even though he had seen the small individual protectors that could be bought to carry eggs safely, he had dismissed them as extra weight and an untested receptacle in his extreme environment. Nonetheless, eggs for breakfast were a rare and unexpected treat—boiled, poached, fried, maybe an omelette? Connor pondered the possibilities and also the potential accompaniments. His larder of dried foodstuffs was not extensive, but, even so, he relished the challenge. He had always prided himself on his cooking prowess, especially on a camping stove. The ability to prepare a meal of different elements and to serve them to the plate hot was an accomplishment. Serving a noteworthy and edible meal also offered a level of satisfaction to the chef. It brought a minimalist angle to cooking, as the post-prandial state of the dishes used in preparation must also be considered. It was akin to the hunter-gatherer instinct; there was no point in exerting effort to harvest foodstuffs that only returned the same amount of energy it took to gather and prepare. Likewise, it was okay to make a mess in the kitchen in making the meal if you had help on hand to clean it up. Connor remembered well the dinner parties he had attended that had been average in content and extraordinary in the havoc they had caused in the making, a factor that had led to many a conversation in the car on the way home.

He had made up his mind. His small stock of dried mushrooms and peppers were soaking in a cup of boiled water whilst he prepared the small, but neatly designed nonstick frying pan with a little of the precious amount of cooking oil that he had. He had decanted the kettle of boiling water into the thermos flask. He whisked the two eggs in a separate bowl with some powdered milk, a little dried egg, and some water. Then he brought the two elements together. The hot oil sizzled and spat as he added the now rehydrated peppers and mushrooms. Connor stirred them around gently in the pan before quelling their hissing with the addition of the eggs. He set about preparing the rest of his breakfast. The water grew dark in the cup as the tea leaves stewed in the steaming water, and he bobbed the infuser up and down as he sought to hasten the process. He sipped at the cup. The liquid tasted metallic again. He put this down to his bout of illness, not the makeup of the tea. Leaning back against the wall, Connor brought his knees up towards his chest and rested the cup atop them, the steam swirling up to the ceiling. He thought back to the stifling heat of the Gambia, the skull-crushing heat that could batter a person to his knees and suck the last millilitre of moisture from his body. Connor recalled the dry, spiced air of northern Morocco and how that gave way to the balmy, salt-laden breeze at the ferry port. Spain had been a myriad of assaults on the senses and had seen the first relief from the heat. Then, on the climb up through the Pyrenées, the cool mountain air had brushed with the icy blasts of the snow-encrusted hillsides. The descent into France had seen the thermometer start to rise. The heady aromas of grape decaying on the vine and sunflowers wilting in the afternoon sun had filled the car as Connor had passed by on arrow-straight roads.

The acrid smell of smoke brought Connor back to the bothy and the cooking of his breakfast. Awkwardly, he flipped the omelette over and felt his mouth salivate and his anticipation rise for the first genuine meal he'd had in some days. This forced starvation had had a dramatic effect on his appearance, and he was more than a little concerned by the protrusion of his hipbones, which before had been a rounded feature of his body. Now, the venous blue seemed to be showing clearer and darker through a translucent quality of skin that was feminine and far removed from his more familiar ruddy complexion, which had a healthy hue. Worst of all was the cold, which was sharp and penetrating and continually there. The layer of fat that had been part of Connor's far from corpulent body had been enough to insulate him from the ravishes of the cold.

Connor turned out the omelette onto his plate. The steam carried the aroma of peppers and mushrooms. He seasoned it well from the small packs salt and cracked pepper that were freely available from services up and down the motorways, and he had availed himself of this facility. The food was hot — that was the most that could be accurately said by way of description. The mushrooms and peppers added texture, but little in the way of flavour, and Connor could hardly taste the salt. This fact puzzled him, and he could only assume that he was deficient in the mineral and smiled to think that this might be the case, considering the health warnings about eating too much salt. Connor admitted to himself that the meal was greater in the pan than on the plate and had not lived up to his expectations. It was this thought though that made him smile when he considered the parody it held against his life, but at least he was making a reach for something better, daring himself to grab the nettle and hope that he would not be stung a thousand times over. Was it possible to shuffle through life cowed by the confines and weighed down with the responsibility of doing the "right thing"? The so-called right thing came as a dictate from someone to subjugate and oppress, dressed in the name of freedom and democracy. The wolf stalked in the pen. Of course, the grass might not be greener on the other side, but that didn't stop Connor from wondering what it would be like in the field across the way, and all the frying pan to fire analogies could not remove the curiosity of those who dared to look further and dream. It was the inertia that Newton identified and that civilisation embraced as being the constant force and state of matter, which required an unbalanced force to act on it and produce a change, a vector. If people were denied this force, they created a comfort zone they were reluctant to leave. The risk was never getting back what they left, so the majority stood still. But some were forced to move when the unbalanced force came. Either out of necessity or desperation, they treaded the path less trod and strove to lift themselves out of the mire to reach that greener field. The pigs and cattle left behind gorged themselves on the troughs of food, happy? Content? Who knew the opiate, in whatever form, that suited the government of the day to keep the masses hushed, Soma for the people. If they drove down the expectation by saying that success could be achieved by those prepared to work hard and risk all, few would. The mind control of populations, the constituent parts who would produce the gross national product, who would pay their tax pound and wage contributions to the gaoler in order to have a few extra luxuries and be looked after a little better. It did not matter whether they perceived their gaols to be open or high security, workhouse or treadmill, as long as their efforts in were slightly less than their wages out, they would continue. Not for Connor. The light had shone, and the dawning of realisation that he was running to stand still had come and made him feel that he had regained his sanity in the lunatic asylum. He had to hide that sanity, to demonstrate a conformity that allowed him to move within the confines without attracting the unwanted attention of the "thought police." He had become society's fifth columnist. He had identified that his cage was gilded and wanted to bend the bars, to escape and see what the cage looked like from without. The views of others were all very well, but a poor substitution for a view and opinion of his own.

Chapter 48

NORTHERN SPAIN

Connor started from the ice-cold water as he plunged in. His desperate jump across the floe had failed, and the creeping, icy water ran around his torso stole his breath.

Connor grasped with his surroundings, and the fading, momentarily very real Arctic sea that was pulling him down into a dark abyss against his efforts vanished to reveal the plastic fascia'd door panel. Connor tried to smile, but the icy water was too real, so he just lay still and luxuriated in the ability to breathe the cool air and waited for his pulse to slow. The light was oblique and dappled by the foliage, obscured by the condensation on the glass. Connor pulled the blanket tight around his shoulders. The lightweight material, though warm, lacked the density of traditional bedding, which gave the squeeze and tied one to the bed. Connor reached over and cranked the engine to life, leaving it to idle and reach its running temperature before turning on the blowers, which chased the opaque veil across the screen and revealed the multitudinous greens as they emerged from the low-lying mist that lurked in the hollows. A zephyr pushed the longer stalks away and set the leaves fluttering on the twigs above the car. Connor rolled down the window to allow the morning air to filter into the car. The sweet air, cool off the mountainside, was all the more sweet compared to the stale, confined air in the car. Connor breathed deep the cedar- and wet grass–laden air tinged with the exhaust of his car engine. He shut down the motor, and the thrum of the engine was replaced with the twitter of birds, the rustle of leaf on leaf, and the creak of boughs. He stretched and yawned, then propelled himself to sit up and adjusted the seat to suit. He opened the door, and the heat from the compartment drained out and twinged his bladder into making its presence and state known. While relieving himself into the hedgerow, he thought of the millions of people who were doing similar, not at the roadside necessarily, but in their various ablutions, and the billions of litres of water that were employed to propel the effluent away. Connor found the world's capacity to cope staggering.

Stretching tall, he turned to take in the view. He had climbed some way into the mountain range that separated the Spanish and French people, ranges that had provided refuge to many throughout man's history in the area. As such, there was a perceptible intrigue and mystery that lingered in the rocky surrounds, particularly in this early part of the day, as the shadows stretched towards the west and easily concealed the absconders of persecution and tyranny, much like they hid the persecutor and tyrant. Connor's neck clicked satisfyingly as he rotated his head around its axis and, although bathed in the glow of the sun, shivered involuntarily at the early morning cold. Climbing back into the car, his spine bent to the shape of the seat, and he knew that it would soon complain of its unmoving confine.

With a small squeal of rubber and scatter of stones, the car rejoined the empty road aiming up into the beckoning mountains and France beyond.

The road signage eventually stopped being multilingual and became wholly French within half an hour of crossing the border, a border that in itself was notional, there being no checkpoints or passport controls to check the movement of peoples between the two countries—or three or four, if one took into account the separatists who laid claim to their own dominions still as yet ignored and resisted by the parent country. The sun was bright and lit the road ahead, which played hide-and-seek as it dipped into and out of the shadows. The lower hills gave way to the grapevines that created optical tricks in the linear patterns they cast across the parched and dust crumbled earth. Pockets of early morning mist skulked into the hollows of the west-facing slopes in vain hope of survival.

Roadside buildings overgrown with verdant ivy and angel share bloom had yet to release their occupants onto the fields to watch the bulbous fruits grow. Soon they would be ready to start the intense harvest period, but for now the quiet before the storm prevailed. Baton bread, coffee, and cognac still had a firm hold amongst the early birds and ruddy-nosed farmers. The sun ducked in and out amongst the rolling hills and valleys that formed the rucked wedding train before the rising of the wedding dress, the mountainous range of the Pyrenées, before ceding to the flat expanses of the southwest sunflower and vine-laden, chalked soil. The sky promised a fine day, and the last of the mountains vanished from Connor's rearview mirrors. Another solid day of driving should have him breathing the tang of salted air.

The day ebbed. The *autres directions* skirted the car around the fortified hill towns and across the castellated protection that guarded the river crossings. Bordeaux beckoned, and the kilometres tripped over on the odometer. The sun was high, and Connor was hungry. The thought of stopping for food was not quite outweighing the need to progress, to rush on and maintain the momentum that would decide his fate his future. It was a craving to get things done not for the outcome alone, but also to see if his thinking was correct, if his hypothesis would withstand the scrutiny to which it would be exposed. Even failure would bring some succour in the scotching of the itch, the gnawing at the bone of the what if. He would know one way or another, and every turn of the wheel, every digital tick delivered him and the outcome together.

The upper tributary of the Garonne, the Gironde, accompanied the road and stole the eye when the banks gave way to allow its sparkling cascade to be seen. South of Bordeaux, it still ran with the Pyrenean waters, which cast the ice-chip prisms that shed myriad rainbows every which way. Connor's car rose and fell along the undulating bank of the river. The traffic had started to get busier as the day had gone on and was growing denser as it approached the city outskirts. The fields gave way to the whitewashed buildings that buffered the city from the surrounding countryside. In turn, there sprang up a mix of industrial and factory units—some traditionally built, others from the modern sandwich-panel construction, bolted and hung from a metal skeleton. Connor recalled that this construction had cost the lives of firefighters in the past and no doubt would in the future. It said more about a government's position with regard to profit over people, or at least in respect to acceptable loss, the collateral damage that greased the wheels of commerce and topped up the coffers of the treasury. He pondered the point. Who calculated the cost? Who decided the levels of acceptable loss or damage? What was the permissible level of destruction that allowed the ruling parties and classes to conduct themselves with seeming disregard for the small person? How many times had the press clamoured for a full inquiry into the latest tragic event that saw pain and suffering for those unfortunate enough to be caught up in the corner-cutting antics of some profit-driven individual, who, knowingly or not, had decided in Godlike fashion that people had to die? If life wasn't fair, then its end was often less so. The government and ministries of the time kowtow to the public outcry and pander to the press, leaking the right documents to skew the thinking at least until the clamour starts to recede. Then, ever so slowly, they closed up the doors and ushered out those it had permitted into its hallowed halls, those it had allowed amongst its underskirts, and now slapped hard the face of the adolescent zeal that had risen in the enquirer on his first serious date. There were other stories on the boil, other enquiries to investigate, but there were no promiscuity here, thank you. And so it would transpire: The fervent ardour expressed for truth was lost to the press. The clarion call had long since subsided and no longer held the front page—or barely any other page, for that matter and so mourning was left to the nearest and dearest to do less publicly. Support groups would be established, even charities registered to help the sufferers, and this would be seen as fitting tribute to the unfortunates who no longer deserved the minute of silence or the commemorative plaque to be polished or the weeds removed from the place of remembrance. If the millions of war dead could be marginalized in the educational curriculum, what chance did the local victims have? The health and safety executive was the government's way of offsetting its guilt for past and future losses.

Hunger pangs eventually convinced Connor to start looking for somewhere to eat. Upon entering Parthenay, as he made his way through the town a small cluster of eateries, he saw each bedecked with brave tablecloths and parasols, which were being tormented by the breeze.

Connor parked up alongside a small square, which had a dried-up fountain as its centrepiece. Around it was some municipal hoarding, demonstrating that the fountain was undergoing some repair or maintenance, but it was coming towards the end of the lunch period and, as such, the maintenance team was most probably on the digestive and third or fourth cigarette.

Connor got out of the car. His trousers were heavily creased from the static driving position and were a visual representation of how his joints were feeling. He stretched out and perused the restaurants that had passed the peak of activity and whose waiters were trying to look busy, straightening tables and chairs and polishing the empty ashtrays. His eye was attracted to a waitress with long, flowing chestnut hair that hung across her face as she collected the cruet set off of a table and collected the tablecloth in short folds. Connor made his way over, his stride increasing in length as his muscles loosened and the blood started to flow. A chalkboard displayed the specials of the day and the *plat du jour.* Connor translated as best he could, but he was not taken by what was offered.

"*Bonjour, monsieur. Comment ça va?*"

Connor looked up from the board, his concentration broken by the lyrical voice of the waitress who had approached him. She smiled at him, awaiting his response.

"Thank you. I am well. *Pardon, ça va bien, merci.*"

The woman smiled again, acknowledging his English and his respect of French. "Would you like a table?" she enquired.

"I was just looking at your menu. *Je regarde la carte.*"

"I am sorry, *monsieur*. The *plat du jour* is now off the menu. We are sold out. Please look . . . *à la carte?*" She proffered a small, bound menu like a professional, just out of his reach, causing him to step across the threshold. Once she had overcome his inertia, she maintained the momentum by turning to present a table set for two.

"Or maybe you would care to sit inside?" she said as she looked to the skies with a small creasing of her features, as though she had been poked on the bridge of her nose. Connor smiled at the waitress and at the way she had hooked him and was now just reeling him in. However, the need to eat aside, the angler herself was very attractive bait. Her traditional black and white ensemble was well fitted, and she had taken the care to keep it presentable and clean. Not in the pre-madonna way— her forearms bore the scars and burns from the kitchen and demonstrated a strength of will and character that added to her attractiveness. She was her own woman and was able to stand alone, self-sufficient. Connor had been cooped up for too long in the car and, although the wind brought a chill to the air, he opted for the table outside.

"Would you like a drink, *monsieur*?" The waitress stood with one hand resting on the table; the other picked off the surplus cutlery and flatware.

"A black coffee and a bottle of water, *sans se pressant, s'il vous plaît.*"

The waitress smiled and vanished into the restaurant, leaving Connor to take in his surroundings.

The buildings around the square were typical—three or four floors with steeply pitched roofs, separated by stubby walls built above the roof lines, which were finished with varying degrees of decoration. The roofs themselves were a combination of clay tiles fading through a swatch of colours, from the newer orangey reds to the more ancient pastels. These, in turn, were contrasted by the slate finish that shone from jet to silver, depending on the sun or shadow in which they were cast. Shoehorned in between was the occasional coppered roof that had a bright turquoise *vert-de-gris* that, in areas, had stained the masonry that it contacted. The combination made the whole square look as if it had been the epicentre of a roofing convention, used to demonstrate the various products and styles available. Below the roofline, the facades of the buildings were more uniform, the masons having less product to choose from. But this did not stop the Gallic flair from surfacing, and apart from some of the larger runs of adjoining buildings, the windows were set at varying heights and widths, their lintels and porticos embellished to differentiate them from each other. It was a wall scape for the eye to wander over, perfect for the lone diner. The southwest-facing windows were mostly shuttered, the fading and peeling boards insulating the room behind. The doorways off the street were almost foreboding, the square being largely non-commercial apart from the restaurants, the remainder given over to offices that did not have to advertise their respective wares other than on the brightly polished plaques affixed to the walls outside, as bold as their base metals allowed them to be.

The waitress reappeared carrying a tray and expertly transferred its load to the table. Lastly she broke the lid seal of the bottled water and poured half a glass before returning to the interior.

Connor plunged the coffee and poured a cup of the hot, steaming liquid into his cup. The aroma was nutty and rich, and the first sip was full, almost oily, and tasted only as coffee that is made from scratch can—great. Connor pondered the thought that he rarely, if at all, could recreate that truly satisfying taste in a store- or restaurant-bought coffee. Granted, there were the industrial coffeemakers of commercial kitchens, but even lesser establishments like the one in which he now found himself had created from base ingredients and widely available equipment a coffee that far out-tasted his own preparations. Of course, he had moved on from the instants to the ground coffee. He had even dabbled in grinding his own beans and keeping the coffee in the fridge, but, regardless, the end product rarely emulated the cup of "joe" served up by some gaudily uniformed, pale-faced kid at the local coffee store. It had to be the fact that it was paid for, that the service in combination with the charge levied in some way gave it an unseen quality that lifted it beyond the hand of the common practitioner, like an Irish-pulled stout beer. The fact that it was charged for was definitely a factor a coffee for free was definitely the last drop, oft quoted, that the rest was good up to.

Amidst the eels and snails that featured heavily on the menu, most likely aimed at the tourist as typically local fare, Connor picked the vegetable soup to be followed by a mushroom omelette. The waitress wrote down the order and offered Connor a copy of the local paper she had brought out with her. Connor thanked her and thumbed through the pages, marvelling at what the stories were about beyond the headline banners, which were written in true newspeak and cryptic at the best of times. The soup arrived, a gutsy stew, almost a chowder, that suited the clamour that was emanating from Connor's very empty stomach. He ate slowly to savour the dish and not to spoil the rest of his meal by becoming too bloated. The square slowly came to life as the occupants returned from their extended breaks, and even the fountain maintenance team returned to talk and point animatedly before shrugging in true Gallic style, striking another light to their cigarettes, and turning to watch the world go by.

Connor had an urge to order some wine, but many years of attending road accidents had kept drink and driving firmly separated. However, there would be little opportunity after he reached the channel. This could be his last chance for many years if things went very wrong. At least it could be a happy memory to tide him over through the inevitable hard days ahead.

"Is everything okay, *monsieur?*"

Connor returned from his mental wanderings and looked to see the waitress smiling at him with a slightly quizzical look about her face, her lips twitching to smile. But something made him doubt the smile was appropriate.

"Yes, yes, *très bien,* I was miles away." He realised that he was deep in thought about his future and his own face must have prompted the inquiry "I was contemplating whether to have some wine to complement the food . . ."

"Indeed, *monsieur,* a meal without wine is only half an affair."

It was an unusual comment and Connor accepted it with a tilt of his head and small smile. "Unfortunately, I am driving and, like affairs, the temptation is great at the time, but the risk is equally great and occasionally fatal." He wondered whether she would understand his response, but was pleased to have drawn the metaphor so quickly and succinctly. There was a pleasing roundness to the conversational interplay.

"It is true, *monsieur,* but a little danger ensures that you are alive, *n'est-ce pas?* It is only a glass or two of wine. What is your hurry? Enjoy your meal, *une petite liaison dangereuse!"*

Connor ceded the point. "Maybe a demi carafe. What would you suggest?"

"*Bon,* we have a very good white that would suit your meal, unless you prefer a red. Maybe un rosé?"

Connor now craved a glass of wine. He ordered the white and waited with surprisingly eager anticipation. His anticipation was quickly sated when the waitress returned with a long-stemmed glass and small carafe, from which she filled the glass. Connor lifted the glass and inhaled the faint aroma and was rewarded with the fresh scent of newly mown grass. The wine was ice-cold and cut through to his palate, bursting with lemony citrus before warming and leaving a slight honeyed undertone as he swallowed. Connor nodded to himself. The waitress was right; this was a good wine. He sat back to relax and wait for his main course. The efforts of the journey thus far had not really surfaced, as Connor had not allowed them to, but this moment, this brief respite, was allowing the suppressed tension to surface and float away. The airy square, the small talk, the food, and wine were all taking effect; he could feel the waves of relaxation pulsing through him. The waitress returned with his main course and replenished his glass from the remainder of the carafe. She smiled once more and, for the first time, Connor noticed a jagged scar that ran down the side of her face, from her eye back towards her ear. It vanished in the hairline. The way that the waitress wore her hair so that the long strand hung forward and down concealed the aggressive and angry welt, which marred the otherwise unblemished skin. In looking up she caught Connor staring and he quickly adjusted his eyes to the plate put before him.

"Is there anything else?" she asked

"Yes, there is. I feel that maybe you are right and I need to experience a little more danger, so if you would be so kind, I would like another carafe of this very good wine and, if possible, a recommendation of somewhere nearby to stay the night?"

The waitress stood up and instinctively turned her scarred side away from Connor as she flicked back her hair. "I know of a nice place not far from here. It is not much, but it is clean and I know the owner very well. The rooms are cheap, and I would recommend it to you."

"That sounds excellent. Perhaps you could give me the directions?"

"I will, but first enjoy and finish your meal before it goes cold. I will fetch you some more wine."

The meal went well and the wine got better, the former leaving a sense of contentment, the latter a warm glow. Connor had resigned himself to the moment, and the wine was headier for it. He felt the rising memory of teenage drinking, that first venture over the line into adulthood. The sweet ciders bought by the tallest in the group when just a few sips led to drunkenness— or some semblance of that condition, at least—or for the more *risqué*, the stolen half pint of vodka decanted from a parent's drinks cupboard, mixed liberally with sickeningly sweet cola to obliterate the taste of alcohol. It was the excitement of the deed rather than the deed itself; it was the expression of freedom and the rebellious nature of the act that was intoxicating. The booze just chivvied the thing along.

Here was Connor. His regime to date had been structured, focused, a place to be and a need to be there, but for some reason he took his foot off the gas now. Stopped. Kicked back. He was rebelling against his own want, demonstrating to himself that he was in charge, in this minute way. This lull allowed Connor to take stock before plunging headlong back into the white water rapids rushing towards the endgame, which, once committed, offered very little chance of pulling out of if he was to keep his sanity.

On the other hand, was this a stalling tactic? Was his mind, his sub conscious trying to warn him away from the path he was travelling. Was this some temptation, some disproportionate distraction to turn again? How could so simple a meal and few glasses of wine invoke such pleasure? It was this ability to enjoy that Connor craved; it was exactly this ability to stop and choose what to do that he was striving to achieve with this whole adventure—to claw back his freedom. The ability to stop was the impetus to carry on. Afternoon drinking, Connor realised, was not such a good pursuit for him. He smiled to himself and drained his glass.

He called for the *"l'addition"* which his scarred waitress delivered, and he paid with a large denomination note, an over-flamboyant gesture, again the product of the wine and time of day. Connor made the change and tipped slightly over the norm, but not flashily. He had enjoyed the occasion, and the waitress played her part well. He still needed the directions from her. She had gone back into the restaurant and, with the afternoon starting to chill, Connor felt suddenly not so content, a little bit used. He had been lured in and steered away from his intended path and had now rendered himself stuck halfway up the west coast of France, too drunk to drive with seemingly nowhere to stay.

He stared into the shaded interior of the restaurant and saw a bartender pushing bottles and glasses around on shelves as he wiped the surfaces with a large cloth.

"*Pardonnez-moi, monsieur, ou est la mademoiselle est servie moi?*" Connor struggled with finding the words, but felt that he had conveyed his question sufficiently for the man to understand. The man looked at Connor in the mirrored reflection before turning to respond

"You want Michelle?" He looked at his watch. "She has finished for the day."

Connor was taken aback. It hurt, for some strange reason. He felt embarrassed, as though he had been stood up, and to add to his injury he had just invited this stranger to witness his embarrassment.

"Is there something you want, *monsieur?*" Was he gloating? Connor couldn't tell, so he said no and turned to leave the bar.

Outside, the first chilled breeze of the early evening fluttered the flags around the square. Their previously bright colours had faded somewhat in Connor's eyes. The whole square, in fact, had dimmed and was less appealing. His bonhomie had faded also, and the alcohol seemed purged from his system. Dejectedly, he resigned himself to the experience and walked the short distance back to his car. *En route*, he spied a street that fed into the square. It offered some hope of accommodation, and he was just going to divert towards it when he heard someone calling,

"*Monsieur!*"

Connor looked up to see the waitress, Michelle, waving to him as she walked briskly towards him. She wore a light cardigan across her shoulders, held together in one hand, a small clutch purse in the other. She was smiling a brilliant smile.

"I thought you wanted directions to the room for the night? 'ave you changed your mind?"

It was wrong, Connor knew, but something just clicked and felt right. Instantly, a euphoric wave rushed over him, a hit that lifted his soul.

"No, I still want the room. I thought you had left. I asked the waiter, and he said you had finished. I thought you had forgotten and left."

They both paused and started to laugh at the situation.

"What is your name, *monsieur?*"

"*Je m'appelle Connor, et vous êtes Michelle, n'est-ce pas?*"

"*Tres bien*, Connor. *Allons-y.*"

Michelle led Connor away from his car after he had gathered and bagged a few belongings. Connor watched Michelle's walk, confident and precise. There was something of the catwalk about it, or at least catlike. She waved casually to some of the shop owners, who smiled and waved back with paternal or maternal familiarity. Connor felt a little awkward and hung back half a pace, but not enough to disguise the fact that he was with Michelle. It felt strange to be with and not with someone simultaneously—not knowing her well enough to walk in tandem like a lover or a friend, he was not fluent enough to engage in chatty banter and be distracting enough not to focus on the awkwardness of the moment. In truth, he felt like some mindless child, perhaps stalker following in the wake of a parent or prey. It became too much. "Michelle, a moment please?"

Michelle stopped and turned to look at Connor, her head tilted to one side. "I appreciate you taking the time to show me where I have to go, but it really is not necessary. You must be tired after your shift. Please do not let me keep you from going home. If you just let me have the directions, I am sure I could find it alone."

Michelle's lips parted into a wide smile, and her hand came to cover her mouth.

"Trust me, Connor, it is no problem. I am going home."

She turned to walk on. Connor just stood on the spot, digesting the information, until Michelle turned and stood with her hands on her hips, her smile replaced with a small pout. "Do not worry Connor. I will not hurt you, I promise." Again the smile returned, and all Connor could do was shrug and follow on. She waited until he was alongside her, and then they walked in step.

"I live with my father and mother. We have a big house, and we have rooms that we let out occasionally. It works well with me being in the restaurant, as I am often asked if I know of anywhere to stay. If I like the look of the person, I will offer them a room at my parents', but if I do not like their look I send them to Madame Bleriot's."

"I passed the test, then?"

"You looked okay, plus you are a good tipper!" Michelle laughed, and Connor smiled at being ribbed by the intriguingly pretty woman. He could feel the energy she possessed, coiled and latent. She was a rifle bullet—sleek, shiny, beautifully engineered, but at the same time deadly, dangerous, a malevolence that could, if unleashed, give someone a very-sad-you-were-born kind of a day. Connor tried to recall her quip about living dangerously.

A few streets on, Michelle led Connor to a path that led to a robust-looking house that sat squat and square amongst a jumble of mixed architectural styles. The house was detached and had a reasonably well-tended garden, not so much the English style of lawn and borders, but a more continental style that turned over to a mix of vegetables, fruiting trees, and bushes interspersed with potted plants that seemed to grow strong, having been left to their own devices.

Connor followed Michelle into the large tiled hallway, and she closed the heavy door behind him.

She called out, "Hello!" A muted reply came from the end of the dark corridor that ran towards the back of the house. Again Connor felt awkward, haunted by the memories of first introductions to girlfriends' parents, that leaden feeling in the stomach when all the reassurance from the girlfriend could not remove the dread of meeting her father or brother. At the end of the day, after all, they were men and knew what men knew. Then, as now, the situation was intensified by the girlfriend suddenly developing a cavalier and confident air that she had not previously demonstrated, that left him susceptible and almost emasculated. He was in another lion's den, and he wasn't sure that he had been invited.

Connor tried to put things into perspective. He just needed a room for the night, somewhere to freshen up and lay his head. He had asked in innocence and followed in good faith.

"I will show you the room." Michelle pointed to the stairs that started with a quarter turn in the middle of the hallway. She threw her bag onto a faded upholstered chair at the base of the balustrade and slipped her cardigan onto the newel post before starting to ascend the stairs. The stairs let onto a landing that followed the plan of the hall below. Connor kept up as he took in the layout of the rooms and decor as he went. The fittings and fixtures were almost grandiose, not quite chandeliers, but elaborate and appropriate for the house. The ornate plasterwork was original and, though in good repair, would have benefitted from a fresh coat of paint. Many of the items of furniture that Connor spied were on the cusp of turning antique and had been in the house and family for at least two generations.

Michelle pushed open a wide-panelled door, which opened into a light airy room. The floor-to-ceiling shutters were hooked back, and the French windows caught the last of the afternoon sun, which shone obliquely across the wide, dark-boarded floor and scattered rugs. A wide and high bed dominated the centre of the room. The plump mattress and deep pillows looked inviting.

Michelle had walked farther into the room and opened another door, which was a small toilet and shower room. "Do you like?" she asked.

"It is very nice, thank you," Connor replied, still looking around the room.

"It is thirty-five euros for the night. Would that be okay?"

Connor had forgotten all about the fact that he was paying for the room, so caught up had he become in the gamut of throwback emotions he had experienced. "Yes, that is fine," he said as he reached for his wallet.

"No, please, you will have to pay my *maman*. She controls the purse, and it is her way of checking out the visitors I select also. But first please freshen up and have a rest. There is no 'urry. Come down later. When you are ready, I am sure my Papa will like to offer you a glass of his beer. He tries it on all our guests, but beware he has a liking for the English, as you have so many different beers!"

Connor said he would be on his guard and thanked Michelle as she closed the door, leaving him to the room alone.

After emerging from the shower, Connor dried himself on the rather thin towels. The bedroom was warm from the fading evening sun, which was dropping behind the tall poplars that stood at the bottom of the garden. Connor jumped onto the bed, the towel tied around his midriff, and stretched out, luxuriating in the sensation of the soft mattress and topper as well as the glow from his skin post-shower. The combined effect lulled Connor, and he felt his eyelids growing heavy. He finally succumbed and drifted to sleep.

When he awoke, the room was crepuscular. The dying sun sent out the last crimson rays and sank into the shadows, giving over to the inky night and waxy moon, a gob of butter high in the sky, haloed in cirrus clouds. The room had grown chilled, and Connor couldn't decide whether to reposition to gain extra warmth, the downside being a loss of the heat he had.

There was a knock at the door. "*Allo*, Connor. Are you okay?"

It was Michelle's voice. Connor looked to his watch and tried to focus on the dial. His eyes eventually adjusted to the dark. He saw that it was quarter to nine. Quickly, he got up and went to the door. Opening the door, he realised his state of undress and stepped back, using the door to shield his semi naked form.

"Hello, Michelle. I am sorry I fell asleep."

"Oh, *pardonnez-moi.* I just wanted to check you were okay." She paused. "We were going to have something to eat, and I was wondering if you maybe would like to join us?"

Caught off guard, Connor stumbled with the information his position, his state of undress. But he also did not want to offend his hosts and demonstrate ill manners.

"Of course. That would be lovely, thank you. I, I, er, need to get . . ." Connor indicated his position rather than having to say, and Michelle was alert to his predicament.

"*D'accord,* please come down when you are ready." She smiled as she stepped back, giving the door a look that barely disguised her ability to imagine what was through it. Connor was glad he had his towel wrapped around him still.

Connor dug some clothes out of his bag. His linen trousers and shirt were rolled up so that the creases were not too bad. They were more in need of a wash than an iron. Connor shook them violently and then sprayed them liberally with cologne before putting them on. Barefooted, he slipped his sandals on and looked like a surf bum trying to look formal. He checked himself in the mirror, took some cash from his wallet, and left the room. The route down the stairs to the back of the house was not lit directly, but rather through occasional lamps that were in rooms off the hall and landing. Connor peered in as he went, looking at the high-ceilinged rooms decorated and furnished to indicate faded opulence and spent wealth. Connor neared the voices he could hear, the rapid staccato of French in a deep but not loud voice, whose counterpoint was Michelle's light and airy voice. Connor knocked gently on the door, which led to the voices becoming hushed. He heard a chair sliding back, and the door was opened by Michelle, who stood in silhouette against the bright light shining from within the room.

"*Bonsoir, monsieur. Entrez, s'il vous plaît.*" Michelle stood back for Connor to enter the room. The first thing he saw was a large table suitable to sit twelve with comfort. At the head sat a woman in her late fifties, her long hair dyed almost black and gathered into a configuration that only French women could make to look casual, but at the same time glamorous. She was petite and had a healthy glow that she accentuated with dark eyes and long lashes. Aside, her looking up at Connor from his paper, sat Michelle's father. He had a balding pate, but the hair he had left was still strong in colour. The baldness put five years on to his sixty or so years, but he looked robust in body if a little tired around the eyes. He smiled broadly at Connor.

"*Bonsoir, monsieur. Comment ça va?*"

"*Ça va bien, merci.*" Connor looked to Michelle, who just smiled somewhat inanely. "*Je m'appelle Connor . . .*" He tapered off, not knowing quite what else to say. The man stood and offered his hand in greeting, the two men shook hands.

"Je m'appelle Jean, et elle est mon femme, Eloise, et ma fille, Antoinette." Connor turned in surprise as Jean indicated towards "Michelle"—or, at least, the woman Connor had taken to be Michelle. Trying to regain his composure, he shook hands with Eloise and then Antoinette, bidding them both *bonsoir.* His face must have been quite telling. Indeed, it prompted Jean to call out, "*Michelle, s'il vous plaît, ma petite.*" In response, the door that led away from the dining room opened, and Michelle emerged through it carrying a large bowl of cut bread. She looked up to see Connor standing in some state of confusion.

"*Allo,* Connor. Are you okay? You look troubled."

Connor was troubled and almost lost for words, so much so that he just pivoted on the spot and turned a quarter turn back towards Antoinette, and then back again to Michelle.

"I thought . . ." His voice trailed away.

"I am sorry, Connor. They are teasing you. This is my twin sister, Antoinette."

The trio all laughed out loud at their playacting, and Connor just looked at Michelle before he laughed along with them.

"*Une boisson,* Connor?" Jean asked above the laughter and waved Antoinette to get some bottles and glasses. "*Asseyez-vous,* Connor," he said as he pulled back a chair and tapped the seat. Connor took the seat, his face flushed a little from the laugh, but more from his reaction and confusion. Antoinette returned with some large bottles of beer and a bottle of unlabelled wine. The beer had the wire and china stoppers, which Jean released. He poured a frothy glass of golden liquid for Connor and for himself. The wine had a plastic cork, which he removed so that he could pour two glasses of dark red wine for his two daughters. Eloise already had a glass set it front of her, half full of some bright green liquid.

Jean raised his glass. "*Salut,* Connor. Cheers."

Connor raised his glass, and the glasses clinked together before he took a drink, watching Jean over the top of his glass so that he did not finish before him. The beer was cold and refreshing; although it was not an ideal beverage to be had on just waking up, it did hit the spot. Connor put down his nearly emptied glass only to have it instantly topped up by Jean once more. It was going to be a long and interesting night.

The night passed, and there was much laughter at the misinterpretation of language and pronunciation. The soup was hearty, and the bread, fresh and pungent, helped absorb the home brew that eventually and inevitably emerged from Jean's cellar. The women were fine company, and they collectively hounded poor Jean so that he good-humouredly acquiesced to the female majority. The shrug of resignation to Connor said all; he was powerless to resist. The matriarch herself had warmed as the evening had gone on. Connor had paid her his night lodgings, and the light, sparkling green drink had been topped up many times since, the effect being that Connor was sure that she had begun flirting with him—or at least trying to provoke Jean into puffing out his chest feathers. The beer was taking effect, and Connor felt himself relaxing a little too much. Though he was enjoying the sensation, he decided that he'd had enough and called an end to his night. He bid his hosts a good night and thanked them heartily for sharing their hospitality with him. Now, standing, he felt the full effect of the beer and steadied himself against the back of the chair. This did not go unnoticed. Jean passed some indecipherable comment, which Connor felt had wrested back his manly honour judging by the slight embarrassment it seemed to cause amongst the women, especially Michelle and Antoinette, who did not wish to know about their own father's ability to drink and still perform. Connor could only guess that that was the gist of the remark, but played innocent and ignorant of the fact. Connor focussed on the gap from the chair to the door and took determined steps to cover the distance. Once there, he said a final *bonne nuit* and slipped through the doorway.

The corridor was cool by comparison. The dark, indirectly lit walkway was bathed intermittently in puddles of warm light that spilled out of the doorways leading into the adjoining rooms. Like luminous stepping-stones, Connor moved from one to the other until he reached the foot of the stairs. The chill air of the hallway had cleared his head somewhat, but he still took a firm hold on the balustrade and climbed purposefully to the head of the stairs. It was a short hop now to the bedroom and the refuge of the waiting bed. The complacency caused by the proximity was Connor's undoing, and the feeling that the floor was tilting away from him and the over-compensation caused him to collide with the half-moon table. This in turn upset the small candelabra, and Connor's best efforts to prevent it falling were in vain and only amplified the inevitable clatter that followed. Automatically, Connor set to restoring the thankfully undamaged candelabra to the table. Straightening the small damask square used to protect the table from the metal base of the candle stand, Connor noticed someone standing behind and to the side of him. The person had ghosted up the stairs, and Connor could not be sure how long he or she had been watching. Connor turned somewhat sheepishly to see Michelle half smiling at him, the sort of look a parent displays to a child who has been caught having done wrong and is trying to restore the damage. Connor fumbled his apology, chagrined by his own inebriated state.

"I warned you about my papa's beer, did I not?" she lectured.

"Michelle, I am sorry, I . . ." Connor did not finish, realising there was no excuse. He just stood there waiting to be rebuked. Michelle's face broke into a smile and a resigned shake of her head. "I think it is time for bed, Connor."

She took him by the elbow and steered him towards the door at the end of the corridor. Trying to maintain his dignity and composure, Connor allowed himself to be led. Michelle reached across and opened the door. She flicked on the light as they entered the room. Connor spun round to sit on the side of the bed before flopping back to stare up at the low-wattage lamp that burned with a yellowing light. The room spun gently, and Connor giggled from the feeling that he was the epicentre of the rotating room. Connor raised himself up to a semi-prone position and refocused his eyes to look at the svelte figure that stood at the side of the bed looking down at him. Her hands rested on her hips below her nipped-in waist, accentuating the hourglass figure with a dominant posture. The slight curve of her breast pushed against her raw silk blouse. Connor felt his blood rush and his focus sharpen.

Michelle crossed to the window and closed the shutters, leaving the French door slightly ajar. The cool air leaked into the room and mixed with Michelle's perfume. Connor breathed deeply the refreshing scent, which washed away some of the alcohol-induced lugubriousness that he was in danger of descending into. Michelle turned, leaned back against the shutters, and stared at Connor—who, feeling her gaze, turned his head to look back. The silence that followed was extended. Michelle seemed to be contemplating something, and Connor felt that staying quiet was the best option. Michelle pushed away from the shutter. She seemed to have reached a decision and walked towards the still semi-prone Connor, who tracked her walk 'til she resumed her previous position so that she was looking down on him once more. She smiled once more.

"I hope we do not regret this tomorrow, Connor. Good night."

Connor found himself staring at the space where Michelle had been standing and, he saw the closing bedroom door instead of her. He sighed and fell back onto the bed, his arms stretched out in cruciform fashion as his misplaced expectation ebbed away.

The morning came all too soon and was heralded by a blank memory, like the projection screen of a home film. The feeder film spooled through, and flashes of numbers and roughly penned words flashed up prior to the frame steadying and the picture fading into firm focus. Connor stirred to look at his watch, causing his head to throb and a wave of nausea to break over him. It was late, and Michelle's parting comment was prescient. He was regretting the state he had allowed himself to get in and was now paying the consequences. Lifting himself up from the bed made the throb in his head intensify, and he waited for the weight of blood to stop pushing at the backs of his eyes. Shafts of light lasered through the shutters; specks of airborne dust floated through the zebra'd light ladder.

The water from the shower played its part in achieving a partial revival. Connor varied the temperature, trying to tolerate as cold a deluge as possible. It seemed that what was good for his head was not good for the rest of his body. He stepped back into the bedroom and towelled himself gently whilst sitting on the edge of the bed, looking at the pile of carelessly discarded clothes. Once dressed, Connor closed the door to the bedroom gently and descended the stairs. At the bottom, he stopped to contemplate whether to steal out and away or to bid his hosts goodbye. The decision was taken away from him when Michelle came in through the front door.

"*Bonjour,* Connor," she said brightly, showing none of the ill effects that Connor was suffering from.

"Papa's beer *est très forte, non?*" she animated this comment with a fist being twisted at the end of her nose, the French sign for dipsomaniac behaviour.

Connor responded in the positive. "It is, indeed. *J'ai mal à la tête.*"

Michelle laughed like the tinkle of glass Christmas baubles, a charming, elfin laugh that ordinarily would have sounded cute and becoming—but, this morning, his thoughts were too self-centred to focus on the world beyond his own suffering. Connor found her perfume, no doubt light and fresh, to be cloying and stifling, causing him to crave the cool fresh air outside.

"I see you are ready to leave, *n'est-ce pas?*" Michelle asked with a casual air, but it was tinged with "stay a little longer." Connor felt the nuance lurking in the question and looked guiltily at the backpack over his shoulder as though it had been sneaked onto him.

"Yes, I am afraid so. I still have quite a journey ahead of me . . ." Connor's words trailed away. He felt he could stay and believed that Michelle would like him to stay longer, but he also knew he had a schedule to keep. The days were moving on; already, his overnight had been an impromptu stop he hadn't scheduled for.

Michelle responded with dignity and a Gallic shrug. "*D'accord.* Would you like some *petit dejeuner* before you leave?" she asked, raising the bag she was holding at her side. Connor felt bilious at the thought of food, but the fear of being rude was testing his etiquette.

"Maybe a coffee?" Connor suggested, hoping that his digestive tract would be able to cope with a shot of hot, caffeine-rich coffee. Michelle smiled and beckoned Connor towards the kitchen door. He turned and followed her as she brushed past, leaving him to follow the scented air that wafted behind her.

To Connor's relief, the kitchen was dark and cool. The window at the head of the table was open, and the cool air that trickled through the sash was tinged with the scent of lavender that grew riotously from an oversized pot at the edge of the small, paved courtyard. Dark in shadow, the tranquil square was tantalising and inviting, like a woodland pool carved by a mountain stream, ice-cold, but still enticing, desirous. Connor breathed deep and felt the throb in his head lift a degree. Michelle rattled utensils and crockery in the room beyond until the acrid aroma of scalded coffee emanated from the room and permeated the house, a clarion call to those within. Michelle came and sat with Connor, smiling nervously. The tick of the clock was heavy and sonorous and filled the gaps in between the staccato small talk. As it was, the conversation was interrupted by the arrival of more of the household, who *bonjour*-ed their way into the room sheepishly, as people can only when they are not quite sure of their actions and conversations the night before. The coffee and selection of bread and cheese focused the attention away from the guest at the table, of which Connor was glad. His head was in the hinterland, a purgatory outside the hell of an incapacitated photophobic, but not in the elysian fields of the holier-than-thou brigade and their temperance values. The trouble was, he was unsure whether he was in the recovery phase or whether his nadir was ahead of him. The coffee was hot and bitter and scalded the lining of his empty stomach, causing an involuntary audible complaint. Connor shifted uneasily in his seat. A flush of heat caused a prickle of dampness on his forehead. Suddenly, the room felt small, and a claustrophobic pang grew within him. He inhaled the cool air lapping over the window ledge. The lavender tones soothed his rising panic. Those around suffered also. Only Michelle seemed free of having to serve any penance; instead, she served up the breakfast offerings to the growing throng of repentants.

The grounds of the coffee were all that remained in Connor's cup, and he swilled them distractedly as the conversations around him grew in volume and intensity to a pace well beyond his comprehension. He decided to take the moment and pushed his chair back. The noise halted the chatter momentarily, but then it resumed. His breakfast companions were obviously used to this awkward hiatus before their guest left, and only the guest, Connor this time, struggled with extracting himself from the temporary arrangement. Connor took his empty cup to the drainer, where Michelle stood moving items of kitchenware around somewhat aimlessly.

"Thank you, Michelle," Connor said as he placed the cup down. Michelle half turned, and a smile flirted on her lips

"You are leaving now?" she enquired

"Yes, I must be going, I have a long journey and a ferry to catch . . ." His voice trailed off. Michelle spoke quickly to the room, which in turn prompted a flurry of *au revoirs* and *bonne chances.* Connor responded in kind, and he was ushered away from an interchange of handshaking and cheek-kissing by Michelle. The sun shone brightly through the fanlight above. The door and the light bleached out the tessellated black and white floor of the hall. Michelle released the latch and pulled back the heavy door to allow the morning sun to fill the corridor and cause squints to form on both their faces, crocodile smiles.

"Well, Connor it has been nice to meet you, and I hope you have had a happy stay?"

"Thank you. Yes, very nice, very nice indeed . . ." Connor felt prudish and awkward running out the niceties, wanting to say more, but he was unable to judge the moment or the mood. Could he expose his feelings, the strange emotional turmoil that was fluttering within? Was it the infatuation of a new place, a new person, and the heady atmosphere caused by the beer— ambience and the opportunity to forget for a few short hours his journey and the task ahead? The pause stretched into a lull in the goodbye and increased the tension, at least as far as Connor was concerned. Michelle seemed unfazed by the issue, and this itself was part of Connor's insecurity.

"Michelle, I have to go back to England, as I have some business to attend to, but maybe I . . ."

Connor stopped and looked into Michelle's eyes to gauge her reaction to his stumbling and ineloquent approach. The coffee-dark liquid pools were warm and inviting, limpid around the dark bean pupils, all set in a white cup and saucer. Connor's memory of youth came rushing back—that first girlfriend, the adolescent ineptitude when asking someone on a date, fearing the rejection, but not quite knowing how to cope with the acceptance, either.

"I have to come back to France in the near future. I thought maybe that if I came here, you could perhaps show me some of the sights . . . ?"

The question hung there. The innuendo was large, but unintentional, and Connor hoped it would not carry over into the French translation that Michelle seemed to be computing.

A smile stretched across her face. "Of course. It would be a delight to see you again, Connor. One moment." She vanished back into the hall and returned with a printed card, which she handed over to Connor. He looked at the card to see the address and telephone number below the words *"Chambres d'Hotes."* Michelle offered her hand, which Connor took to shake goodbye, but she leaned forward to offer the more traditional *au revoir* kisses. Connor breathed deep the gentle perfume of her hair and skin, an intoxicating blend of woodland honey and mountain stream.

"Hurry back, Connor . . ."

Michelle closed the door—abrupt, finished, gone. Connor stood alone with the card in his hand and a small void forming inside of him. Confused by her sudden exit, he started to smile as he pieced together the moments before. For now, at least, he put a positive interpretation on them. He turned on his heel and, looking back occasionally, made his way back to his car.

The square was quiet. The tables were, as yet, undressed. The chairs were stacked against the restaurant frontages, which were dark and semi-shuttered like sleeping dogs with half an eye on the passing world. Delivery lorries were off loading vittles, viands, and many crates of drink, a prosaic restocking done with quiet efficiency with no thought to the eventual destination of their products, the romantic meetings, the joyful reunions, or the tearful departures that the forkfuls of food and glasses of wine would play a part in. At the moment, they were just commodities in boxes stacked on the pavement and sack barrows—the Christians being filed into the coliseum unaware of the drama they were about to play a part in.

The sun was lighting the upper floors of the southwestern side of the square, the buildings awaiting their daily bleaching. Far below in the lake of shadow, Connor climbed back into the driver's seat. The inside of the car was cool, damp. The plastic fascia and trim were tacky, and the inside of the windscreen had a tidemark of condensation rising from the dash board. Connor turned the key, and the engine fired into life. He wound down the windows, allowing fresh air to circulate the dank interior. Whilst the engine warmed, Connor studied the map. His route ahead was due north, through the town of Samur on the Loire, aiming for Le Mans before easing gently northwest to Caen, where he would return the car to the hire company. He anticipated that he should make the rental office by about mid-afternoon, and if all went well, be back in the small harbour and on board *Little Star* by early evening. Connor released the handbrake and pulled out of the square into the warming morning sun.

The exchange at the car rental was curt and grudging. The level of inspection around the car was excessive to the point of ridiculousness and almost, as far as Connor was concerned, to the point of annoyance. He maintained his temper, conscious that he did not want to linger in anybody's memory more than necessary. The fees paid for the petrol top-up were, again, over market value. *They get you coming and going,* thought Connor as he doled out the euros to the greedy hands, which totalled the notes into separate denominations before depositing them in the underused till. Credit cards were the universally accepted currency, crossing the divide of countries and continents.

Connor left the office in bad humour and made his way to the bus station he had seen on his way into town. The weather was closing in, and the skies were strewn with what looked like old men's white shirts, creased and greying. The rising wind was chasing the depot detritus along the pavements and gutters. Connor sought the maps and route boards to identify which bus he needed before seeking the departure point, where he then stood alone, glancing periodically at his watch as the minute hand edged round towards the hour, the publicised time of departure.

With a little time to go, the single decked bus hove into view and pulled alongside Connor's stop. The doors hissed open and flapped noisily against each other to reveal a less-than-interested bus driver. Connor climbed aboard and paid the fare to Bayeux. It was late in the day, and the bus was fairly empty, with only those who were on the return journey from their shopping trips—those who fell between the haves and the have-nots. Not rich enough to own a car, but still able to travel further afield to shop. The aged and those whose friends and families lived too far away to accompany them, but would be assured by the phone call that meant they had gotten home safely after their day out. The greyed-out look on their Eleanor Rigby faces showed that they had spent their lives living for others. Their greater duty was to mankind to propagate the population, to do the expected thing and to do so without fuss or nuisance, to move along and not obscure the view or guilt-trip their progeny into reaching back and lending funds or favours. These jackal offspring sucked their mothers dry and then feasted on her mortal remains so that they could carry on in turn to be the feast in famine. Once more, Connor saw the shackles of society that bound the population to the machine formed link by ponderous link. The weight of expectation was of ball-and-chain proportions. Sure, one could move, shuffle along, but he'd dare not swim, let alone fly. Society could ignore a person for a while, knowing well he could travel neither far nor fast. The harpooned whale, stuck firm on an immovable spike that would release only at great cost to the flesh, possibly irrecoverable, possibly fatal. How great was the fight to be free, knowing that the end saw demise, death, and destruction, be it now or later. How long could the suffering continue, the yoke of oppression was religious, financial, and societal? It was an ingrained fundamental need to nurture the whelps, which were products of the loin, and protect them unquestionably. This was applauded by the caring society as right and proper: Practice the natural way until life drifted from the body and the final thought was, "Where was my life?"

Connor pulled out of the spiral of dark thought, necessary in part to bolster him for his road ahead. Not for him. The stale urine stink of aged decrepitude lumbered with the thoughts and memories of an empty life. No, he would soar. He would walk as giants, loud and proud—in his mind, at least. His heart would be content for having experienced life outside of the cage, for having tasted the freedom that life should offer and having run the gambit of failure in the hope of success. The Elysian fields were reached through offerings to the gods, and there were many gods who might grant such a gift.

The bus had long since departed and the road was, as French roads oft are, straight and direct to the point, as roads should be. This hangover from Roman or Napoleonic times served the country and users well; pragmatism over aestheticism was the call of those who had somewhere to go and wanted to be there. For the rest, life's tourists, they had reached where they needed to be. The view changed then; the veil was lifted to reveal the true purpose, hopefully justifying the means. For those people, the wending road had attractions and views that were lost for time on most others. The short trip ended in the darkening evening in a market square, where the business of the day had long finished. Street cleaners where driving their vehicles to and fro across the litter-strewn expanse, whilst boiler-suited colleagues corralled the wind drift into weighted piles for shovelled removal.

Lights were starting to glow from the windowed fronts of the shops, bars, and restaurants that hemmed the square and hoped to attract the night time tourists and those that chose to tarry after work amongst the blue haze of the bars.

Connor followed his fellow passengers off the bus into the cooling evening air. He breathed deep to help clear his mind and went in search of a taxi. This was an exciting part of the day, the day's work done and the night creeping forward. The heady aromas drifted from the eateries and the spilled laughter from bustling bars as doors opened to admit more revellers to the throng. The beautiful people emerged from their photophobic hideouts to dazzle those who gazed upon them, moth and flame in suicidal proximity. The perfumes trailed like irresistible pheromones, assailing the senses and beguiling the recipients like pied piper rats and children. Nonchalant gaggles of young beauties strode confident paths bolstered by their linked-arm unity, their hydrogen bond strong, but ultimately breakable to release the volatile element that togetherness hid. *Look at us,* their gallant posture screamed. Their brief, mayfly beauty was stunning, but waning like the day-old sun. Connor passed many on their way to tears and laughter (some to both). The hope of the evening ahead brought the birth and death of the future, and fate held the dice cup firmly.

The cab rank was empty. Connor waited on point and watched the world pass him by. He checked his watch three or four times before his taxi rounded the corner. He moved to the boot to unload his backpack before climbing into the backseat.

"Port-en-Bessin, *s'il vous plaît, monsieur,*" Connor said. The driver glanced at Connor in his rearview mirror with a quizzical look on his face, his brow furrowed somewhat.

"*Oui, d'accord,*" he responded, and engaging first gear, pulled from the kerb. The dashboard lights glowed a gentle luminous orange that Connor longed to bathe in. The day had been tiring, and the warm glow was inviting, comforting. He laid his head back against the headrest.

"*Pardonnez-moi, monsieur. Nous sommes arrivés.*"

Connor sat up, startled from his brief slumber, shocked and surprised to see the driver twisted around, shaking him by the knee. Collecting himself, Connor shuffled across the seat to the door.

"*Combien, s'il vous plaît?*" Connor asked. Once the driver had responded, he passed him notes from his wallet as he helped retrieve his bags from the boot.

"*Merci. Au revoir,*" the driver called as he returned to his door. Connor was lifting his backpack onto his shoulder as he oriented himself. The smell of the sea was being pushed inland by a freshening breeze, and the damp air felt laden with rain. Having spied the path, Connor crossed the road obliquely and descended to the little harbour on the far side.

Striding along the echoing jetty, Connor counted off the boats, his eyes searching ahead for *Little Star.* His eyes came to rest on the mast that he had stared at for so many hours, a familiar shape below, where his small sanctuary lay. He stepped aboard, and the boat dipped to welcome him. He moved to the hatch and unlocked the padlock, allowing the last of the fading light into the cabin below and letting out the bottled-up damp and fetid air. He stepped down into the dark and fumbled to locate the main power switch, which supplied the low-voltage lights that offered up an off-white glow. By the softened light, he removed a hatch and primed the engine before turning over the cold lump of glistening metal, never really having much faith that the batteries would overcome the resistance and inertia that lay like a dead hand on a cold day in the engine pit. The relief and gratitude that followed the first spark of the engine firing was all the greater for the doubt that Connor felt before. The anxiety that lay like a soured lemon in the pit of his stomach melted away.

The lights in the cabin brightened, and Connor moved around the cabin, stowing kit in some of the lockers and removing items from others. Soon the stove was hissing, and the indigo flame tinged yellow at the tip as it bent around the base of the bubbling kettle, its lid barely containing the excited steam as it escaped its captive cauldron.

The time was moving on, and the sun had taken its leave. The evening light wove through the small harbour. The boats nestled close to their moorings as the breeze sang gently over the taut wired rigging and stays, safe for another night inside the harbour wall.

The steam of the hot poured tea mingled with steam from the reconstituted meal that Connor had taken from the small stock of dried food he kept on the boat. On the table before him lay spread out a set of charts and tide tables, along with a calendar on which the Saturday two days hence had been circled. Checking the date and time on his watch, Connor sat back against the bulkhead and smiled slightly before clearing away the remnants of his meal and making his bed for his last night in France. Tomorrow was the start of the walk on the dark side, and if all went well, he would be an invisible and nonexistent entity with a licence to use his tightly woven cloak of obscurity to his own nefarious ends.

Connor awoke to the gentle rocking of the boat and the blackboard screech of the gulls that shouted at each other as they played off ground touch on the mastheads. The surroundings pulled slowly into focus and he took reference of his position amongst his jumble of bedding. It felt cold—no, not cold. Damp. Yes, that was it. The damp penetrated his bones and caused a deep ache that would leave only when it was ready, good and ready. Connor stretched as if he had been asleep a hundred years, an expanding stretch where the pain was good, but only just, and too fast tilted the needle back to the pain scale.

Up on deck, the sun was trying to cast some shadow, but the clouds were doing their utmost to throw an opaque shield around the hemisphere of sky that enclosed the harbour. The horizon looked dark and metal-grey, deepening to a line of black along the rim of the sea, a view that would convince all, but the most hardened sailors that the world was indeed a sphere and that the edge would go on to infinity.

Connor fired the engine and moved with quiet efficiency as he loosened the painters and mooring lines, letting the boat steal away from the floating pontoon jetty like a guilty lover from a morning bed. He increased the throttle and pulled the helm hard across. *Little Star* turned until her bow was pointed towards the gap in the harbour wall and the confusion of the open sea beyond. The boat slipped from her sanctuary and left behind the sleeping world of continental mainland Europe to head home.

Connor steered the boat northeast, wrestling with the sails and the continual pitch and roll as the boat was caught in a swell that came onto the port quarter. The yaw caused by the wind, waves, and Connor's poor seamanship put many more miles on his journey, but fortunately he had allowed for this. Tempted as he was to strike his sails and revert to his engine, he resisted, choosing to conserve the fuel load that he had. The day crept on, and he decided he had made sufficient headway to allow himself the opportunity to lay up a while. He was off the main sea lanes, and the English coastline, if his instruments were correct lay just over the horizon. Taking the time to prepare himself a hot drink and a meal, Connor once more, with an almost obsessive compulsion, checked his calendar watch and small sailing diary. The late afternoon started to give way to the evening, and the darkening sky grew up and over the boat, seeping across the sky with oil-slick persistence to the ruddied scar of a sunset. Connor lit his navigational lights, and the emerald and scarlet jewels that adorned the little boat shone out like talismans against the evil that lurked in the inky darkness of the night. Wrapped against the cold, Connor sat in the cockpit with a warming cup of tea. The wheel was locked off, and the boat turned naturally into the wind. The bucket anchor offered just enough resistance. The first stars broke the cloud cover, and Connor tried to join the dots, but the frustration of the overcast skies and increasing pain in his neck caused him to slop his chilled remnants of tea over the side. Taking one last look, he descended into the womblike shelter of the cabin.

Sleep eluded Connor for most of the night. Fitful at best, he pursued the asylum of oblivious unconsciousness only to be pulled from the edge by an errant wave or imagined noise that grew in the mind to engines, voices, or foghorns. Resigning himself to his fruitless pursuit, Connor watched his watch wind round and the dark give way to the new day. He checked his satellite navigation against his chart, across which two broad red lines had been drawn approximately two inches apart, between which an "x" was also drawn in black china graph pencil. Monitoring the time, he hauled in the sea anchor and set his sails so that he tacked into the wind. Taking the satellite reading and then transferring the position onto the chart Connor kept a check on his progress and a keen eye towards the horizon on the English side of the channel.

The sun was lifting the veil of the night and ushering in the new day. On the port quarter, Connor could just make out the shadowy landmass of the south coast of England. The occasional speck of light still shone like a grounded star in its death throes, brought on by the day. Sitting in the shadow of mast and sail, *Little Star* beat against the wind. Connor's progress was slow, but time was on his side. As the morning wore on, the tips of masts and pennants peeped over the tops of the waves, and Connor steered his little boat towards the English coast. His timing was not crucial, but it was important.

The Isle of Wight sat like a discarded stone in a puddle, a calved land mass separated from the parent, an apron-string offspring that wouldn't quite let go. The island, which sat in the Solent, was a mecca to the sailing world, the epicentre of the sailing nation that had once ruled the seas. It was now an eclectic mix of the visiting sailing set with their swollen bank accounts and the less fortunate locals who fulfilled the visitors' seasonal needs. There were the diehard sailors who stayed year-round and immersed themselves in their pursuits and the local customs. The ferry ran to and from the mainland and disgorged its payload of commuters and visitors onto this charmed isle, beloved by the Victorian age, and by none more than by the eponymous matriarch herself.

Connor checked his watch. He was early, so he turned the helm so that the boat came about and the French coastline, or at least the line of clouds that hung above, passed across the peak of the bow. Connor once more tacked his way away from the little isle, figuring that another hour or so would be about right.

The minutes ticked by. The sun had climbed just short of its midway point and was dodging the grey-tinged cumulus, sending its beams of light to set ablaze the tinfoil sea. *Little Star*'s bow rose and fell as the waves cut across her. The boat twisted in a yaw as it peaked the high point of the rolling wave, and the wind ran full against the freeboard of the hull. Connor nudged the helm over to counter the deviation and brought the boat back into the wind, the tell tales on the rear edge of the main sail flying straight as the wind spilled from the sail.

The time had come, and Connor took a large breath as he gibbed the boat and turned down the wind. The sail cracked across, threatening to tear the kicker out. Connor tightened the sheets and inspected the damage. Thankfully, there was nothing discernible. "Careful, Connor," he chastised himself, "not now."

Little Star felt the moment and seemed to know that this might be her last chance to feel the breeze and the swell of the sea, and she seemed determined to have good memories. *Carpe diem.* To die doing something beloved must be the best way to go. Not for *Little Star,* the face down in the gutter whimper and fade away, the close-up of piss-stained tiles or peeling wallpaper. No, *Little Star* would fill her sails and sprint ahead of the Valkyries, her mast bending against the wind. She'd be found if she fell, having died in glory or slipped peacefully from the mooring hitch, floating away on the evening tide, but never the insipid grey in between.

Connor held the helm tight as he steered northwest, aiming at the southeastern end of the island. Forty-five minutes saw the flotilla hove into view. There was a multitude of colours that could not be imagined as they glinted and fluttered in the midday sun, a veritable riot, a phalanx spread across the line of sight to obliterate all. Dodging and darting, the boats charged, each with its planned course affecting those around it. Brownian motion writ in the play of the world's biggest sailboat race, and *Little Star* was about to join the melee.

The boats were making their penultimate turn, having beaten the wind along the seaward southern edge of the island, and the strategies were coming into play as some sailed close and others took the wider turn, and others took anywhere in between. Connor was coming in off a starboard tack and was now running down the wind as he met the main bulk of the fleet and was quickly lost, invisible as a single fish in a shoal, there but gone. Falling in with those around him, Connor held his way and steered clear of harm from the more competitive. This was not his race.

There was some banter and waving between the boats and their crews, as well as a few curt remarks when boats were not obeying the racing code and giving water where and when it was needed. The boat with right of way would raise its objections formally or animatedly across the gunwales. Connor watched with the luxury of the unbiased view and the careless mentality of a true neutral. Thousands of boats moved on the silence of the wind, and amongst them *Little Star* stole into British waters unmolested and unchallenged by custom patrols or, for that matter, harbourmasters. Connor had sailed into Cowes amidst a small flotilla of boats of mixed pedigree and sought a mooring at the farthest edge of the harbour. It was an undesirable location this early in the day, with the post-race celebrations that would go on late into the night. Berths closer to the centre of activity were prime location and highly sought, but they came with the encumbrance of having neighbours clambering across the decks in the small hours in varying states of drunken revelry. Connor had secured a first-position berth, which was more than he had hoped, as it meant that he would not hamper the departure of any boats had they been landside of him. He moved quickly to gather his backpack and secure his boat. Stepping ashore, he gave the boat a last look, a faint smile of thanks, and then turned his back as he set out along the pontoon, passing the cocktail-stick buffet of boats as they made the sanctuary of their moorings. Connor strode out towards the harbour centre.

The town centre bars were fast filling with the returning sailors, doing what sailors do best. They wore gaudy-coloured sailing regalia as a badge of merit, as if the wind-burned ruddy cheeks were not sign enough. Cigarette smoke and stale beer emanated from the dark interiors, and bawdy laughter punctuated high sea tales of derring-do. Pretty little things stood by at elbow's edge and played the role of ultimate accessory, wishing to be back in Berkshire or under the glow of the Sloane streetlights, but the social calendar had to be followed and the face had to be seen.

Connor watched his reflection as it followed him in the shop front windows. The pedestrianised high street was quiet, and soon the side street that led to the ferry appeared. Connor turned down it and cut across the small square, reaching the ticket office ahead of the service bus, which decanted its passenger load of tourists and locals making for the mainland. With his ticket bought, Connor made his way past a small queue of cars waiting to embark and stood near the front of the foot passenger line, allowing him to look out to the approaching ferry as it cut a swathe through the dirty water and congested seaway. He wondered whether the skipper of the ferry had the level of tolerance to obey the laws of the sea and give way to the sailboats, which seemed to run the gauntlet with his bow and his patience, a frayed edge he expressed through repeated blasts on his ship's klaxon. If ever a monotone could project an almost polysyllabic set of instructions, then the klaxon was the epitome of discourse and left nobody unsure of its message or intentions.

"Make way you laggard, coming through," it seemed to shout. The circling gulls swooped and dove, adding to the visual and aural chaos.

Men materialised, as if six or seven "Mr. Bens" had stepped through the door at the back of the changing room and onto the quayside to take up their respective positions and receive the incoming ferry. Lines were cast and caught, wound around and over polished bollards as the ferry snuggled into its berth. Ramps folded down and a small procession of cars lightened the boats load, followed by a gaggle of foot passengers who dispersed quickly to the waiting bus and beyond, carrying their spoils of excursion.

Connor made his way inside the boat and up a set of stairs to the weather deck so that he could see back over the island towards the mainland. The wind was still fresh, a blessing for those still trying to make the harbour—and there were still many trying to do just that. Never had Connor seen so many sailboats at one time. The island population must have quadrupled over the course of the whole week, as must have the coffers of the hoteliers and hostelries. But who could blame them for making hay when the sun shines, especially when there were many long weeks when it didn't?

Cables and lines were cast off, and the ferry shook as the engines pushed the vessel away from the mooring. Once more, it entered the fray. The ship horn warned those who thought of running the gauntlet. The down draft washed the decks with the odorous diesel exhaust fumes and saw a few hardy souls migrate to the windward side of the ship to receive the fresh air. Connor watched through the Perspex window, stained white at the edges to form a porthole field of vision, nature mocking the built world. The ferry pushed harder as it emerged from the cover of the sea wall, and the trail of turbulent white frothed behind the boat's stern, tracer for the gulls to dive-bomb.

The trip back to the mainland was short and not unpleasant, as it gave a brief glimpse of the British navy, old and new.

These machines of naval warfare were instrumental in putting the "Great" before Britain, and in turn the Brunel's ironclad leviathan bore the name with pride, being the vanguard of the industrial age's incursion to suck the wealth of the world back to the sceptre-isle. Those gloriously dark days. The exploitation of the weak. Suppression of the masses. It was capitalism writ large, commercialism at its finest hour. The wealth of the nation was controlled by ports such as Portsmouth, Bristol, Southampton, and the other great ports of the country that disgorged from the holds of the oceangoing vessels, exotic colours and smells, mysterious voices, and wide-eyed immigrants. Many made their money on the gamble of the sea, entrusting their cash to some unknown broker to return it many fold more than when it first left the sweaty hands of the spectacular. Whether earned by stint of hard work or through ill-gotten means, the money bought goods and products provided by forced labour on some foreign shore or plantation, and every sea mile put between the producer and the user was penance and absolution for the suffering caused. The industrial-age streets were hemmed in by grandiose edifices built with the money of various continents' wealth, fought for and protected by the redcoat armies of mother England.

The ferry docked once again in its perpetual shuffle between shores. The shoreline was once more in a state of change. The industrial warehouses were, where possible, being converted to "prestigious quayside apartments," and those that couldn't were being replaced with bijou marinas with executive apartments for the fair weather sailors, or at least their mistresses. The polished glass and chrome were the architects' nod to the influence of the sea and the vibrancy of the docks. Truer, it was if they were over painting Botticelli's vision of Dante's hell. How many reached these shores to pass into the cities of woe and eternal pain to find blessed relief through expiration?

The sky was blue, but it should not have been. Connor's melancholia wanted to see grey vistas with steeples of oppressive, angry, purple-tinged, anvil-headed clouds. There should have been at least a silent for ever drizzle, falling, enveloping the middle distance in a mist of mystery, a place of dark deeds. But no, the sky was blue and the few clouds were white and almost edible-looking. Moving with the queue, Connor left the ferry and wound through the streets to the train station. The route was fairly straightforward, involving a change and short hop on the underground in London before emerging on the other side back into the leafy 'urbs of the shires.

Wherever possible, but without trying to attract undue attention, Connor would try to avoid the field of vision of the security cameras that guarded the public places he crossed. Conscious that not being seen was virtually impossible, he changed his appearance whenever he could. While passing the various stores, Connor would enter and make a purchase—a hat, a coat, or a bag. When the moment was right, Connor would enter a toilet in one garb and minutes later emerge in another. It was not much, he knew, but he thought it sufficient to throw any future follower off his trail. Too often, luck played a part in the detection of the unwitting criminal, the culmination of circumstances, that thousand-to-one chance that chose that moment to turn up. *No,* Connor reasoned to himself. If ever the tapes were reviewed, then the chances of his form being linked to a cross-country journey from a channel coast port would be small to say the least. The discarded items were buried in the bottom of bins or locked in abandoned luggage lockers. They were untraceable and of no intrinsic value, so even if they were found, they should not raise any suspicion and might even make the finder's day.

The day had been long, and the evening was drawing in as Connor paid the taxi driver and watched him pull away before crossing the road and making his way through the industrial estate towards the lockup. The business of the day was done, and the lights were being switched off as the factories and offices released their occupants back to their respective lives. The grey mundane. Far removed from the brave new world that had been promised in their halcyon days, the hubris of youth faded and morphed, manifest in the frustration of the "nine to five." To become part of the oppressed masses and not to realise it was the biggest con that the establishment could pull. The constant distraction of life, the cycle of holidays and events that kept a person buoyed with hope for the future, but made him miss the fact that, all the while, his life was sliding by. The magician's misdirection, the squeeze on a man's arm just before dipping in his pocket so that he would not feel the latter. There was something for everyone—the summer holiday, the weekend, Christmas, the football season, Olympics, the next birthday or anniversary. There was always something coming over the horizon that could be focused on with hope or trepidation, but the effect was always the same: It stopped a person from focussing on the now.

Connor walked through the crowd of people making their way home to their fish supper, always on a Friday, and the latest instalment of TV serial. The lockup was dark and quiet. Connor pushed the door shut behind him. A fine layer of dust lay on the rich livery and dulled the reflection of the buzzing fluorescent lights. Making his way to the rear of the lockup, Connor cast his eye over the discarded equipment that had propelled him to this stage. He filled the kettle and, after plugging it in, slumped in the beat-up armchair he had inherited with the hire of the lockup. The four walls with no windows were a welcome sanctuary— no prying eyes, no need to be guarded or ultra-aware of his surroundings and actions. Connor felt, physically, the knot of tension untie. He breathed deep and let the angst drain down his spine and pool around his ankles to seep into the cracks of the rough concrete floor. The click of the kettle pulled Connor back from the edge of slumber and left him sitting there, deciding whether the effort of getting up outweighed the comfort he had carved out in the armchair. Comfort won.

He awoke four hours later. The lights were bright. He squinted to see the dial of his watch; it was nearly midnight. He stood and stretched away the stiffness that had crept into his body and, once again, started the kettle.

Chapter 49

SCOTLAND XIV

The sunlight was watery and cold. It promised warmth, but failed to deliver Connor watched the yellow light creep slowly around the room. The wooden walls of the bothy had been bleached by the sun many times before, but not today. Connor's moisture-laden breath sent steaming clouds out into the centre of the room to vanish and travel unseen to the inside of the windows. He was comfortable, warm, snug, cocooned in his sleeping bag.

The plastic-wrapped bundles sat squat and heavy in the bottom of the rucksack. Like a radioactive isotope, his load irradiated out and could not be contained by any guise, nor shielded from creeping into Connor's consciousness. Having carried it for many miles with the literal weight on his shoulders, he realised that the time had come to offload his burden. In his wanderings, his eye had cast around many nooks and crannies as he passed, but always the nagging doubt of accidental discovery haunted him. Obviously, the fear of losing the hard-won fortune was his primary concern, but a close second was the lead it would give to the police. The opportunity to start to piece together a timeline, a starting point, or more accurately an endpoint to work backwards from would narrow the window down and allow the circumspect thought to be more factual, allowing the strands of evidence to form up into the Turk's head of knots, around which Connor was the standing part. One possibility had arisen, but he had dismissed it as too theatrical to be worthy of merit. However, faced with the options, the idea was growing into a tangible concept. After retrieving his well-thumbed maps, he scanned the coloured charts in an ever increasing radius, with his current position as the central point. Twenty minutes later, he had marked up the map with four circles, which he now pondered.

The days passed and slowly. Connor's strength returned. When his appetite allowed, he would eat as much as he could, with a mind to striking a balance between eking out his stock of comestibles versus trying to rebuild his strength and lost body weight. He kept his mind busy by servicing his kit, cleaning and airing his tent, and in between listening to his radio. The hours crept past on the scale of normality, but when there was no time agenda, no comparisons existed. Time did not hang heavy, as there as nothing to hang it off of. The days and nights were broken up by an unimposed ritual of eating, sleeping, and ablutions. The childhood indiscipline of not waiting for the next thing to happen stole around the periphery of thought and prised its way into Connor's consciousness whenever his mind was devoid of subject matter. In order to push away from the shores of boredom, Connor would scull across the placid lake of possibility to which his newly gained wealth had allowed him access. His house in the country was a very real possibility; shiny cars and fine wines were within his grasp. More tempting was the potential to turn his back on the world of work. The devil stalked and sowed his seeds across his trodden fields, and in his wake grew the fields of temptation. The pendulous fruits hung ripe ready for picking. How could the starved resist such bounty. It was easier to live in Sparta surrounded by kith and kin than to walk in the Garden of Eden and have to return to Spartan surrounds, where cupboards were full of nothing but echoes. Connor looked at his Eden, plastic-wrapped and cuboid. If not Eden itself, it was at least the passport to the better place and, at the same time, a passport without a visa. If he tried to use it, it would flag his presence to the authorities, so it was both a route to freedom and incarceration at the same time.

A week had passed, and the bothy had been unvisited by anyone. Connor was lord and master of all he surveyed, or at least the temporary leaseholder. The paradox was that it was ideal; the setting and environment were all that he would seek if given the opportunity to purchase such a place, and yet here he was in it, and it was his for nothing. If he could tolerate the occasional guest, there was very little reason not to stay put, and although it was a consideration, his socialist tendencies did not quite stretch to commune living. For this reason, Connor was restowing his backpack and removing his wardrobe from various makeshift pegs and hangers he had adopted in the little wooden cell where he had taken sanctuary for the last twelve days.

He took a last scan around the building before stepping out onto the veranda and into the watery sunshine, which dripped through the black coniferous boughs that cast the bothy into mottled shade. Connor closed the door behind him and eased the heavy latch into its stay. The ground and trees were still covered in snow, and this caused an involuntary shudder within Connor in light of the task ahead of him. Shouldering the bag, he stepped off onto the path, leaving behind the bothy and a set of fresh footprints in the snow.

It took a while to find his pace and settle into the familiar gait, which, prior to his stay in the bothy, had become almost second nature. Whether it was the snow covering the path or his lack of practice, he could not be sure, but the outcome meant he was labouring more than he should. He was also stiff, which caused him to tense further until the small of his back started to complain, exasperated as it was by the load of the backpack. Connor slowed further. The covered ground hid the rocks and potholes that could turn ankles and twist knees, and he could not afford to be rendered lame this far from anywhere near civilised. As he had not cut across any other footprints, Connor was sure that he could be here a long time alone if things did go bad. So, slower and leaning heavily on the walking poles, he picked his way amongst the hills. Occasionally, the hills would peel back to give an unencumbered view of the way ahead a sweeping vista of fields of snow that cut and dove into the burns, and re-entrants that shaped the hills. A panorama of a child's unfinished project in plaster—fat, rounded shapes gorged in their snow cloaks, a veritable frosted Christmas cake into which Connor, a Wenceslasian character in search of winter fuel, stepped.

The sky had dulled and now bore the leaden pallor of the ill. The wind danced around, an annoying invisible dog that snapped at his heels. The terrain had undulated, a frozen storm of sea that Connor had navigated across, with perilous peaks and cavernous troughs. His journey had literally ended on the shore: An expanse of black water extended away from where Connor stood. Like a bullet hole in a bed sheet, the loch looked stark amongst the snow-clad surrounds. The wind swept the loch and ruffled the water, the only animation in the bleak vista.

Connor scouted around for a campsite and decided on a spot under a slightly overhanging rock shelf. Although in the full teeth of the wind, the loch was also in full view from that position. He fought with the wind to pitch his tent, and the gods played with him he recalled the days when it would have caused a fit of fury, a rage that would have seen the tent cursed and thrown aside until the futility of his actions were realised and his anger had cooled. *Where have those feelings gone?* he wondered. Was it that there was no one else to blame and that only he suffered for his predicament? Connor just smiled and plodded on. There was no expectation of him; his gender role had been neutralised. Years of indoctrination of fulfilling his "manly" role were gone. There was no crowd to play to. He did as well as he wanted, when he wanted. So he smiled some more as he untangled the guy lines, stretched the fabric into the shape of the tent, and emptied his belongings into the fabric shelter, which was to become his home for a couple of days.

From the inside of the tent, Connor sat cross-legged and peeped through the opening of the partially unzipped door.

The edges of the zippered door framed the edges of the loch without, and Connor could quickly scan the expanse of water and compare the real landscape to the coloured chart he had on his lap. He located visual landmarks, inlets, gullies, and featured rock formations on the map and drew on the chart a number of straight lines across the loch from one identified feature to another. After a few hours' work, the map showed a number of fanned-out lines emanating from each individual point. Each line had an alphanumeric reference, which Connor had transposed into a small pocket notebook. Content with his work, he stretched before crashing back flat out onto his sleeping bag. He stared at the chart and at the intersections formed by the lines crossing it. He was searching for a point where at least three lines crossed and that was not too far towards the centre of the loch. *Approximately thirty metres. That would be ideal,* he thought. Two options presented themselves, and Connor put an asterix by them in his notebook.

The light was starting to fade, so Connor set about his housework in preparation for his night time needs and fired up the little stove. His mind started to wander as he watched the shadows thrown into animation around his tent walls, which rippled in the evening breeze. The shadows shrank and elongated as the material wall was bellied in and out, and the mundane took on the grotesque. Extraordinary appearances lurked amongst the subconscious mind. It was in his subconscious that Connor realised that his character had been seeded, deep and beyond his waking ability to amend or alter. His lifetime exposure had been hardwired in an unerasable set of primitive reflexes to a given set of conditions. Of course, the more obvious ones were just that—obvious. He could accept, and largely rationalise, his fight-or-flight response or fear of the dark or heights as intrinsic survival traits, most likely primitive in origin. But what was it that caused him to dislike crowded places, his need to be in control, his inability to let go, and his obsessive pursuance of too many things? What about his ability to suffer in silence and persevere alone, or his inability to work alongside someone who was trying to help? The closer the relationship, the less tolerant he became. There were many facets of his behaviour that this sojourn away from society, for the most part, had brought to the fore of his mind and made him consider whether community living was a beneficial factor for someone with his seemingly antisocial disposition.

Connor disliked cats, not a hatred that would have him kicking at a passing feline, but a dislike of their surly approach to life. The way in which they were almost parasitic, taking what they needed primarily, and if the host benefited in some way from this relationship, then it was a symbiotic affair. But the truth was that the cat was at the top of its list and always came first. Connor had heard it said, "You dislike the people and things that you most recognise in yourself." He wondered whether he had become a cat, a feral tom that stalked the wilds, a beast of some Godforsaken moor, forest, or heath that, for the large part of its existence, remained unseen, but would occasionally dip into the communities that it came across to take what it needed before scuttling away back into solitude and obscurity. Uncomfortable with this depiction of his existence, Connor could not altogether deny the similarities. He had hermitised himself. Granted, at the time his goal had been evasion and escape from criminal prosecution, but it could not be ignored that to a greater degree, his current solitary existence was his ultimate goal, an isolation with which he was content. But if the truth be told, he could have achieved his current position without carrying out the crime in the first place. So why could he not have just taken the step? It was, he decided, his catlike principles, if that was not an oxymoron. He was selfish, top of his own list, and as such was prepared to take some risk to climb the tree to raid the nest, steal the cream, sprint from the fishmongers with ill-gotten gains, and even look at the queen. All were carefully calculated against the exertion necessary to achieve the required outcome. Cats in management would be accountants, loss adjusters, and insurance brokers—takers, not creators, the kind of social parasite that Connor disliked. Now he was beginning to realise that the root of his dislike, the reflective traits, were hardwired in him and most probably everybody else, and it was an effort to rise above the sea of selfishness and aspire to the lofty heights of charity and giving, be it in mind or deed. Connor recognised that he had laid a middle path for himself. Of course, there were no selfless acts. It was just a matter of doing what he liked and wanted to do primarily, and if that helped others, then symbiosis was achieved. Connor resigned himself to being a cat.

The next few days passed quickly, and there was a repetitiousness about them. Connor visited and paper-plotted each of his sites for likely lines of sight. Following the static survey, Connor would spend the best part of a day walking the circumference of the loch and checking his calculations against the view from the ground, systematically discarding those that were not up to the required needs and, by default, promoting those that were. The weather had been a mixed bag—no, a rummage sale—of climatic conditions that would have a weatherman's report sounding like an astrologer's prediction, covering all the bases. The wind was perpetual, and it brought the rain, sleet, and hail at varying degrees of angle. Clouds sailed the sky-seas like Spanish galleons, full-sailed and heeling dangerously under their black shadows. But every now and then, the ships of the sky would relinquish their hold and let through the watery golden rays of sunlight that painted the earth canvas in honeyed hues that denuded the lurking shadows and darkened valleys of their sinister cloaks. Connor strode on, sighting the way, and marked out crops along his compass. Then, he would triangulate against other significant promontories.

His work done, he sat in his little tent, going over the previous day's notes and findings as he sipped at the warming cup, causing involuntary body shakes, or his future grave stone was experiencing a lot of footfall. From his recordings it became apparent that the first loch offered the best options, so he would relocate there tomorrow. He could not decide what the best weather would be for him to carry out his next intentions, but he knew none would make the task particularly nice—not at this time of year, at least.

The sun was trying hard to show its face through the scudding clouds. Shadows danced across the green-grey mottled loch, and a distorted reflection of the crucible that held the water stood out through the eddies and ripples when the wind took a breath. Connor stood at the edge, hands buried deep in his jacket pockets, and his chin sunken in the turned-up storm collar. If ever a body of water looked as cold and uninviting as the one that lapped at the shore on which Connor stood, he would not want to see it. However, he had been away some time now, and the task he had set himself he felt was, although somewhat dramatic, suited to the script as it had unfurled.

Having positioned a large, flat rock on the shore, Connor sat upon it and unlaced his boots in a slow, deliberate way in an attempt to stave off the inevitable task ahead. A bundle of green nylon parachute cord trailed across the stone-strewn shore and lay in a loose coil alongside the rock on which he sat. Standing somewhat gingerly due to the sharp-edged stones under his feet, Connor unzipped his jacket and let it fall to the ground before picking up the coil and stepping towards the loch. He was clad in a thermal base layer, and the wind bit with a razor-sharp chill, which was beat soundly into second place by the icy grip of the water as it flowed through his toes and around his ankles. Connor looked down at his feet, which had already turned a larded white as every red blood cell evacuated the extremity of his feet to the warmer climes of his core. Connor stepped forward and pulled the cord taut behind him. The chill crept up his calves, and clouds of silt and sand obscured the water as he waded tentatively forward. The wind blew full in his face and caused wavelets to rise to higher levels and force him to take involuntary gasps. Bending his mind to the moment, Connor visualised himself back in the steaming heat of the Gambia, the breathless, parched air and the trickle of sweat running down his spine to soak his belted waistline. He had read that extreme swimmers could raise their core temperatures in order to overcome the freezing conditions to which they exposed their bodies. It seemed a trick too advanced for Connor as he struggled to control the gasping intakes of breath as the water crept up around his groin. Pausing, he reached his hands into the torturous waters, cupped an icy handful to his face, and repeated the process twice more before shaking the droplets from his head as he ran his hands through his hair. His skin fizzed with the sensation. He took a half step forward and ducked into the water so that it rushed over his shoulders as he sank into a squat. He tried to sit still, but his whole being screamed and jigged to escape the confines of water and shudder involuntarily. His breath was rapid and shallow, and as hard as he tried, he could not force more air into his lungs than his panting diaphragm would allow. His bladder reacted to the cold and, pretty much beyond his control, expelled what transpired to be a more pleasant experience than he had anticipated as the heat from his urine stole around his body. He felt quite lightheaded and could feel his muscles start to tighten and become unresponsive. He could no longer feel the cord in his hands. Taking as big a breath as he could, he ducked his head into the water. Even then, his body and mind would not let him totally submerge. His temples screamed in pain as though ice cubes were being forced into his skull. The nape of his neck pulled tight, and an instant headache flashed through his head. His shoulder muscles clamped as though an ice pick had been spiked in between his shoulder blades. Connor struggled to the upright and turned back to the shore, speeding as the water lessened in depth. He stumbled through the shallows and fell to all fours as he freed himself of the water's grip. He shook loose the gripped cord from his hand and lifted the flat rock onto it before gathering up his coat and boots as best he could. The wind, now in league with the water, pursued him back towards his tent, and Connor would swear that his vision was starting tunnel. He breathed deep as he crossed the last few yards to the open flap of the tent and dove through. He ripped off the thermal layers. Once inside, he rubbed his deadened skin with the towel as he tried to restore his circulation. Using his unresponsive fingers and his teeth, he pulled on the tether attached to the zip to pull the flaps of the tent together and shut out the sniping wind. Once he was as dry as he could get, he pulled on his jumper and sleeping bottoms before crawling into the undone sleeping bag. Connor pulled his legs up to his chest and lay as still as his shivering body would allow. Gradually, he felt the heat start to return to his dermis. Some half an hour passed before he stopped shaking sufficiently to light the stove safely. The heat rose in thermal waves of the dancing flames and collected in the roofline apex of the tent. Connor breathed deep the heated air before he poured steaming tea, sickeningly sweet with sugar, from his flask. The hot vapours stole across his face as he raised the cup to his bruise-coloured lips. The tiny hairs on his face and nose hairs bent to the change in temperature caused by the steam. The hot liquid flushed through his system and purged the last vestiges of cold from his pallid body so that a pink flush crept across his skin. The air in the tent grew warmer and warmer until it started to grow uncomfortable to breathe. Connor pulled down the zip four or five inches, allowing the cooler fresh air to blow into the stuffy confines.

Connor sat sipping at his cup and reflecting on his experience, contemplating what lay ahead. He questioned himself over his planned course of action. He still believed that the water route was best. He accepted that the summer months would have been better to carry out his task, but be that as it may, he was where he was when he was. The colder months of winter offered solitude and, most importantly, no prying eyes—or none that would believe what they were seeing, were they to see Connor thrashing around in the snow-bordered loch.

He dressed and luxuriated in the warmth each additional layer offered. Once fully clothed, he donned his boots and, taking his water bottle, went back to the water's edge.

The silt had settled, and he was pleased to note that very few of his footprints could be seen on the bottom of the loch. Connor bent down to the length of cord clamped beneath the rock and tied a figure-eight knot in the bight before straightening out the line. There was a disappointingly short amount beyond the knot, but Connor tied the running end to his water bottle, which he filled to the brim from the loch. Having done so, he threw the bottle out into the loch and slowly trawled the line back in until the knot was against his hand. Connor waited for the water to still and the dragged-up silt to settle and clear once more. Staring in to the loch, Connor could see the aluminium-bodied bottle lying on the bottom, pretty much as he had expected, but he wanted to gauge the conditions he was dealing with. His experiment completed, Connor retrieved the bottle before throwing it as hard as he could back into the loch. The cord extended out and unfurled as it followed the arc made by the water-filled bottle. With a satisfying splash, the bottle once more sank to the bottom. Once again Connor scanned out across the water to see if he could spy the bottle in the depths. Failing to do so, he moved away from the water's edge to higher ground before turning back to see if the new vantage point allowed him to see the bottle's position. He was not able to see the bottle's whereabouts, even with the telltale cord floating out across the water before sinking down to the murky depths. Connor returned to the shore, took up the slack in the line, and tied a second figure-eight knot. He then dragged the line and bottle in a couple of metres before repeating the viewing process. Each time he repeated the task, he would tie a new knot and untie the last. Eventually, the bottle could be seen once more from the raised vantage point, but not from the water's edge. Connor tied the new knot and then measured out the distance between the two knots, much like a market stall fabric seller approximating the length across his body from his chest to his fingertips. All told, he reckoned on about ten metres. Allowing for the depth, he guessed that he would have to go out another five to seven metres before going down. It was not an endearing thought.

After returning to the tent, Connor brewed a hot mug of sugary tea, which he drank as hot as he could bear. The scalding liquid brought a sheen of perspiration to his brow as he sat in the windless calm of the tent. He finished the tea and moved quickly to the water's edge. He disrobed as before and once more entered the ice-cold, heat-sapping waters of the loch. Paying out the knotted cordage as he hyperventilated his way into the loch, Connor was determined to go beyond his previous depth. The water once more stole above his groin, and again the urge to urinate was strong. This time, he reasoned to hold in the body-hot liquid, his reasoning being that the specific heat capacity of his urine was better losing its heat conductively through him than being lost to the greater mass of cold water through which he waded. The knot slipped through his fingers, and still he kept taking tentative half steps, his feet obscured by the rising billows of silt. Two, three steps saw the water lapping in between his taut nipples and tendon-stretched neck. Eventually, his natural buoyancy caused his feet to float away from the muddied bottom, and, taking stunted, small strokes, Connor floated in the water on the edge of panic as his breath rushed in and out of his restricted chest, where a sharp pain was developing just left of his breastbone. Grasping the line tight, he turned back towards the shore, which he was surprised to see he had moved so far away from. Concentrating and willing his body to respond, he reached forward in the water and kicked as hard as he could. His legs were leaden, like two chilled ham hocks, dead and hanging almost unresponsive from his hips. A flash of fear coursed across his mind, and the world immediately around him became intensely focused in micro detail. The ripples and froth of the splashed water were sharp and fascinating. The distance to the shore looked infinitely far and beyond his claw-handed reach. This was it, was it? This was to be the demise and worldly exit, his final view of his earthly existence? The edge of his vision greyed and blurred, and his sight became tunnelled. The shining wet rocks reflected the weak sunshine as it was washed from the waves by his thrashing, the ever -increasing circles of disturbance reaching the shore whilst the epicentre seemed not to be gaining any forward momentum. Straining his neck backwards, up and out of the water to keep his mouth clear of the suffocating cold water, throwing his body in uncoordinated arcs, he could not gauge whether he was moving at all. His vision was now of the wintry sky and scudding clouds. A cough and choke allowed the first mouth of water to antagonise his epiglottis and a new spike of panic to cease his mind. As Connor thrashed wildly and uncontrollably, his hand came into contact with the muddied bottom. The realisation of what he was touching did not register, such was his panicked state. Indeed, there was no conscious reaction to the final stages of his near drowning, as his survival instinct had kicked in and gone into an autopilot mode, not trusting the cognitive processes to take the rational steps the situation demanded. Legs stumbling for purchase on the shifting bottom and hands reaching out to maintain balance as they sunk into the sucking silt, Connor fell from the loch, crashing onto the stony shore. His lungs reached with blessed gasping relief of the unadulterated thin air that his cramped, aching body craved.

His paroxysms were uncontrollable and debilitating as his body tried to contract his muscles to generate heat, to kick-start the stalled part of his motor systems. Dizzy and confused, as if drunk, Connor struggled to cover the ground back to the sanctuary of his tent that stood alone, a beacon of safety on the cold and barren shore. He grazed his knees, hands, and cheek as he tripped, stumbled, and fell the ridiculously short distance back to his sanctuary. Connor felt none of the damage he was inflicting on himself. His whole being was focused on achieving his goal: a few microns of coloured nylon and the warmth it offered within.

The worm of an idea wriggled into his confused consciousness and somehow commanded centre stage amidst the noise and hubbub that existed there. *Lie down,* it said. *Have a rest and gather yourself for the last push.* The words were warm and inviting, sugar-coated temptation that would be so easy to succumb to, but still he fought his way across the boulder-strewn plateau towards the fluttering tent, only yards away. Wishing he had opened the tent doors on the end that faced the loch so as he would have had less distance to travel, he skirted the rock-held guidelines to the far end of the tent before he crashed into the windless womb and the downy embrace of his sleeping bag. He was beyond cold. He knew his core temperature had dipped as he wrestled the quilted sleeping bag around his body, still in the wet nylon thermals he had worn in the loch. He had neither the energy nor the manual dexterity to remove the garments, so he hunkered down, covering himself as best he could, as the zipper was well beyond his waxy white and senseless hands. With his head covered by the bag, he brought his knees up as best he could to his chest, and in this foetal position he tried to bring his body and breathing back under his control. Connor realised he was very vulnerable, and at any time he could slip uncontrollably into the grasp of hypothermia. If that were to happen, by the time he was discovered, he would be beyond saving. He would probably be found semi-naked, lying out on the shore of the loch—which would be a cruel paradox, as it was hypothermia's final mindfuck to cause the sufferer to believe that he was indeed hot. For those who had been brought back from the edge of hypothermic expiration, it was not an unpleasant last state—if one had to go, that is. But the physical cold was one factor. Hypothermia preyed not just on the physically weak; indeed, it was the mentally weak that were its first victims, and Connor was not going to cede that battle, as he knew it was one he could win.

The shaking grew violent, but at least now, he reasoned, the effort of the shaking and the heat generated was insulated and no longer escaping on the thief wind or cut-purse loch waters. He breathed under the cover of the bag so that the air became stifled and uncomfortable. He tried to recycle every valuable joule of energy back into heating his frozen body. Memories of lying in his boyhood bedroom with his head beneath the bedclothes whilst real and imagined ghosts stole through the shadows, which had morphed into sinister, little boy–torturing creatures entered his mind. The atmosphere became almost irrespirable, so he had to burst from his self-imposed confinement to breathe the cool, sweet air and face his fear simultaneously. Sleep always followed swiftly after. Connor just peeled back the edge of the sleeping bag and inhaled the cold air before shutting out the light and chill to pull tight, the bag around him once more. Slowly, slowly the shivering abated, and a buzz of pins and needles tortured his extremities as the tepid blood made its tentative way back through the restricted vessels that served his appendages. Staying deep within the confines of the sleeping bag, he gently flexed his fingers. The digits responded painfully, but they did respond and opened from their claw-like state into something that more resembled a hand. The dexterity was still not there, though, and Connor continued to grasp and flex to bring the warming blood back. He needed to light the stove and get something warm into him. He needed to shed the thermal underwear, which, although now warm, was still damp and sapping heat from his body that he could ill afford to lose. He also needed to close the zipper on the tent flap. None of these tasks that would speed his recovery were at all possible whilst he had no feeling in his fingers, and he had to maintain his discipline not to try too soon, as he would lose all the cocooning heat built up in the bag. If things went bad, he could double-dip his core temperature, and whether or not he had the inner strength and wherewithal to come back from that, he did not know. Whereas he might be physically able, the frustration of watching his own hands failing to achieve quite menial tasks would be mentally damaging and would lower his morale into the reach of the hypothermic devils, a clasp he was striving to escape. The light darkened as Connor just lay shivering in his tent. Eventually, a gentle wave of sleep washed against the back of his eyes and became an irresistible force. Connor succumbed to its call and gentle massage, his eyelids growing heavy 'til they met and stayed closed.

The unaccustomed flapping of the tent nylon registered deep in the sleeping Connor's subliminal consciousness. He resisted the call back to the awake world, preferring to reside in the temperate zone of his sleeping state, but his eyes reluctantly opened and tried to focus through the dark to the source of the unfamiliar sound. The blackness was impenetrable. As hard as he stared, there was no focus, no shade of black or grey. A slight panic seized him. Had the cold had some neurological effect and stricken him blind? He fumbled in the dark and pressed with desperation at the watch strapped to his wrist and, more by luck than any precision, felt a blessed relief as from the darkness the backlit watch glowed. His eyes struggled to adjust to the relatively bright light emitted by the watch. Connor lay back, gathered his thoughts, and took stock. The cold was still there, but limited to the extremities. He rubbed his hands together, gently at first, but increasing the intensity until the friction generated a palpable heat. His fingers throbbed as the blood was forced to circulate. Forcing himself out of the bag, he moved as quickly as he could to locate his head torch and turn it on. This would allow him to draw down the zipper as far as he could reach before turning his attention to his stove. The controls seemed impossibly small, and his hands were alien to him as they struggled to eject a small shower of sparks from the reluctant lighter in the vicinity of the hissing stove, which suddenly caught alight, sending a flame front across the tent floor through the escaped gas that had started to pool at the stove's base. The resultant heat washed up over the crouched Connor, and, although an unwanted event, the captured heat was a welcome addition to the cold tent. The stove flame sent out a radiating wave of heat, which Connor held his hands over. His shoulders gave an involuntary shudder. Scoping round, he located items of clothing he had left out before going to the loch. He now pulled these on over the now dry thermal underwear. Fully dressed, he placed the kettle on the stove and, whilst waiting for it to boil, rifled through the stock of food until he located a cellophane bag, in which was rolled a mixture of oats and dried milk powder. Connor shook a quantity into a metal bowl as best he could and then tore open a number of paper bags containing granulated sugar with his teeth. He added these to the mix, and the occasional grain exploded with sweetness on his lips and tongue. The tent filled with the fumes of the stove mixed with the whiffs of steam. But, more importantly, he was breathing in heated air; his skin tingled as the capillaries dilated and the wet heat caused the fine hairs to move and tickle as though unseen insects were crawling over his skin. Unable to wait for the kettle to reach its full boil, Connor poured the hot liquid into the bowl stirring the dried mixture into a lumpy white soup. Almost instantly, he started to spoon the mixture into his mouth, not caring about the heat burning his mouth. He swallowed the sweet porridge, and the effect was almost instantaneous. The sugar coursed his digestive system and, as if an engine starved of fuel had suddenly been injected with petrol, burst in to a full-throttled revving. Connor felt the heat spreading around his body. He cast the empty bowl aside and crawled back into the bag, the stove glowing gently and keeping back the dark in the shadows. He lay in the half-light and considered his options. All said and done, he felt that the loch was the best option, but it had nearly cost him his life. The alternatives carried their own risks. Indeed, he discarded his original choices due to the complications or mental turmoil they would create if chosen. His bundle of cash was not something he could explain away if he were caught with it—not that there was much chance of being caught, but accidents happened, as well he knew. Waking up in a hospital bed with broken limbs or damaged parts was one thing; waking up with a suited police officer holding a bundle of plastic-wrapped money and an inquisitive look on his face was quite another thing altogether. The bank system was a nonstarter, as were left luggage lockers. The torment would be insufferable. Burying the stash here in the barren wilderness was, he thought, the most viable option—and in keeping with the ethos of the whole adventure to date. The boulder-strewn plateaus, the hillsides and mountaintops, the streams and bogs he had crossed had all offered potential sites to hide his stash, but Connor had decided they were ultimately unsuitable, the basic reason being that, if he had discovered the potential repository, then it followed that others could also find it. It was a chance he was not prepared to take. The bottom of a loch, Connor rationalised to himself, was not the sort of place you would accidently trip over a bundle of money, especially if he could secrete it as he had intended. His problem, though, was in trying to hide the stash. He had nearly been overcome by hypothermia. A compromise had to be struck between finding a safe hiding place and being able to safely accommodate his stash in it.

Resolved to follow his plan, Connor had decided on a strategy. Having studied his map, he had located two towns large enough to support a village store. These he would visit and, once he had stocked up with sufficient provisions to sustain an extended loch-side vigil, he would carry out the secretion of his valuable bundle—but only when the weather would not add to his suffering. It would have to be a day when the sun was shining and the wind was not blowing, and these were rare conditions here in the high hills.

With his larder stowed to overflowing with sugar- and carbohydrate-rich foods, Connor sat and waited for the clement weather that would allow him to carry out his plans. He took the time to experiment with his piece of line, to measure the optimum distance off the banks of the loch, to submerge and bury his bundle of cash and then take an armpit-to-fingertip measurement of the distance. Eschewing the fact that the number thirteen was the count, he chose to add one for luck.

The wait was long and arduous, but at the same time, it offered the opportunity to contemplate the situation. His survival high in the Scottish wilderness had run to just over three months now. Apart from planned encounters to restock, Connor had only physically come into contact two or three times with other people as they traipsed across the highlands. A hello here and there and maybe a brief conversation about the mountainside staple of weather and the where and whence of travel. People did not come to the wilds to have conversations; in fact, the opposite could be said. The societal fugitives gathered alone together, amidst the mist and rain where their voices went unheard, blown away by the wind and rendered tiny in the amphitheatre glens, like mice in a cathedral—lost, like their opinions, on the cold, hard rock that remains impassive and inert to the thought of man. A metaphysical footprint in the memory of time. Distant flecks of colour passed across the field of vision, which was framed by the small aperture Connor had created in the door of the tent as he sat cross-legged and stared at the sky and loch as they systematically changed places with each other. People went their way with their world on their backs, hoping to escape the four-walled conformity for the contemplative, agoraphobia-inducing skies and grunt challenges laid down by the precipitous hills and mountains. The breathless inclines stole their minds to be singularly focused to the task at hand and to buy them time away from the stress and strain of monotony, to walk in the world of the kings of Nirvana. And those same kings could reward their labours with views that lifted their hearts, letting them soar free, unfettered, and unencumbered of the chains of society as they looked out on vistas that are theirs alone to behold, a personal panorama where they could do as they wished. To sit silent and watch the ebb and flow of the clouds and light as they swept across the glens and washed up against the weighty masses of the damming mountains, as they corralled the elements within their enfolding arms or allowed them to wash around their stalwart presence. To share the moment with a loved one, to make vows or give enlightenment to an excited mind as it stood on the shores of life's seas, preparing to wade in to the unknown—those pearls of wisdom that might be cast before swine, but should nonetheless be cast. Life's universities accepted all comers, so the doors must be forever open, allowing Jack with his handful of beans and Solomon with his sword to wander in when they wanted. There were too many hard knocks out there, and though fathers and mothers might point out the worst, they should similarly stand by with the bandage as they saw their offspring's cocoon stripped away and their unique character revealed and taking shape. The mountain could be like life: The summit one set out to scale could often morph into the false peak, and the previously unseen challenge beyond became the intent of that person's labours. The path wended many ways and guaranteed nothing other than to absorb time and energy. For the lucky few, topping out allowed the reward of the unparalleled view both back and forth, to see the peaks and troughs of the route to the current vantage point, and to be able to see the horizon ahead and plan the future route. For others, the cloud and mist would prevent them from languishing on the fruits of their labours and leave them uncertain of what lay ahead and how to progress. The chilling wind would snap at their heels to make them move along and vacate their spot for those young hopefuls coming up behind. So off they stepped, fumbling into the future with a hand-drawn sketch of where to go and life's compass pointing unerringly in one direction. The only solace was that the way was pretty much downhill from here, and they could free-wheel into oblivion if life had sucked the aspiration out of them.

Connor scanned the sky to the west and decided that another day would pass without his plan advancing beyond its current stalled position. The plastic wrapped-bundles sat inanimate, but still managing to emanate a source of fear and hope combined— yin and yang, a tangible block that could damn the beholder as well as provide relief and succour to escape the treadmill monotony that beckoned. Connor pulled the cube towards him and, raising himself, sat upon the dais that afforded him no better view of his future, but allowed him to sit in more comfort, at least for a while.

Days and nights passed. Connor had adopted a pattern of existence with a natural rhythm, and he was not going resist the flow. The mealtimes were the highlights of the day, interspersed with ablutions that he had extended somewhat unnecessarily to include full-body immersion in the loch as a means of conditioning himself to the cold. Maintenance of the campsite and his kit also helped to while away the day. The nights were made somewhat bearable through the use of his small radio, which inexplicably would work sometimes and not others. This introduced an element of will-it-won't-it, and when it did not there was a frustrating amount of repositioning to improve, often fruitlessly, the level of reception. On these radio-less nights, Connor would ponder the thumbed maps and re-read labels he had read many times before. Often, he would run through elements of his plan and test the variables. Through a process of binary decisions, he would arrive at various outcomes—some good, some bad. In turn, he would contemplate the alternatives that would lead more often to good outcomes, but the spectre of failure always existed. He thought that the hard part had been done, the deed of taking and to some degree the avoidance of capture, but the crux of it was the level of self-control that was needed. The burden and mental torture to maintain the facade of innocence and remain out of the limelight of suspicion would be, at the very least, testing, but it was a cross he was going to have to bear until he could slip the final shackles.

The morning crept into the tent and swirled around the sleeping figure, prodding him awake with unseen fingers. Connor stirred, noticing the lack of noise, the absence of the continual ruffle of nylon and bowing of the wall of his tent. The stillness bordered on eerie, causing Connor to unzip the door and look at the loch as it appeared from the nighttime shadow. A blanket of mist swirled over the calm waters, a steaming cauldron coming to the boil. The stillness was uncanny for all that had gone before. The animated, twitching heather and gorse, the ripple-distorted reflections that shimmered across the loch, had stopped. Still. Stock-still. Looking up, he saw that the sky was obscured by a bank of mist that hung some thirty or forty feet above the ground and stretched off towards the vanishing point at the bottom end of the loch. The sun was there, given away by the brighter white that stained the greyer mass it hid amongst. She would have to find a thicker bushel of cloud to obscure her light. Pulling down the door flap further, Connor emerged from the tent, stood, and pirouetted through 360 degrees with his hands on his hips and an incredulous look on his face. It was if someone was playing a meteorological prank and had cancelled the weather, or it was an apocalyptic forewarning of darker days ahead, and the weather was just on hiatus prior to an exhalation of foul-breathed fury. Today might be the day; it would be one of those rare, so rare days and reward for the long loch-side sojourn. Connor set about preparing himself. He made a sugar-laden bowl of porridge, which he consumed whilst he put together the ingredients to make a rough soup—or, more accurately, a watery pottage. He combined dried onions, mushrooms, and peppers with some stock cubes and crumbled dried noodles. With the soup set to simmer, he filled his kettle to set on the stove, which he had repositioned at the rear of the tent porch, the entrance farthest from the loch. After arranging the inside of the tent, he opened up the sleeping bag and placed his pack towel down at the water's edge.

He took the line and fixed it with a snap hook around the large boulder he had designated as his reference point, then counted out the fourteen arm- and body-width measurements he had previously calculated. At the point of the fourteenth spread, he tied a large figure-eight knot and into the bight of the knot, attached a second snap hook karabiner, and to this he affixed his empty water bottle. Just over six feet further on, he tied the line around an elongated spike of loose rock he had found for the purpose, using two clove hitches. He left the whole line affair on the large waterside boulder.

Upon returning to the tent, he checked and seasoned the soup before transferring it to the wide-mouthed flask and stowing it just inside the tent. Connor turned down the stove and replaced the soup saucepan with the kettle. Before leaving the inner sanctuary of the tent, he attached a piece of looped parachute cord to the zipper of the tent door and pulled the zipper up a quarter of the way, which was sufficient to allow him to step through even in a near hypothermic state—at least, he hoped so. The makings of a cup of hot chocolate were left in a cup by the stove and kettle. His preparations complete, Connor took his cube of cash contained within a water-resistant bag, to which he had added a couple of large pebbles, down to the loch-side. He stripped down to his thermal underwear, but retained his boots and smiled at his "Max Wall" appearance of tight leggings and big boots. In truth, the smile was tinged with a nervous tension caused by the apprehension of the task ahead.

Taking the coil of rope, Connor edged into the water just as the first direct rays of sunshine pierced the mist overhead, causing the ripples that radiated away from him to sparkle and glint. Connor had to hold up his hand to shield his eyes. Keeping the line taut, he continued to edge in a shuffling manner deeper into the breath-taking cold as it inched up his legs towards his groin, refrigerating his skin as it went. Forcing himself deeper and deeper so that the water reached his midriff, he finally took the plunge and swam out to the length of the line at which the bottle, now floating, changed direction vertically downward, towards the rocks resting on the silted bottom. Trying to regain his breath, Connor tread water, but struggled as he felt his muscles contracting and restricting his movement. Taking a large breath, he duck-dived down the rope to complete a submerged handstand. Whilst inverted, he dug furiously around the rocks so that they sunk into the mud, shale, and light gravel on which they had previously rested. Connor lost all vision and had nothing to focus on other than the immense cold, which took piranha bites into his flesh whilst icicles were being nailed into his temples. Too much. He pushed away and surfaced. Striking out for the shore, he was surprised how well he progressed compared to his last attempt. The sunlight was reflected by the shoreline snow and the diamonds of water that scattered in front of Connor as he fell clumsily from the loch. When he reached the rock, he grabbed the towel and rubbed his head, face, and hands vigorously as he was able. All the while, he jogged around on the flat piece of ground between his tent and the water's edge. His body responded to the physical jerking, feet stamping, and arm swinging, all done in the warming beams of sunlight. These caused a steam trail, which would engulf him if he stood still long enough, to follow Connor's erratic path.

In the tent, Connor poured himself some of the near boiling water into the prepared cup, topped the kettle with cold water, and reset it on the stove. He took a longing look at the warm, cosy glow of the inside of the tent and returned to the loch-side, sipping at the steaming drink as he went. The water bottle that had floated above the loch was now submerged six or so inches below the surface, the rock tied below having sunk into the hole that his frantic underwater excavations had created. Unfortunately, it was still not enough. In Connor's mind, at least another four inches, maybe six, would be needed to "bury" his bag, which he eyed as it lay at the base of the big boulder to which his line was tied. Another excursion into the loch was required.

After finishing the hot, sweet dregs of the cup, Connor completed some final stretches and bends. Although his thermal clothing was wet, it had warmed due to his activity and the unseasonal sun's beneficence. Steeling himself, he once more waded in, every step torturous because of the physical pain as well as the anticipatory mental anguish of progressing against

the very will and fibre of inner sense. Once more, he duck-dived.
He located the bottom of the sunken line and dug furiously at
the thankfully giving bottom of the loch. The clouds of silt
again billowed up and stole the light, creating confusion within
Connor's mind. The gravitational pull was nullified by the
water, and his physical orientation was hampered by his lack of
vision. The confusion creeping into is mind due to the crippling
cold and oxygen deficiency was such that only the line against
his shoulder and his hands in the cloying mud allowed him to
know which way was up. Soon his lungs were aching with the
pressure to release the intolerable build-up of carbon dioxide
and replenish the body's craving for oxygen. Connor pushed up
towards the brightness above his head, exploding through the
water and instantly expelling the stale air. He breathed in the
sweet, chilled mountain air whilst simultaneously stretching for
the shore, pulling on the tied-off rope to make some headway, as
his legs were cramping with the cold. Once more he stumbled
out of the water. The edge of his vision was blurred and his
movements were slow, laborious. He tried to take the towel to
dry off, but his fingers were locked into pugilistic fists, and he
stared at his own hands as though they were phantasmal for the
control that he could exert over them. The thought that he had
pushed too hard once again flashed through his mind. He turned
towards the tent, thankful for his earlier preparations, but as he
turned his eye caught the bag at the base of the rock. He found
himself looking at the bag, which he could not pick up, lying
in the open. He needed to get to the sanctuary of the tent. He
shivered involuntarily and had started to curl his body into a
stooping bow. He was caught in two minds, and his dithering
was exposing him further.

Connor turned his back on his bag and made for the tent.
He lifted his leg through the partially done-up flap, twisted,
and fell into the womb that offered sanctuary and succour—an
inverted birth. The stove had heated the inside of the tent with
an encompassing warmth that Connor savoured. He struggled,

but eventually shed his wet clothes and pulled on his fleece jacket and dry trousers. He dumped the wet garments, along with his boots, out of the tent, taking the opportunity to scan the horizon for anyone approaching and, in the foreground, the stark and blazoned bag he had abandoned. He noticed that the edge of his vision had cleared, and although still shaking, he could manage to straighten his lard-white, gnarled hands. With a little difficulty, he wrestled off the lid of the flask and slopped its contents into its accompanying cup. The savoury steam assailed his nasal cavity and, trying not to drop or spill the contents, he took a mouthful of the hot, fibrous liquid. It gave up its inherent warmth as it descended through his oesophagus before the more complex sugars and carbohydrates set about reheating his chilled muscles. Connor hunkered down as best he could, drawing up the sleeping bag around his shoulders so that he could still see the bag lying abandoned on the snow- and gravel-strewn shore. A wave of tiredness flushed through him as he felt the warmth of the tent and the soup start to take effect after the cold-water exertions. But he fought the strengthening impulse to lie down and curl up inside his bag in order to keep vigil over the bag outside. The gnawing anxiety grew as his shivering subsided, until he could no longer bear the exposure and, Gollum-like, he dragged himself out of his cave and sank his bare feet into his cold boots. He shuffled down to the bag to bring it back under his control, his "precious."

The weight of pressure that the collection of the bag brought and the closure of the tent so that no stray eyes could steal a view of his world brought with them an irresistible tide of sleep. Connor crashed into the welcoming softness and fell into a deep slumber.

He woke early. His limbs were aching and his muscles stiff from the exertion and immersion in the loch the day before. It was still dark, and he found his way around the inside of the tent by torchlight and the glow of the flame on the stove. Connor was hungry despite the high-calorie diet to which he had subjected himself. The outdoor living and his cold climate exposure ensured that the extra intake was not making him any fatter, as it was being converted directly for the immediate needs of his body—and that was predominantly the generation of heat. He now understood the ability of the ancient and modern polar explorers to eat almost indiscriminately foodstuffs that, in normal life, would be repugnant to all but the most ardent glutton. He would not have thought to mixing savoury and sweet, but now the matter was not the abhorrence. It might once have been and was, in part, the reason he was considering how to combine the remnants of soup from the flask with his craving for a sugar-loaded bowl of porridge, the powdered milk over-watered to produce Scrooge-like gruel. In the end, he kept with convention and sat through two courses for his breakfast. The soup course, however, was prepared and served in the residue of the porridge so that the savoury tang was occasionally lifted by the smattering of sugar—which, if he considered the matter, was not an unpleasant addition.

Once he had finished his meal, Connor extended the tent flap zip from one that allowed the steam of cooking to escape to almost halfway down so that he could explore the view over the loch from his seated position. The sun was inching up, and its warming glow was lighting the skies to the east, which Connor could just see through his portal. The dark greys were giving way to a mustard mist, which diffused the hard edges of the mountain-framed horizon. Here and there, stray shafts of light threw into stark relief the undulating re-entries of the monochrome mountainsides. The snow had melted back a little, receding like an old man's gums to reveal the darker rock below. The immediate foreground was still dark and uninviting, the sun being denied access as the trolls of the night packed away their games and sought dark refuge under the hem of the mountain's skirt, which formed the easterly shore of the loch. Connor cast his eye across the loch itself. It was a spill of Indian ink, a black hole that sucked the light from the air, and a vacuous sinkhole that just lay impassive, flat, and uncaring. There today and forever, shaping itself to its environment, waiting for nothing just doing, in an infinitesimal way, the thing that water does as it moves through the water cycle from cloud to sea time after time after time. The atoms and molecules being vaporised, liquidised and solidified. Consumed, swallowed, breathed, regurgitated, and excreted. Polluted, purified, and bottled, having travelled farther than the imagination could imagine. This was no virgin pool; this was the bastard, bastard of all bastards, and it cared not where it went. To sit on the tables or to flow through the taps of the greatest names the world has ever known. To have been the by-product of the respiratory action that fired the synapse of creation or destruction mattered less than the irregular orbit of its electrons, as long as its molecular combination remained the omnipresent, life-giving cradle and support mechanism for earth. As far as Connor was concerned, it was the solvent for his tea and the cloak and barrier for his secret.

An involuntary shudder crept across his shoulders and caused him to take a slurp of the hot, sweet liquid. Thankfully, the wind was still light, barely casting a ripple on the glossy black tar pit that ran away to vanish in the dark. Looking up, he saw that the sky was turning a whitish-blue that threatened to be an azure hemisphere if the semi-opaque mist allowed. Taking stock, Connor decided today would have to be the day. The cold and suffering caused by the loch was becoming a mental barrier that was increasingly difficult to overcome. The season was moving on, and soon the mountainside and hills would become busier with walkers and climbers plotting courses with maps and compasses across the currently sterile environment. Then Connor's activities would provoke unwanted attention. It was then that he spied the carelessly discarded pile of wet thermal underclothes lying against his boots. A less inviting or motivating sight would be hard to imagine at this early hour, especially from his current position of warmth and relative comfort. Reaching forward, he picked up the clothing and squeezed the material so that the chilled water ran over his hands. When the garments were as dry as he could render them, Connor stretched them out and placed them in the loft so that the heat would at least take the chill off the damp clothing. He shuffled forward and opened the tent flap fully, then pulled his boots onto his bare, stockingless feet. The chilled fabric and leather pressed hard against his calloused skin. Loosely laced up, he climbed out of the tent, his joints aching and complaining as he brought himself to the vertical. After retrieving his coat to fend off the early morning chill, he crunched his way through the remnants of snow to the water's edge. He skirted around the loch until he reached the boulder, from which the line stretched out into the darkness of the loch. Connor climbed up onto the boulder and sat so that he was staring out towards the water along the vanishing line. If seen, he would to all the world look like someone practising yoga or semi-mystic shamanism.

The hour hand of his watch crept around, and gradually the light strengthened to reveal the simultaneously beautiful and sinister landscape. The towering slopes were awe-inspiring. Connor was tempted to scale and view the world from their shoulders. At the same time, the bleak escarpment could become a place of torture and torment for the unprepared or the unaware—and, all too often, that combination existed in the same person. The line of light crept down the mountainside at Connor's back, a laser level tide mark that chased the shadow of night as it drained into the pool that he looked out over. A tinge of warmth tickled his scalp as the earth's azimuth allowed the sun to appear over the facing mountains. All too quickly, Connor was fully bathed in the morning light, his body was being heated, and the last vestiges of the night time chill were exorcised from the bottom of the cold cauldron in which he sat. He could hear the tinkle of running water as the snow and ice reached the mysterious triple point, became undoubtedly the liquid point, and started to flow towards the greater mass calling to it. From his vantage point, Connor watched the light creep along his line out into the languid water that lay unsullied beneath him, until it moved beyond where the bottle should have been floating. Happily, Connor could not make out a clearly discernible image of the submerged vessel. He deduced that this meant that the hole he had created was of the required depth.

Connor climbed down off the rock and set about preparing himself for the final stage of his plan. Having prepared the tent and hot soup as before, he changed into the damp clothing and jogged gently around, slowly raising his core temperature. As he did so, he would occasionally pick up a suitably sized rock and transport it to the landward side of the line. When he had accumulated a sizeable stock, he threw the rocks as accurately as he could out into the loch, following the direction of the line—as far along it as he was able. Starting to sweat from his exertions, Connor checked that everything was in place before retrieving the waterproofed and weighted bag from the tent. The moment had come.

Once more, he edged into the loch, and again the cold waters rose up around his legs as he progressed further in. When he was knee-deep, he lowered the bag into the water and let it go. Giving up a few bubbles, it sank silently and came to rest amongst the stirred-up, silted bottom. Happy that it was not going to reveal itself by floating to the surface of the loch, Connor retrieved it from the muddied waters and continued deeper in.

All too quickly, the cold was clamping his head and body as he pursued the line downward, assisted by the weighted bag until he reached the hollowed pit he had created. With one final scoop, Connor pushed the bag into the oozing, yielding mud before taking two quick swipes at the surrounding mud, pushing it back over the bag. He pushed up and away from the bottom and replenished the depleted, spent air in his lungs. Diving again, he scrambled blindly in the swirling murk, feeling for the rocks he had thrown earlier. When he found them, he would lay them over the half-buried bag. The cold was creeping deeper as he located the last stone, which concealed the bag (as best as he could tell) more by touch than by vision. Connor pulled the line, released the tied rock, and surfaced to begin his struggle to replenish his body with life-giving heat. He followed what had become nearly a routine of drying and seeking the heated sanctuary of the tent. To his surprise, his recovery had grown quicker. Perhaps it was true that a person could condition his body to cope with the ravages of the ice-cold water. Who knew? What was indisputable was that he did not feel as bad as he had on the first two occasions. That said, he ensured that he took on plenty of hot food and drink.

Feeling recharged and dressed in dry warm clothes, Connor walked down to the loch. The line floated where the gentle slip of a breeze chose to send it. He retrieved it from the water and coiled it onto the boulder. Standing on the same rock now, with the sun coming over his shoulder, he scanned the water for signs of his labour. The cloudy silt had billowed and dissipated, and once more the water was clear and reflected the world around. Sky and cliff were inverted in its mirror finish. Moving from rock to shore and skirting around, Connor tried to spy his subaquatic excavation, but he was pleased to see that, wherever he stood, it was to no avail. The source of his joy and anguish was set free and nearly beyond his control, as he had to resist the temptation to go splashing back in to bring it back to his hot grasp. The thought of the icy depths was literally cold water on the idea. Connor went back to the tent as the sun brought the artificial twilight to the glen. A few more days and he would be turning his back on the mountains for some time. He needed to prepare for his departure.

The following morning saw Connor scaling the slopes directly opposite the bearing on which he had buried his prize in the loch. He found a comfortable spot and hunkered down to watch the loch as it changed with the rising sun. The colours morphed from black through the grey scale and then, as the clouds above gave way, bloomed into a turquoise green that occasionally had a handful of pearls scattered across it as the sun's light bounced joyfully off the rippled expanse of water. He stared hard at the point of his cold-water trials and, seeing no evidence of any suspicious activity, repositioned himself at the next natural vantage point, where the mountain explorer would stop to take a photo, rest after a short scamper up the hillside, or just stand to admire the view. At each point, he would wait for the trailing sun to catch up so that he could examine the effect the changing angle of the light had on the water and the clarity of view. On no occasion could Connor see any obvious disturbance—none, he thought, that would arouse suspicion and lead to further enquiry. Having moved 180 degrees, he started to descend the slope back to his tent. The sky was tinged red like a dripping razor nick that splashed into the bowl and diffused so that the colour ran to nothing. He contemplated the day. Not a soul had passed by. Only the shadows had moved and colours had altered. The harsh, cold blues of the morning, the tight, up-to-the-line colour that stopped before the next colour took over gave way to the flat splashes of the middle hours, which then merged with the mauve reds that knew no boundaries as they smudged into one another before being consumed by the creeping black of the dusk.

The sanctuary of the tent beckoned as Connor tripped across the darkening scree and bouldered slopes. The ever moving and eroding slopes could easily catch out the unwary, weary traveller, especially in the half-light in which he was now making his way back. A broken ankle now would be disastrous on so many levels, and potentially fatal given the exposure and lack of passing population. But the real threat, other than death, would be whether he would seek help, as that would inevitably lead to unanswerable questions being asked—unanswerable, at least, if he wanted to maintain his secret existence.

Acclimatised as he had become to the outside temperature after his daytime exposure, the inside of the tent felt almost stifling. The lack of air movement meant that he quickly grew uncomfortably warm, and as the blood flowed back to his extremities in an effort to expel the excess heat, the capillaries swelled and painted a swathe of ill-applied rouge across his already ruddy face. His skin felt tight, and he had to undo the flaps of the tent to allow a flow of cooling air. It was as though he had opened the door of a sauna. Connor considered how risible these comparisons were between the cold of the days before and now, by contrast, the relative heat that was making him uncomfortable. *Never happy,* he thought. Always too much of one thing or not enough of another. When would he find the sweet spot, the blessed neutral state? Or was it just a utopian idyll that was always on the horizon and unreachable? A false hope, an empty promise that was never realised, the negative motivator, a stressing factor that caused a person to act. He stared out at the loch, which had once more turned as black as the night that it mirrored and as dark as the secret it helped to conceal. Connor smiled in the dark of the tent. He might never be satisfied, but at least now he could afford to explore the options and not be unhappy or frustrated by never knowing how unhappy achieving could make him. It was, he rationalised, better to be unhappy and well off than unhappy and poor!

The following day saw Connor once more on the hillside, but this time moving against the previous day's arc of travel. The morning had been cold, and a fine mist of rain had all but obscured any view, at least from the higher perches. But it eventually gave way to a brighter sky, and by the end of the day, Connor was bathed in the warming but waning sunlight. Two days of watching the loch had set his mind at rest. If someone discovered his treasure trove, then it would be due to factors beyond his control, and fate's intervening hand was not his to stay. He had planned long and hard and considered every practicable eventuality, at least within the realms of what was foreseeable. The months of preparation and investment financially and emotionally had been considerable. Granted, they had exposed him to new vistas and challenges that had not killed him, so they must have made him better, if only to ponder on when the grey years took over and the evening fire cast shadows and shapes that ignited the memory. The self-contented smile that crept over old men's faces as they cradled their beer alone in the corner of the bar and reflected on their youth, misspent or otherwise. To go with memories worth going with, to leave that collection of fading photographs and trinkets that spoke of firm, muscular bodies and derring-do. To have blazed a trail—not that others should follow it.

It was not about trendsetting. Why aspire to be what you don't want to do yourself? No, walk your own path at your own pace to your own destination, planned or otherwise. Contemplate your success and failures with good grace, and be thankful that they can be contemplated by the person who invoked them. Take another mouthful of beer, move closer to the fire, and smile once more the smile of the contented traveller.

Connor had a more than vested interest in ensuring the safety of his cache. He had one shot. That was the beauty of the plan, to come from nowhere and to vanish back there. Vampirous, to creep out of the dark of night to feed undetected and to slip back undercover, leaving the puncture wounds for the victim to puzzle upon on awakening. Any additional attempts increased the chance of capture by a factor not beyond calculation, but definitely beyond consideration. No, he had one chance, one shot to get it right, so whilst he could, he would secure every possible favour he could.

This night would be one of his last. Tomorrow, he would pack up and start making his way back out of the cover of the mountains and towards the claustrophobic world of civilised existence. Back to the noise and the grime, the litter and pollution. Back to the selfish, uncharitable, me-first, first world of cold-shouldered, cold-staring proximity of fellow man. The seething cesspit of corrupt exploitation and suppression, the one-upsmanship survival that pitted neighbour against neighbour and colleague against colleague. Sure, there was a place for competition and reward for those who earned it, but whereas the greed of Midas might have cured the hungry king, his lesson was lost on the fat cat, pension portfolio'd brokers who wallowed in their pits of opulence whilst too many others struggled to feed themselves and heat their homes.

The walls of the tent and the scant few belongings that lay scattered around the inside of Connor's cell were suddenly very inviting and comforting. Here he had little, but enough. He had no responsibility, agenda, or expectation made of him. Here he was happy. In pursuit of his goal, he had failed to realise that it was a false God that he idolised. He was living the life that he sought, the paradox being that he had to go back to what he did not want in order to achieve that which he did. "The lord giveth and the lord taketh away."

"Shit!" Connor shouted aloud to everyone and to no one, and flopped down into his sleeping bag to escape the torment of the situation in sleep.

The morning dawned, announced by the patter of rain on the tent fabric. Connor lay still, warm and content in the knowledge that he was no longer in possession of anything incriminating. Sure, he had more cash than one would expect for someone roaming the hills, but very soon that would not be the case. Then he would be as any other in the mainstream. He would redeposit his unspent traveller's cheques back to his bank account along with some of his cash, but on the whole he would deplete his "loch money" as and where he wanted, letting the bank deposit take care of the ennui, the quotidian transactions when he got back to his mundane and work-a-day life.

The thought of returning to his previous life was oppressive and depressive—that Sunday-night feeling when school loomed the following day, the job interview when you really needed the job, the funeral. All of the dread and fear that manifest and lurk in the mind's empty spaces to fill the voids left by the thought of the moment. When you woke from luxuriant sleep, and as the layers of sleep were cast off like the wrappings of a pass the parcel, you revealed the cause of your apprehension, your source of woe. A dog turd of a worry left on your doorstep, which shouted to be dealt with or left you having to step over it every day. Either way, the thing was repugnant, both ends of the stick shitty.

Connor looked at his watch and, for the first time for a long while, summoned the day-date function. Six months had passed, all but a few days. Six months effectively alone—apart from the occasional pleasantry, very little meaningful conversation. He had exiled himself from the mainstream and ostracised himself from people, a self-inflicted hermitage. He had been content in his loneliness, responsible to himself and nobody else. The freedom to stay or go, to change direction as he felt on a whim or due to a perceived necessity, unquestioned and unchallenged, was truly liberating, but also incongruent with his previous professional and personal life. He had travelled on two continents, crossed two seas, and used all modes of transport to cover the miles from Africa to his loch-side abode. He had moved overtly and covertly as he placed himself within and outside the law. He was now in possession of a tidy pile of money and faced the need to return to work to maintain the pretence of being an innocent man. A wave of lethargy washed over him as he contemplated the reunions ahead and the conversations that he would be forced to engage in. It would be anathema juxtaposed against the solitude he had so long enjoyed. The rain was blown hard against the tent, causing Connor to pull tight the enveloping warmth around him and to seek escape from his tormenting thoughts in sleep.

The descent from the hills was eventually forced on Connor. He had run out of excuses and had almost run out of food. The days were ticking by. He had contemplated just flitting amongst the mountain bothies, surviving on the offerings left by other users and truly becoming the nomadic man that legend would grow from. As appealing as it was in part, the practicality of sustained existence could not be guaranteed, and it would not be long before his absence would lead to questions, and nobody liked an unanswered question. No, better if he returned and faded from public view like a member of the audience leaving early than to be the act that never turned up. So Connor wound his way across the upland, the rocky escarpments, showing defiance to time and weather. The softer rolling hills were shrouded in the ethereal mists that hung languid above the snow-patched gorse and heather, a blanket thrown over a sleeping, fat Dalmatian. The hills sloped off into the glens, through which a silvered ribbon lay, haphazardly strewn towards the horizon. There, on the edge of vision, specks of light gave away the presence of a hillside village, the first step back into civilisation. Connor strode down through the glen, drinking in the vistas, committing them to memory so that they would be ready to recall in the grey days ahead. A path started up alongside the babbling infant of a stream. As though walking with an excited child *en route* to his first day at school and the great big world beyond, the waters burst with gurgling excitement, fresh and pure, racing innocently onward to the mass of seething, polluted, and corrupted seas that lay unavoidably ahead.

Connor stepped onto the metalled road and paused whilst he looked back and up into the hills, the sanctuary that he was leaving behind. From here on, he was casting off his cloak of invisibility and leaving it at the roadside to walk in the full glare of the public spotlight.

The bus was not long in coming, and Connor sat alone— or as alone as he could, given that the driver was within a few metres of him. The grim, road-weary man had not wanted to talk, and that suited Connor fine. The bus wound through the villages, magnetically pulled towards the supporting town that lay at the bridged confluence of rivers that flowed down from the mountainsides into the basin below. Connor disembarked and, deciding that the day was late, sought the tourist information office to arrange a bed-and-breakfast for the night. With the arrangements made and finder's fee paid, he took a pamphlet map of the town and set off in search of his bed. *En route*, he stopped off to buy some articles of clothing; his current get-up, though suitable for the hills and mountains, was slightly more conspicuous in the town environment, especially given its worn state.

The room was, to most, small but comfortable, but to Connor it seemed palatial and luxuriant considering his previous months' existence. The novelty of running water, let alone hot water, was an alien a concept. The bedside light, the sprung mattress, and clean sheets were all flicked, prodded, and sniffed as if Man Friday had come across Crusoe's abandoned encampment. His shower was beyond description. The grime accumulated over the months washed away in the heady perfume of a frothing soap. He washed and rewashed until the soap scum was no longer tinged with the greasy dirt that had started to insulate his body despite his cold-water immersions. Connor positively glowed as he rubbed himself dry with the warmed towel. His hair, now grown out, hung limp across his face, which was now scraped clean of facial hair and soft, silken to the touch. His whole body bristled. It was as if he had been un-entombed and set free by a fossil hunter's hammer. He just lay naked on the bed. Some bits he realised he did embrace.

The night had passed. Connor lay awake in the quiet house, the only noise being the creak of the pipes as the central heating geared itself up for another day's exertions. He had not slept well; the air in the room was warm and stale, and the sheets and bedclothes felt restrictive, cloying. Connor's head throbbed as though he had the start of a hangover. Whichever way he turned, he could not escape the discomfort, like following someone into a toilet when you desperately need to go—his smell was there, inescapable, and you had to breathe. The light, weak as it was, filtered through the thin curtain, the nondescript pattern doing little to prevent the passage of the light from the low-slung sun. He swung his feet out of the bed and sat still, taking stock. Once he had reached a decision, he moved quickly and efficiently to collect his meagre set of belongings into his backpack and dress in his newly acquired clothes.

The stair landing was dark, and it creaked as he crossed it and descended the carpeted stairs to the front door. In the hallway, he heard the cold metal scrapings of a kitchen being urged into life by a reluctant galley hand, the lash of the cat needed to get the oars working. Connor approached the door, which was ajar from overuse. A middle-aged woman, dressed perfunctorily to meet her clients' needs for underdone bacon and overdone eggs, was twisting cooker dials and flicking switches on kettles as she gathered foodstuffs from cupboards, fridges and freezers. Connor coughed his presence into the room, causing the woman to start slightly and step back half a pace before her short-term memory could catch up and recall the face at the door from the previous day. She relaxed slightly, having reversed herself into a flight cul-de-sac. She now drove forward into the proprietor role and the fine line between hotelier and housekeeper. She stepped from the formidably independent woman, that chance and circumstance had led her to play the role of a friendly and welcoming hotelier. She was a woman who did the basics well, but went beyond the minimum grudgingly and warily. She was a "meat and two veg" tourist and maybe a glass of ouzo.

"Good morning," she greeted Connor, and a more defensive opening would have been hard to find at such an hour. This was out of the ordinary, and she wanted to prepare herself to say no and "I'm afraid not" as politely as she could muster.

"Good morning," Connor responded. "I just wanted to let you know that I won't be needing any breakfast, thank you. I need to get away, I'm afraid."

Of all the responses that she had expected, this one threw her somewhat. "Is everything okay?"

"Yes, fine. I have a long way to go and wanted an early start, so I'll probably just grab a coffee down at the station."

"If you're sure?" She seemed to hope that he was and that he wouldn't change his mind. One less breakfast was less work and more profit, and more profit meant she could sell up all the sooner and have others wait on her, catering to her needs.

"Yes, I'm sure, thanks. I'll be off now." Connor turned awkwardly due to his backpack in the small vestibule.

The woman followed him. "I need to let you out . . ." She held up a bunch of keys by way of explanation.

Another moment of awkwardness followed as the woman tried to squeeze past Connor, as she did not want to relinquish the bunch that obviously held more than the key to the door. Connor smiled inwardly as he watched the woman struggle with the etiquette of the moment. The personal space between the two was nonexistent, and Connor could not help but notice a frisson of sexual tension, his sensitivities having been heightened purely by the lack of opportunity. He would not have been surprised if the same feeling was being experienced by the woman, trying to make up her mind how to overcome the situation before her. Connor played the innocent; he was encumbered by his backpack and the confines of the corridor. She was torn between the two evils of the submissive position, with her back to the slim but muscular stranger or the face-to-face personal and suggestive position, having to find somewhere to look during the moment of ultimate proximity. Connor could almost see the woman wrestle mentally with the choice, an inner turmoil. Part of him enjoyed the dilemma, if only due to the fact that he knew, as most likely did the woman, that dead-locking the door and removing the key was a bit of a fire safety no-no. It was strange that the thought should come to him from so long ago. A decision had been reached and the nettle was to be clasped. She pushed herself with her face against the wall and brushed gently against Connor as she moved, pigeon-stepping sideways. For a fleeting second, Connor breathed out as she passed, a subtle trickle of air disturbed the fine hairs on the nape of her neck. An instant hot flush coursed through her, and a pink splash grew on her cheeks and emerged from the top of her blouse. Quickly, she undid the lock and pulled back the door to let in the morning air. The ardour-cooling chill sought to redress the equilibrium of passive neutrality, but they both knew.

Connor stepped the early morning streets, breathing in the cool air, and watched as the town started to come to life. He headed towards the small train station along with the earliest of commuters, who trod the same journey in the same shoes to the same office desk or workbench so that they could continue to live in the same house and make the same journey each day and do mostly what they had settled into doing in such a way that the repetition was barely noticeable or, in some cases, had become the required repetition that they didn't notice they craved. The latter being those with the shiny suits and battered sandwich boxes carried in the equally dog-eared briefcases—or, worse, the carrier bag that had lost its logo through overuse. Push bikes with mudguards and spring -loaded luggage racks, bicycle clips, and sensible shoes—and always the same bloody tie.

The train stood quietly against the platform. The Hornby-like setting was something to behold: the backdrop of rolling fields merging into the uplift of the hills and mountains on the smudged horizon. The cleanliness of the platform and smartness of the guard talking to the driver as they shared a cup of something hot. The lay of the track as it stood both rusting and shining before running off across a series of unfathomable points towards the blips of coloured lights away on the edge of the bend further down. The closed clunk of the heavy carriage doors as the travellers took up their usual places on the train. Out came the newspapers and the awkward unfolding as they tried not to upset the neighbouring passengers. Connor watched over the rim of his insulated coffee cup. The sotto voce conversations of those who boarded together were interspersed with the "good mornings" of the regular travellers. Seemingly looking out the window, Connor watched the reflection of a young woman applying her makeup, the train carriage an extension of her dressing room and, therefore, allowing an extension of her beauty sleep. What the sleep couldn't deal with her, compact and lipstick could. Connor enjoyed the view, the attention to detail and self-absorption that she demonstrated. It was only the very confident who could achieve this level of "look at me." There had to be an amount of latent beauty to go public with first. Onto this lily the gild could be applied. The outcome was not in the eye of the beholder, but the creator, the singular, critical eye that scanned the reflection offered by the small portal of a folding hand-held mirror. At what age did this stop? Connor pondered this as, by contrast, a young schoolboy got on the train. He demonstrated the epitome of a lack of self-awareness, at least here. Here, out of the view of his peers and absorbed in his book, his battered schoolbag bulged with the requirements of the day. A games lesson was no doubt on the timetable, if the mud-encrusted laces trying to escape their dark confines were anything to go by.

A whistle, a short hiatus, and the inertia-overcoming jolt that he could not be prepared for, even though he knew it was coming. For that short time, no drinks were drunk, no lipstick applied, and those that chose to stand took an extra grip as the train rolled gently away.

The towns grew in size the farther the train travelled. People joined the train, resigned to the conditions, and then departed as they arrived at their various destinations. On the whole, the numbers disembarking were less than those that fought their way into the increasingly crowded interior. Connor was trapped into his seat in the corner of the carriage. For months, he had wandered unencumbered with more space than he could have ever used and nobody to share it with. Now, he smiled to himself, well, just look. He had once read or heard that it was possible to get the whole world's population, theoretically of course, onto the Isle of Wight, and that each person would have only a square foot to stand up in. It appeared that this carriage was part of the training course should that eventuality come to pass.

The suburban landscape started to change as the train wound its way into the outskirts of Glasgow. The bright morning sun and blue sky did their utmost to lighten the view, but there seemed to Connor a dour heaviness in the view through the picture window, against which he rested his forehead. The corporation housing was sprawling and monotonous, and even the attempts at individuality that some had tried—a splash of colour or half built extension—seemed desperate, a drowning man's final gasp before sinking into a sea of anonymity. The high-rise blocks looked more forlorn. To be trapped with what must be an inspirational view must be torture itself. Connor shifted his focus back to the carriage. He had taken the step to try to ensure that the confines and imposition of others would not be forced upon him. He had made up his mind that, if it were true that everyone had a choice, he was going to make his even though it did not comply with the norm. It was his life, his choice. Therefore, he reasoned, his parameters, utilitarianism and pragmatism, combined to shape the now and mould the future.

The passengers started to grow restless, reacting to the visual cues that were lost on Connor. Bags were gathered, papers folded, and watches checked as the trained slowed and eventually pulled into Glasgow Central station. The doors of the carriages popped, and the passengers emptied onto the platforms as the venous system fed its oxygen-starved contents into the aortic thoroughfares of the ventricular city before being pumped back out to the capillaries at the end of the day. This perforated heart of a city that produced the great and the good, those that had shaped the world and driven humankind forward, also produced a level of partisan and religious zealotry that fostered hatred and damnation of their fellow man due to demarcation and ideology. As a city, it was not alone in its troubles; the bigotry of the population was manifest and widespread up and down the country and indeed across the international borders. How could the security of the individual be attained through the group when the group itself became the host of the malevolence that harmed the individual?

Connor climbed out of the now empty carriage. The roof of the station stretched out above him, and the pigeons flew amongst the cast iron and glass, spying out the dropped morsels and discarded crusts. Leaving the station, he followed the signs for Queen Street. It was a pleasant morning, and the sun filled the busy squares before being expelled from the valley bottom paths that wended their way through the grey-stoned buildings. The statuary seemed to ponder the passing throngs, which bustled by almost oblivious to the contribution that the person immortalised in stone had made to their present condition. Indeed, they showed less care than the pigeons that adorned its advantageous perches. To give so much, to be so forgotten.

The hubbub of the high street was like any city. The traffic struggled to shuffle along roads not designed for the volume that was struggling to use them. The outlets splashed their corporate frontage with scant regard for the historic facade in which they had imposed themselves, and that the city planners had allowed them to abuse in order to build the wealth of the city. Pedestrians flowed with apparent randomness, with disregard for each other as they changed direction and thought, serving the "me"-centrism. Interacting with the light-controlled traffic, knotted crowds allowed the pickpocket to operate before being green-lighted to continue on their journeys. Connor was amongst the moving mass, his gait interrupted by those around him. He sought the kerbside route that diced with the vehicles. Truth be known, they were on the whole moving slower than he was. As he crossed a small side road, a flash of orange signage caught his eye and caused him to divert off course. He entered the shop to the sound of an electronic beep announcing his presence to the back of the store, from which a young woman appeared and cast Connor a quizzical look. Her hair, makeup, even her nails were pristinely done, no doubt the product of a lot of downtime between customers.

"Can I help you?" she enquired in a light sing-along Scottish accent, the rising inflexion ubiquitous in women of a certain age and cultural background, as if asking the question twice.

"Hi. Yes, I was wondering about your prices." Connor was looking at the list on the counter whose menu style showed the variety of costs for the various services.

The girl broke into a well-rehearsed patter that followed the "menu," but was suffixed with her personal take on the process. Connor interjected when she reached the ten-minute all-over body booth, which at £30 she seemed to acknowledge was good value. As he was led behind the counter to a changing area, Connor received instruction. After declining the exfoliating brush, he emerged in his provided dressing gown feeling self-conscious and somewhat odd when he considered that he was next to naked in a side street with someone he did not know in a throbbing city centre. Business like and detached, the woman led him to the booth and directed him further in the process before handing him a set of glasses, which she said only to put on before, immediately before he pressed the timer start button.

"You'll be unable to see anything if you put them on too soon, and worse if you don't put them on at all."

The woman left the room. Connor placed the goggles over his head and stepped into the booth. He pulled the wraparound door closed. He located the start button and, standing in just his underpants, pressed it as he pulled the glasses over his squint-shut eyes. The bright light washed over his body, and he studied his skin under the critical glow. The ten minutes crawled by, and Connor's mind just wandered over the previous, how long was it? He totted up the time—nearly six months, he reckoned. He was now on the homeward leg, though home was a misnomer, as he had no designated address. Stephanie's was the nearest that he had, but a long time had passed and, though he had written, there were no guarantees that she would still be there for him. The communication had been all one way. He had kept it that way, deliberately. Deep down, if she had moved on, that wouldn't be so bad and would involve much less explanation and probing of his non-existent story. He had sent the postcard packages, which he hoped had been forwarded by Beril as agreed, so that as far as all were concerned, he had been working hard on various projects alongside working on his final thesis, ready for submission on his now imminent return. The truth was that he had received his final assessment results and an adequate "B" pass, which he had sent to his work address and was waiting for collection on his return.

The future for Connor was more the dilemma. He was rich, richer than he had expected to be, richer than he needed or wanted to be. He had survived, especially in the last five months, on little or no money and had felt free from the everyday pressure that imperceptibly crept into one's life, much like the cancer that took a toehold within a person's body and then penetrated and rooted itself, malignant, pervasive, a hostile takeover. If the person was lucky, early detection and invasive intervention could eliminate the disease, but the subtlety of stress was that it grew until it became intrinsic. It drove someone, willingly or not, and felt as much a part of him as his name. It was only when it became absent that a person started to question its presence. That sleeping bliss of a holiday, that hankering for a lifestyle change before returning to the treadmill existence of the nine to five. Those halcyon days, where were they now?

For Connor, though, he tried to focus on his position. He was what he was, the grey man. He had come from nowhere and gone back into the same non-world where he attracted no overt attention to himself and gave no reason to become a subject of their agenda. The temptation was very real to just slip away, never to return to his starting point, but that was the paradox. To become really invisible, he had to be visible; to enjoy his wealth, he had to live in relative poverty. He had to maintain the pretence; he had to walk and live amongst his peers convincingly enough not to arouse suspicion. He would be the man next door, in the flat above you, the guy you saw down the pub or at the newsagent. He was just like you. He could *be* you. He was the fish in the centre of the shoal around which the predators stalked, and that predator would have to pass a lot of other fish to get to Connor. The probability of that happening was very, very slim, but as soon as he started acting differently, he might as well paint a large "x" on himself and start limping. He had to stay strong and true to his plan. The timer binged and the lights went out.

Back on the street, Connor felt no discernible difference to his pre–tanning salon state, but as he walked towards the station, his melatonin production was changing and his body was going through its defence and starting to darken his skin tone. His convoluted journey home via some of the larger cities and further tanning booths had given him a tan not unlike someone who had tried to cover himself from the sun's ravaging rays. He hoped that people would take that look for someone returning from the African continent.

A week out of Scotland saw Connor arrive back at his home train station. The familiarity of the setting was strangely unfamiliar. He knew what was left and what was right of him; no more did he have to study signs or tourist maps or rely on taxi drivers. He could become self-reliant, which he had exemplified in his ability to survive. But strangely, in the hubs of societal living, he was most vulnerable due to his lack of local information and, rendered so, he stood out the more for it. Now, though, he was vulnerable due to his lack of personal information. He needed cover—an address, a base to work from. He was of no fixed abode, a status that was undesirable in modernity and tantamount to unacceptable vagrancy, and a condition that required explanation and incongruent with how he wanted to be. He gave the taxi driver Stephanie's address, and soon the taxi was turning down the once familiar roads, eventually stopping in the road outside her door. An estate agent's board stood in the little front garden like a shoddily erected gallows and advertised To Let. After paying the driver, Connor stepped to the door and rang the bell, recognising that it was most likely a futile gesture, as the lower glazed section of the door, though obscured, showed a pile of unclaimed mail. He looked through the letter slot, and the cold, damp air leaked out. The oblong, framed view was of an empty corridor.

Searching his backpack, Connor retrieved a pair of brass keys and tried the locks. Pushing the door, he snowploughed the pile of mail and junk fliers back against the wall before quickly crossing the threshold and closing the door behind him. The stillness of the empty house amplified every shuffle and footstep as Connor walked through the rooms. Questions tumbled through his head—the whats and whys—whilst he tried to work out whether this was a good or bad thing. He returned to the pile of mail and sifted through until, as he suspected, he uncovered a small photograph-size package with his penned handwritten address and three Gambian postage stamps affixed. A sad smile crept across his face, which he erased with a shrug of his shoulders before slipping the package into his pocket.

The time had passed, but the effects were difficult to perceive. The fire station stood sentinel as it always had, guardian to its community, who benefited unknowingly from the invisible shield responding to the hour-of-need call. Those within were largely unchanged; the faces had aged a little and some new had joined the happy band of "grubby-faced heroes." Connor trod familiar stairs and corridors to pass by and through equally familiar rooms and offices. The conversations had quickly moved on from his sabbatical—politely, but they had moved on nonetheless. He was keen not to have to regale his crew with unlived experiences. The events of the day were far and away more interesting and pertinent to all, and the reminisces of a holiday bore were much less appealing. This suited him. Even though Tony feigned interest, Connor did not punish him and allowed the conversation to move on quickly to other subjects.

Days, weeks, months, and years passed by. The roller coaster of life was ridden and watched from the queue from those waiting to get on. The trials and tribulations that came and went with the seasons and the changing tides of fortune washed over all, but through all the ups and downs, Connor's ship managed to stay on an even keel. His neutrality in regard to issues that were previously hotbeds of conversation and argument now seemed to wash off and around him. If it was ever commented on, it was attributed to his experiences in the underprivileged regions of Africa. The economic turmoil that threatened to undermine the stability of whole countries and their interconnectivity saw many tighten belts that most felt were too tight already, and new holes were being made in virgin leather. But even against this backdrop, it seemed that Connor's fortunes were unassailed; in fact, they positively thrived, taking advantage of the downturn in the building trades to have an extension added to his modest semi, which was set down a leafy lane. Indeed, the international turmoil, currency fluctuations, and grounded-out interest rates allowed him to buy a holiday home, which was explained away against a windfall inheritance from a distant and long forgotten relative. A modest lottery win earned him the sobriquet of "Lucky" and explained away the car purchase and somewhat elaborate wedding to a French woman he had met on an extended period of leave. Professionally, he played the game and sought the advances that were offered, but was unaffected by the letters that contained the "unfortunately this time" line. A wry smile and a shrug saw the letter cast to the recycling. There still existed a vein of rebellion, and it was a continual presence that he actively suppressed so as not to raise his profile to such an extent that questions would be asked that he wished not to answer. It was often said that behind every great fortune there existed a crime. It could now be said, if it hadn't already, that the same could be said of modest crimes and associated fortunes.

***

Deep in the police archives of unsolved crimes, a file detailing the theft from a variety of establishments exists, and occasionally it is reviewed and quickly set aside, remaining unsolved due to lack of any new evidence and the paltry amount, when compared to other crimes, that was involved. The officer reviewing the case thought to himself that he would earn the amount stolen within the next fifteen years and wondered who would be stupid or desperate enough to risk what would most likely amount to fifteen years' imprisonment for so little. You'd have to be crazy or absolutely sure that you would get away with it, and he knew there was no such thing as a perfect crime, nor one that could deliver the assurances to pursue seemingly fatuous outcomes. He'd rather keep his nose to the grindstone. That said, it's hard sometimes to explain away the wealth that exists amongst those deemed to be less deserving—unless, of course, they have had an undeclared lottery win or fortunate inheritance from a distant relative?

Lightning Source UK Ltd.
Milton Keynes UK
UKOW04f0853311013

220153UK00001B/176/P